'I'm not the woman for you.'

While today's misgivings hinted that Pen might be right, his pride flinched under her rejection. 'We know each other so well—'

She sighed. 'Cam, you need a duchess with dignity and decorum. You must have forgotten all the times you dragged me from disaster.'

'You're still young. You can be trained,' he said, before he recognised that such a comment would hardly forward his suit. Usually he said exactly the right thing, but this encounter rattled his sangfroid.

Her momentary softening congealed to frost. 'I'm not a hound to come at your whistle.'

He sighed again. 'You know that's not what I want in a bride.'

'Do I?' she asked, arching her eyebrows. 'You've devoted your life to rising above your parents' disgrace, the scandals have guided your every action.'

He winced under the compassion in her gaze. 'That makes me sound like a complete idiot.'

'No, it doesn't. You can help me. You'd make a capital duchess.'

'You're mistaken. He'd never imagined that worldly smile on Pen's face. His reluctant desire deepened. 'I'm too independent to be anyone's duchess, *especially yours.*'

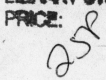

THE SONS OF SIN
by Anna Campbell

Seven Nights in a Rogue's Bed

A Rake's Midnight Kiss

What a Duke Dares

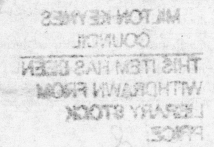

WHAT A DUKE DARES

ANNA CAMPBELL

MILLS
BOON

Published in Great Britain 2014
by Mills & Boon, an imprint of Harlequin (UK) Limited,
Eton House, 18-24 Paradise Road, Richmond, Surrey, TW9 1SR

© 2013 Anna Campbell

ISBN: 978-0-263-25095-4

009-1114

Harlequin (UK) Limited's policy is to use papers that are natural, renewable and recyclable products and made from wood grown in sustainable forests. The logging and manufacturing processes conform to the legal environmental regulations of the country of origin.

Printed and bound by
CPI Group (UK) Ltd, Croydon, CR0 4YY

Anna Campbell was the sort of kid who spent her childhood with her nose buried between the pages of a book. She decided when she was a child that she wanted to be a writer. When she's not writing passionate, intense stories featuring gorgeous Regency heroes and the women who are their destiny, Anna loves to travel, especially in the United Kingdom, and listen to all kinds of music. She has settled near the sea on the east coast of Australia, where she's losing her battle with an overgrown subtropical garden.

The first book in THE SONS OF SIN series, *Seven Nights in a Rogue's Bed,* has generated some wonderful reviews and a number of awards, including favourite historical romance from the Australian Romance Readers Association. Anna was also voted favourite Australian romance author at the ARRA Awards.

Anna loves to hear from her readers. You can contact her through her website at www.annacampbell.info.

WHAT A DUKE DARES

Prologue

Houghton Park, Lincolnshire, May 1819

Every young lady dreamed of a proposal from the heir to a dukedom. Especially when the heir was rich, feted, in possession of his wits, and still young enough to have all his teeth.

Every young lady except, apparently, Penelope Thorne.

From the center of her father's library, Camden Rothermere, Marquess of Pembridge, eyed the girl he'd known from the cradle and wondered where the hell he'd slipped up. He straightened and summoned a smile, struggling to bridge the awkward silence extending between them.

Damn it. He never felt awkward with Pen Thorne. Until now. Until he'd spoken the fatal words.

Until, instead of radiating delight at the prospect of marrying him, Pen's black eyes sparked with the rebellious light that always boded trouble.

"Why?" It wasn't the first time this afternoon that she'd asked him the question.

Stupidly he couldn't summon an adequate answer. He'd blundered into this half-cocked. It was his own fault. Knowing Pen as he did, he should have prepared a comprehensive list of reasons for their marriage before broaching the subject.

Right now, he wished he'd never broached the subject at all. But it was too late to retreat, or too late if he hoped to salvage a shred of self-respect from this dashed uncomfortable encounter.

"Devil take you, Pen, I like you," he said impatiently. Despite her inexplicable and irritating behavior today, it was true. There wasn't a girl alive that he liked so much as the chit currently regarding him as if he'd crawled out of a hole in the ground.

He knew her better than any other girl too, even his sister, Lydia. Through their childhood, he'd rescued Pen from a thousand scrapes. She'd been a hellion, riding the wildest horses in her father's stables, climbing the tallest trees in the park, throwing herself into brawls to defend a friend or mistreated animal. Cam had long admired her spirit, loyalty, and courage.

Those were qualities he wanted in his duchess. And if she needed some guidance in deportment, he was perfectly prepared to teach her proper behavior. She was a Thorne and Thornes weren't renowned for their prudence, but while Pen might be impulsive, she was intelligent. Once she'd become the Duchess of Sedgemoor, he was sure she'd settle down.

Or he had been, until her unenthusiastic response to his proposal.

"I like you too," she said steadily, regarding him with unwavering attention.

Cam wondered why her admission didn't reassure. Inhaling

deeply, he strove for forbearance. "Well, there you have it, then."

That bitter note in her laugh was unfamiliar. He could hardly believe it, but the possibility of failure hovered. Pen was clever, determined, headstrong—he'd get that out of her soon enough—and stubbornly inclined to take a positive view of events. Or at least so he'd believed until today.

He'd also believed that she'd leap at the chance to marry him.

Clearly he'd been wrong.

He wasn't used to being wrong. Confound her, he didn't like it.

Her voice remained curiously flat. "I'm sorry, Cam. 'There you have it, then' won't pass muster. You'll need to do better than that."

From where she stood before the high mullioned window, she studied him much like a schoolmistress surveyed an unpromising student. He only just resisted the urge to run a finger under his unaccountably tight neckcloth.

Good God, this was *Pen*. She wasn't a female who put a man through hoops before she fell into harness. She'd never demand more than he could give. She'd never subject a fellow to emotional storms. She'd never lie and cheat and betray.

She was the absolute opposite of his late mother, in fact.

Cam was unaccustomed to feeling like a blockhead, especially with the fairer sex. By nature he wasn't a vain man, but he'd anticipated a better reaction to his proposal. Pen's father Lord Wilmott had been in alt to hear that his daughter would become a duchess.

Most definitely, Pen was not in alt.

And she bloody well should be. After all, she was a mere baron's daughter—and a ramshackle baron at that—while Cam was heir to the nation's richest dukedom.

The Thornes were an old family, but had always had a justified reputation for trouble. In times of political unrest, they backed the wrong side. If they managed to lay their hands on any money, they lost it, usually in some disreputable pursuit. "Wine, women, and song" should be the family motto instead of the much more staid and highly inappropriate "steadfast and faithful."

The previous generation had spawned a handful of eccentrics, including an uncle who had married his housekeeper. Bigamously as it had turned out. Lord Wilmott had squandered his wife's dowry on a succession of greedy strumpets. Pen's aunt ran with a dissolute crowd on the Continent. Peter, Cam's friend and the current heir, was devoted to the gaming tables and disastrous investments. If Cam's mother hadn't been great friends with Lady Wilmott, the families would have had little contact.

What made Pen's tepid response to Cam's suit even harder to understand was that she'd always worshipped the ground he walked on. Was he a fool to presume on childhood adoration?

A horrible suspicion struck him. Was he presuming on far too much? Despite his parents' scandalous behavior and the gossip about his legitimacy, the ton lionized Cam as the future Duke of Sedgemoor. Had endless flattery turned him into a self-satisfied ass?

If Pen thought him insufferably arrogant, no wonder his proposal hadn't bowled her over. He sighed with self-disgust and impatiently ran his hand through his hair. "I'm making a dashed mess of this, aren't I?"

Pen's slender body lost its rigidity as a wry smile curved her lips. Lips, he reluctantly noticed, that were pink and full and lusciously kissable.

As shock shuddered through him, he wondered why he'd

never noticed before. Pen had been such a constant in his life that he hadn't taken the time to mark how she'd changed.

Still unwilling to admit that Pen wasn't the girl he remembered, he looked more closely. To his dismay, the coltish adolescent hovered on the brink of becoming a true beauty. Even more dismaying, he felt the unwelcome, unmistakable prickle of desire.

"Yes, you are. But it's not totally your fault." With a grace he hadn't seen in her before, she gestured toward the leather chairs ranged around the unlit hearth. "Sit down, for heaven's sake, and stop looming over me."

Actually he wasn't looming, although with his height, he loomed over most people. Pen had always been a long Meg, closer to a boy than a girl in his mind. But in this discomfiting instant, when for the first time he saw more than his friend Peter's occasionally annoying younger sister, there was nothing boyish about Miss Penelope Thorne.

Since he'd last seen her—and for the life of him, he couldn't recall when that had been, such an ardent suitor he was—she'd grown up. The thin body had gained subtle but fascinating curves. The vivid, pointed face that had always seemed too small for her decisive features had refined into striking attraction. When had she tamed her tangled mane of hair into those gleaming ebony coils?

Apprehension tasted sour on his tongue. God help him, this new Penelope was a bloody disaster. He narrowed his eyes on the siren who had mysteriously supplanted a hoyden as daring as any of his male friends. And saw that she was blossoming into a woman who made men stupid.

Categorically he didn't want to marry a woman who made men stupid, the way his mother had made his father stupid. How insulting to his chosen bride that part of her appeal had been her lack of overt attractions.

His father's example proved what catastrophes resulted from choosing a tempestuous beauty as a wife. Cam had grown up hearing salacious gossip about his mother's affair with her husband's younger brother. Nobody, including Cam, knew who had fathered him. He was a Rothermere, but not necessarily the late duke's son.

Long ago Cam had decided to marry someone he could be friends with, not who became a challenge to every deuced roué in London. Cam wanted a wife who would help him establish the Rothermere name as one to be respected, not a cause for snickering and dirty jokes as it had been all his life.

Gossip about his parentage had dogged Cam from boyhood. School had been a nightmare, and while he made a fair job of pretending he no longer cared, he knew whispers of his bastardy still spiced the tattle whenever his name was mentioned. He'd be damned before he subjected his own children to similar torments.

He reminded himself that this was brave, honest Penelope Thorne, she who risked her neck to save a kitten from village boys twice her size. But looking at her now, he didn't see the girl who had launched a hundred escapades. Instead, he saw a woman who other men would pursue. A woman who perhaps would succumb to temptation, as his mother had done. Pen's burgeoning loveliness made Cam burn to bed her, but it beggared any chance of an unexceptional domestic life.

Feeling slightly ill, Cam accepted Pen's offer of a seat and watched her take the chair opposite. Dear heaven, when had that smooth glide replaced her eager gallop? This was Pen, yet it wasn't.

Even as he questioned his old playmate's suitability as a bride, he couldn't take his eyes off her. When had she become this intriguing creature? Where the hell had he been when the transformation took place? At nineteen, she was a little late to be approaching her first season, but he could already see that she'd set society on its ears. She'd prowl into London's ballrooms on those long legs, like a tigress set loose amid a host of pretty little butterflies.

"I appreciate that you're doing your duty by your mother and mine. A match between us was always their greatest wish." The earnestness in Pen's regard was familiar, but still he felt as if he'd been tossed high into the air and come to land in a different country. "But let's be realistic. I'm not the woman for you."

While today's misgivings hinted that Pen might be right, his pride flinched under her rejection. "We know each other so well—"

"Which is why I'm convinced that any match between us would be a debacle."

"Why?"

Her lips twisted, and he realized that her earlier bitterness hadn't entirely vanished. "Isn't that my question?" She sighed. "Cam, you need a duchess with dignity and decorum. You must have forgotten all the times you dragged me from disaster."

"You're still young. You can be trained," he said, before he recognized that such a comment would hardly forward his suit. Usually he said exactly the right thing, but this encounter rattled his sangfroid.

Her momentary softening congealed to frost. "I'm not a hound to come at your whistle."

He sighed again. "You know that's not what I want in a bride."

"Do I?" she asked, arching her eyebrows. "You've devoted your life to rising above your parents' disgrace. You've never made a secret of the fact that your wife must be beyond reproach."

He bared his teeth at her. Mention of his mother's adultery always raised his hackles. "Pen, this isn't something I wish to discuss."

She made a sweeping gesture. "Whether you want to talk about it or not, the scandals have guided your every action."

He winced under the compassion in her gaze. "That makes me sound like a complete widgeon."

"No, it doesn't."

"You can help me. You'll make a capital duchess."

"You're mistaken." He'd never imagined that worldly smile on Pen's face. His reluctant desire deepened. "I'm too independent to be anyone's duchess, especially yours."

"You can change," he said desperately, wishing he'd taken Lord Wilmott up on his offer of a brandy earlier. Cam wasn't used to being so wrong-footed with a woman, with anyone. Where had his famous social assurance buggered off to?

"Perhaps I can. If I wanted to change. I don't." She sighed with a tolerance that made his skin itch with resentment. "You'd be trading your family's scandals for mine, and the rumors would continue to dog you all our lives. I follow my heart before my head. I speak my mind. Before the ink was dry on the settlements, I'd do something to upset the old tabbies. You'd find yourself knee-deep in gossip and you'd hate that. You'd start to hate *me*."

"You're the only woman I've ever pictured as my wife. I decided as a boy that I'd marry you." He straightened in his chair and bit out each word, before remembering that he came to woo, not browbeat her. "Our families expect me to make you my duchess."

The regret in her smile did nothing to bolster his optimism. "I'm sorry, Cam. For once in your life, you'll have to disappoint expectations." Her gaze sharpened in a way that he didn't completely understand. "I know you don't love me."

He flinched back as though she'd struck him. Damn, damn, damn. *Love*. He'd thought Pen too smart to fall prey to mawkish sentimentality. "I esteem you. I admire you. I enjoy your company. You know the Fentonwyck estate. You know *me*."

"All very gratifying, I'm sure." Her smile turned sour. "But I won't marry without love."

He surged to his feet. "We both have parents who married for love. As a result of *love*, my father descended into cruelty and obsession and my mother became a byword for promiscuity. Pardon me saying so, but your parents aren't much better. Doesn't that convince you that friendship and respect form a stronger basis for marriage than passing physical passion?"

"I doubt that either my parents or yours understood what love truly is." Emotion thickened her voice and strengthened his premonition of failure. "Love means wanting the best for the beloved, whatever the cost. Love means sacrificing everything to achieve the beloved's happiness."

"You're an idealist," he said disdainfully.

"Yes, Cam, I am." She rose with more circumspection—an adjective he'd never before associated with Pen Thorne—and regarded him with an unreadable expression. For a woman who confessed lack of control, she was remarkably controlled. "I believe love makes life worth living and nobody should marry without it. You're too young to settle for second best."

He placed a short rein on his temper. He was rarely angry, but right now, he wanted to fling one of the smug Ming dogs on the mantelpiece into the fire. "I'm twenty-seven."

She released an impatient huff. "Well, I'm only nineteen. I'm definitely too young to settle for second best."

"I hardly think becoming the Duchess of Sedgemoor

counts as second best," he said frigidly, wondering just where his childhood friend had gone.

Pen sighed as if she understood his turmoil. "It is when the duke offers only a lukewarm attachment."

Resentment tightened his gut. He didn't want to be understood. He hoped like hell she hadn't noticed his bristling sexual awareness. Having Pen recognize his unwilling desire just as she sent him away with a flea in his ear seemed the final humiliation.

"Would you rather I lied?" he growled.

She winced as though he'd hit her. "Even if you lied, I wouldn't believe you, Cam. I've known you too long. And you set your mind against love long ago."

He struggled for a reasonable tone. Blustering would only make her dig her heels in. The encounter verged dangerously close to a quarrel. "Pen, think of the advantages."

Her jaw set in an obstinate line. "Right now, aside from the obvious fact of your riches, I can't see any."

His appeal to her worldly interests disappointed her. Shame knotted his gut. With regret, he recalled the days when in her eyes, he could do no wrong. He drew himself up to his full height and glared.

"There's no point going all ducal, Cam," she said curtly, not, blast her, remotely cowed. "That look lost its power over me before you went to Eton."

She shifted closer, stretching one hand toward the mantel. When he noticed how her fingers trembled, he faced the unpleasant truth that despite outward calm, this encounter upset her.

Of course it did. She felt things deeply. More than once, he'd caught Pen crying alone after her brothers' teasing had struck a painful spot. She was proud, Penelope Thorne. Another desirable quality in a cracking duchess.

But clearly not his duchess. Pen didn't have a monopoly on pride. Cam regarded her down his long nose and spoke as coldly as he'd speak to an overweening acquaintance. "I gather that you're refusing me."

The knuckles on the hand clutching the mantel turned white, although her voice remained steady. "Yes, I am." She paused. "I appreciate your condescension."

That was so obviously untrue that under other circumstances, he'd have laughed. But pique shredded his sense of humor. Through his outrage, he knew that he behaved badly. However unfairly, he blamed Pen for that unprecedented state of affairs too.

He bowed shortly and spoke in a clipped voice. "In that case, Miss Thorne, I'll waste no more of your valuable time. I wish you well."

Something that might have been pain flared in her dark eyes, but he was too angry and, much as he hated to admit it, wounded to pay heed. She stepped toward him. "Cam—"

"Good day, madam."

He turned on his heel and stalked off.

Pen watched Cam march out of her father's library, his back rigid with displeasure, and told herself that she'd done the right thing. The only thing she could in honor have done.

Right now she didn't feel that way. She felt like she'd swallowed toads. She clung to the mantel to stay upright on legs likely to crumple beneath her.

Her anguish didn't change merciless reality. Cam didn't love her. Cam would never love her. Nothing in today's awkward, painful encounter had convinced her otherwise.

As a foolish child, she'd dreamed of him tumbling head over heels in love with her. What girl brought up in close proximity to the magnificent Rothermere heir wouldn't imagine a fairy-tale future? Especially when her mother encouraged her.

But that was before Pen had grown up and recognized the stark truth. A truth ruthlessly confirmed when she was sixteen. One summer at Fentonwyck, she'd overheard Cam talking to his best friend Richard Harmsworth about discouraging a local belle's advances. When Richard had blamed the girl's antics on love, Cam had responded with cutting contempt and said that was even more reason to steer clear of the unfortunate lady.

Romantic love has no place in my life now or ever, old chap. Let other fellows make asses of themselves. I've seen too much of the damage that poisonous emotion can wreak. It's a trap and a deceit and a damned nuisance. I'll never marry a woman who expects me to love her.

Pen felt sick to recall that self-assured pronouncement. Perhaps she might have dismissed his remarks as a young man's bravado, except that in the three years since, everything she'd seen of Cam confirmed that he'd meant every word.

Even with those closest to him—Richard, his sister, Pen—he kept some element of himself apart, untouchable. Over the years that distance had only grown more marked.

Camden Rothermere was rich, handsome, clever, honorable, and brave. And completely self-sufficient.

Pen had prayed that Cam would ignore his late mother's matchmaking, but of course, he considered it his duty to offer for Penelope. Just as he considered it his duty to inform her that his interest was purely dynastic.

If she'd harbored the tiniest shred of hope of melting the ice in his heart, she'd disregard questions of her notorious family and headstrong inclinations. She'd even try to make herself anew in the image he wanted.

But she knew Cam as she knew herself, and she'd never been a fool.

Cam wouldn't countenance a marriage based on love and she couldn't countenance a marriage that wasn't. She never went into anything halfhearted, and a loveless union would destroy her.

Pen remained trembling near the fireplace, knowing that her family awaited news of her engagement. Her refusal of the greatest marital prize in the kingdom would set the cat among the Thorne pigeons. Right now, her control was so precarious; she shied from her mother's bullying.

She fought a childish urge to cry. If she cried, there would be endless questions and more bullying. Her mother saw tears as opportunity for manipulation, not for comfort.

Pen sucked in a shaky breath and although she'd sworn that she wouldn't, she rushed to the window facing the long drive.

Cam cantered away on his magnificent bay horse. He didn't glance behind to catch her staring after him. Why would he? He'd want to get as far away from her as he could. For a famously self-controlled man, he'd verged very close to losing his temper this afternoon.

That had been a surprise. She hadn't imagined that he cared so much about marrying her. In truth, she hadn't imagined he cared at all.

But then, he'd expected her to say yes without hesitation. Despite the fact that Penelope Thorne was wrong for him on every count.

Except perhaps one.

The fact that she'd love him until she died.

Chapter One

Calais, France, January 1828

Through the bleak hours between midnight and dawn, the candles burned low in the shabby room high in the dilapidated inn. Wind rattled the ill-fitting windowpanes and carried the creaking of boats at their moorings and the reek of salt and rotting fish. The man lying in the narrow bed gasped for every breath.

Camden Rothermere, Duke of Sedgemoor, leaned forward to plump the thin pillows in a futile attempt to offer his dying friend some relief. When Cam sank into his wooden chair beside the bed, Peter Thorne's eyes opened.

Although he and Peter hadn't been close in years, Cam knew about his friend's numerous reverses. The Thornes were famously rackety, and a son and heir who gambled away his fortune was hardly the worst of it.

Cam had arrived in Calais a few hours ago and rushed straight here to find the doctor in attendance. He'd cornered the man before he left. The harassed French medico had been blunt about his patient's prospects.

At first, Peter had drifted close to unconsciousness, but the eyes focusing on Cam now were clear and aware. Eyes sunk in dark hollows in a face that carried no spare flesh. It was like staring into a skull.

"You...came."

The words were hoarse, slow in emerging, and ended in a fit of coughing. Swiftly Cam fetched some water in a chipped cup. After a sip, the sick man collapsed exhausted against the hard mattress.

"Of course I came." Anguish and outrage gripped Cam. Peter had been a companion in childhood games, a participant in university hijinks. He was only thirty-five, the same age as Cam, too bloody young to die.

"Wasn't sure you would," Peter gasped before succumbing to another coughing fit.

Cam offered more water. "We've always been friends."

"From boyhood." The response was a papery whisper. "Although you'll wish me to the devil tonight."

"Never."

"Don't speak...too soon." He closed his eyes and Cam wondered whether he slept. The doctor had said that the end would come tonight. Looking into Peter's bloodless features, Cam couldn't doubt that conclusion.

Grief stabbed his gut, made his hand shake. He placed the cup on the crowded nightstand before he spilled the water. He wasn't a religious man, but he found himself murmuring a prayer for a swift end to his friend's sufferings.

"I need your help."

Cam started to hear Peter speak. Spidery hands plucked fretfully at the threadbare covers drawn high on this cold night. If Cam thought it would do an ounce of good, he'd shift his friend to the best inn in town. But even without the doctor's warning, he saw that Peter's time was measured in hours, perhaps even minutes. Relocating him would be cruel rather than kind.

"It's Pen."

The moment he'd received Peter's summons, Cam had harbored a sinking feeling that it might be. "Your sister?"

"Of course my damned sister." Another coughing attack rewarded Peter's irritable response.

Cam slid his arm behind Peter's back to support him while he caught his breath. "The doctor left laudanum."

Peter coughed until Cam thought surely he must suffocate. The cloth pressed to his mouth came away bloody. Rage at a fate that turned a once-vital young man into a barely breathing skeleton clutched at Cam's gut.

When Peter could speak again, it was in a whisper. Cam leaned close to hear.

"I don't want to sleep." He winced as he drew a breath. Cam saw that every second was excruciating. "I'll have rest enough soon."

Staring into his friend's face, Cam recognized the futility of a comforting lie. They both knew that Peter wouldn't see the dawn.

"Pen's in trouble." Peter fumbled after Cam's hand, gripping with surprising strength. His clasp was icy, as though the grave already encroached into this room.

Cam's expression hardened. He hadn't seen Pen in nine years, since his proposal. The only proposal he'd ever made, as it had turned out. If the chit was in trouble, she probably deserved to be. "I'm sure that she's been in tight spots before."

Penelope Thorne had never had the chance to make a splash in London society. Instead, she'd joined her eccentric aunt on the Continent and stayed there. She hadn't returned to England even after her parents' death in a carriage accident five years ago. Cam gathered she'd been somewhere in Greece at the time.

He hesitated to admit that her refusal had undermined his confidence to such an extent that he only now seriously contemplated marriage again. He needed a wife to help restore his family's reputation, which was even more appalling than the Thornes', and at last he'd found the perfect candidate. His recently chosen bride was as dissimilar to his hoydenish childhood playmate as possible.

Thank God.

By all reports, Pen had become rather odd. There had been nasty rumors from Sicily about her sharing a shady Conti's bed, and of a liaison with a Greek rebel. Goya had emerged from seclusion to paint her both clothed and naked in imitation of his famous *majas*. Not to mention her week's sojourn in the Sultan's harem in Constantinople.

She'd published four volumes of travel reminiscences, books Cam had read over and over, although he'd face the stake before confessing that publicly. A man would rather be flayed than claim a taste for feminine literature.

Peter's hand tightened. The desperation in his old friend's face was unmistakable. Unfortunately. "Lady Bradford died last October. Pen's gone from disaster to disaster since. She's on her way north to Paris to meet me, but she's a woman alone on a dangerous journey."

Serves the hellcat right, Cam wanted to say, then wondered at his spite. He was accounted an equable fellow. The last time he'd lost his temper was when Pen had refused him. If she'd lost her chaperone, however inadequate, Pen should easily find alternative protection. And he meant that in the Biblical sense.

"Peter, I—" Cam began, not sure how to respond. He guessed that his friend meant to charge him with rescuing Pen from her irresponsibility. Although, hell, after a lifetime of friendship, how could he say no?

As if reading Cam's reluctance, Peter spoke quickly. Or perhaps he knew that he had too few breaths remaining to waste any. His urgency seemed to suppress his cough so he managed complete sentences. "In her last letter, she was in Rome and running out of money. That was a month ago. God knows what's befallen since."

"But what can I do?"

"Find her. Bring her back to England. Make sure she's safe." Peter regarded Cam like his last hope. Which made it damned difficult to deny him. "Elias will have his hands full inheriting and Harry's not up to the job, even if I could get him away from the fleshpots."

Peter forestalled Cam's suggestion that another Thorne brother could undertake this task. Cam rose to pace the tiny room. "Confound it, Peter. I've no authority over Pen. She won't pay a speck of attention to me."

"She will. She's always liked you."

Not last time they'd met. "I can't kidnap her."

Shaking, Peter shoved himself higher against the pillows. His black eyes, so like his sister's, burned in his ashen face as if all the life concentrated in that blazing stare. "If you have to, you must. I won't have my sister bouncing all over Europe, called a whore by ignorant pigs who should know better."

Bloody hell.

His stare unwavering, Peter clawed at the blankets. He gulped for air and gray tinged his skin now that brief vitality faded. "There's no man I trust more than you. If you've ever considered me a friend, if you've ever cherished a moment's affection for my sister, bring Pen home."

A moment's fondness for his sister? Aye, there was the rub. Until she'd treated him like an insolent lackey, he'd been fond of Penelope Thorne.

Pausing by the window, he stared into the stormy night. An endless forest of masts ranged against the turbulent sky. It was a night for making deals with the devil. Except in this case, Cam would wager good money that the devil was the woman at the end of the wild goose chase.

He caught his reflection in the glass. He looked like he always did. Calm. Controlled. Cold. The habit of hiding his feelings had become second nature. But he was sorrowing and resentful—and that resentment focused on one trouble-some woman. Behind him, hazy in the glass, he saw Peter watching him, suffering stoically through his last hours.

How could Cam refuse? Futile as the quest was. Pen would go her own way, whatever her dying brother asked, whatever pressure her childhood friend placed upon her.

Cam leveled his shoulders. Duty had guided him since he'd been old enough to understand the snide whispers about his mother's affair with her brother-in-law. Duty insisted that he accept this task, however unwillingly. Slowly he faced his friend. "Of course I'll do it, Peter."

And was rewarded by an easing in Peter's painful tension and a hint of the formerly brilliant smile. The Thornes were a famously handsome family and fleetingly, Cam glimpsed his rakish old companion. "God bless you, Cam."

God help him, more like.

Chapter Two

During nine years of travel, Penelope Thorne had been in more tight spots than she cared to remember. None quite so restricted as this one in the rundown common room of a flea-ridden hostelry high in the Italian Alps.

Battling to steady her hand, she raised her pistol and pretended that facing down a pack of miscreants was an everyday occurrence. Instinct insisted that betraying her fear would only invite rape and robbery—perhaps murder.

A dozen men leered at her. All desperate. All drunk. All drawing courage from their cohorts' belligerence.

"The first man who moves gets a bullet," she said in fluent Italian.

Unfortunately the denizens of this godforsaken village spoke some outlandish dialect. Their speech bore little resemblance to the melodious Tuscan that she'd learned in Florence's salons.

Pen cursed the bad luck and bad weather that stranded her so far from civilization. Behind her, her maid and coachman cowered against the wall. The innkeeper was nowhere to be seen. He was probably in on the plot. He'd looked just as villainous as these thugs.

A heavily whiskered brute swaggered forward, expression contemptuous. Through the blast of incomprehensible patois, she made out the words "one" and "bullet."

She kept the gun straight, despite crippling fear. "One bullet does a lot of damage."

His lip curled in disdain and he took another step. She cocked the gun, the sound loud in the fraught silence. "Any nearer and I'll shoot."

He proved his scorn by approaching so close that she smelled the stale odor of his hulking body. Her stomach, already churning with dread, revolted and she only just stopped herself from faltering back. Behind him, the others shifted. Whatever the leader said prompted laughter. Laughter that made her skin crawl.

"I warned you." She forced herself to meet the glittering excitement in his piglike eyes.

Her finger tightened on the trigger and an explosion rent the air. She jerked back and her ears rang. The hot stink of gunpowder filled her nostrils.

"*Porca miseria*—" He staggered into the gang, who heaved and growled like an angry ocean. A bloody hole punctuated his forehead and astonishment froze his features before his eyes rolled up in his head and he slumped motionless.

Dear heaven, he was dead. At her hand.

Pen desperately wanted to be sick. In her twenty-eight years, she'd never killed anyone.

As the rabble coalesced into a menacing unit, she fumbled

in her pocket for her second gun. She felt a presence at her shoulder and realized that at last her coachman Giuseppe displayed some backbone. If only he displayed some backbone while carrying a rifle. But his weapons remained in her carriage outside. All he had were his fists.

"*Brava*, milady."

The men surged on a wave of rage. Pen raised her pistol with a hand that proved unexpectedly firm. Stinking bodies surrounded her, blocked the air. Cruel hands grabbed her, pinched her breasts. A blow landed hard against her ribs, stealing her breath.

Terror gripped her. She had one bullet left. Was this time to use it?

Giuseppe was somewhere in the melee. She couldn't help him. She could barely help herself. Gasping and struggling she lifted her gun, bleakly aware that once she shot, she was at the mob's mercy.

When a gunshot rang out, she first thought she'd fired. Yet the pistol remained cool in her hand.

The groping hands stilled. The angry roar faded to silence. The attack had lasted seconds, but it had felt like a lifetime.

Another gunshot and the horde fell away like a tide withdrawing down the beach.

"Get away from her."

Cam?

Astonishment turned Pen to stone. Even after nine years, his voice was familiar. The authoritative baritone caught at the heart that she'd kept on ice since their last meeting.

Sullenly her assailants retreated, creating a path between Pen and the doorway where her unlikely rescuer stood. Pen sucked in her first full breath in what felt like hours. Sweat, blood, and the reek of her fear tainted the air.

The tall man wearing an elegant cape and a beaver hat tilted at a rakish angle seemed to belong to a different species from the bandits. Cam carried two horse pistols, a rifle hung over his shoulder and a sword dangled at his hip. Snow brushed his hat and shoulders.

"Get out and don't come back." As he stepped forward, his tone sent a chill oozing down her backbone. "This lady is under my protection."

His Italian was as good as hers and this time the thugs understood. Although his arsenal of weaponry undoubtedly spoke more loudly than words.

One of the men remonstrated about their dead comrade until Cam raised the gun. The fellow skulked off with the rest, the dead man hoisted between them.

Shaky and ill, Pen extended a trembling hand toward Giuseppe. To her consternation, Cam gripped her arm. Even through the leather glove he wore, she felt the heat of his touch. How could he affect her like this after so long?

"I'm all right," she forced past rising gorge.

"Like hell you are." His hold tightened.

If only the room stopped revolving. If only she caught a decent breath. If only she saw something other than Cam's endlessly disapproving expression and the face of the man she'd shot.

"I've...I've never killed anyone before."

"Don't waste your pity." He sounded livid.

Wonderingly she stared into his face. That beautiful, sculpted, austere face that still haunted her dreams, no matter how she'd struggled to forget him. "You're angry with me?" she asked in bewilderment.

"Damn right I am." His mouth flattened. "I'd love to take you over my knee and give you a good spanking."

"I can't imagine why," she said faintly, her voice coming

from the end of a long tunnel. Cam's face became the only fixed point in a reeling world.

She closed her eyes. Then her stomach gave a nauseating swoop as Cam swept her up in his arms. She managed an incoherent protest before blackness claimed her.

"Take this." Fumbling to hold Pen, Cam shoved the horse pistols at the useless cur who had cowered behind her. He firmed his grip on Pen's motionless body. She was a bonnie fighter. How his heart had leaped when he saw her courage, even while his belly twisted with terror.

He stared down into her face. The promise of the girl had flowered into the sort of beauty that started wars. He still remembered how disturbed he'd been all those years ago to discover his childhood shadow transformed into a striking woman. Now the long slender body was curved and soft in his arms. Her scent teased him. Something fresh and floral. Warm and womanly. Smoky. A trace of gunpowder, by God.

Long black hair flowed around her. Outrage threatened to choke him as he recalled those savages tearing at it and pawing her. If he'd had more bullets and some men at his back, he'd have done a damned sight more than chase the brigands away.

"Fetch the landlord," he said to the girl he assumed was Pen's maid. She hunched on the stairway, dark eyes wide as if expecting Cam to take up where the locals left off. She rose and managed a wobbly curtsy before disappearing down a corridor.

Pen stirred as he laid her carefully upon a wooden bench under a shuttered window. Looking at Pen, a turbulent mix of emotions assailed him. Relief at her survival, of course. Anger at her being in this place at all. An unacceptable physical awareness.

An awareness that only built as he bent over her, checking for injuries. Scratches marked her neck and shoulders. He couldn't see much else wrong with her. Horror clenched his gut as he imagined what might have happened if he hadn't arrived.

Inky eyelashes fluttered against pale cheeks, but she didn't wake. What shocked him wasn't her sensuous beauty. What shocked him was that she still contrived to look innocent.

His gaze fell to her lips, parted slightly as she inhaled. Something that felt disconcertingly like lust shuddered through him. As he pulled her torn bodice over her shift, he struggled not to notice the satiny skin under the tattered dress. He was a scoundrel to think of her as a desirable woman, rather than as a duty to hand off as soon as possible.

Blast it to hell. The moment his eyes dropped to her breasts, she stirred.

"Have you seen enough?" she asked in English.

The Duke of Sedgemoor was famous for his self-assurance. Nobody made him blush. But heat prickled along his cheekbones as he straightened and regarded Penelope with what he hoped was his usual detachment.

"You don't appear seriously hurt." He flung away his cloak and set his sword and rifle on a table. He was prepared for this lawless corner of the world even if Pen wasn't.

"Not on my bosom at any rate." Clutching at her bodice, she struggled to sit.

He stifled a quelling response. After all, he had been ogling her. "What in heaven's name brought you to choose this hovel?"

One slender hand brushed her tumble of hair back from her face. To his dismay, he saw that she was shaking.

"Try the weather." Her tone was sharper than his sword.

"I know you could barge through an avalanche without creasing your neckcloth, but we lesser mortals must seek shelter when snow blocks the roads."

She was a fool to travel through the mountains in February, but her pallor silenced his scolding. The landlord bustled in, carrying a tray.

"Mi dispiace, mi dispiace..." The fellow burst into an emotive explanation from which Cam gathered that the brigands had locked him in the cellars.

Cam seized the tray, pleased to see a bottle of brandy and two glasses. After the last half hour, he deserved a drink. Once the landlord assured them that he'd arranged for some stout villagers to guard the hostelry—a matter of civic honor apparently—Cam reserved a bedroom and sent him away.

Pen had remained quiet through the innkeeper's recitation. So quiet that when they were alone, Cam tilted an eyebrow in her direction. Unless she'd changed beyond all recognition, quiet wasn't her natural state. "Are you all right?"

He had a sinking feeling that the answer was "no," but typically, she lifted her chin and glared at him. He wondered what she saw. Nothing she liked, if he read her expression right.

"Perfectly."

He'd believe that if her gaze hadn't skittered away from the blood on the floor. A girl carrying a bucket crept into the room and kneeled to clean up the mess. The strain on Pen's face eased.

These flashes of understanding were odd. Cam thought she'd be a stranger after all this time. Yet she wasn't. In many ways, she was still as familiar as his sister.

Peter had given Cam all Pen's recent letters so he had

an idea of where to seek her. It was how he'd tracked her to this backwater. He'd struggled against falling under the spell of the woman who wrote with such humor and vitality. She hadn't mentioned any amorous intrigues. But then, she'd been writing to her brother.

She swallowed and stared at him, he suspected in preference to the bloodstains. "What a coincidence that you turned up."

"A lucky coincidence," he said drily, lifting the brandy bottle.

"I hope you're pouring me one."

Another reminder that she wasn't the innocent he'd proposed to. "As you wish."

"I wish."

He passed her a brandy and tried to hide his surprise when she took a confident swig. In his world, unmarried ladies of good family didn't indulge in strong spirits. But of course, Pen no longer belonged to his world.

He thought of Lady Marianne Seaton, the woman he'd chosen to marry. Lady Marianne wouldn't drink brandy. But then he couldn't imagine Lady Marianne having the fortitude to shoot a bandit either.

He'd never seen Lady Marianne less than perfectly turned out. Pen sat before him completely disheveled. Her bodice sagged, revealing the lacy edge of her shift. It seemed a betrayal to acknowledge that of the two women, Pen struck him as considerably more beddable.

The devil of it was that the years hadn't diminished his reluctant sexual interest. The moment he'd seen Pen again, he'd wanted her. And now he was stuck with her until he got her safely back to England. What a hellish situation.

No matter what she'd got up to over here, she was his childhood companion and his friend's sister. She deserved courtesy and respect. If he took Pen for one night, he was honor-bound to take her for life. He'd grown up enough to recognize his foolishness in offering for her all those years ago. The last thing he needed was a permanent entanglement with a notorious Thorne.

Empty glass dangling from one hand, Pen slumped against the wall. The brandy had restored some color to her cheeks.

"It isn't a coincidence, is it?" Pen's voice was flat. The maid slipped from the room.

"No."

"Why are you here, Cam?"

Like a coward, he reached for the brandy bottle and refilled his glass. And hers. "Peter sent me. He was worried about you after Lady Bradford passed away." He paused. "I'm sorry about that."

Something that might have been grief flashed in the remarkable black eyes. She'd learned to guard her thoughts.

"Thank you." A hint of warmth entered her voice. "I miss her. She was excellent company."

As a boy, Cam had met Isabel, Lady Bradford. She'd possessed a vast fortune, and after a short, disastrous marriage, no interest in a second husband. Cam had liked her. She'd been eccentric and funny and opinionated. But nobody would consider her a suitable companion for an impressionable girl.

"Pen, I've got sad news." His gut cramped with regret and pity. Pen loved her brother dearly. "I'm so sorry, but Peter died a month ago in Calais."

Pen sucked in a breath. Her eyes went blank. What color she'd regained faded to ash.

Curse him, he was a bumbling idiot. He should have broken the news more gently.

Cam sat beside her on the bench, curling his arm around her shoulders. She was as stiff as a corpse. He firmed his grip, worried at her rigidity.

"Pen?" He hadn't thought about her seriously in years, except as the woman with the temerity to refuse him. This enforced intimacy revived older, sweeter memories of comforting her as a child. "Pen? Speak to me."

Slowly, she turned, blinking as though waking from bad dreams. "I was meeting him in Paris." Her voice was thready and raw. He wished he could do something to help instead of feeling so confounded helpless. "That's why I'm traveling at this ridiculous time of year." She sucked in a breath as if she needed to make a conscious choice to take in air. "What happened?"

"He collapsed on the quay."

"Oh, dear God." She started to tremble. "I didn't know he was ill. He should have told me."

"You know Peter."

"He wouldn't want to burden anyone." Tears thickened her voice as her unnatural composure cracked.

"He was a brave man." Peter might have been a numbskull in worldly terms, but at heart, he was as true as an oak tree. Once Cam had thought much the same of Pen.

"Yes."

Cam shifted closer. His heart ached with sorrow for her. She'd hardly come to terms with shooting a man. Now she faced the loss of a beloved brother.

She wriggled free. "Please—"

As he stood, he stifled a pang that she rejected his sympathy. He had no right to touch her. And given his unwilling attraction, it was better for both of them if he didn't. "What can I do?"

Usually he knew how to handle any situation. Not in

this case. Not with this woman so familiar, yet essentially a stranger.

The glassy look in her eyes made him wonder if she saw anything. His gut knotted when he saw how bravely she battled to dam her tears.

"Cam, can you please leave me alone?" Her hands twisted in her lap.

He shouldn't be hurt. Clearly she was distraught. But as a little girl, she'd always turned to him with her troubles. "I can't abandon you."

She shook her head and her voice cracked. "Just a little privacy, for pity's sake."

Inwardly he flinched, although he retained his cool exterior. "Of course."

He turned to go, before recalling that he had more to tell her. He caught her curling up against the wall as if shutting the world away. The impulse rose to haul her into his arms. He beat it back. She'd made it clear that he was the last man she wanted to touch her. "Pen, there's something else."

She didn't glance up, but her hands stiffened into talons in the dark blue skirt over her upraised knees. "Not now."

"I must." He felt like the world's biggest bastard. For once, not just because of the doubt surrounding his parentage. He straightened as if facing a dangerous foe. "Peter asked me to fetch you back to England."

"I don't need an escort." Her voice was lackluster as she stared blindly at the shutters.

Sarcasm tinged his response. "That was apparent when I arrived."

The tilt of her chin lacked defiance. "That's never happened before."

Any fool could see that she was near breaking. "I just wanted to say that we'll go on together."

He knew he'd said the wrong thing the moment the words left his mouth. Her eyes flashed with anger. It was an improvement on dumb grief. "Still giving orders, I see, Your Grace."

"Don't cross me on this, Pen," he said steadily.

She cast him a look of pure dislike. "Go away, Cam."

Chapter Three

The problem with small inns in the back of beyond was that one had a devil of a job finding somewhere private to observe comings and goings. Particularly during an ice storm of Biblical proportions.

Even after weeks of rough lodgings, this shabby inn was the worst Cam had encountered. He was reluctant to intrude upon Pen's grief. But nor did he want to sit outside in the snow, turning into an icicle. He couldn't retreat upstairs to his room for fear that the bandits might return. The villagers had rallied, but he couldn't entrust Pen's safety to people he didn't know.

Now he roamed the rooms like a lost dog, hungry and cold and unaccountably depressed by his reaction to Pen. And by her unenthusiastic reaction to him.

When she finally appeared, Cam was in the kitchen, suffering a glass of the pungent local red. The landlord's wife cooked dinner and the savory smell made Cam's stomach grumble. Confounding malefactors gave a man a powerful appetite.

"Good evening, Pen," he said evenly, standing. "Would you like some wine?"

"Perhaps later," she said without venturing inside.

She'd tucked her torn bodice into the neck of her shift. It reminded him, should he need reminding, that she'd faced down violence. It also reminded him, sod it, of her sweetly curved body. This continual, itching awareness of Penelope Thorne was tiresome. It wasn't the response he'd expected— or wanted. "Are you looking for me?"

"I want Maria. I'd like to wash and change." Her tone was almost as frigid as the weather.

"If you aren't using the taproom, let's bring our guardians inside for a meal. It's a perishing night."

"*Noblesse oblige*, Cam?"

He tried not to prickle under her mockery. Care for those who served him was bred into him. "If you wish to put it like that."

"*Poverina, poverina.*" Their landlady abandoned the stove and bustled forward to place her arms around Pen. Pen sagged against her substantial bosom and Cam caught unguarded vulnerability in her expression.

No wonder she'd skulked in the doorway. She'd made a valiant effort to hide her grief, but he immediately saw her red eyes and spiky eyelashes. While he'd cursed the inconvenience, she'd been crying her heart out. He felt like a rat.

He watched, admiring her strength, as she gathered herself and straightened, towering over the dumpy, gray-haired woman. Their landlady gently led Pen to the table. Within moments a glass of wine and a bowl of steaming soup sat before her.

"*Grazie.*" Pen's thanks were husky. She stared at the meal as if expecting poison.

"Eat it while it's hot." Cam cut her a slice from the hearty loaf in the center of the table.

Pen dipped her spoon in but nothing more. "Isn't eating in the kitchen beneath the superb Camden Rothermere?"

"Stop trying to skewer me. You're giving me indigestion." Despite her bristling hostility, he touched her hand. The contact shivered through him, even as he told himself he offered comfort. "Eat, Pen. It will work out."

"To your advantage, you think."

Silence fell, thick with animosity. Such a pity. He and Pen had always got along famously. Until he'd proposed.

"I'm sorry about Peter," he said quietly. He spoke in English to create some privacy. Around them, the business of the inn continued with maids carrying trays to the taproom.

"So am I." She didn't glance up, but her tone was less confrontational. "Thank you for saving me."

He didn't want gratitude, although God knew what he did want. "Any man would do the same," he said uncomfortably.

"*Noblesse oblige* again?"

He didn't respond. Instead he cut himself more bread. "Peter thought you were in trouble. From what I saw today, he was right."

"You must have cursed him for involving you. Seeking out an old friend's wayward sister wasn't on your agenda. Especially when we didn't part under the best circumstances."

Just like Pen to refer so bravely to their last awkward meeting. Cam sipped his wine and decided to be equally frank. "You needn't have run away. I had no intention of pestering you."

Color tinged her cheeks and to his relief, she ate a little, if only to avoid his gaze. "I wasn't running from you. I was running from my mother."

Ah. He should have guessed. "She bullied you?"

Pen's laugh was acerbic. "Into the ground. She even told my father to beat me until I agreed to marry you."

He should have approached Pen before seeking her father's permission. But in his arrogance, it had never occurred to him that she'd refuse. "Hell, Pen, did he?"

"Of course not." For one poignant moment, they shared a knowing glance like the friends they'd once been. "Can you see my father raising a hand to me?"

The late Lord Wilmott had been a weak man who had avoided his shrewish wife. "No. He'd scuttle up to London and hide in his club."

"He went to ground with his latest mistress. Mamma was not pleased."

"I'm sure." Just as he was sure that Lady Wilmott would take that displeasure out on her daughter. "So your aunt's offer arrived at the right moment."

"I'd always wanted to travel and I was rather dreading my season."

He wondered why. "You would have been the toast of London."

"I doubt it." Her lips twisted in wry denial. "The consensus in the county was that I was too headstrong for my own good. I can't imagine that the London beaux would have differed." She paused before he could protest. "I had no idea that I'd wounded your vanity so badly."

He shrugged, resenting the effort it took to speak lightly. "I daresay the experience was good for my soul."

Her expression didn't ease. "I'm sorry, Cam."

"You're not sorry you said no." He should drop this subject. Harping upon her refusal smacked of injured pride.

"It's a long time ago," she said softly. That was something new in her. The Pen he'd known would have met that incendiary remark head on. She bent to her soup again and ate with more relish.

"Will you fight me on returning to England?" he asked once she'd emptied the bowl.

He was pleased that she didn't look nearly so defeated. He hated to see her proud spirit cowed. "Do you want me to?"

He frowned. "However my high-handedness annoys you, I gave Peter my word that I'd take you back."

"Peter wasn't my keeper."

Although you need one. "Perhaps not, but he loved you and wanted to see you settled."

The bitter laugh reminded him of the day he'd proposed. "With a husband and children, no doubt."

"Is there something wrong with that?" Cam asked sharply.

"It would be wrong for me. I'll never marry."

She sounded so certain. And why shouldn't she? She'd established a life she liked, doing exactly what she liked with whom she liked. He'd almost applaud her audacity. Except that illogically, her impudence made him want to punch something. Preferably one of her damned *cicisbei*.

She cast him an assessing glance. "I'm well past my majority and as I have neither husband nor father to compel me, I'm a free agent."

He kept his voice even. "I intend to honor my promise."

The dangerous glint in her black eyes was familiar. "By hitting me over the head and tying me up?"

"If necessary," he said in a hard voice. Although God knows what he'd do if she refused to cooperate.

Her body sagged and he saw again the grief-stricken girl who had come into the kitchen. "It won't be necessary."

A mixture of surprise and pity made him set his glass down so roughly that wine sloshed onto the pine table. "What the hell?"

Faint amusement curved her lips. Those damnably kissable lips. "You're easier to tease than you once were, Cam."

"Why, you—"

She pushed back the rickety wooden chair and stood. In spite of her smile, sorrow dulled her eyes. "Peter and I were meeting in Paris to discuss Aunt Isabel's will. He was to be my legal representative in London. Now I must represent myself. You have my word I'm going home. But if we travel together, people will gossip."

Even before meeting this disturbingly attractive version of Penelope Thorne, he'd devised a strategy. "We'll avoid the cities until we reach my yacht at Genoa."

"Genoa? That means retracing my steps."

"Be damned if I'm crossing the Alps in February, Pen. We're heading south."

"I can head south on my own."

He was tempted to agree, if only to escape this attraction that had him counting her every breath. Some corner of his mind kept exclaiming in astonishment, *But this is Pen Thorne! With her untidy plaits and her muddy dresses and her skinned knees. How can Pen Thorne throw me into such a lather?* "You'll run into trouble. You were careless to set off with only that spineless coachman as escort."

Her eyes turned to black ice. "I don't owe you excuses or explanations." She turned to go. "I wish you good evening, Your Grace."

He surged to his feet. "Wait."

He caught her arm. When she was younger, he'd touched her a thousand times. Still, her soft warmth shuddered through him. Dear God, this was a catastrophe. He struggled to bring Lady Marianne's face to mind, but instead of her cool beauty, all he saw was gypsy-dark hair and eyes flashing insolence.

She stopped. "Let me go, Cam."

"Do I have your word that you won't disappear into the night?"

She jerked her arm and he released her, if only because touching her threatened his precarious control. "The snow has closed the roads north. I wouldn't be surprised if the roads south are impassable too."

"So we're trapped."

Her eyes narrowed. "Exactly, Your Grace." Drawing her cape around her like an ermine cloak, Pen marched out, spine straight and hips swaying with a sinuous impertinence that set his heart cartwheeling.

Damn her.

Chapter Four

Oldhaven House, London, February 1828

Harry Thorne took one last puff on his cheroot and tossed it with a contemptuous flick into the bushes lining the terrace. He hadn't enjoyed it, although smoking was the craze for the young bucks he ran with.

Just lately he didn't enjoy much. The malaise had set in last month after his older brother Peter's death. The exciting life that a fellow of twenty-three with no responsibilities led in the capital had lost all savor.

Guilt added to his depressed spirits. Hell, if he'd known the truth about Peter's troubles, he'd have rushed to his brother's side. But Peter had kept his difficulties to himself. Still, it was a damned bitter pill to swallow that his brother had breathed his last, alone in a foreign country, and Harry hadn't had a chance to say good-bye.

Harry wandered away from the ballroom into the dark garden. The violins scratching out the latest waltz faded until the music was a whisper.

Somewhere out here Lady Vera Standish waited, finally ready, if he read the signals, to surrender her plump prettiness. She'd challenged him to find her. After months of dogged pursuit, he damn well hoped she wasn't trying too hard to hide.

Except even the prospect of exploring Lady Vera's much admired, and much caressed charms didn't dispel his megrims. He reached the garden wall, well away from the house. When he heard a rustle, he turned, struggling to muster a flicker of excitement.

Then a sound he didn't expect. A sniff and a muffled sob.

Not Lady Vera.

He retreated to grant some privacy to whoever huddled in the bushes.

Another sniff. Another choked sob.

He took a couple of steps down the white gravel path. If someone cried out here alone, it was none of his damned business. If he delayed, Vera Standish would turn to some other swain. She wasn't noted for her patience.

His shoe scraped across a rock. Silence descended. Whoever was hiding now knew that she wasn't alone.

Harry recognized that he was incapable of leaving someone to suffer. As a rake and roué, he was a rank failure. With a sigh, he turned toward the holly-smothered alcove. As he battled through the prickly greenery, he couldn't help thinking of the prince struggling through thorns toward Sleeping Beauty.

"Please don't come any closer," a soft, broken voice whispered from mere feet away.

"Too late," he muttered, bursting through the hedge into an enclosed hollow. His eyes had adjusted and he easily made out the girl in a light-colored gown cowering against the wooden seat.

"Go away." Although he couldn't see her face, she sounded very young. Her lace handkerchief twisted in her hands.

"Are you all right?" He ventured closer and she pressed back.

"Perfectly."

There. He'd asked. She was fine. He could now find Lady Vera. "Why are you crying?"

"I'm not crying." Her quaking voice proclaimed her a liar.

"You sound like you are."

"It's a bad cold," she said stiffly.

"You shouldn't be sitting outside, then."

"And you shouldn't be talking to strange women without an introduction."

The show of spirit intrigued him. He could make out very little apart from her slenderness and the constant tugging at the handkerchief.

"Are you?"

"Am I what?" she asked with a hint of snap.

He hid a smile. "Strange."

She stood. The full moon chose that moment to emerge from behind a cloud, granting his first glimpse of his damsel in distress.

He felt like someone had punched him in the gut.

How in hell had he missed her before this? Had he been so fixated on the pinchbeck of Vera Standish when somewhere in that ballroom waited pure gold?

"I'm not strange." She surveyed him with wide eyes in a delicate face under a pile of thick golden hair. "I'm beginning to think you might be."

His damsel was breathtakingly lovely. "Why the devil are you sitting out here all alone?" he asked roughly. "You don't know who might come upon you."

Tentative mischief lit her expression. He'd been right to suspect liveliness beneath her distress. "Well, you did."

He should say something rakish. But when he looked at her, his heart stopped. She was the prettiest girl he'd ever seen. Who on earth was she? Damn it, he'd been out in society since leaving university and he had a reputation as a dog with the ladies. But this girl stole his ability to do more than mumble and act the looby. He managed a smile, quite a feat when his heart performed somersaults in his chest. "I'm generally accounted quite benign."

She stared at him as if she'd never seen a man. "I should go."

He chanced a step nearer and felt a surge of triumph when she didn't retreat, although even in the uncertain light, he saw her wariness. Not quite as innocent as all that, apparently. "You don't want to go back into the ballroom with red eyes."

"Nobody would notice."

His laugh was short. "This is your first season, isn't it?"

"Yes."

"Then take advice from someone older and wiser—the old tabbies notice everything. And they pass it on. If you don't want the world to know that you've been crying, you'll enter that room utterly composed."

Her lush lips turned down. "I don't like London."

"You will."

Daringly he reached for one of her gloved hands. She started, but even through two layers of fabric, he felt her warmth. The urge to strip away both gloves and test the softness of her skin beat like a war drum in his head. But one false move and she'd scarper for the ballroom, red eyes or not.

"I'm not so green that I don't know a stranger shouldn't hold a lady's hand," she said drily.

"Yes, remiss of you not to tell me your name."

To his surprise, she laughed. He was glad to see her regain her cheerfulness. "It's better that you don't know who I am."

"Won't you tell me why you're crying?"

She raised shining eyes to his and he suffered another blow from an invisible assailant. "You've just told me I can't trust anyone."

Hoist by his own petard. "You can trust me."

An unimpressed look crossed her face. "I'm sure every untrustworthy person in the world says that."

Good Lord, she was sweet. "Where does that leave us?"

"With plans to return to the ballroom?"

"Are you deserting me?"

Another faint smile. He had a delicious sense that she tested her power. "Yes."

He fleetingly wondered whether perhaps he'd dipped too deeply into the punch. But when her smile widened and his heart lurched like a drunken sailor, he recognized that this intoxication reached far beyond lowly alcohol's power. "Cruel beauty."

"How can I be cruel when you've been so very kind?"

He groaned. "That makes me sound like an aged uncle."

This time when she tried to withdraw, he let her. "Nevertheless, it's true."

"Will you save me a dance?"

Her poise revived with every second. "My card is full."

"What about tomorrow night?"

"We mightn't be at the same party."

It was his turn to smile. "Oh, that we will, my mysterious miss."

The moonlight was bright enough to reveal the flash of unhappiness that crossed her face. "There's no point flirting with me."

"There's every point."

She shook her head and he wished he believed that she teased him. "I'm spoken for."

Spoken for? "You're not married?"

Thick sheets of lead coated the heart that had been lighter than air. Something had happened to him tonight in this garden, something momentous.

"Not yet."

Not yet? What the hell did that mean?

Before he could question her, she turned and hared off through an opening in the hedge that he'd missed. And bugger it, he still didn't know her name.

Something in him insisted that she'd seen him as clearly as he'd seen her. That she'd felt the immediate connection. Stronger than attraction. Affinity, and an odd recognition, as though their encounter was preordained.

He sighed and sank onto the seat. Could a man's world change in an instant?

When Harry rejoined the party, he immediately located the girl. He'd wondered whether to blame the moonlight for his enchantment. Now that he saw her clearly, she still took his breath away. Candlelight revealed details that he'd missed. The precise shade of her gold hair. The creamy skin. The pink flush on her cheeks.

A pink flush that heightened when she cast one nervous glance to where he stood near the doors.

Satisfaction that she'd sought him out flooded him. His eyes followed her as she twirled around the room, graceful as a flying bird in her white dress. She was dancing with the Marquess of Leath. Could his rival be James Fairbrother? The man was filthy rich and from a powerful family.

Across the crowded room, Lady Vera scowled at him as if she'd like to skin him alive. He shrugged and sent her a regretful smile. How could he explain that after a chance meeting, he was no longer the same man?

"Who is that pretty girl with Leath?" he asked with studied nonchalance when his friend Beswick sidled up.

Beswick took a few moments to locate her. The man must be blind. She outshone every woman here the way the sun outshone the moon. "The blonde?"

The goddess. "Yes."

"That's Sophie Fairbrother." Beswick regarded him in disbelief. "That's setting your sights too high for a penniless younger son with no prospects, chum. She's Leath's sister. Word is that she's promised to Desborough, although nothing official's been announced."

Another punch in the guts. Was that why his beauty had been crying? Her family forced her into an unwanted match? "Earl Desborough?"

Beswick laughed derisively. "Is there another? He and Leath are political pals and this will unite the two great fortunes. The chit comes with a fat dowry. Surprised you haven't heard talk of her."

"Does she love Desborough?" Harry asked, then cursed himself for the betraying question.

Another scoffing laugh from Beswick. "Who cares when she brings all that gold? Good God, I'd make a play for her myself if Leath didn't know that my pockets are to let. Wish he'd forget about fortune hunters and concentrate on his spat with Sedgemoor."

Without shifting his attention from Sophie Fairbrother, Harry asked, "What spat?"

"Have you been living under a rock?"

Harry cast his friend a look of cordial dislike. "No, just

attending Peter's funeral and helping Elias settle into his role as the new Lord Wilmott."

Dismay filled Beswick's good-natured face. "Beg pardon, old man. I forgot. Blame it on my frustration at seeing such a fat pigeon fly to someone who already has a full dovecote."

Reluctantly Harry smiled. Beswick's financial woes were long-standing. "Buck up, Beswick. It's always darkest before the dawn."

"Especially if you can't afford candles," his friend replied glumly. "You must have heard about Richard Harmsworth and Sedgemoor exposing Neville Fairbrother, Leath's uncle, as a thief? Fairbrother shot himself before charges were laid, but the investigation has filled the papers. Jonas Merrick gathered most of the evidence—as you'd expect with his contacts. That man knows before a mouse farts in the wainscoting, I vow."

Perhaps Harry had been living under a rock. "The uncle's doings have tainted all the Fairbrothers?"

"Pretty much. The word is that Leath hopes this spectacular marriage will restore the family prestige."

"So she's a sacrificial lamb." Poor Sophie. The dance finished and her brother returned her to a group of grandees including, he noticed, Desborough.

"Sacrificial virgin, more like." Beswick's voice lowered. "Desborough's a lucky dog. Brass doesn't usually come in such an appealing package."

"Watch your mouth, Beswick," Harry snarled.

Even without looking, Harry knew his friend regarded him like he was going mad. The way he felt, perhaps his friend was right. "Steady on, man. She's a pretty girl who's completely out of reach. We've admired plenty of those in our time."

The Thornes were inclined to sudden, but lasting passions. Sophie Fairbrother had no idea what she'd sparked tonight. As if she sensed his thoughts, Sophie looked up sharply and immediately found him. Even across the room, he saw the hectic color in her alabaster cheeks. Dear Lord, she was a peach.

Harry held her eyes. He meant to make her his. Let the rest of the world go hang.

Chapter Five

Val d'Aosta, February 1828

Very carefully, Pen inched open the door from her chamber on the upper floor. Despite exhaustion, roiling turmoil had stopped her sleeping. Grief for Peter. Anger that he hadn't confided in her about his illness. Resentment at Cam's arrogance. Impatience with herself for finding Cam as compelling as ever, even when she burned to crown him with the nearest stewpot.

Just seeing Cam confirmed that agonizing truth. She hated to admit that she was still that most pathetic creature, the lovelorn female yearning after a man who would never love her back.

Since refusing his proposal, she'd done her damnedest to forget Camden Rothermere. Her aunt had led an active and interesting life, mixing with people who found English manners too restrictive. In the past nine years, Pen had met poets and painters and musicians, wandering aristocrats and antiquarians, travelers and scientists.

She'd learned that her idiosyncratic character, too individual to meet approval at home, appealed to those who appreciated intelligence and spirit. Her broken heart had found some small solace in the admiration of brilliant, sophisticated men. Cam didn't want her, but that didn't mean she was undesirable.

Occasionally she'd wondered if someone might usurp Cam's place in her affections. But to her despair, she was a true Thorne. She loved once and she loved deeply.

Which meant she couldn't bear to spend the next weeks cooped up with Cam. Last night, she'd told Giuseppe and Maria to be waiting at five, whatever the weather. Luckily, the storm had died overnight and when she checked out her narrow bedroom window, the road from the village looked passable. Even if it wasn't, she'd damn well walk rather than suffer Cam's company all the way back to England.

Now that Peter wouldn't meet her in Paris—she stifled a pang, she'd grieve once she was out of this pickle—she'd go south as Cam suggested. Then she'd make her way to London.

The corridor outside her room was black as a cave in Hades. She edged forward. Once she made it downstairs and outside to the stables, she was on her way.

"Going somewhere?"

She jumped and dropped her bag to the wooden floor. Gasping, she whirled toward the shadows near the door. "You scared me."

"Not enough, apparently," Cam said drily.

She ignored the remark. "What are you doing outside my room?"

"What are you doing dressed for travel?"

"How do you know I'm dressed for travel?"

"Aren't you?" he asked coolly. "Shall we continue this discussion in private?"

"We have nothing to say to each other," she said crisply, marching past.

"After so long? You wound me." He caught her arm and bustled her into her room.

"You have no right." She struggled to break free. He'd touched her too often since he'd saved her. And every time he set her pulse racing.

"Perhaps not. Will you stay and listen?"

"You're such a bully," she said sullenly.

"Sticks and stones. Do I release you?"

She wanted to kick him. "Yes."

Cam let her go and moved past. He paused before the window, his tall, lean shape silhouetted against the light reflected from the snow outside. After some clicks and scrapes, the candle on her nightstand bloomed into light.

"I hate to mention your dignity again, but isn't it degrading for a duke of the realm to sleep across a lady's threshold like a servant?" she asked with pointed sweetness.

He glanced up with a faint smile. Despite her irritation, her heart lurched. How she wished he wasn't so beautiful with his narrow, intense face and his glinting green eyes and his level dark brows. After nearly ten years without him, he still dazzled her. It just wasn't fair.

"I didn't have to prostrate myself on your doorstep." He paused. "Giuseppe told me your plans."

Blast Giuseppe and his flapping gums.

She didn't realize she'd spoken aloud until Cam laughed. "You should give him his marching orders. He's worse than useless."

"Perhaps you should offer him a place in your household," she asked with more of that dangerous sweetness.

"Not on your life. I value loyalty too much to employ that

weasel. Pen, do you really want me trailing you all the way back to Dover?"

He made her sound absurd. "You'd do that?"

"I would."

Of course he would. He'd accepted the obligation of her safety and he wouldn't relinquish the burden short of death. Cam's principles were a deuced nuisance. She released a long-suffering sigh. "Were you always this annoying?"

"Probably." He glanced around. "Shall we go?"

"Now?"

He lifted the candle. "Your carriage awaits. I paid the landlord last night."

"What about your carriage?"

"I rode."

Aghast, she stared at him. "Through the snow?"

"Through the snow." He paused. "You've put me to a deal of trouble, Pen."

Her lips tightened even as guilt pricked her. It had been a horrific winter. He'd faced weeks of peril on her behalf. "I didn't ask you to come."

"Perhaps not, but set aside your stubbornness and admit that you'll be better off with a man to ease your way."

Patronizing swine. She left the bedroom and gingerly descended the insecure staircase, careful not to grip the makeshift banister too hard. "What a typically male thing to say."

"Which makes it no less true." His voice warmed a fraction. She wished to heaven she wasn't so attuned to every nuance. She wished to heaven she'd never met him again.

On the ground floor she faced Cam, illuminated in candlelight at the top of the stairs. God save her, could he look any more appealing? She bit back a bitter laugh.

If he'd suborned her coachman, she didn't have much

choice about going with him. Still, she didn't like to admit defeat any more than His Grace, the Duke of Sedgemoor. "We need to set some rules."

He cocked his eyebrow with familiar mockery as he descended, carrying her bag. "That's not like you, Pen. You usually prefer everything free and easy."

Ouch. "Just because I didn't settle into middle age before I hit twenty doesn't make me a complete flibbertigibbet. I've traveled for years without major problems."

"Yesterday was a close call."

She wished he hadn't arrived to find her at such a disadvantage. On the other hand, without his intervention, she doubted that she'd be here this morning. "Are you going to dine out on that rescue all the way to England?"

"You've got a nasty tongue, my girl." He sounded like he appreciated her barbed responses.

Oh, no. Oh, no, no, no. They weren't falling into the habit of private little messages. They weren't going to act like intimate friends. She glared. "I've developed many unfortunate habits," she said flatly. "Are we going?"

"Your eagerness for my company fills my heart with elation."

"Give yourself a day or so in a carriage with me and see if you feel the same," she snapped and flounced outside to where the perfidious Giuseppe waited in the driver's seat. A high-bred bay gelding was tied to the back of the coach. The snow might have stopped, but it was bitterly cold. Pen hoped Giuseppe froze.

When Cam entered the vehicle, she was bundled under fur throws with Maria beside her. The lamps inside were lit. He settled with his back toward the horses. Again, the perfect gentleman.

He banged on the ceiling to tell Giuseppe to go. Pen bit

back a snide comment about him taking charge. Even as a small boy, Cam had been inclined to command. Seven years as Duke of Sedgemoor had only fortified his dictatorial tendencies. If she bridled at every order, she'd be a wreck before they reached the foot of this mountain, let alone England.

Maria curled into the corner and closed her eyes. Cam shot the girl a disapproving glance. Servants at Fentonwyck displaying such *lèse-majesté* would be dismissed without a character. Pen stifled the impulse to justify herself. In Maria's defense, Pen saw little point making the girl sit up when she had nothing constructive to do.

Already Cam threatened to become a tyrant. If he was hers, she'd bring him down a few pegs. But to her everlasting regret, he'd never be hers.

"Does your maid speak English?" he asked once they were on their way.

"No." The mountain road was bumpy. Pen grabbed the leather strap against the jolting.

"Good." He extended his closed hand. "Here."

Automatically she reached for what he offered. He dropped something small and round and warm onto her palm. She looked down. It was the Sedgemoor signet ring, carved with two rearing unicorns, their horns crossed to make an X.

Shocked, she looked up. "What are you doing?"

"It's a loan."

Her fingers closed around the ring. For centuries, it had been the tangible symbol of Rothermere power. "Why?"

To her surprise, he looked uncomfortable. He hadn't looked at all awkward when he'd pushed her around. "Wear it on your ring finger. I don't imagine anyone will recognize us and we'll use false names. But we'll attract less attention if people think we're married."

Feeling sick, she stared at the gold ring gleaming in the lamplight. It taunted her with the cruel reality that she'd never be his bride. "How...practical."

He heard her implied criticism. His lips tightened. "You know the consequences if we're discovered." His tone bit. "It's not as if you want to marry me."

She sighed, depressed that he held a grudge when they both knew she'd done him a favor by refusing him. "Cam, you can't still be angry about the proposal. That makes no sense. Especially when now we've met again, you must see that I'd make the worst wife in the world."

His jaw hardened. "Don't flatter yourself, Pen. I got over any youthful pique years ago."

She wasn't convinced, although it seemed out of character for Cam to be such a poor loser. Mostly he'd won their various games, but if he hadn't, he'd taken defeat in good spirit.

"Well, stop harking back to it," she snapped.

"I'm offering you a ring. I'm inevitably reminded of the last time I did that."

Her heart lurched with futile longing. If he'd offered love along with the ring, they'd have been married nearly a decade. Gracelessly she shoved the ring onto her finger. "Life was easier when I traveled alone."

"Stow it, Pen. We're together until we reach home soil. You're always cranky when you lose." He settled into his seat, folding his arms across his powerful chest. His black superfine coat was so beautifully cut, it didn't strain against the movement. The boy she'd known had been quick and strong, but nine years had turned Cam into a man ready to take on the world and win.

"I haven't lost," she said coolly. "I've retired to regroup."

More displeasure blasted her way. He'd perfected the

crushing effect of his stare since their last meeting. "Don't cross me on this, Pen. I promised Peter I'd get you to England."

She strove to remain uncrushed. "What happens when we arrive? Will you dog my footsteps until I perish of old age? Or irritation, which is more likely."

His smile held no amusement. "Once you're safely home, as far as I'm concerned, you can go to the devil."

Chapter Six

Chetwell House, London, February 1828

Harry marked the moment that Sophie slipped from the crowded ballroom. Hardly surprising when he'd observed her every move.

All week, he'd waited impatiently to catch her alone. The burning need to speak about something more significant than the weather had built until it threatened to explode.

The night they'd met, he'd obtained a formal introduction. He'd managed a country dance and a schottische with her since—quite a feat when she rapidly became the toast of London. During their dances, he'd confined himself to platitudes. He'd had to be satisfied with touching her hand and delighting in the shy attraction glittering in her blue eyes.

Tonight, neither the watchful marquess nor Lord Desborough attended. Under other circumstances, Harry might admire Leath's protectiveness. In worldly terms, an undistinguished younger son from a ramshackle family was no fit match for the Marquess of Leath's sister. But surely Sophie should marry a man who adored her, rather than one who treated her as Desborough did, like a pretty pet to fuss over or ignore at his whim.

Harry didn't move in Desborough's exalted circles. But he had eyes and a brain, however rarely he'd exerted it. While he discerned no dislike between Sophie and the man touted as her husband, he discerned no genuine attraction either.

Damn it, she deserved better.

Whether she deserved Harry Thorne, well, that was her choice.

Harry tracked Sophie into the gallery. The long room faced the gardens with doors open onto the terrace. Fortunately, for February, it was a mild night, but even so, away from the crush, he shivered in the chill air. At the far end of the room, a couple he didn't know bent their heads toward each other.

Sophie paused before a portrait of a bewigged, double-chinned gentleman. She looked beautiful tonight in rose silk and with pearls tangled in her upswept hair. Harry stopped a few feet away, waiting until the couple wandered into the garden without sparing him a glance.

"You followed me," Sophie said, without turning.

What point prevaricating? "Yes."

As he'd stalk a skittish animal, he edged closer. He stared at her vulnerable nape, wanting desperately to kiss her there. Wanting to kiss her everywhere.

It was too soon.

Still she didn't glance back. "My brother warned me against you."

Did the bastard, by God? "What did he say?" Harry kept his voice soft. He and Sophie might be alone, but they were still in public.

"That you're a fortune hunter."

He laughed dismissively. "You know I'm not interested in your money." While he'd love to see her face, there was a delicious suspense in standing so near, catching the soft drift of her fragrance, flowers and beautiful girl.

"That's what a fortune hunter would say."

"Probably. But in my case it's true." He paused. "That wasn't all he said."

She shifted and spoke reluctantly. "He said your family was—"

"Shady?"

Finally she turned. She didn't look annoyed or flustered. She looked curious. "After Uncle Neville's villainy, our family can't boast."

He was impressed that she broached the scandal. Harry had always sensed that Sophie Fairbrother was made of stronger stuff than society suspected. Which meant that something more important than a petty disappointment had made her sob her heart out in the Oldhavens' garden.

Despite his determination to remain within the bounds of propriety—just—he took her arm. She gasped in surprise without pulling away. Beneath his touch, her skin was smooth and cool. A bolt of heat sizzled through him, startling him with its power.

"If I drag you into a private room, will you scream?" he murmured.

He wasn't sure what reaction he expected. Certainly not a soft giggle. "That depends on what you intend to do."

For a beat, shock held him silent. She wasn't afraid. Instead she looked interested and eager. Heaven help him. Clasping her slender arm and drowning in eyes as blue as a summer sky, he didn't feel like a gentleman. He felt like a starving man presented with a table groaning under lashings of food.

"Not as much as I want to," he admitted.

He whisked her behind the nearest door. The latch's click sounded like thunder. His heart thudded with excitement and uneasiness. If they were discovered, there would be the devil to pay.

"This is dangerous." His grip softened to a caress and instinct alone led his hand to her other arm. This room was as dark as a coalmine.

"It is. My brother is a famous shot."

The warmth of her skin under his hands set him trembling. "For a few minutes alone with you, I'll take any risk."

"Will you think that when he puts a bullet into you?" In the quiet gloom, the rasp of her breathing was audible. She was more nervous than she pretended. That hint of vulnerability contained Harry's rocketing desire as nothing else could.

"Even then, it's worth it."

"Such a flatterer."

He knew he deserved the mockery, but he couldn't like it. How to explain that this time everything was different? Sophie wasn't one of his women. She was *the* woman.

"I'll be missed if I stay too long."

He smiled. "That sounds promising."

"How so?"

"That you mean to stay at all."

She offered no coy protests. The more he saw of her, the more he liked her. "Are you a fortune hunter?"

He breathed unsteadily too. Not because of fear, but because her nearness set his heart galloping like a wild horse across the moors. Her scent tinged the air. Something fresh like running water. "What do you think?"

"I think I've spent far too long thinking about you."

Triumph flooded him. He exhaled and cupped her

face, feeling her silky cheeks beneath his palms. "I can't stop thinking about you either. Are you going to marry Desborough?"

She started, but didn't move away. "My brother wants me to."

"Do you?"

"It's a good match," she said unenthusiastically.

He released her. "So good it makes you hide away and cry."

"That wasn't—"

"Don't lie, Sophie. Not to me."

"You can't call me Sophie."

He laughed softly. "I can't address the woman who shares my cupboard by her title. It's a rule of society."

Her gurgle of amusement made his blood fizz with happiness. "You don't strike me as a man who follows rules, Mr. Thorne."

The need to kiss her surged, but despite her unexpected if hesitant cooperation, he didn't want to frighten her away. "You've listened to too much gossip. And my name is Harry."

The pause that followed vibrated with significance.

"Harry..." she breathed, turning his prosaic name into music.

His heart crashed against his ribs. Dear God, he was in trouble. "Lovely, lovely Sophie," he whispered and despite the risk of taking everything too far too fast, he curled his arms around her.

"Oh!" She jerked from the brush of his lips.

He set her free and withdrew as far as the cupboard allowed. "Forgive me."

To his astonishment, she caught his shirt. "You took me by surprise."

"I had no right—"

"You're a very chivalrous rake, Harry Thorne," she said drily.

Her tone piqued his curiosity. Ignoring common sense and self-preservation, not to mention the gentleman's code, he placed his hand over hers. "Don't you want me to be chivalrous?"

"Not right now."

"You deserve better than a furtive courtship," he said helplessly, even as his other hand snaked around her slender waist to arch her against him. "But since the day we met, I've dreamed of you."

Her sigh conveyed wonder. "Really?"

His voice deepened into urgency. "I've dreamed of kissing you."

And other things, but he couldn't sully her innocence with his wanton fantasies.

"I'd like to make your dreams come true." She leaned closer, her breasts grazing his chest. "Will you kiss me, Harry?"

"Sophie—" Her scent filled his head like wine, overwhelmed thought. His hand tightened around her waist.

"Don't you want to?" she asked in a small voice.

"Of course I bloody want to," he said roughly, then dragged in a breath. "I'm sorry. I'm not acting the gentleman."

This time her sigh was disgruntled. "You're acting too much the gentleman."

"Sweetheart—"

She interrupted before he pointed out that he cared for her reputation. After all, how convincing could any avowal sound when he embraced her in a cupboard in the middle of a ball?

"I don't want to hear it." Her voice softened. "Unless it's 'Kiss me, Sophie.'"

Oh, hell. How could he resist? "Kiss me, Sophie."

Harry lashed her to him and pressed his mouth to hers. Her lips trembled beneath his. Her fluttering uncertainty hinted that this was her first kiss. Tenderness stabbed at his heart.

Automatically he gentled, nipping and licking at her, until her breath hitched and she leaned closer. His tongue slid into her mouth, tasting her fully. Her flavor blazed through him like lightning.

The world beyond Sophie's clumsy but ardent responses vanished. All Harry knew was her warmth and the way her tongue danced around his. Her broken moans. Her soft, quivering body pressed into his.

It took him longer than it should to realize that she'd stopped participating. He raised his head and struggled to see her through the darkness. "What—"

"Shh!" Her hands formed claws in his shirt. Now she trembled not with passion, but with terror.

There were voices outside. Damn. His arms tightened and he drew Sophie against him. Anyone within a mile's radius must hear his heart. He wasn't frightened for himself but for her. Only a bloody fool would risk this encounter.

He strained to hear if the people outside mentioned the Marquess of Leath's sister. They discussed supper arrangements. If Harry hadn't been thickheaded with delight, he'd have recognized his hostess's voice immediately. She seemed to be talking to her butler.

Fleetingly, he relaxed. Until he wondered if the butler needed supplies from this tiny storeroom.

In vibrating silence, Harry and Sophie clung together until the voices faded. Eventually he whispered in her ear. "I need to get you out of here."

With a trust he didn't deserve, she laid her cheek upon his chest. "I thought I'd die when I heard them."

"I shouldn't have brought you in here. But I've been desperate to see you, and your brother's like a collie with a ewe lamb."

"He's terrified of fortune hunters spoiling his plans."

"To be fair, that's his duty."

"But you're not a fortune hunter."

"I'm not." He paused. *"I'm not?"*

"A fortune hunter wouldn't hesitate to ruin me to force a marriage."

Marriage? The word clanged through him like a great bell.

The malaise dogging his heels disappeared in Sophie's company. The sight of her turned his day to brilliance. That left the choice of taking himself off and leaving her to the man her brother chose. Or ruining her. An idea which made every cell in his body revolt.

Or marriage.

"Harry?" she asked on a thread of sound. "What's wrong?"

It was too early to mention lifelong commitment. Already she'd surrendered more than he'd hoped. His heart kicked as he remembered those wondrous kisses.

He eased his grip. "We've been here too long."

"Yes." Regret weighted her voice. "Will I...will I see you again?"

Despite the last fraught moments, he couldn't contain a laugh. "What do you think?"

"I don't know. I'm not experienced with flirtation."

Another pang of painful tenderness. He wasn't experienced with love. In this glorious new world, they were both innocents. "When can I meet you?"

"The park." She sounded relieved. "I ride tomorrow morning."

"With your brother?"

"He's away this week."

"I'll find you."

"I hope so." He caught a quiver of uncertainty.

"I swear it," he said.

"I don't want to leave you."

How he basked in hearing that, however difficult it made this parting. "I don't want to let you go. But I must."

He kissed her quickly. He meant the contact to be sweet and brief, but he found himself drowning again.

Luckily for failing willpower, she broke away and opened the door a crack. "Tomorrow," she whispered, slipping outside.

"Tomorrow," he confirmed, then waited in the dark while she shut the door with a soft snick. Right now he wasn't fit for civilized company. He hoped Sophie was. He had a horrible feeling that she'd look mussed and thoroughly kissed.

Chapter Seven

Fontana dei Monte, Italian Alps, February 1828

I t was snowing again. As this purgatorial week proceeded, Pen began to think that the world contained only snow and ice and wind. And flea-ridden inns. And rude servants.

And men who tried to push her around.

Or more accurately, one man who pushed her around. His overbearing Grace, the Duke of Sedgemoor.

Pen and Cam traveled as Lord and Lady Pembridge, using the Sedgemoor heir's courtesy title. She supposed that now they left the mountains behind, the inns would become busier. She and Cam would need to be more discreet than ever in case they met someone who knew them.

Their coach bumped its way into the tiny hillside village where they would spend the night—or rather where the man who had assigned himself lord and master had decreed they'd stay. Idly Pen wondered when she'd finally break. Would this be the day when she pushed Cam headfirst into one of the towering snow drifts lining what was optimistically termed a road?

Cam sat beside her now, staring out the window as if the acres of white formed a glorious vista considerably more appealing than his companion. They'd had a long day. Not that they'd covered much ground. It was discouraging how much time they took to traverse every mile. Cam had been right, much as she hated admitting it. Crossing the Alps in February had been an asinine plan.

Over the last days, the temperature inside the carriage had been colder than outside. In public, Cam might treat Pen with deference that set her teeth on edge, but their infrequent private conversations had been stilted and tinged with hostility.

The coach shuddered to a stop, jerking Maria awake on the seat opposite. Pen had developed enormous envy for her maid's ability to sleep through anything. Strangely Maria had immediately accepted the news that her mistress and the duke traveled as a married couple.

Desperate to stretch her cramped legs, more desperate to escape the oppressive atmosphere, Pen opened the door and jumped out before Paolo, their new coachman, could help her. Despite herself, she glanced back at Cam, expecting the usual disapproval.

But the expression in his watchful green eyes troubled her. In another man, she'd interpret the gleam as reluctant interest. But Cam treated her as a troublesome obligation, not a woman he wanted. Still, that level gaze made her shiver like someone brushed an icy hand across bare skin.

After weeks of rough travel, Cam was no longer a polished specimen of British manhood. His linen was grubby, his clothes crumpled, his boots cloudy with dirt. And he looked tired. He pretended that he rose above human weakness, but the man in the carriage looked exhausted to the bone. She'd always thought his impossible pursuit of perfection made for a lonely life. Right now, he looked heartbreakingly alone.

She resented Cam's bossiness. She resented, much good it did, his inability to love her. Even so, he'd undergone considerable trouble for her and she'd rewarded him with a fit of the sullens. Her tone was friendlier than usual. "Cam, are you coming inside?"

Paolo disappeared to secure rooms. Cam regarded her with familiar coolness. "Of course."

He sounded assured and dismissive. Much as he'd sounded all week. She bit back a sigh. Their easy communication had gone forever. She should be glad. The last thing she needed was a reminder of what a wonderful companion Cam could be. But good sense was difficult when one was stuck with a grumpy nobleman on an endless road to perdition.

"Well, do it soon. I'm freezing."

Grim humor lit his face as he left the carriage and extended his arm. "As you command, my lady."

Reluctantly she laid her hand upon his forearm, disturbingly aware of the muscles beneath her gloved palm. His physical reality was a perpetual torment. Over the years, he'd faded in her memory to an over-idealized cipher. Real Cam was more complex, more powerful, and more compelling than any fantasy.

Paolo chose that moment to return, his round, good-natured face troubled. "Milord, milady, there is a question."

Surprised, Pen turned to the man she'd learned to respect for his ability to make the best of unpromising circumstances. However arrogant Cam had been to dismiss the craven Giuseppe without her permission, he'd unearthed a treasure in Paolo. "What is it?"

"A storm has hit the inn and only one room is fit for sleeping."

"That's unacceptable," Cam said sharply while the nightmare ramifications of Paolo's news invaded Pen's mind.

Paolo flinched at Cam's displeasure—and looked understandably puzzled. He'd never shown any curiosity when his employers requested separate rooms. He probably attributed it to English eccentricity. But surely at a pinch, a married couple could share a bed.

A freezing February night with deteriorating weather counted as a pinch.

"We shall travel on," Cam said coldly.

The prospect of driving further prompted even imperturbable Paolo to protest. "*Signore*, the next village is ten miles away, over the mountain. There will be heavy snow tonight."

"With fresh horses—" Cam began in his "I won't shift even for stampeding elephants" tone.

"Cam, we can't go on. It's dangerous."

"Your courage fails?" He turned a supercilious expression upon her and Pen suppressed a shiver unrelated to the rapidly dropping temperature. "You were all set to drive single-handed across every glacier between here and Paris."

Oh, how she itched to shove him into the snow. Deciding that convincing Cam would take too long, she spoke to Paolo. "If there's only one room, we'll take it. Thank you for your care."

Paolo went pink with pleasure. "*Grazie,* milady."

"Shall we go inside, madam?" Cam continued in an undertone, "I thought you'd be the last person to welcome tonight's arrangements."

She snatched her hand from his arm and cast him a fulminating glare. "It's stupid to struggle on in the dark through an ice storm."

"It's stupid to share a room."

"Perhaps you can sleep in the taproom," she said sweetly.

"Perhaps you can," he sniped back.

Fortunately the innkeeper arrived to greet his distinguished guests, rescuing Pen from divulging her opinion on that suggestion.

After a surprisingly good dinner in the taproom, Cam climbed the oak staircase to the single habitable chamber. So far, this establishment proved an advance on the other places they'd stayed.

Apart from that one impossible circumstance.

That one impossible bedroom.

Despite his threat to make Pen sleep in the public room, crammed with stranded travelers—Paolo had been right about the snowstorm—Cam had always intended her to have the bedroom.

Which left him at a loss.

He'd checked if the damaged rooms were as damaged as reported. They were. He'd tried to sleep in the taproom, but it was unbearably crowded and his failure to join his wife in comfort and privacy upstairs stirred curiosity that, even in this obscure hamlet, he wanted to discourage. English travelers attracted enough attention anyway. An English husband refusing to sleep with his beautiful wife became a little too remarkable.

The irony was that he'd cut off his right arm for the right to sleep in Pen's bed. Desperately, he summoned thoughts of Lady Marianne Seaton. While he was yet to propose, his marked attentions had signaled his intentions to the lady, her family, and society. Nobody would be surprised when Cam returned to London and requested the Marquess of Baildon's permission to marry his daughter.

But during this journey, Marianne became increasingly difficult to remember as more than a shadow. The only face in Cam's mind was Pen's.

Damn it all to hell.

And damn his protective urge. His fellow travelers looked exhausted, but villains might lurk among them. So here he was ascending the stairs. Expecting a scolding for his good intentions. Pen wouldn't want him sharing her room. Even if he wasn't the first man to enjoy that privilege.

He'd spent far too long stewing over her lovers. Surely he was better off not knowing details. But not knowing allowed imagination free rein. He loathed where his imagination roamed.

Outside the closed door, he inhaled deeply and reminded himself that he was a gentleman. He'd hoped that the rigors of travel would stifle this inconvenient yen. He'd hoped that Pen's unfeminine independence and sharp tongue would shift fascination to dislike. He'd hoped that his managing manner would keep her at a distance.

There at least he'd been successful.

The unwelcome truth was that a prickly Penelope was just as alluring as a polite Penelope. God help him if she moved from politeness to amiability. His goose would be well and truly cooked.

She might choose her lovers where she pleased, but she was still a girl from a good family. If the Duke of Sedge-moor bedded Lord Wilmott's daughter, he'd pay with a wedding ring. Standing outside her room all hot and bothered, he almost thought that price might be worth it.

On a sudden fit of temper—confound her, she treated him like a beggar—he crashed the door open and barged into the candlelit room.

And stumbled to a standstill as if struck with an ax.

Rising from a small wooden tub like a goddess from a spring, Pen was all gleaming white skin. Naked as the day she was born.

His heart slammed hard and heavy. Lust pounded in his ears.

Her back was to him. Her thick dark hair gathered untidily, revealing her elegant neck. The straight, stubborn shoulders. The graceful spine. The subtle curve of her hips. And God help him, a perfect pear-shaped arse.

His hands curled at his sides, preparing to frame that luscious roundness. He'd never seen anything so beautiful as Penelope Thorne in the bath.

Until she turned.

Perhaps he'd made a sound, although the breath jammed in his throat. Perhaps cold air eddied through the open door.

"Maria, I—" Black eyes huge with horror, she stared at him.

For a second that extended into eternity, they regarded one another. He should leave. He had no right to absorb every glorious, forbidden detail and imprint it on his mind to remember forever. The wet skin shining like a pearl; the high breasts crowned with beaded raspberry nipples; the delicate triangle of dark hair guarding her sex. Cam had never suspected what bounty lurked beneath her dark, plain jackets and narrow skirts.

Outrage replaced her shock. With a dizzying mixture of relief and disappointment, he watched her fumble for the worn towel on the small table beside her.

"Close the door." Her voice was low and shaking.

Without shifting his attention, he reached behind him to obey. Penelope's violet soap scented the air. Until now, he hadn't realized how her perfume had permeated his senses.

"With you on the other side," she said sharply, hitching the towel.

He could have told her that she wasted her time covering herself. Transparent with dampness, the skimpy towel extended from breasts to thighs. She looked more sexually available in the strip of linen than standing naked.

Her throat moved as she swallowed. She eyed him as if expecting him to pounce.

"I'm sleeping here," he said gruffly.

"Over my dead body," she snarled, trembling hands gripping the towel.

Perhaps discretion was the better part of valor. "I'll come back in ten minutes."

"I don't want to see you tonight."

He shrugged. It felt unreal to argue as they'd argued so often on this journey, while she stood before him like every dream come to vibrant life. "If you're asleep, you won't see me."

She grabbed for the soap dish and raised it in a threatening gesture. He just reached the corridor before pottery shattered behind the hurriedly closed door.

Damn her for a shrew.

A beautiful shrew.

A shrew whose eyes, for one blazing moment, had flared with desire.

Even as Pen lay in bed struggling to sleep, she was still blushing. Despite his threat, Cam hadn't reappeared. She wasn't sure whether to be relieved or piqued. And still those incendiary moments played over and over in her mind, making her stomach lurch with horror. And forbidden excitement.

For one stolen moment, she'd read desire in his eyes.

In that searing instant, she'd seen endless hunger beneath his cool manner. Then good old common sense had asserted itself. She was a naked woman. His reaction was a purely physical reflex.

On that sour reflection, she sat up and reached for her thick blue robe. It was a bitterly cold night. Even in this room with its fire and blankets, she shivered. Cam might want her, but she trusted his self-control. It was churlish to leave him freezing while she kept the bed.

She wrapped herself in a paisley shawl, as much for modesty as warmth. She hoped to encounter an obliging maid before she braved the taproom. Carefully she opened the door and checked the lamplit hallway.

Time reversed, leaving her giddy. It was like the morning when he'd caught her trying to escape.

"What's wrong, Pen?"

She scowled at where he huddled against the opposite wall, using his greatcoat as an inadequate blanket. "Are you afraid I mean to run?"

"No." With one hand, he rubbed his eyes.

Even in the dim light, she noted his weariness. Did endless craving play on his nerves? Or was that wishful thinking? "Then what are you doing here?"

One eyebrow tilted. "I'm not welcome inside."

Guilt stabbed her. The corridor was considerably colder than the bedroom. "I thought you'd go downstairs where there's a fire."

"And about a thousand people, most of whom have fleas and only passing acquaintance with soap and water." With a wince, he stretched against the wall, then stood without his usual lithe smoothness. Her guilt strengthened. He hadn't said so, but she guessed that he stayed close to protect her.

"I don't have fleas," she said softly, hitching the shawl around her shoulders. Despite the velvet robe and the grandmotherly flannel nightdress, she felt naked when she looked into his eyes. She couldn't help recalling his gaze on her body. Dear Lord, if this awkwardness persisted until they reached England, she'd go stark, staring mad.

"Not yet," he said drily. "It's miles to Genoa, with lavish accommodations every night."

She'd have to speak plainly. Which was strange. With Cam, she rarely needed to spell things out. Squaring her shoulders, she told herself to forget that he'd seen her in the bath. "You can come in."

To her surprise, he didn't leap at her invitation. "I'm safer out here."

She sighed and stood back, leaving him space to enter the firelit room. "I haven't got another soap dish."

His lips twitched, although the tension across his broad shoulders hinted that he too felt the swirling undercurrents. "Instead you've got armor."

How she wished his eyes didn't crinkle when he smiled. How she wished his face didn't brighten to brilliance. How she wished her heart wasn't so susceptible. "Armor?"

"The head to toe covering." He didn't approach. "What changed your mind about inviting me in? Earlier you looked ready to flay me."

The heat in her cheeks could warm the inn. "I'd rather ignore that incident."

The smile lines around his eyes deepened. "I can imagine."

"So are you coming in? I'm getting cold."

He folded his arms across his chest and leaned with elegant nonchalance against the wall. "In that get-up? No chance."

She growled deep in her throat and started to shut him out. Let the rogue freeze.

"Wait," he said softly. He caught the door.

For a blazing interval, they were close enough to touch.

Looking deep into his eyes, she couldn't mistake his desire. He wanted her, all right. A question sizzled in the air. A question that made her skin tighten with yearning.

Fleetingly she considered yielding to what they both wanted. Then she recalled her misery after leaving England, her futile attempts to forget him, the emptiness she carried with her constantly. If Cam used her body, she'd never escape this agonized longing.

Worse, if he besmirched his honor in his childhood playmate's bed, he'd never forgive himself. Then she'd never forgive herself. He had enough burdens without despising himself as yet another Rothermere scoundrel.

What a damnable mess.

She nearly left him shivering, this time from cowardice rather than exasperation, until she told herself that she was better than that. Not entirely convinced that she was, she gestured him inside. This time he cooperated.

"You can sleep on the right," she said irritably, slipping the shawl from her shoulders and dropping it over a chair. "I hope you don't snore."

He looked troubled. "You'd share the bed?"

She glowered. "Purely a humanitarian gesture. It's as cold as charity."

"Do you trust me that much?"

Oh, God save her. She'd always trusted him. She'd trusted him before she loved him. Nothing since had shaken either trust or love. Even his recent arrogance. Even tonight's revelation that he wanted her. "I promise not to demand my wicked way. Would you rather sleep on the floor? I'm not giving up any of my blankets."

Grimness thinned his mouth. "We need to talk."

She stopped straightening a bed chaotic with her restlessness. "It's the middle of the night."

He stood as straight as a soldier on parade. "I must say this now."

A bleak premonition knotting her belly, she sat on the bed. Nobody said "we need to talk" before good news. "How very ominous, Your Grace."

His expression didn't lighten at her mockery. "Listen to me, Pen."

Fear made her rush into speech. "What happened tonight was an accident. Better to forget it."

He shook his head and stepped forward. "I can't forget it." He paused. "And forgive me if I'm presumptuous, but I doubt you can either."

"You've seen a naked woman before, Cam."

"We've traveled in close confines—"

"And very annoying it's been too," she said quickly.

One commanding hand rose to silence her. "Something unexpected has happened. When I saw you again, I—"

Cam was never lost for words. With another man in other circumstances, she might believe he meant to declare his love. "Can't this wait until morning?"

Or forever?

Stubbornness firmed his jaw. "No." He stared hard at her, green eyes opaque. "Pen, God forgive me, but I never expected to want you."

Like a seedling reaching for the sun, joy unfurled. Until native cynicism made her hesitate. "You don't sound very happy about it."

His lips flattened. "I'm not."

Her laugh was acid. "So this isn't the prelude to another proposal?"

He flinched. "You had good reason to refuse me."

Yes, she did. She still did. "A lucky escape for you."

"I wouldn't be so ungallant."

Her lips twisted and she stared into her lap, covered in thick white flannel. Strangely, this was the closest they'd ventured to a frank conversation in a week. "Never you, Your Grace."

"Stop sniping. I'm struggling to do what's best."

She regarded him with dislike. "You always do."

Her ironic tone nettled him. "Our circumstances are trying, but not impossible."

"Glad to hear it."

He plowed on. "I've always tried to be honorable."

Of course he had, she thought wearily. Another snide remark rose, but his expression stifled it. "That's good."

"Pen, I have to keep my hands off you."

Pain crunched her heart. "Because I'm an unsuitable bride?"

Waiting for agreement felt like the pause before someone punched a bruise.

He shook his head. "Because I'm courting another lady." He stared over her head as if the crucifix on the wall provided enormous interest. "When I return to England, I'm marrying Lady Marianne Seaton, the daughter of the Marquess of Baildon."

Chapter Eight

Hyde Park, London, February 1828

After that miraculous encounter in Lord Chetwell's cupboard, Harry was too restless to sleep. Too restless and too happy. Sophie mightn't love him yet, but she was interested. To the point of defying her powerful brother.

Harry had wandered home from the ball in a daze. The memory of Sophie's kisses fizzed in his blood. The sound of her voice filled his ears like music. Her scent haunted him.

He was head over heels, madly in love. And he didn't give a tinker's curse.

Anticipation had him saddling his horse—he wasn't selfish enough to wake a groom so early—and riding to the park before dawn. He settled his mount under a tree with a view of Rotten Row. There was a special luxury in being here on a misty February morning, knowing that his beloved might appear any moment. The sun just peeped above the horizon, shooting long golden rays through the bare trees.

Into this magical glade trotted his Sophie, controlling a fine gray mare with a light touch. She wore a neat dark blue riding habit, and the jaunty angle of her hat made him want to kiss her.

Harry straightened from his slouch, an uncontrollable smile spreading across his face. His heart performed a jig.

She smiled back. "Mr. Thorne, what a surprise," she said in an unnaturally lilting voice for the benefit of the groom plodding behind.

Stifling a laugh, Harry doffed his hat and bowed. What a hopeless conspirator she was. "Lady Sophie, a delightful chance."

"The park is quiet this morning." She glanced at Harry under her long lashes. "Are you alone?"

"Yes. Perhaps we could ride a little way."

"Your ladyship, I'm not sure—" the groom began before Sophie cut him off with a laugh. A very unconvincing laugh.

"Mr. Thorne and I are old chums, Jones. Why, we danced together only last night."

"Very well, my lady." The man settled into the saddle, his stare unwavering. Leath had chosen a diligent guardian.

Harry had hoped for more kisses. What man wouldn't? But he saw that a brief and decorous conversation was all he could expect. "It was quite a party, wasn't it?"

He wheeled his horse to amble in the same direction as Sophie's. The park must contain other people, but as far as he was concerned, he was alone with his beloved.

"I enjoyed myself immensely," Sophie said with another sideways glance. "A memorable occasion."

Harry was more convinced than ever that she was a minx. He liked her all the more for it. The thought of her harnessed to a dry stick like Desborough made the gorge rise in his throat. "Is this your first visit to London?"

"No, my brother always comes up for parliament. The last few years, he's brought me too."

Leath was touted as a future prime minister, wasn't he? Or at least he had been, until his uncle's criminal activities had stained the family name. The marquess must be seething over the gossip, and all of it so public, thanks to Sedgemoor's intervention.

Leath would place Harry in the Sedgemoor camp. After all, the Rothermeres and Thornes had grown up together. Years ago, there had even been talk of marriage between Cam and Harry's sister, Penelope. What a disaster that would have been. Pen was headstrong and unconventional, whereas Cam was the model of gentlemanly restraint.

"That explains the town bronze. Most young ladies are wide-eyed with wonder during their first season."

She giggled delightfully. "I'm quite the sophisticate now that I've seen Astley's Circus and the menagerie at the Tower of London."

Color brightened Sophie's cheeks. She had the most exquisite skin. Harry's blood heated when he imagined that skin bare to his exploration. As his hands tightened on the reins, his horse shifted.

They'd moved ahead of Jones, who seemed prepared to give Harry the benefit of the doubt. For now. Harry leaned to pat his horse's gleaming neck and spoke in a murmur. "I want to touch you."

She responded in a whisper. "I couldn't get away on my own."

"Neither you should. London's full of scoundrels."

"Including you?"

"Yes, including me," he said gloomily. Then more loudly for the sake of Jones who edged closer, clearly suspicious, "Do you live in the country the rest of the year?"

"I've been at school in Bath. Now I live with my mother at Alloway Chase in Yorkshire."

"Your mother doesn't come to Town?"

"She isn't well." She stared at his black armband. "I'm sad to see that you've recently lost someone."

"My brother died in January. I'm surprised you hadn't heard." If Leath had warned Sophie away, surely he'd mentioned Peter's financial woes. Peter's calamitous mismanagement of the already sparse Thorne coffers threatened the family's ruin, making Harry an even more unsuitable match for this lovely girl.

"I'm sorry."

"Thank you." He met her compassionate blue stare and his love, already powerful, deepened into something richer. "He was marvelous company and he'd go to the wall for the people he loved."

"He sounds wonderful."

"He was." Harry found himself saying what he hadn't said to anyone else since Peter's lonely death. "I've lost my taste for pleasure. The whole world is gray." Except when he was with Sophie.

"I felt like that after my father died."

The late marquess had passed away four years ago. The nation had mourned the loss of a brilliant politician. As with his son, there had been talk of him becoming prime minister. Just up from Oxford, Harry had paid little heed. He'd been too busy kicking up his heels and adding a few more smears to the family reputation.

He reached to comfort her before Jones cleared his throat. Winning Sophie from the dragons who protected her wouldn't be easy. For the first time in his shallow life, Harry burned to meet a challenge.

He glanced around and noticed that full day had broken.

Riders emerged for their morning exercise. To save Sophie from talk, he must ride on. "It was a pleasure seeing you."

She bent her head with a grace that hinted at the grand lady she'd one day become. Under the brim of her stylish beaver hat, Harry caught a gratifying flash of longing in her eyes. "I'm engaged for Lady Carson's ball tonight."

"Perhaps I'll see you there," he said, not meaning perhaps at all. He bowed. Jones's watchful expression warned him that a kiss on her hand would take things too far, damn it. "Good morning, Lady Sophie."

Hills above Genoa, early March 1828

Pen stood on the inn's terrace and stared at the rugged coastline below. The night was clear and she easily made out Genoa's lights in the distance. Around her bloomed pots of spring flowers. After the frozen wastes, this seemed nothing short of miraculous.

The grueling journey drew to a close. Tomorrow, they embarked for home. This last week had been almost easy. The weather had been kinder and the roads in the more heavily populated areas showed considerable improvement from the goat tracks higher up. Even the inns were more luxurious, saving her from sharing a room with Cam again. Thank God. She still remembered lying awake, eaten with useless jealousy, while he'd stretched silently beside her, no more asleep than she.

The announcement of Cam's marital plans should have eased the tension between them. She'd always known he'd marry, and now that his bride had a name, she should finally be able to crush her painful longing.

Instead, since that endless night, the atmosphere had weighed heavier and heavier. Until tonight it had become so unbearable, she'd barely finished dinner before rushing outside to escape him.

She flattened her unsteady hands upon the stone balustrade and stared blindly into the night. She wore a favorite gown, a sea-green silk purchased last year in Florence. Even as she'd asked Maria to find it, she'd recognized her pathetic purposes. She flaunted herself, taunting Cam. *This will never be yours, however much you want it.*

Definitely pathetic.

"Has my conversation driven you to throw yourself off a cliff?" a low voice asked behind her.

Slowly Pen turned. She should have guessed that Cam would follow. Lamps lit the terrace, lending enough brightness for her to see him in the shadows near the doorway. He'd dressed with care too, as if aware that tonight marked some kind of ending.

She'd been so reluctant to travel with him. It seemed absurd to be sad that their time together was nearly over. "You don't talk enough to drive me to self-harm."

He approached with the loose-limbed stroll that always set her heart racing. She really was a besotted idiot. He passed her one of the glasses of red wine he carried. "Let's toast old acquaintance."

For once, prickling hostility was absent. Instead, Cam seemed like the kindhearted boy she'd known years ago. Her determination to maintain her distance faltered. She raised her glass. "To friendship."

"Our journey ends," he said musingly.

"We have the voyage ahead."

"We're safe from scandal on the *Windhover*. My crew is paid to keep their mouths shut."

How he must want this marriage with Lady Marianne. Unworthy chagrin cramped Pen's heart. She wanted to tear every hair from the woman's no doubt perfectly coiffured head. Pen had devoted too many futile hours to wondering about Cam's choice. Beautiful, Pen was sure. Impeccably behaved. Circumspect.

"We've made it." She tried and failed to sound happy.

Thankfully Cam didn't appear to notice her glumness. He sipped his wine and stared out to sea with a pensive expression. "Yes. And without killing each other."

"We've come close."

He studied her. "I wish you well, Pen. I've only ever wished you well."

She knew that. Her rejection of his proposal might sting. Her independence and obstinacy undoubtedly infuriated him. Perhaps he even regretted that they'd never explore the desire simmering between them. But the bonds of childhood affection persisted.

"I wish you well too, Cam," she said softly.

"What do you intend to do when you get home?"

"Settle my aunt's affairs."

"After that?"

She shrugged. "Return to Italy. I have friends here and places I'd like to see."

"You won't stay in England?"

And witness, even from afar, Cam's wedded bliss? Cam becoming a father? She'd rather cut out her liver with a paperknife. "No."

"Elias and Harry would love to have their sister home."

"They have their own lives. They're used to doing without me."

"Now they have to do without you and without Peter." He flinched at her distressed inhalation. "I'm sorry. That was insensitive."

She stared at him. "Goodness, Cam, was that an apology? I thought you'd lost the knack."

His lips firmed, but he remained calm. Pity. Her longing was so much easier to control when dislike crackled. Except what vibrated between them wasn't exactly dislike.

"I've been a brute."

Her laugh was wry. "Not by anyone's definition but your own."

His gaze remained unwavering. "You know why I've been difficult."

"You told me."

Then he'd retreated to silence on the subject. Thank heaven. It was excruciating, knowing that he wanted her, but knowing also that only a fool would succumb.

"I'd hoped honesty would simplify things."

"It didn't." The air tautened until she felt suffocated. Would he kiss her? Just one kiss to last a lifetime wasn't too much to ask. Except she already had too much to remember.

"Is that because you don't want me?" The flickering light was more deceptive than true darkness. She could almost imagine desperation in his eyes. Cam was never desperate. He'd never let himself become desperate. "Or because you do?"

She jolted back, spilling wine over her hand. "Cam, I—"

"God knows this is wrong. I'm courting another woman. You're my friend's sister. We grew up together." His voice shook. "But tell me you want me. Not knowing is driving me mad."

She didn't want to hear this, partly because a wicked, wanton part of her burned to fling herself into his arms and beg him to do a thousand wild and forbidden things to her. She retreated against the balustrade. Fear beat high and fast in her throat.

The threat of betraying her secret hovered close. He must never know she loved him. His pity would be worse than death. "There's no point to this."

Cam took her glass and placed it with his on the balustrade. "I need to know."

"No, you don't," she said, then groaned when satisfaction flooded his face. On this breezy terrace, with his usually immaculate dark hair ruffled and his eyes glowing with passion, he was the handsomest man she'd ever seen.

He grabbed her hand. "If you don't want me, you'd say so."

She knew to her bones that if he kept touching her, she'd lie in his bed tonight. "Someone might see."

"I don't care. Tell me."

His touch set her blood ablaze, shooting hot and urgent to the pit of her belly. "What use is this?" she asked in angry despair, struggling to withdraw. "You're marrying Lady Marianne."

His gaze focused on her lips, making them tingle as if he kissed her. "Once, I wanted to marry you."

Bitterness welled. "When you thought you could mold me into what you wanted. Before my family's eccentricities tumbled over into full-scale scandal with Peter's ruin."

She'd cut off her right hand to hear him deny her assertions, but of course, he didn't. He wouldn't lie to her. She respected that even as she loathed it. "Lady Marianne will make the perfect duchess."

Pain lanced through her as she acknowledged that he'd never have said that about Penelope Thorne, even before her bohemian wanderings. "Do you love her?"

He snatched his hand free and his jaw hardened with the rejection familiar whenever anyone mentioned love. "You're mistaken to think that love is a requirement for a happy marriage."

"You're mistaken to think that it's not," she snapped back.

"My parents were in love. For a short time."

"Your parents were always children dressed as grown-ups."

He glared down his daunting nose. "You venture on dangerous territory."

She drew herself to her full height. Temper made her speak in a rush. "Why? You speak freely to me." Her tone eased. "Cam, I know this...attraction is a pest. But it's not so surprising. We're two healthy adults confined to each other's company. It would be unnatural not to demonstrate a little curiosity."

A bitter smile twisted his lips. "That's a facile explanation."

For a sizzling interval, their eyes met. She knew that, like her, he remembered her standing naked before him.

Then the shutters crashed down over his expression. She felt disoriented. He'd lured her up to a door, then slammed it in her face.

Still, she was grateful when Cam's fierceness ebbed. It had been torture to hear him speak his need aloud and know that it wasn't enough, it could never be enough.

As if by common consent, they turned toward the sea that tomorrow became their highway. Somewhere down there his yacht lay at anchor. If winds were favorable, they'd be in England within a fortnight.

A silence descended. At first, it was heavy with suppressed passion, but gradually it became something softer and kinder. As his voice was softer and kinder when he spoke. "Pen, why are you so determined to go into exile? What are you running away from?"

You.

She'd spent the last nine years fleeing this man she loved but who could never love her. Despite excitement and adventure, despite playing a sophisticate in a sophisticated world, she hadn't run toward anything. What a lowering admission.

"I enjoy my life." Apart from a constant ache that no spectacular scenery or charming admirers or glamorous intrigues banished.

"You'd enjoy London."

"I doubt it. People at home are more conservative than here. English society won't accept me with open arms."

"I would."

Pen couldn't help herself. She laughed. It was either laugh or cry. If she cried, he might guess how it would crush her to leave him. "No, Cam. I'm not throwing myself into your arms under any circumstances."

He didn't laugh. He looked disturbed and angry. That dangerous hum in the air returned. Fatalistically she recognized that it had never gone away. "Pen, I'm trying my best to remember that I'm an honorable man."

She sobered, telling herself that she couldn't allow him to compromise his principles. But how easy it would be to ignore what was right when for the sake of a little sin, he could be hers. However briefly. Physically if not emotionally.

She could cross a mere foot of space and kiss him. If she knew anything about men—and at twenty-eight, she should—the slightest encouragement would shatter his restraint.

"Unfortunately," she whispered before she could stop herself.

The hum rose to overwhelm every other sound.

Then he stepped back and bowed. Even as hunger darkened his eyes, he spoke with the chill politeness she'd heard too often on this journey. This evening, they'd spoken like friends. Or lovers. Now she watched Cam draw the shades over that intimacy. "I won't act the cad. My family's reputation is at stake. If I tumble you, I prove that all my work to restore the family honor has been in vain."

She'd known that. Still, rejection hurt. She bent her head, not wanting him to see how he wounded her.

A couple emerged onto the terrace from the inn. The lady paused and spoke with joyful recognition. Even worse, in the clipped accents of an upper-class Englishwoman. "Miss Thorne, what a wonderful surprise."

Chapter Nine

Prescott Place, Wiltshire, March 1828

She came to him through the sweet new greenery like a forest spirit, although there was nothing unearthly about the woman he seized in his arms. She was all warm, passionate femininity.

Harry kissed Sophie until they were both breathless. Then he kissed her some more. "You got away."

His asinine comment sparked amusement. "Obviously."

This past week, Sophie had joined a house party given by one of Leath's political cronies. Despite Harry's best efforts, his pursuit of Sophie had attracted attention. Leath had removed her from London to separate her from young Mr. Thorne. A note channeled via Sophie's maid had put paid to that plan.

Harry kissed Sophie again. His blood heated as she answered with eager dips and swirls of her tongue. Still a little unsure of herself but gaining in confidence every minute.

"Sweetheart, I've missed you so much," he said brokenly, punctuating every word with kisses.

They'd only kissed once before, and the craving to do it again had kept him sleepless and grumpy. They'd managed three more meetings in Hyde Park and a couple of circumspect dances. Here in Sir Garth Burton's woods on a sleepy afternoon, nobody was likely to interrupt. Harry had sworn he wouldn't lose his head. But after one glimpse of his beloved, moderation flew to Hades.

"I've missed you too," Sophie murmured unsteadily, her hands working on Harry's shoulders as if she hardly believed that he was there.

"It's been an eternity." He trailed his lips down her throat, nipping the curve of her shoulder until she trembled.

"It's only a week."

"You speak lightly of my pain," he whispered into her skin.

"I've thought of you every minute." She slid her hands under his coat, bringing him closer.

"I've thought of you too."

He backed her into a conveniently placed tree and touched her in earnest. Learning the curve of waist and hip, the slender line of her back. Careful of her innocence, he kept his hips from sliding against hers.

Her hands slid daringly lower. Astonished gratification shook him, although those eager fingers digging into his buttocks threatened control.

He stared at her through dazed eyes. Passion flushed her creamy skin and her blue eyes were heavy with desire. She looked rosy and approachable, a different creature from the golden-haired debutante he'd first met. She wore a cobalt walking dress, fastened down the front with hussar frogging and with a high collar, askew thanks to Harry's attentions.

He rested his forehead against hers, sharing her breath. She smelled marvelous. Like the vibrant spring that burst into life around them. She'd brought him to life. He wondered if she knew.

"Harry?" He caught the confusion in her voice.

He lifted his head. "Sophie, I'm trying to act the gentleman."

She smiled, her lips moist and swollen. "You don't have to."

He groaned. He really didn't need to hear her say that. Not if he meant to retain some honor. "Of course I do."

Her smile broadened and the light in her blue eyes filled his world with color. More, painted his world with rainbows. "I want you to touch me."

"You test my restraint." He kissed her again, hot and voracious. His heart crashed against his ribs as she curled into him.

"I don't want to be restrained." She clutched his shoulders.

With shaking hands, he parted the frogging on her dress. He'd take things a little further then stop. Dear heaven, let him find the strength to stop.

Control shuddered closer to fraying as her dress sagged open. The pink pearls of her nipples pushed against her delicate shift. With a groan, he bent and sucked one perfect bud. Her choked cry echoed in his ears. Knowing he ventured toward the point of no return, he cupped her other breast and rubbed his palm across her nipple. She arched until her belly bumped him.

With sudden ruthlessness, he pushed the lacy edge down to reveal her breasts. Better than his dreams. Thoughts of her nakedness had fueled his fantasies, waking and sleeping, since he'd found her crying in Lord Oldhaven's garden. He drew back to feast upon the sight.

"You're so beautiful." Reverently he stroked her pale skin.

He kissed the tip of her breast. The act conveyed homage more than desire, although desire surged powerful enough to shake his principles.

She breathed unsteadily. "I feel beautiful when I'm with you." She bit her lip. "I never have before."

Her vulnerability defeated the ravening beast inside him. Grateful and disappointed in equal measure, he sighed and stepped back. Because he loved her, he said what he'd always known to be true. "You deserve better than me."

She looked suddenly distraught. "Have I disgusted you?"

Harry's gut lurched. If anyone should feel ashamed, it was him. "Hell, no, Sophie. You're glorious, perfect, an angel."

With shaking hands, she tugged at her bodice but the complicated fastenings were beyond her. "No angel lets a man strip her naked in public."

"Sophie, you're human." Very gently—and with a wicked regret that he couldn't stifle—he restored her to respectability.

"A little too human today," she muttered.

"Don't be so hard on yourself. Desire is perfectly natural." It was too early for declarations. They'd only known each other a few weeks, and their meetings had been short and snatched from the teeth of scandal. But she needed to know that he wasn't toying with her. "Desire is part of . . . love."

She went completely still. Her hands dropped to her sides and her eyes opened wide as if she strove to see him with absolute clarity, perhaps to check whether he lied. "Love, Harry?"

Hell, he hadn't blushed since he was in the nursery. Meeting her eyes, he spoke with the steadiness of complete conviction. "I love you, Sophie."

To his consternation, she didn't smile.

She took a long time to answer, which worried him even more.

Had he mistaken her? Trepidation sank sharp teeth into him. She could be flirting. After all, she enjoyed her first season and flattery had turned the heads of girls less admired than Sophie. Perhaps she collected hearts like trophies. The thought made him feel sick.

The delay became unbearable. "Say something, darling."

Still she didn't smile as she straightened away from the tree. Her shoulders were level, her chin was up. She looked every inch the young aristocrat. "I love you, Harry."

For a moment, he stared at her in disbelief. Could he be so fortunate? She looked like she meant it.

Another close examination of her expression. By God, she meant it. Troupes of angels danced a gavotte in his soul.

What could a fellow do when the woman he adored told him she loved him? Nothing except sweep that woman into a wild kiss.

Harry surfaced from joy to discover that he lay over Sophie on the soft grass and that her hands tangled in his hair. "We have to stop."

She pouted in a way that made him desperate to go further, but some thread still moored him to reality. That reality didn't encompass Harry Thorne taking the Marquess of Leath's sister in the woods like an amorous gypsy. "I can't believe the world talks about you as such a rake. I'm disappointed."

His laugh cracked as he rose on his hands. "Shall I promise to be rakish only with you until death do us part?"

She went rigid and the teasing light drained from her eyes. "What...what do you mean?"

He should be nervous. But he'd been committed to this

woman since their first meeting. Everything following had only confirmed that he was eternally in her thrall.

"I mean—" Even when he was certain, a man tended to stumble at such a moment.

Poised over her like this, he couldn't do justice to his intentions. Struggling to ignore how beautiful and damnably available she looked spread out on the grass, he rolled away and kneeled beside her. He tugged a crushed daisy from her wantonly tumbled golden curls. "Sit up, Sophie."

She frowned in puzzlement. "What is it?" Nonetheless, she sat, folding her legs beneath her.

Taking her hand, he rose on one knee. "Lady Sophie, I knew the moment I saw you that I want to spend the rest of my life with you." He swallowed and stared into her shining eyes. "Will you do me the inestimable honor of marrying me?"

Hills above Genoa, early March 1828

Damn, damn, damn.

Cam knew he was devilish reckless playing these games in public. And now the time had come to pay the piper.

As the horse-faced woman with the loud voice and deplorable taste in hats bustled toward them, he stepped away from Pen and tried to act as though their acquaintance was purely casual. At least, thank God, the woman hadn't appeared while he'd been manhandling Pen.

He'd battled so hard to keep his distance, but in the end, the temptation had proven too strong. Especially now he knew that Pen wanted him too. Even when there was bugger all he could do to satisfy his craving and still call himself a gentleman.

Awake, Pen was constantly in his mind. Even worse,

he dreamed about her at night. Hot, sweaty, ribald dreams, where he used her hard. Like an experienced woman, not a delicate lady of his class. He woke shaking and ashamed, hard as an oar.

If he could make his yacht fly back to England, he would. Surely once he didn't see Penelope every day, he'd become again the measured, sensible man he'd been before he fell under this gorgeous termagant's spell. Part of him still looked at her with astonishment. *This is Pen of the scraped knees and broken dolls. You have no right to tumble the girl whose childhood tears you dried. Not only tumble her, but have her in every filthy way your imagination can conjure.*

When the woman reached them, Cam caught speculation in her beady eyes. The man, obviously also English, approached with less dispatch but equal curiosity. Luckily Cam knew neither of them. Although that wouldn't save him from a scandal, unless he came up with some reason why he and an unmarried girl from a good family were alone together.

"Mrs. Barker-Pratt, what a surprise." Pen tried to sound enthusiastic.

The two women exchanged kisses on the cheek and Pen turned to Cam. "My lord, permit me to introduce Mr. and Mrs. Barker-Pratt, dear friends of my late aunt." She paused infinitesimally, but only someone who knew her as well as he did would guess how rattled she was. "Mr. and Mrs. Barker-Pratt, this is Lord Pembridge who has been touring the lakes."

He bowed, wondering whether the game was finally up. Anyone familiar with noble English families would recognize that heirs to the Sedgemoor dukedom took the courtesy title of Marquess of Pembridge. "Mrs. Barker-Pratt, Mr. Barker-Pratt."

"My lord." Mrs. Barker-Pratt curtsied while the husband, a little man who faded into invisibility in his wife's dominant presence, bowed.

"The Barker-Pratts hail from Shropshire, but have lived in Tivoli for many years," Pen continued with false brightness. "Mr. Barker-Pratt is an expert on Roman funerary monuments."

"How interesting," Cam murmured. Pen's skill at weaving through the introductions filled him with dreadful fascination. It was like watching someone cross a gorge on a high wire while a river full of hungry crocodiles snapped below.

"We haven't returned to England in forty years, despite war and revolution. We'd feel quite foreign in London. Although with so many English friends here, it's like being at home." Mrs. Barker-Pratt's laugh could shatter glass. "At home with only the most interesting people, of course. Don't you agree, my lord, that the best of the English are those who leave the country?"

Cam smiled at Pen. "In Miss Thorne's case, that's definitely the case."

Pen sent him a withering glance. "So gallant, my lord." She turned back to Mrs. Barker-Pratt. "His lordship is a childhood friend. We met by chance this evening."

If she wasn't careful, the story would unravel. The staff knew that they'd arrived together. Still, he'd do his best to play along. "A pleasure to see dear Miss Thorne again."

Mrs. Barker-Pratt looked puzzled. "We heard you were meeting your brother in Paris, Miss Thorne."

Pen paled. During these last weeks, her grief for Peter had been a palpable presence.

Cam saved her from having to talk about Peter. "Lord Wilmott has passed away."

"Oh, my dear, I'm so sorry."

Mrs. Barker-Pratt might be an unwelcome intruder, but Cam felt a surge of gratitude when the woman swept Pen into a motherly embrace. For weeks, he'd longed to extend a similarly generous response. Once he wouldn't have hesitated. But they'd both grown up since then, damn it.

Cam stepped back. "I'll wish you good night. You have much to discuss, I'm sure."

As he walked away, he couldn't help wondering what might have happened if he and Pen had remained alone in the lamplight. Nothing to be proud of, that was sure.

Prescott Place, Wiltshire, March 1828

"Yes," Sophie said immediately and her hand tightened around Harry's. "I'd love to marry you."

"Oh, my dear!" Harry raised her fingers to his lips and kissed them. He could hardly believe that the space of an afternoon had delivered not just this glorious creature's vow of love, but also a promise to be his. "I'll speak to your brother the instant he returns to London."

Sophie snatched her hand back and regarded him with horror. "No, you mustn't."

The abrupt change left Harry bewildered. "You're under twenty-one, Sophie. I need his permission."

She scrambled to her feet and stared down at him as if he'd suggested some unnatural practice. "My brother wants me to marry Lord Desborough."

More slowly, Harry rose from his knees, his gaze never wavering from Sophie. "You can't marry Desborough. You love me."

For a moment, he thought she might hurl herself into his embrace, but she curtailed the movement and wrapped her arms around her crushed bodice. "My brother is determined on the marriage."

"Your brother is a reasonable man. He'll—"

She interrupted him. "He is a reasonable man. He's arranged a match with a kind gentleman of great fortune who's fond of me."

Harry glared at her. "You sound like you want to marry the sod."

"Oh, Harry," she said on an exhalation of despair. "You don't understand."

He folded his own arms, fighting his hurt. To think, five minutes ago, he'd considered himself the world's happiest man. "I understand that you said you'd marry me and now seem to say that you won't."

She curled her hand around his tight forearm. "Let's not quarrel."

"I can't let you marry Desborough."

"I don't want to. But my brother is in a state because of Uncle Neville's suicide and because Sedgemoor is working against us and because he thinks the scandal may end his political career. It's not the time to tell him that his carefully laid plans won't eventuate."

"You're frightened of him."

The suggestion shocked her. "Of course not. But open defiance now, when he feels like the world turns against him, would hurt him."

What about me?

Harry bit back the childish question. "So what do you propose?" Moments ago, "propose" had conveyed a completely different meaning.

She stared up with a sweet entreaty that, if he was less upset, would have him back on his knees. "We wait."

"I can't wait." He made a sweeping gesture. "I need

everyone to know that you're mine. Living without you this last week nearly broke me."

"Please don't be angry," she said softly, changing her grip into a caress.

"How long until you turn twenty-one?" Although even then if Sophie married without Leath's approval, there would be a brouhaha.

Devastation darkened her blue eyes. "Nearly two years."

Two years? That was an eternity. He stared at her in anguish. "I can't bear to think I might lose you."

"You'll never lose me," she said with a certainty that should have surprised him, but didn't. She was young, but she was steadfast. Which was a double-edged sword. A flightier girl wouldn't spare a thought for her brother. "We can continue as we are."

"Meeting in secret? Lying? Snatching moments that only serve as a painful reminder that moments are all we have?" He swung away. "The longer we wait, the more the world believes that you'll marry Desborough."

"Do you want me to release you from our engagement?" she asked miserably, stepping back.

A cold wave of dread turned Harry's blood to ice. "Do you want that?"

She looked on the verge of crying. "Of course not."

He crossed the chasm separating them and discovered it only measured a pace. He seized her in his arms and kissed her hard. For an instant that lasted an eon, she resisted before kissing him back with a fervor that threatened to send everything but passion to hell.

She leaned back to see his face. "I want to marry you, but I don't want my selfish pursuit of happiness to burden my brother with more scandal."

"Does that extend to marrying Desborough?" Harry

asked harshly. "When I met you, you were crying over your brother's plans. Don't pretend that suddenly you're prepared to play the dutiful sister."

With a sigh, she laid one hand against his cheek. "I *was* prepared to play the dutiful sister. That's why I was crying."

Fear dug its talons into his aching heart. "You can't enter a loveless marriage to save Leath's pride."

She stiffened. "You demand so much."

His hand tightened on her waist as if Leath emerged from the undergrowth to steal her away. "Meeting like this does us no credit."

Temper lit her face to vivid beauty. "You should be used to deception. I've heard gossip."

Harry's resentment of Leath ratcheted up another notch. "I'll wager most of it came from your brother."

When Sophie avoided his gaze, he knew he was right. "Did James lie?"

Harry had never been ashamed of all his dashing widows and bored wives before. He was ashamed now. "Hell, Sophie, you're the only woman I've ever loved." His voice shook with sincerity. "That's what's important. That, and how these meetings stain your character and mine."

Resentment shadowed her expression. "You're cruel."

"No. I'm a man in love." He paused. "I want to shout that love from the rooftops, not meet you in corners as if my feelings are a dirty secret."

"Harry, I'm sorry." She rose on her toes and peppered his face with kisses. Each one eased his outrage, until he caught her and pressed his lips to hers.

"I can't be angry when you kiss me."

"That's good." She trailed her lips along his jaw with a tenderness that melted pique. "When we're married, I'll kiss you all the time."

She spoke as if merely by promising to marry him, their difficulties vanished like mist across the morning meadows. He wasn't nearly so convinced that delay would change her brother's mind.

For the sake of his future and his love, Harry must brave the dragon and claim the maiden.

Chapter Ten

English Channel, late March 1828

Cam stood clinging to a rope on a deck that bucked up and down. He wiped stinging, icy rain from his eyes and reminded himself that the yacht had withstood worse. His gut tightened with foreboding only because they were so close to journey's end.

They'd experienced rough weather since leaving the Mediterranean and sailing into the Atlantic. Thus far, the *Windhover* had coped with raging seas like the thoroughbred she was. Spring gales had tossed the ship until Cam didn't know which way was up. Much the way he felt when he encountered his enigmatic passenger.

Now they were only hours from Folkestone, the port he'd chosen in preference to Dover. At Dover, he was too likely to run into someone who recognized him. After that inn above Genoa, Cam was more careful than ever. Pen had assured him that she'd headed off Mrs. Barker-Pratt's curiosity. If she was right, Cam had achieved a miracle. He'd managed to bring Pen home without jeopardizing his plans to marry Lady Marianne.

Even more miraculous, he'd managed to keep his hands off Pen. Despite a case of blue balls unlike any he could remember, he'd resisted the ravening hunger that kept him awake at night, and restless and cranky all day.

A wonder indeed.

Now he just had to deliver Pen to London. Then, given her plans to return to the Continent, he'd probably never see her again. He was a damn fool to regret that. But regret it he did. Losing her before he discovered what all those lovers had taught her made him want to gnash his teeth and break something.

Even in the last minutes, the storm had worsened. The wind through the rigging shrieked like lost souls in hell.

"Can we turn back to France?" he shouted to his captain, who was lashed to the wheel. The usually imperturbable Scotsman fought to hold the helm steady, the set of his jaw betraying their danger.

"Too far." Through the gale, the man's brogue was barely comprehensible. "Better we race for the nearest port and wait the storm out."

"Do as you think best," Cam shouted back.

For years, he'd sailed with John MacGregor. If anyone brought the *Windhover* through, it would be the dour Aberdonian.

"Go below, Your Grace." His tone held no deference. If Cam hadn't been worried sick, he'd smile. "Ye're proving a wee distraction up here."

It was an indication of their perilous situation that Mac-Gregor admitted to needing all his concentration to keep the yacht afloat. "I want to help."

"Ye'll help by bundling up somewhere safe. If the bonnie Duke of Sedgemoor drowns on my watch, my bluidy wife will never let me hear the end of it."

Cam acknowledged the man's dry humor, surely the only dry thing left on the ship. He clapped MacGregor's shoulder then turned. Staggering from one handhold to the next, he struggled against the clawing wind toward the hatch.

Below decks, he'd thought the din would lessen, but it was somehow worse for being contained. The creak of timbers, the water pounding against the hull, the deep, irregular bang as the *Windhover* struck the bottom of a wave. He wondered how the fragile wooden structure survived.

In the saloon, he shook off the water drenching him. Like the crew of five above, he wore oilskins. Not that they provided much protection. Swiftly he undressed to shirt and breeches, shivering in the cold.

Pen was in her cabin. Throughout this trip, she'd borne every inconvenience without complaint. But in such a storm, even a good sailor with a courageous heart would be frightened. Whatever her distaste for Cam's company, he couldn't leave her terrified while they plunged through this turbulent ocean. She was alone—Maria hadn't wanted to come to England.

Bumping drunkenly from one wall to another, Cam made his way down the short corridor to where Pen's cabin faced his. During their fortnight at sea, that proximity had plagued him. Now, all he could think about was extending comfort and reassurance.

Although it was only early afternoon, the hallway was as dark as the pit. Cam knocked on Pen's door, received no reply, knocked more loudly, then realized that he'd need to bash the polished teak with a hammer for her to hear. Feeling like a trespasser, he depressed the brass handle and stepped inside.

All day he'd breathed air sour with salt. How was it, then,

that the moment he entered this shadowy room, he caught Pen's violet scent? Sweet, womanly, alluring. He closed his eyes and reminded himself that he was here purely to provide assistance.

"What do you want?" Pen asked sharply from across the cabin.

As his eyes adjusted to the gloom, he saw her braced in the porthole embrasure. He'd imagined she'd be in bed, but of course, that would be devilish uncomfortable, given the yacht's lurching.

"I wanted to see if you were all right." He raised his voice over the bedlam. He shut the door, hoping that might help. It didn't.

"Of course I'm all right."

Disappointment and self-disgust weighted his gut. He'd been a fool to imagine she might want him with her. "I'll go to my cabin, then."

He faced the door, catching the lintel for balance, when she replied. "No. Stay."

From Pen, that counted as a major concession. Slowly, he turned. "I don't want to intrude."

"Cam, don't be a numbskull," she snapped. "I've never been so scared in my life."

"Oh, my dear..."

The endearment escaped before he could stop it. He prayed that the storm muffled the words. With a few unsteady steps, he covered the space between them and, knowing it was a mistake, wrapped his arms around her. As he pressed into the opposite side of the embrasure, lightning flashed, revealing her face as she jerked her head up.

"Cam, what are you doing?" Like her expression, her voice was wary, but her eyes betrayed flaring heat. Even without the lightning, near the window the light was better.

"Stopping you from falling." They balanced inside a narrow nook, porthole on one side, cabin on the other. The restricted space offered at least an illusion of stability.

Was his world reeling because of the tumultuous ocean or because he touched this woman? His hands tightened on her waist and he couldn't even pretend that he held her for safety's sake. She was tall and strong, but he felt her tremble.

"They'll give you a medal," she said with a dryness that wouldn't have disgraced John MacGregor.

"Is there a kiss with my medal?"

More lightning illuminated the way she nervously licked her lips. She shifted backward, but their nook was so small, she had nowhere to go unless she returned to the cabin.

"How can you flirt when we're about to find a watery grave?"

"How can I not?" His voice roughened into urgency. "If the ship goes down, I'll be damned if I die without kissing you."

She started without moving away. "This is a mistake."

He laughed, wondering how his demise became cause for amusement. Perhaps Pen's courage bolstered his. Most people would cower at the raging seas, but valiant Penelope Thorne met the storm and the man who wanted her with her head high and a smile on her lips. At that moment, if he'd been capable of love, he might imagine that he loved her.

"The thought of kissing you has tortured me."

Her hands linked around his neck. To steady herself or because she wanted to touch him? He hardly cared as long as she stayed near.

"I thought you were bored with this journey."

He snorted his disbelief. "We've battled brigands, avalanches, bad roads, nosy English travelers, and fleas as big as cats. Boredom would be a relief."

"You acted bored."

He'd never seen her like this. Like she yearned for his touch the way he yearned for hers. Desire pounded harder than the waves outside. Thunder cracked close.

"Oh, hell, Pen," he groaned, firming his grip on her. He was incapable of gentleness. The storm outside was a pale echo of the storm in his blood.

On another guttural groan, his mouth crashed down.

As the ship plunged like a wild thing, Cam's mouth ravaged hers. Astonishment held Pen captive as a fierce mixture of sensations struck her harder than the waves against the hull.

Since she was a girl, she'd imagined Cam's kisses. The reality was earthier, more intimate, more passionate, more...exciting than anything she'd conjured in fantasy, no matter how lurid. His mouth was hot and commanding. His hands were ruthless and inescapable. The storm beat around her until she wasn't sure whether the chaos was outside or within her.

Pen was no longer the nineteen-year-old innocent who had turned down his proposal. She knew how a man behaved toward a woman he respected. In Cam's kisses, there was neither caution nor care.

Some distant corner of her mind urged her to protest. He treated her the way he'd treat a strumpet from the docks. But how could she demur when she basked in endless heat? All her life, she'd felt so cold, so cold.

His tongue plunged between her lips, demanding a response. Helpless to resist, bewildered and giddy with arousal, she gave it to him. She opened her mouth wide, sucking his tongue, tasting this man she'd always wanted. Her senses flooded with his rich flavor, his salty scent of storm and ocean and clean male sweat.

She moaned and arched into his damp clothes, frantically seeking the searing heat beneath. She'd set him alight and the flames of his desire lashed her. His hard length jutted into her vulnerable belly.

The knowledge of how much he wanted her set up a throbbing between her legs and she wriggled, wanting more. He rocked against her in an imitation of the sexual act. The breath scraped from her throat and she closed her eyes, reveling in incandescent sensation. Never had she felt like this.

Still his mouth explored hers as if he claimed a private kingdom. She could hardly breathe, sinking into untamed delight. She clung to his shoulders as her knees threatened to collapse. He was shaking too. If he wasn't braced so firmly against the window frame, they'd tumble to the floor.

His hands roamed over waist and hips and thighs. She didn't hear her dress rip, so she was startled at the sudden coolness across her chest. When his hands closed greedily on her breasts, she cried out in surrender. His long fingers plucked the beaded peaks, teased the areolas, stroked and squeezed and pinched. She'd recognized his desire weeks ago, but had no idea he wanted her so ferociously.

His hands pushed her to the edge of pain, but the agony was glorious. Never had she felt this intensity. Awe lanced through her.

Still he wasn't tender. She was past caring. She'd permit him anything, as long as he kept kissing her, touching her, panting his appreciation into her neck. She burned to touch him. Return this bliss. Conquer him in turn.

Hesitantly she slid a shaking hand between their bodies, cupping him. He was large, vigorous, daunting in her hand. She shuddered to feel the vibrant life. The thought of all that power thrusting inside her made her head swim.

"Damn it, Pen," he groaned into her bare shoulder and nipped her sharply.

Shock sizzled through her with the sting. His savagery appalled her, scared her, but spiked her excitement to a level where she threatened to combust.

"Should I stop?" The storm made her feel as though they were in a world of their own. She nibbled a line up his neck and along his strong jaw. "Tell me to stop."

"Hell, no," he groaned and drew one pointed nipple into his mouth. More exquisite pain flowed into intoxicating pleasure. To share this delightful hurt, she clenched her other hand in his tangled, wet hair.

He sucked her other nipple. Heat flooded her as every muscle tightened into a delicious coil. Through the haze, she felt his hand on her leg above her stocking. Another hitch against the ship's movement and his fingers curled around her mound. She jerked at the intimacy.

She tugged at his shirt until her lips skimmed hard pectorals, kissed the mat of soft hair. When one long finger invaded her body, she released a sharp inhalation and sank her teeth into his chest. He jerked and returned the favor with a sharp bite to her throat.

With a stagger, he swung her from the window. Away from the embrasure, the ship's pitching was dizzying. Or perhaps Pen was dizzy with passion. Cam tumbled her toward the luxurious bed where she'd slept alone for two weeks, tormented to know he lay just across the corridor.

Breathless with excitement, she toppled back onto the mattress. Then she was doubly breathless when Cam flung himself on top of her. His weight was unfamiliar, thrilling. The boat's tossing rolled them together so they wrestled like puppies. Inside her, a great emptiness yearned. She ached for Cam to fill her. She grabbed his shirt and ripped it off, desperate to feel his bare skin. She was as fierce as he was. Even now when it was clear that he was mad for her, she still feared that this glory might end before she'd drunk it to the dregs.

Cam fondled her breasts, pressing them together, kissing her nipples. Response rippled through her like fire as she bowed up toward the hot rasp of his tongue.

He kept speaking, broken words of praise and encouragement. *Kiss me. Touch me. Hold me. There. There. Ah, just there. You're beautiful. I want you. That's right. More. Harder. Tighter. Don't stop.* A feverish litany of demands that set her wayward heart pitching like the yacht.

With an urgency that stoked her craving, he slid down her body, setting his mouth wherever he reached. Throat. Breasts. Stomach, still covered by her shift. She'd had no idea her skin was so sensitive. Somewhere between the window and the bed, she'd lost her corset. She still wore her dress. Barely. Her skirts frothed around her hips.

His hands were everywhere. She jolted as he ripped her drawers away. His touch commanding, he caught her thighs and parted her. The ship gave a mighty kick as though protesting at his action.

Chest heaving as he rose, Cam caged her between his arms. "You drive me insane."

Gasping, she hooked her hands around his neck and held on hard. Making love in this storm was like embracing on a galloping horse. "I think we're both insane."

Lightning flashed again and again, turning the room continually bright. He looked desperate, as she'd never seen him. She thrilled to think that she, Penelope Thorne, did this to him. He dipped his hips until he rubbed against the place where she wanted him.

"I need more than this." Urgency made him sound angry.

"Don't talk." She pressed higher into that intriguing hardness, gathering her courage to unbutton his breeches. Above, there was a deafening crash as if a mighty tree fell. The yacht plunged, setting Pen bouncing. If Cam had been naked, he'd be inside her.

His hands on her waist were insistent, holding her firm against the shifting mattress. "Say you'll give me more than this."

What on earth? She frowned at him, struggling through her lunatic arousal to understand what he asked. "Of course I'll give you more than this."

"Having you once isn't enough. Give me a month." He pressed his face to her naked breast. "We'll go somewhere. Somewhere nobody knows us. Cornwall. The Highlands. France. A month will make no difference to your aunt's bequest."

Bewilderment, passion, recklessness vanished within the second. Like freezing seawater, stark reality crashed down. "A month," she repeated flatly.

He didn't notice her tone or that her body no longer curved toward his in welcome. Instead, she lay stiff as the planking on the deck.

"A month. Say you'll give me that much." He shifted to cradle her face in his elegant hands. "I promise you more pleasure than you've ever known."

Quickly and thoroughly, he kissed her. There was still no tenderness. Minutes ago, she wouldn't have minded. Stupid, brainless, needy little fool she was. Even now, her heart raced, her skin yearned for his touch.

"What's wrong?" He raised his head and stared at her in concern. "Is it the storm? This is hardly the best place to start an affair, but I see you and I can't keep my hands to myself."

"Apparently."

This time, he noted her tone. Slowly he sat back on his knees and she stole the chance to scramble up against the bedhead. She curled one hand over the carved top while the other clumsily struggled to restore her dress.

Lightning revealed Cam's wary expression. The flash also showed her how she'd devastated his clothing. How mortifying. His shirt hung in tatters over his powerful shoulders and chest. She struggled not to glance at his breeches, after a nervous glance revealed that he was still mightily aroused.

He ran a hand through his hair and his lips twisted in self-castigation. "You told me not to talk."

"You should have listened." She blinked back corrosive tears of anger and frustration. And hurt. When would she learn to keep her distance? Venturing closer to Cam always shredded her into bloody gobbets. But never so agonizingly as today when he'd asked her to be his temporary mistress before he married another woman.

"What did you think I offered?" He no longer sounded like her ardent lover, but like the authoritative man who had escorted her through the Alps.

"I didn't think," she admitted grudgingly. She still had trouble making her mind work. Anger and pain had doused passion, but her blood still pumped hot and ready.

"What in Hades is this, Pen?" Cam growled low in his throat. "You don't want to marry me. You made that clear nine years ago. I can't believe you've changed your mind."

Had she changed her mind? The awkward truth was that if he loved her, she'd swim a mile through the heaving ocean outside to marry him. With one arm tied behind her back.

The even more humiliating truth was that if he loved her, she'd sneak away in the blink of an eye to his love nest. If he loved her, she'd give up her last drop of blood to make him happy.

But the sad and unalterable reality was that he didn't love her. He'd never allow himself to love anybody.

He suffered a bad case of unsatisfied desire, a stronger reaction than she'd expected from phlegmatic Camden Rothermere. But love had never been part of the equation.

She spoke stiffly. "No, I don't want to marry you."

Another crash from above, violent enough to shake the deck. It sounded like a herd of elephants thundered up and down playing football.

"If you don't want an affair, what the hell do you want?" Because of the noise, his voice emerged more aggressively than perhaps he intended.

A fair question. So fair that it made her lash out in disappointment. "I don't want you to relieve your itch for me in some shabby little hideout before you go straight to Lady Marianne."

Lightning revealed him looking particularly ducal, all supercilious lowered eyelids and lips curled in aristocratic disdain. "My dear girl, you do me an injustice. There would be nothing shabby about our retreat. My mistresses never complain of my generosity. You won't surrender your doubtful virtue for a mere shilling."

She slapped him hard enough for the impact to echo over the wailing wind. Glaring, she rubbed her palm. It stung like the devil. She hoped his cheek felt worse.

Despite the noise, a vibrating silence descended.

When lightning streaked through the sky, she clearly saw the imprint of her hand on his face. He looked ready to murder her.

Good. She felt the same. If she could arrange it, she'd happily push him into the ocean and laugh while he drowned.

She should feel horrified at hitting him. But outrage still writhed in her stomach like a cobra, making her feel sicker than the rolling ship ever could. She'd never imagined him addressing a woman of his own class like a courtesan.

Damn Camden Rothermere to hell.

Another crash from above shattered his paralysis. He rolled off the bed to stand, clinging to the base of the bed. The rage drained from his expression, leaving him tired and unhappy. She told herself she didn't care.

"I'm sorry, Pen."

Pen wished he'd go, then realized that he awaited absolution. He could wait until hell turned into green meadows. "There's no excuse."

Her uncompromising response flattened his lips. "I haven't acted as a man of principle."

"And that irks you," she snapped.

He looked surprised, although to do him credit he didn't sidle away from responsibility. "Yes, it does. You know how I've struggled to prove that a Rothermere isn't necessarily a scoundrel."

She sighed, suddenly deathly sick of it all. "Cam, grow up and accept that you're not perfect. You made a mistake."

He knew he wasn't off the hook. "Around you, I make nothing but mistakes."

"Then perhaps it's better that we never meet again," she said dully.

"That might be best."

His ready agreement shouldn't sting. Of course he wanted to be rid of her. She'd been nothing but trouble, and now she'd teased him into a lather, then clouted him for good measure. "So get out of my cabin."

A lurch of the ship had him grabbing for the bedpost. Fortunately the furniture was nailed down. "You said you were frightened."

"Now I'm frightened of you," she said with a spite that later she'd regret.

He paled and his hand clenched on the carved column. "Pen, I—"

She stared blindly at the paneled wall, hoping he'd take the hint. Still he didn't go. Couldn't he tell that she didn't want to see him?

A splintering sound rent the air. A more fanciful woman might say it marked the splitting of her heart.

"Pen, I never meant it to be like this. Please forgive me."

Cam sounded like the boy she'd grown up with. She'd fallen in love with that boy. She'd trust her life to that boy. She turned ready to scream like a harpy, then stopped astonished as the door behind Cam slammed open and an oilskin-covered Goliath barged in.

"Your Grace, Your Grace, come above. The lady too. Cap'n says the *Windhover*'s about to founder on Goodwin Sands. The mast's gone and we're taking water. We must man the boats if there's hope of saving ourselves."

For a burning instant, Pen stared into Cam's eyes. "Cam, are we lost?"

"Never." The mad courage in Cam's response made her heart surge, despite all the anguish and hatred of the last hour. "Give me your hand."

Then the world turned to chaos as the yacht slammed into a solid obstacle.

Chapter Eleven

Leath House, London, late March 1828

By God, Leath's butler was a superior bugger. Harry fought the urge to stick a finger in his neckcloth to loosen it. He stalked through the door that the haughty fellow held and into an extravagant library.

The tall man who rose from behind a vast mahogany desk bore an expression even more forbidding than the butler's. By the hard set of his jaw and the shuttered eyes, he looked ready to boot young Mr. Thorne back into Berkeley Square. Harry gulped to moisten a dry mouth, then told himself to buck up.

"Thorne." Leath's voice was particularly deep and resonant.

Only with difficulty did Harry stop himself from jumping like a nervous cat. He'd heard innumerable stories of the marquess's lethal tongue and razor-sharp brain shredding any members of the House of Lords rash enough to set themselves against him. "My lord."

No invitation to sit. Instead Leath prowled around the desk to prop his hips against the edge. Harry supposed Sophie was upstairs. He hadn't informed her of this afternoon's call.

Harry swallowed again and struggled to keep his voice steady. He felt colder inside Leath House than outside in the squall slapping rain against the windows. "I'm sure you've guessed why I requested this appointment."

The marquess's expression remained discouraging. "Perhaps you should tell me."

Harry had devoted the last week to planning his campaign. He'd arrived dressed in his best and armed with an array of arguments to melt a bronze statue's heart. Now he stared at the man he hoped would become his brother-in-law and couldn't recollect a word.

Impatience drew the marquess's fierce black brows together. "I'm a busy man."

The world accounted James Fairbrother a handsome fellow in the brawny, saturnine fashion. Right now, Harry just thought he was terrifying.

Harry drew himself up and spoke from the heart. Which was the last thing he'd intended. He'd long ago realized that no appeal to sentiment would win over the marquess. "I'm here to ask permission to court Lady Sophie. I love her and I'm sure I'll make her happy."

To Harry's mortification, the marquess laughed. He folded his arms across his dauntingly wide chest and bent his head and snickered fit to send a man mad.

"My lord, I see nothing amusing in my request." Harry cursed himself for sounding like a pompous blockhead.

Abruptly Leath stopped laughing. This time Harry couldn't mistake the animosity in his eyes. "When I got your note, I wondered if you were moronic enough to declare yourself. Surely even the stupidest member of England's most imprudent family couldn't be that foolhardy." Another snide laugh. "I overestimated you. Although nothing I've seen since you started sniffing around my sister indicates that I should have."

"You're offensive, sir," Harry said coldly, before remembering that umbrage wouldn't forward his cause.

"I'm offensive?" Leath didn't raise his voice, which made his contempt all the more powerful. "I'm not a useless fribble of a spendthrift who imagines he'll win a great heiress just for the asking. An heiress who happens to be the sister I love. On his deathbed, I promised my father that I'd look after Sophie. Entrusting her future to a wastrel would make me a vile liar."

Harry struggled not to retreat under this tirade, all expressed in a *basso profundo* that set his teeth vibrating. "You need to give me a chance to present my case, my lord."

Leath's fist banged hard upon the desk behind him, setting the inkwells rattling. "The devil. I do not need to give you anything, except an order to leave my house and stop bothering my sister."

Every rule of politeness insisted that when a man requested a guest's departure, the guest was duty-bound to depart. But Harry was angry enough and desperate enough to defy the marquess's decree.

"There is some justice in your accusations, my lord," he said through lips so stiff that they felt made of wood. Nobody had spoken to him like this since he was an unpromising schoolboy at Eton. He squared his shoulders and stared directly at Leath. "I won't make excuses for my behavior or my family."

"There are no excuses," Leath snapped.

Harry told himself that he couldn't close this interview

by punching the overweening coxcomb in the nose. "I am a young man who until now has had no call on his talents. I've done no harm to anyone. My vices are those of any sprig about Town. If you inquire, you'll discover I'm addicted to neither the bottle nor the gambling tables. I'm not in debt." Barely. "I love your sister sincerely. I believe I can make her happy."

Leath regarded him like a cockroach that had crawled from beneath the rich Turkey carpet. "And I believe that you're a rake without income or prospects who intrigues to set himself up in luxury, courtesy of my sister's fortune."

Harry flinched before he recalled that any display of vulnerability placed him at the marquess's mercy. Not that mercy seemed part of the man's repertoire. "I'd take your sister in her shift, sir."

"Gallant words, Mr. Thorne. Ones you'll never need to prove."

"She ought to marry a man who adores her." Harry retained enough grip on strategy to know that mentioning Desborough would only infuriate Leath.

"She ought to marry a man who offers steadfastness and care."

"I am that man, sir." Harry straightened his spine, although he knew nothing would help him. Damn it, Sophie had been right. He should have listened. She'd be furious when she discovered that he hadn't. "We should ask Lady Sophie's opinion."

At least Leath didn't laugh, although his smile was derisive. "You've turned her head. You have a charming manner, Mr. Thorne. Not charming enough to gain this heiress."

"You harp upon her fortune, my lord, as if that is all Lady Sophie has to offer. You do her a grave injustice."

Was Harry optimistic to notice a softening in Leath's

contempt? "You've got more backbone than I expected, Thorne. Perhaps you do fancy yourself in love."

Harry didn't bother gracing that comment with a reply. "So I have permission to court your sister?"

Leath's eyebrows arched. "Be damned to you, you do not. She'll marry a man who can give her the life she deserves. That, sir, is not you."

"You are mistaken, my lord."

"I doubt it." He stalked around his desk to sit in the imposing leather chair. "I'm no longer at leisure." Briefly Leath's tone had thawed to slightly above glacial. It was back to icy now.

Knowing he'd made a fool of himself, knowing he might have made an irredeemable mistake in declaring his hand too early, Harry stared helplessly at the marquess. "Is there nothing I can say to change your mind?"

"Nothing." Piercing dark eyes blasted him with antipathy. "Now I suggest—*again*—that you leave."

He'd failed. Dear God, he'd failed.

Now Leath would be more watchful than ever. Why the hell hadn't he listened to Sophie and ignored his masculine impulses to stake a claim? He'd said he cared about honor, but he now realized that self-importance had driven him to this ill-considered meeting.

"Thank you for your time." He prayed that he concealed his turmoil. He dearly wanted to retain a scrap of dignity.

"I can't say it was a pleasure."

"Good day, my lord." Harry bowed, defeat settling sour and heavy in his belly. He'd made a complete mull of everything. He hoped like hell that Sophie forgave him. He hoped like hell that he had a chance to see her so that she could forgive him. Leath might exile her to Timbuctoo to keep her from unwelcome suitors.

Leath didn't do him the courtesy of standing for his departure. Instead, he drew a folder of papers closer and began to read.

He dismissed Harry like a tradesman. Keeping a rein on his temper, Harry turned on his heel and marched out, back straight as a ruler even as despair battered him.

Kent Coast, late March 1828

The small boat tossed like a cork in a whirlpool. Pen hunched in the stern, soaked and clinging to the gunwales with frozen hands. Cam and Captain MacGregor rowed like demons to steer the dory toward the dimly visible coast, a mere line on the horizon.

The wind whistled past, ripped at her hair and the cloak she'd grabbed to save her modesty before Cam had rushed her on deck. It provided little defense against the thrashing waves and the horizontal rain. Her teeth chattered and after half an hour of this hell, she could no longer feel hands or feet.

She couldn't bear to look behind at the empty space where Cam's magnificent *Windhover* had once commanded the sea. The ship had gone down with astonishing rapidity moments after Cam had flung Pen into the tiny craft they now shared. The fall had left her bruised, but grateful to be above the waves, not below. The sick chill that she'd felt watching the graceful yacht sink like a stone still thickened her blood.

Two crewmen hadn't made it. Pen had hardly known one, but the other had been a cheerful presence. If she survived this ordeal, she'd mourn his death. Of the two remaining sailors, one had been hit by the falling mast. Moaning and barely conscious, he huddled beside Pen. The other crewman

Williams bailed madly in the bow. The strange dim light of the stormy afternoon revealed his losing battle. With every second, they wallowed deeper.

Bile flooded her mouth. Not sea sickness. Sheer terror.

Except that the Thornes were famous for courage, if not good sense. Stiffly Pen uncurled her cramped limbs and crouched at Cam's feet. She began to bail with her hands.

"Pen!" Cam's voice was thin in the wind, although he sat so close. She'd thought the noise in the cabin was deafening. Here, she could hardly summon thought, it was so loud.

She met his eyes. Not long ago, they'd fired cruel words at one another. Through the driving rain, his expression defied their destruction. He reached down and produced a tin dish. For the first time since they'd met again, no shadows darkened his smile. Ridiculous as it was in the middle of a tempest and with drowning likely, she smiled back.

"Good for you," he said.

Such simple praise. He'd said it so often when they'd been children and she'd bowled a straight ball or taught one of her mongrel dogs a trick. The accolade warmed her heart, on a day cold enough to freeze lava. She stared into his eyes and realized that if fate decreed her death, she couldn't ask for a better companion.

Then she started to bail furiously. The boat climbed each wave, then descended with a nauseating thud. Thunder cracked again and again. She was soaked to the skin. Her hair clung to her face like sticky icicles. The air she inhaled was jagged ice. Her hands didn't seem to belong to her. Still they went on. Dip and throw, dip and throw, dip and throw.

She reached a point where anything more than rote movement was beyond her. Somewhere in her soul, she knew that Cam was here. With death breathing wet and cold down her neck, his nearness meant the world.

She didn't look up. There was little point. Visibility had worsened until it was like heading into a cloud. Still she kept going. Dip and throw. Dip and throw. Dip and—

The boat crashed into something and the world turned topsy-turvy again. For an instant, Pen stared up at the lightning-riddled sky. Then choking darkness engulfed her as she sank beneath the waves.

Chapter Twelve

Cam surfaced to a wave smashing into his face. The capsizing boat had tossed Pen free. That had been the most terrifying experience in a day of terrifying experiences. Spluttering, he searched the wild seascape.

Nothing.

He dived, opening his eyes against stinging salt and cold, but saw only gray and black. Sand churning in the water abraded his skin. He stayed down until his lungs screamed with pain. Then he kicked toward the surface, gulped for air, and went under again.

He bobbed up, gasping, to watch the upturned boat shatter into jagged spears of wood against the rocks. The impact was loud enough to rise above the wail of the wind and the roar of the waves.

Cam couldn't see his crew. He had a sick feeling that Oates, the injured man, wouldn't make it.

"Pen!" he shouted, but the wind whipped the cry away.

The sea wouldn't take Pen. His thoughts extended no further than that. Nothing, not even nature's fury, would gainsay his claim.

The current shoved him closer to the jagged rocks. He'd gone beyond the point where he cared about his safety.

Down he went into freezing darkness. Up through the swirl. A glimpse of sky. Coughing to clear the water splashing into his face. Snatching air. Down again. Hands closing on an empty universe of ocean.

No lithe female body. No obstinate woman who drove him to madness. And made him feel more alive than anyone else ever had.

His legs turned to rubber. His arms lost the strength to pull through the water. Still he dived. Still he searched.

So spent that even breathing tested him, he surfaced once more. A sensible man would save himself now that it was clear that she was lost.

Bugger sense.

He inhaled and ignoring the agonized protests from every sinew, he pushed down. Down. Down. Not sure if he could fight the suck of the water.

His lungs burned. The cold made him sluggish. He couldn't see. The idea of floating into oblivion beckoned.

He reached into the void. Praying like a madman. Stupid, mindless, incoherent pleas to the Almighty.

Please. Please. Don't let her die. Let me find her. Take me instead.

The only answer was the roar in his ears as he started to drown.

Still he reached. Still he struggled.

When long strands brushed his icy skin, he thought they must be seaweed. Debris filled the water. Wreckage from the *Windhover*. Nets threatening to entangle him.

In air-deprived stupidity, he delayed dangerously before he realized that no seaweed was this silky. With lunatic hope, his hands closed on Pen's hair.

Triumph delivered one last spurt of power. With an ungainly kick, he shot forward, using her hair to guide him.

All the while, his heart hammered one word. Over and over. *Penelope. Penelope. Penelope.*

Something bumped his hands. Something that felt like a body. Numb fingers fumbled to catch her. She still wore the cloak. Its weight must have dragged her down.

He ripped at the strings around her neck. They resisted, but so close to saving her, he wasn't giving up for the sake of a few knots. Finally the strings parted and the cloak flowed away.

With one final push, he kicked toward the surface. Noting with dread the lack of movement in the body lashed in his aching arms.

He burst through the rough sea and wrenched Pen upward until she bobbed, facing the sky. Lightning revealed how pale and still she was. That seemed wrong for someone so vivid. Her eyes were closed and blue tinged her parted lips. Her features were so wan, she could be carved from marble.

Using a clumsy sidestroke, he battled the current to swim for the shore.

Then the miracle happened. On top of a wave about fifty yards off, he saw a light. The light turned into a boat with searchers sweeping lanterns across the turbulent water.

"Over here!" he shouted, but his voice emerged as a mere thread.

Beside him, Pen floated lifeless as a spar from the *Windhover*.

He summoned his last strength and raised one arm, waving wildly, praying that he'd be visible over the choppy sea. "Over here!"

Even then, he wasn't sure it was enough. A towering wave hid the boat. Despair, fatal as the icy water, gripped him. He'd failed to save her.

Then the boat crested another wave and he saw that it headed toward him. Only when the boat was almost upon them did he hear the team of oilskin-clad men shouting encouragement.

"Take her," he gasped, lifting Pen and getting a mouthful of dirty salt water.

"We've got her, laddie." A man's hands closed around Pen and hauled her up.

"Here." Another man extended a hand to Cam, who grabbed it with a gasp. He was too weak to be more than dead weight, but eventually, he flopped into the rowboat. Beside him, one of his rescuers had turned Pen over and pressed rhythmically on her back.

For a terrifying interval, she didn't respond. Cam had prayed in the water. He'd never prayed as hard in his life as he did now.

Still no reaction.

Dear Lord in heaven, he'd been too late.

One pale, slender hand, weighted with his signet ring—how had that stayed on her finger?—twitched. Within seconds, she jerked and coughed and vomited up what seemed like an entire ocean.

Thank you, God.

Simple words, but he'd never felt them so sincerely. Groaning at the effort it took—all energy faded now that they'd been rescued—he reached across to touch her heaving shoulder. He needed to feel the life flooding back into her. His desolation when he'd thought her lost still fermented in his belly.

He sat up, although every aching muscle begged him never to move again. A sailor handed him some water and only after a few sips could he speak. "Five men were on the ship."

Since the boat capsized, he hadn't seen MacGregor or the other crewmen. But he'd focused solely on Pen. If John MacGregor had floated a yard away, Cam doubted he'd have noticed.

The fellow who had tugged him from the water like a floundering haddock spoke through a beard of such thickness, Cam couldn't see his mouth. "There's another rescue boat out, but I don't 'old much 'ope for survivors. It's a terrible day, terrible."

Cam recognized the cruel truth of that. "Can we search for them?"

The man's snort might have contained amusement or express derision for someone stupid enough to expect anyone to brave this storm. "We've seen nobody else. And we need to get you and your lady to shore. We've plucked two live uns from the waves. Reckon that's our bounty." He paused. "The lads are done in. As dangerous for rescuers as for drowners."

While he recognized the sense in what the sailor said, Cam's heart cramped with regret. John MacGregor was a good man, and the crew had been under Cam's charge.

He moved closer to Pen. Gently, he turned her over and was shocked to see that she was barely covered. Drawing her into his arms, he spoke to the man who had saved him. "Do you have a blanket?"

"We've got some in the basket in the stern. No promises 'ow dry they be," the man said gruffly. "They'll warm your wife."

Cam didn't bother to explain that they weren't married. The rower behind him passed word down. Soon Cam had wrapped Pen in a damp, prickly, but serviceable wool blanket.

Cam braced himself against the side of the boat. Pen only gradually returned to consciousness. She moaned and

Cam pressed her icy face into the curve of his neck. He told himself he shared body heat—she was alarmingly cold and didn't feel much more alive than she had as a drifting wraith. But the truth was that he needed to touch her to fill the void inside him that had opened when he'd thought her dead.

"You're hurting me," Pen muttered into his bare chest, her breath like a kiss.

"I'm sorry." Reluctantly he loosened his grip. "How are you feeling?"

He took a moment to recognize the choked sound she made against his skin as a laugh. God above, she was magnificent.

"Awful." Her voice was scratchy, as if she'd screamed for him again and again and he hadn't come. Despite her earlier protest, his hold tightened.

"I'm not surprised." He raised the flask of water to her lips. After she drank, choking a little, he spoke. "What do you remember?"

She showed no urge to move away. "I remember hitting the water. I remember trying to swim, but the cloak was so heavy. I should have taken it off, but the strings were tangled." She leaned back to stare into his face. A jagged flash through the sky revealed a vulnerable expression. "Thank you for saving me."

He gave her more water, pleased to see she managed better. "How do you know I did?"

Despite everything they'd been through, she found a smile. "You always saved me. Even if it meant fighting an army of village boys for the sake of a flea-bitten cat. Don't you remember?"

"I remember." Around them, the men rowed like demons. Inches away, the sea clawed at their boat. But he and Pen were cocooned in intimacy. "Don't speak, Pen. Rest."

For a woman who had nearly drowned, her gaze was remarkably steady. "No, there's something I must say."

"It can wait until we're on land."

"Please, Cam." She rested her hand over his heart, the heart that had cracked at the thought of losing her. "Let me speak."

He already knew he wouldn't like what she said, but he wasn't proof against her pleading. "Very well."

"You will always be the dear friend of my childhood." Despite her hoarseness and her pauses for breath, her voice was as steady as her gaze. "And now you've saved my life. Again."

He took no comfort from what she said. Her manner hinted that she spoke of endings, not beginnings. "Rescuing you is my mission."

"No longer." Regret stabbed him when she lifted her hand from him. Her lovely face was drawn and tired—and heart-breakingly sad. "This journey hasn't been easy on either of us. But it's over. Let's forget the anger, and remember one another with generosity. Let's say our farewells without rancor."

Penelope was right. And wise. Wiser than he.

He tucked her head under his chin and stared unsee-ingly toward the approaching coast. As Pen said, once they reached England, their dealings were done. His life would return to its assigned path. Playing the omnipotent Duke of Sedgemoor. Restoring some respect to the family name. Running his estates and investments. Marriage to Marianne Seaton.

He should be delighted. Instead, he felt like red-hot pin-cers ripped out his guts.

Chapter Thirteen

As the boat slid into the stone harbor, the cessation of pitching seemed a miracle to Pen.

Her body felt made of wet string. Battered wet string. Even breathing hurt. She was shaking and her teeth chattered, despite Cam's best efforts to keep her warm. He must curse her for the loss of not only his yacht, but his crew.

He should have let her drown.

But of course he wouldn't. He was too honorable. The offer he'd made before the ship foundered was the exception that proved the rule. She'd been so furious with him. Right now, having come so close to dying, it was hard to reawaken her outrage. Especially when he'd nearly died himself trying to save her.

The boat bumped against the pier and rocked as the sailor at the bow tied it to a metal hook. Daylight gradually returned as the storm abated.

When Pen struggled to stand, her legs folded beneath her. Predictably Cam caught her.

"Let me help you," he said softly.

Once they were safely on the dock, Cam swept her into his arms. She curled into his powerful body against the onlookers' curiosity. Taking those first painful gasps of air after nearly drowning, modesty had been the last thing on her mind. Now despite the weather, a crowd surrounded them and she was grateful for the concealing blanket.

"Come away to the Leaping Mackerel, sir," a man said at Cam's shoulder. "There's food and a fire and we'll fetch the doctor."

"Thank you." Cam sounded remarkably like his usual self, instead of the shaken man who had rescued her. He spoke over her head to the crew who had saved them. "And thanks to you. We owe you our lives."

"It's nothing, laddie," the bearded man said.

Pen couldn't imagine anyone calling haughty Camden Rothermere "laddie" since he was breeched. Probably not even before then. "Nonetheless, your gallantry won't go unrewarded."

"Thank you," she choked out.

The man nodded before turning away to stow the boat. Her hands tightened around Cam's shoulders as he strode along the quay. Rain sheeted down, but they were already so wet it made little difference.

Cam's ordeal had hardly been less taxing than hers. "I can walk."

"Don't be a fool." His grip tightened as if he'd fight anyone for the right to carry her.

Pen surrendered to the forbidden luxury of his touch. She was too tired and sore to resist. Feeding her senses with his salty, clean scent and the heat of his body, she hid her face against his bare chest. For a dangerous interval, she floated in a world where Cam's arms welcomed her forever.

Cam marched through the crowd, responding briefly to

congratulations and good wishes. Pen's contentment was short-lived. The onslaught of noise and warmth when they entered the inn dazed her as if she'd stumbled into civilization after being lost in the wilderness.

"Is the doctor here?" Cam shouldered his way through the packed taproom. Gently he placed her on a padded bench near the fire.

"Aye, sir." A thickset middle-aged man appeared behind Cam. "I'll see to the lady." Although she missed Cam's arms, Pen sat quietly while the doctor took her wrist to check her pulse.

"She'll want a nice cup of tea. And you'll have brandy, I'm sure, my lord." A woman who must be the innkeeper's wife bustled forward with a brimming glass that she shoved at Cam. "I'm Mrs. Skillings. Welcome to the Leaping Mackerel, Ramsgate's finest inn."

Cam looked like a ragamuffin, wet and filthy in his tattered clothing. But Mrs. Skillings hadn't mistaken his accent or bearing. Cam could stand naked surrounded by polar bears in Greenland and he'd still appear exactly what he was, an English nobleman of the highest standing.

"Thank you." He accepted the brandy, but instead of drinking it, he offered it to Pen.

"You're too kind." How true that was.

Wincing, she extended one hand from under her blanket to take the glass. She felt like she'd been through twelve rounds with Tom Cribb. And the boxer had won. Now that she was safe, she felt the sting and ache of innumerable scrapes and bruises. Despite the fire in the hearth, she shivered. The chill extended to her bones. When she drank, the spirits settled in her belly and stirred her sluggish blood.

"My lady needs a coat," Cam said to the room at large.

"So do you," Pen said softly. Cam looked magnificent

with his bare chest and torn breeches. Like a marooned pirate king. But he'd been immersed in cold water as long as she had.

Mrs. Skillings addressed the man behind her, obviously the innkeeper. "Take the lady to our best chamber, John. I'll bring her one of my dresses to tide her over."

Pen caught a flash of quickly hidden amusement in Cam's eyes as she returned the brandy glass. Three of Pen would fit into anything that went around the woman's ample figure.

"I haven't finished my examination," the doctor protested.

"Aye, Frederick Wilson, and what sort of lady would she be to let you fuss over her in the middle of a public taproom? Can't you see she's quality? Do your poking and prodding once she's upstairs, away from nosy parkers and resting in a nice featherbed."

"Thank you, Mrs. Skillings," Pen said gratefully, clutching her blanket. "Is there any word of our crew?"

"Oh, dear me, you wouldn't know, would you?" the woman said. "The other boat came in before yours with three men. They're in the private parlor waiting for Dr. Wilson."

"Thank God," Cam whispered. He addressed the stocky sailor who had steered them to safety. "Two more men went missing when the ship sank."

"I'm sorry, laddie. The sea was bloody cruel today."

Cam was still "laddie." She noticed that he was careful not to reveal their names. Here in England, the Rothermeres were so well-known that the Pembridge title would provide no protection. After just escaping death, Pen found it difficult to care about scandal. But Cam had so much more to lose if word emerged about their travels. The thought soured the brandy in her stomach.

"Hiram Pollock, watch your language. There's a lady present," Mrs. Skillings snapped.

Remembering that two good men had perished made Pen want to cry. "Mr. Pollock, after what you did tonight, you can say anything you like."

The man laughed. "Well said, my lady." He shifted closer. "May I carry you upstairs?"

"That's my privilege." Cam passed his empty glass to the innkeeper and bent to lift Pen.

Gratefully she turned her face into his chest. The crowded room, stinking of wet wool and people of dubious cleanliness, made her feel faint. That, and her pummeled, aching body.

Cam hitched her higher and followed Mrs. Skillings. The crowd parted reluctantly. Pen had visited enough small towns to recognize the hunger for excitement that infected people who led generally uneventful lives. The *Windhover*'s wreck and the rescue of these well-spoken strangers would fuel conversation for years.

"I've had word of a yacht lost in the bay." A pompous tenor cut through the babble like a knife through butter. "I demand a report. I take it most amiss that I am the last person to learn of this disaster."

Cam's breath caught in dismay. The muscles beneath Pen's cheek turned hard as stone.

"Sir Henry." Mrs. Skillings's lack of welcome was audible. "We were about to settle his lordship and his lady in their rooms where they can recover in peace. I'm sure you'll agree that was our first duty."

Mrs. Skillings stood firmly in their path. Pen couldn't see past her bulk, although she had a suspicion that Cam knew the man.

"Your first duty was to inform the local magistrate. Just who are these people you call lord and lady?" Sir Henry's doubt of the castaways' status was clear.

"Why, here they be." Mrs. Skillings made a triumphant gesture.

"Who, sir, are you to claim the privileges of the peerage? You might gull a parcel of ignorant fisherfolk, but I'm a member of parliament and a regular visitor to London. I'm familiar with our ruling classes." Rudely Sir Henry shoved Mrs. Skillings aside.

After his blustering claims to know the great and good, Pen had expected to recognize him, if only from sketches in the papers. But the red-faced, rotund man dressed too fussily for a country inn was a stranger. She sucked in a relieved breath.

Until she saw astonishment then delight transform his expression. "Your Grace!"

"Good evening, Sir Henry," Cam said coolly. Only Pen, held close in his arms, knew how his heart raced. "I owe my life to the brave men of Ramsgate and Mrs. Skillings has been the soul of hospitality. If they delayed notifying you, they had due cause."

"Your Grace, this is an unexpected pleasure. But what odious circumstances bring you to our humble town! I'll make immediate arrangements to transport you to Kellynch House. The Leaping Mackerel doesn't befit your dignity." His eyes sharpened on Pen, who struggled to hide her sick apprehension.

After weeks of subterfuge, their efforts came to nothing. They were trapped in a scandal. Cam's grand plans lay in ruins and she loved him enough to regret that to her soul. He'd spent his life compensating for his parents' notoriety. Now, he'd face public disapproval as a man who, at the very least, kept a mistress even as he launched his courtship.

"I hadn't heard that you'd married, Your Grace. May I wish you and the new Duchess of Sedgemoor every happiness?"

"Thank you." Cam's arms were like steel. There wasn't a chance in Hades of containing the news that the Duke of Sedgemoor had survived a shipwreck. Not only that, but he'd gallantly rescued a female companion.

Pen waited for Cam to deny the marriage, until she saw that Sir Henry's glittering eyes focused on the gold signet. Strange that so much had been lost in the wreck, yet that lying proof of their union remained.

"Or have I mistaken the situation?" Sir Henry's voice lowered as no introduction to the new Duchess of Sedgemoor eventuated. "If so, you may rely on my discretion."

Pen had no idea how he meant to fulfill that promise. Fifty people must have heard Sir Henry identify Cam as the Duke of Sedgemoor.

"Not at all, Sir Henry," Cam said as coldly as she'd ever heard him speak to anyone. Then words that rendered her dumb with horror. "My wife has undergone a terrible ordeal. She requires quiet and privacy. I'll take her upstairs and tend to her. Should you require details of the wreck, you may call tomorrow." He marched past an openmouthed Sir Henry. "Mrs. Skillings, pray direct us to our rooms."

The throng fell completely silent to witness Cam at his most ducal, although curiosity swirled around them as powerful as the lashing sea that had nearly drowned her.

"Cam—" she began, uncertain how to avert catastrophe.

"Later, my dear." His words sounded more reprimand than endearment. "Your servant, Sir Henry."

Cam bowed to the magistrate with insulting brevity. Carrying a quaking Pen, he followed the innkeeper from the taproom.

Chapter Fourteen

I won't marry you, Cam." In the three days since the ship-wreck, Pen felt like she'd repeated those words a thousand times.

She stared uncompromisingly across the small parlor that linked their bedrooms at the Leaping Mackerel. Cam lounged against the windowsill, the mullioned window open to the busy street below and the salt-laden breeze ruffling his thick dark hair. Morning light shone on him, as though heaven itself informed the unworthy Miss Thorne that this man was completely out of her sphere.

He still looked like a pirate, although a better dressed one than the drenched ruffian fished from the Channel. Cam had managed to borrow some clothes that almost fitted, but Pen still got a surprise whenever she caught sight of the elegant Duke of Sedgemoor wearing the rough shirt and trousers. Strangely the cheap clothing made him look even more aristocratic. She'd never been so aware that he was born to be a duke.

At a disadvantage sitting, Pen rose from the table where

she'd been reading last week's London papers. She had a nasty feeling that Sedgemoor's shipwreck and mysterious bride featured in more recent editions.

Cam had just come in from checking on Oates, the injured crewman. Captain MacGregor and Williams had left yesterday. Tragically this morning they'd received news of the missing men's bodies washing up further south.

"The world believes we're married," Cam responded implacably. He must be as sick of this subject as she was. But gentlemen accepted the consequences of their actions. Not for the first time, Pen wished she'd been shipwrecked with a man of fewer principles.

She squared her shoulders, sensing the difference in Cam. She'd seen his face when he learned about the two dead sailors. She'd read guilt, anger, regret—and ominously for her, immovable determination. They had no further reason to linger in Ramsgate. They were both close to recovered, barring a few bruises. He knew this was his last chance to convince her to marry him.

"Nobody has identified me. A glower down that long nose will quash any impertinent questions. You can blame the misunderstanding on the chaos after the wreck. The world will shrug its shoulders and assume that you traveled with a mistress. A small scandal. A diamond or two will smooth Lady Marianne's feathers. No harm done."

He slumped on the windowsill, looking uncharacteristically defeated. "But harm is done, Pen. You're ingenuous to suggest otherwise."

"It will be a five-minute wonder at best," she said desperately, because somewhere at the back of her mind, a voice insisted that he was right.

"You forget that I'm a child of scandal." She hated when Cam looked at her as though he needed her help. "Now I'm caught in a compromising situation, all the old stories will resurface." His eyes sharpened on her. "And if you imagine your role will remain secret, you underestimate the press. You forget we were seen together near Genoa."

"When I'm back in Italy, tattle in England won't bother me."

"I'm staying here and it will bother me. The world wants me to prove myself as rackety as my forebears. Do you mean to throw me to the wolves, Pen?"

She whirled away to escape his grave regard. To gain her cooperation, Cam played upon her guilt. When he'd proposed a marriage to save her from ruin, she'd stubbornly resisted. With her father's indiscriminate womanizing and Peter's extravagance, there was already scandal aplenty in the Thornes. More, while unwelcome, wouldn't make much difference, especially as Pen had no intention of marrying.

Now Cam deployed his final weapon—their long friendship. Despite his words, she knew he wasn't selfishly concerned for himself. Although he should be. After his struggle to restore pride to the Rothermere name, he'd now undergo trial by gossip.

He was a manipulative devil to enlist her conscience against her. Fathoming his game made his tactic no less effective. She hated to think of Cam suffering because of her actions. He'd hurt and infuriated her when he'd asked her to become his mistress. Remembering that scene before the shipwreck, she was still hurt—and restless and embarrassed and wickedly curious about what might have happened.

"That's not fair, Cam."

"Isn't it?" he asked softly.

The room fell so quiet that she heard a mother scolding her child on the street below and the creak of boats moored in the harbor. Still she refused to answer. Knowing that if she did, she was lost.

When she was nineteen, she'd fought this agonizing battle. If anything, her reasons for saying no to everything her heart desired were stronger now. Except that Cam didn't offer everything her heart desired. Whatever passion they mustered between them, there would be a coldness at the center of this marriage arranged purely to appease public opinion.

Pen couldn't live with Cam day after day hungering for his love. She'd seen her mother become a bitter harridan through yearning after a man who didn't return her affection once the first reckless rapture had passed. It was a terrifying example of the price of unrequited love.

With a grim sense of inevitability, she heard Cam padding toward her. Even in borrowed boots, he still moved like a cat.

"Pen, look at me."

"No." It was childish, but she couldn't bear that concerned stare, as if he only pursued her best interests.

"If you won't look at me, will you at least listen?"

"I don't want to." More childishness.

"I won't give up. I won't have the world calling you vile names."

That had her turning. "You could convince a spider to weave you a shirt, but you won't change my mind."

"At least you're looking at me," he said calmly.

"I won't marry you."

"So you'll let me become a public laughingstock?"

Oh, he was cruel. Her throat felt dry and tight. "That won't happen."

"If not a laughingstock, then a byword for villainy. A man who ruins a childhood friend and abandons her to face her disgrace alone."

"Nobody who knows you will believe that."

A muscle flickered in his cheek. She couldn't doubt how deeply he wanted to save her, even at the sacrifice of all his hopes for a different life. "But it's true."

"You're exaggerating."

"No, I'm not. Your reputation will be in shreds. And it's my fault."

His remorse on her behalf stripped another layer from her defenses. She felt like she waged a losing rearguard action. "We didn't do anything wrong."

His level stare stirred unwelcome memories of their kisses. "Not for want of trying."

Mortifying heat rose in her cheeks even as her temper stirred. "If you recall, that encounter was an absolute shambles. Instead of proposing marriage, any sane man would run for the hills."

"You were right to hit me." She supposed that was the closest he'd come to an apology. "Pardon my frankness, but there was no lack of heat between us."

"That's no basis for marriage," she snapped and caught a flash of satisfaction in his eyes at her unwitting admission.

How could she marry him, loving him and knowing that he'd never love her? He hadn't changed from that young man who had dismissed love so contemptuously in her hearing. She just needed to remember his reaction when she'd asked if he loved Lady Marianne to recognize that Camden Rothermere was as set against love as he'd ever been.

Pen was a passionate creature who when she cared, cared wholeheartedly. A lifetime pining after an unattainable man who remained a hand's reach away would destroy her. She'd be like a dog choking on a chain too short to reach the water bowl.

"It's a start." He stepped closer, making her aware of his

height and strength. His evocative scent filled her nostrils. "Desire is on our side."

"Desire is on *your* side," she corrected sharply. "I'm trying to be sensible."

The affection in his smile knocked a few more bricks off the walls of her refusal. "No, you're trying to be obstinate."

Oh, dear God, she was so susceptible. The slightest warmth from Cam and she wanted to curl up at his feet and beg for his love. That humiliating image made her scowl down her nose in her best imitation of his imperious glare. "I refuse to marry a man who won't take me seriously."

To her complete astonishment, he burst out laughing. "My sweet Pen, I take you as seriously as an epidemic."

She didn't smile. "Charming."

The time he took to sober didn't advance his cause. "Fate seems set on us marrying. Nine years ago, you escaped. You won't escape now."

"This isn't cosmic destinies colliding. It's you wanting your own way," she said sourly.

She understood that he found her implacable opposition puzzling. After those torrid moments in the cabin, he knew she wanted him. He could cope with desire. Her love would horrify him. If she could suffer his pity, she supposed she could confess her feelings to drive him away. But she and Cam were both proud beyond bearing. His pity would be the last straw.

"We have more than physical attraction."

"What? Childhood memories?"

"Yes," he said steadily. "You know me so well, despite our long separation. I think we'll go along very well together. Producing an heir won't be a hardship." He paused. "And you don't expect any lovesick romantic nonsense from me, which will give us a good start. I like you, Pen. I always have. I distinctly remember telling you that I liked you better than any girl I knew."

Oh, heaven lend her strength. She supposed he meant to flatter her. To her, the lukewarm declaration twisted a knife in an open wound. How he'd cringe if he knew that "romantic nonsense" powered her every breath. "That was nine years ago."

"You remember?"

She remembered everything he'd ever said to her. That was just another curse of this futile, painful love. "I remember you wanted a conformable wife."

His laugh was wry. Long ago, she'd recognized that he didn't laugh enough, weighed down even as a boy with old scandal, an unhappy family, and an overdeveloped sense of responsibility. The overdeveloped sense of responsibility hadn't faded. Why else would he be so set on marrying her?

"I know when I'm beaten. Conformable is no longer part of the deal."

A wave of her hand dismissed his response. "Cam, you talk about the Rothermere scandals. What about the Thornes? We've become more ramshackle with every year since you proposed, and we were no shining example of respectability even then. My father ruined himself chasing whores. Aunt Isabel was decidedly eccentric. Peter died in penury. From what I gather, Harry plays the rake. I can't imagine the ton approves of my junketing." Even though the words pierced like darts, she forced herself to say them. "Far better you weather the gossip and make your peace with Lady Marianne. You need a duchess to enhance your name, who meets general approval, who fits the neat, useful, proper life you want."

This description left him less than delighted. "How dull I sound."

Her fight drained away. Instead she felt deathly weary, as though she'd walked twenty miles in ill-fitting shoes and found no welcome at journey's end. "Not dull, Cam, just not for me." In so many ways that she could never explain. "Confess everything to Lady Marianne. If she's the woman you think she is, she'll stand by you. Marry your perfect bride and forget me."

"No," he said stubbornly. "We must marry."

"Don't you like Lady Marianne?" It hurt to say the woman's name. Pen wondered if she'd ever overcome the excruciating wrench of knowing that Lady Marianne would be with him every day; she'd bear his children, she'd accompany him into old age.

"Of course I like Marianne. She's a paragon."

Naturally. If Pen married Cam, she'd always know she was his second-best bride. "I'll never be a paragon, even if you sacrifice your happiness to save me from social ruin."

His expression hardened. "I'm not saving you from social ruin, I'm saving myself. Everything I've worked for since I was a boy will turn to dust if I don't make this right. I beg of you, Pen, marry me. Only you can rescue me."

Oh, the villain, the scoundrel, the cad. At this moment, she hated him.

She stared at him, telling herself she wouldn't cry. "Cam, it's mean to play upon old obligations."

He shrugged. "You're my only hope of emerging with my reputation intact. A man with one hope doesn't surrender lightly."

She backed away as if distance would bolster her resistance. "You're inviting years of misery."

The tension eased from his face, leaving him somber but adamant. "I'll live with that."

"I'm not sure I can."

He paled and she was shocked to see that she hurt him. "I'll do my best to make you happy, Pen."

In a low, trembling voice, she repeated, "It's not enough."

He didn't pursue her. He didn't have to. He knew he'd won. "It must be."

Well, that was an epitaph for a marriage if she ever heard one. Harshly, because the grief ahead loomed like jagged mountains, she asked, "Even if we marry, I don't see how we'll avoid scandal."

"That's easy."

His confidence didn't soothe the dread stamping around inside her stomach. "It always is for you."

He winced at her jibe. "Not always. You've made me wait nearly ten years."

"Don't count your chickens," she said sharply, although they both recognized that she argued for pride's sake. "While the world thinks we're married, we're not. If anyone learns the truth, our children will be exposed as bastards."

The thought of creating those children made her sick with apprehension, although this marriage could never have been a chaste arrangement. Cam needed an heir. Given the gossip about his birth, he'd countenance no doubts about that heir's legitimacy.

But how could she lie in his arms and know that duty alone brought him there? How could she lie in his arms and pretend mere *liking* when every beat of her heart echoed his name?

"Credit me with some sense," he said equally sharply. "We'll say we fell madly in love in Italy and married in a Roman Catholic ceremony in some obscure village because we couldn't bear to wait."

"How romantic," she said flatly.

He ignored her interjection. "We'll arrange a quiet cere-mony at Fentonwyck to confirm our marriage under English law. You're in mourning for Peter so nobody will question a quick, private wedding."

"That's...interesting." Actually it was brilliant. If Cam wasn't playing skittles with her life, she might applaud. "The sticklers will question the validity of the Continental ceremony."

He shrugged. "Most people will accept our story, especially once our first child arrives."

She raised her eyebrows. "Just how many children are you planning, Your Grace?"

Mockery curled his lips. "The prospect of fatherhood makes me feel quite dynastic."

"It makes me feel ill," she snapped.

The amusement drained from his eyes and he regarded her searchingly. "Pen, I'm sorry. I know this isn't what you want. If I hadn't barged into your life, you'd still be free."

Pen straightened her spine and staunchly told herself that she could endure a future with Cam. Perhaps marriage wouldn't be too bad. Many ton couples lived separate lives. Surely once Cam had got her with child, he'd pursue other interests.

Oh, damn, she didn't want to think about those interests. He'd take a mistress and she couldn't insist otherwise. This wasn't a love match and she had no claim on his emotions or fidelity. This was a marriage of convenience. A business contract.

Dear Lord, if she didn't stop, she'd be sniveling like a lost puppy.

Courage, Pen.

But as she stared down the empty years ahead, she wanted to scream and cry and insist that it wasn't fair. "It's not your fault the ship sank. It's not even your fault that Peter asked for your help."

Cam's gaze was wary. "That's remarkably reasonable of you."

The smile she summoned felt like a rictus grin. She had the sensation of entering a long, dark tunnel. "You've chosen a remarkably reasonable duchess, Cam. I hope you appreciate her as she deserves."

Chapter Fifteen

Leath House, London, late March 1828

I begged you not to go to James. Why didn't you listen?"

Vibrating with fury, Sophie paced the small Chinese summerhouse. The swish of daffodil yellow skirts added an incongruously sunny note to her tirade.

"I'm sorry." Harry slumped onto the bench and endured his beloved's perfectly justified temper. He hadn't spoken one word to Sophie since his disastrous meeting with her brother three days ago. "I loathe sneaking around. I wanted everything aboveboard."

"I told you he wouldn't countenance your suit. I told you he wanted me to marry Desborough."

Of necessity, she kept her voice low. Discovery remained a whisper away, however well concealed this pavilion. It was late afternoon and the gardeners had finished for the day. The servants had dinner inside the house. Leath plotted parliamentary maneuvers at his club.

"I hoped he'd give me a chance."

She stopped prowling and glared at Harry until he winced. "You should have trusted me when I said he wouldn't."

"Yes, I should have." Self-disgust twisted his gut. "But, Sophie, an honorable man doesn't risk compromising the woman he loves."

Her rage didn't abate. He hadn't expected that it would. "Now James is sending me to my great-aunt in Northumberland."

He'd expected something like this, but hearing about it still struck him like a blow. He fought back the despair that had gripped him since Leath's brusque dismissal. "I'll follow you."

She shook her head. "My great-aunt is a dragon and she lives in the middle of a village full of busybodies. James told her that I'm allowed to go to church and that's it."

Harry surged to his feet and seized her hands. "When do you leave?"

Halfheartedly she tried to pull away. "Tomorrow."

His heart plunged. "So soon?"

"Yes."

Still Harry refused to accept that Leath had won. "And how long are you away?"

"A month." Tears trembled on Sophie's long eyelashes. "If I'm good."

Harry wanted to curse Leath's tyranny, but he was worldly enough to recognize that the man acted in what he considered were Sophie's best interests. "I'm up to circumventing a mere aunt."

An unconvincing attempt at a smile. "She's not a mere aunt. She's a bluestocking and a man-hater and she has huge dogs."

"For you, I'd brave a pack of hungry lions. What's a dog or two?"

"Harry, stop it," she said on a pleading note. "When we're parted, you'll forget me."

Shock made him drop her hands and step back, drawing up to his full height until he towered over her. "What the hell do you mean?"

She twisted her hands in her filmy skirts. "There are so many pretty debutantes this year."

"Oh, my darling." Devastation flooded him. How could she think him so fickle? He caught her in his arms. "Never, never think that."

"How can I help it? James does nothing but talk about your intrigues." She stood stiffly in his embrace. "You're so handsome and charming. Every girl in London wants you."

He was appalled to realize that this vulnerability pre-dated today's quarrel. "You're the only woman I've ever loved." His voice lowered. "I've laid my heart at your feet, sweetheart, and there it will stay. I'll kindly ask you not to kick it."

"Of course I won't kick it." He was mightily relieved to see the doubt fade from her eyes. "I'm glad that you'll love me forever."

"Forever. So what's a month?" Endless purgatory, but he didn't say that. "We can write."

She rested her head on his chest. Touching her made Harry's world revolve in the right direction. Heaven help him if she succumbed to family pressure and accepted Desborough. Harry would be useless to man and beast.

"No, we can't. I need to buckle down and behave or James won't let me finish the season. He said he's happy to let me rusticate until I marry Desborough."

Harry's heart pounded in frantic denial against her cheek. "You're not marrying Desborough."

"I don't want to." She released a broken sigh. "Why is this so difficult? I think I hate James."

"No, you don't. He's just trying to protect you."

"But he won't let me marry you. He was scathing about your request to court me."

Harry grimaced. "I'll wager he was more scathing to my face. It was perfectly clear that he'd give you to a rabid dog before he'd give you to Harry Thorne."

She stared at him. "If he knew you as I do, he'd understand."

"Perhaps." Harry was far from sure. "He isn't completely wrong, my darling. I have no fortune and the world considers me a wastrel. Even if we marry, I only have my allowance from Elias and even that's looking devilish shaky right now." His voice descended into glumness. "Perhaps you'd be better off marrying someone else."

She frowned as if he'd offered her an insult. "Do you love me, Harry Thorne?"

"You know I do."

"Then that's the only qualification you need to be my husband." She watched him steadily. "We'll work the rest out."

He smiled. "You'll make a dashed fine wife, Sophie."

She smiled back. "Because I sew a fine seam and I play the piano like an angel?"

"Do you? By Jove, those are useful skills if we're left on our uppers."

"Don't joke, Harry," she said.

His smile broadened, even as his heart ached at their looming separation. He'd had three days of living in gray limbo without her. A month seemed like torture. "And because you're the bravest girl I know."

The teasing light in her eyes dimmed. "I'll have to be brave if I'm in Northumberland."

He couldn't resist kissing her. "Courage, Sophie. If we're true to one another, nobody can part us."

"Do you believe that? It seems too optimistic."

"I'm a man in love. I eat optimism for breakfast."

As he'd hoped, his silly response raised a smile. "You're a fool."

"I'm your fool." With one hand under her chin, he tipped her face until he drowned in her huge blue eyes.

He desperately hoped that he deserved the trust he read there. Nobody had ever relied on him. As the youngest and most charming of the reckless Thornes, he'd never taken responsibility for anything. He swore that lack of practice in responsibility wouldn't scuttle his plans. He intended to become the world's best husband. If he had his way, Sophie would never suffer a moment's unhappiness.

"Now kiss me good-bye." He forced a smile. He wanted her to retain a memory of pleasure amidst all the turmoil. "Make it good. It needs to last me until you return."

She rose on her toes and laced her hands around his neck. "If you put it like that."

His brief humor dissolved to ash under her passionate assault. After a surprised hesitation, his arms lashed around her and he pressed her full-length against him. He wanted to remember her warmth and scent, and the soft sounds of her excitement.

His hands firmed on her hips and he kissed her back, telling her with his lips that he loved her and he'd miss her and the hours without her would feel like eternity. He also silently assured her that in time, they'd be together.

Eventually he raised his head, knowing that if he didn't stop now, he wouldn't stop until he'd lost all pretensions to honor. He pressed her against his heart, resting his chin on her head. Breathing unsteadily, he struggled for calm.

"You must go," she said with audible regret. "If James catches us, he'll send me further than Northumberland."

Harry kissed her briefly. "I'd follow you to the ends of the earth."

Disconsolately she surveyed him. "If James gets his way, you may have to."

Chapter Sixteen

Upper Brook Street, London, late March 1828

Cam bowed as Lady Marianne Seaton entered the sunny morning room of her father's house in Mayfair. He felt damnably awkward. He hadn't seen her since spending Christmas at the Seaton estate in Dorset. An indication of his intentions and her family's acceptance of those intentions, although he was yet to make a formal offer.

As Lady Marianne curtsied with her famous grace, he was startled to notice how lovely she was. God forgive him, he'd forgotten. With her widely spaced blue eyes and full lips, she looked like a Renaissance Madonna.

While he might have only a vague recollection of her appearance, Cam had remembered her air of tranquility. It was among the reasons he'd chosen her. After his chaotic upbringing, the prospect of marriage as a haven of calm was devilish appealing.

Ironic that he ended up with an independent miss who stirred turbulent currents wherever she went.

"Your Grace, what a pleasure." Lady Marianne's voice was low, like a cello. That voice would never challenge him or tease him or warm with wry humor.

Whatever else Pen was, she was entertaining. Five minutes with her and his skin prickled with physical awareness, his brain fired with stimulation, he was laughing.

He couldn't imagine laughing with Lady Marianne. She was too like one of the Meissen figurines that his mother had thrown when no dinner plates or Chinese vases lay to hand. In the Rothermere residences, numerous shepherds lacked their shepherdesses, thanks to the late duchess's tantrums.

"Good morning, Lady Marianne," he said.

Lady Marianne sank onto an azure chaise longue. Her back was ruler straight, her hands laced decorously in her lap. She looked like she sat for a painting. Her pale yellow gown complimented her creamy complexion. Immediately Cam pictured Pen as he'd last seen her, wearing an ill-fitting, borrowed dress. She'd been fighting him. Why was that immeasurably more exciting than Lady Marianne's serenity?

Clearly he was mad.

He'd been set on marrying this lady, to a point where he'd quarreled with his closest friends Jonas Merrick and Richard Harmsworth. Both were converts to the joys of married bliss and they hadn't approved of Cam's coldhearted plans for an alliance with the Seaton family.

Yet now he felt like he faced a stranger.

Lady Marianne gestured toward a chair upholstered in matching blue. "Please sit down. I heard about the shipwreck. I'm sorry about the loss of your yacht. And the brave men who perished with her."

She must have heard about his bride too. He'd expected this, but it was a devil of a way to discover that her suitor jilted her.

Wishing desperately he was somewhere else, he sat. "Thank you. You perhaps also know that I traveled with a lady."

The steady cobalt gaze didn't waver. She was better at concealing her emotions than anyone he knew. Or perhaps she had no feelings to hide. Neither had harbored any illusion that their marriage was more than a dynastic merger. Cam had been grateful for that. A wife who wanted his love—even worse, a wife who would be hurt by his inability to love her—was his definition of hell. His father had loved his mother and unrequited passion had warped into anger and cruelty.

At least Pen knew that love wasn't on the agenda. Lord, she didn't love him. Most of the time, she could barely stand to have him around. He would never experience that glorious closeness with a beloved partner that Jonas had found with Sidonie, and Richard had found with Genevieve. And from the bottom of his frozen heart, he was relieved.

"Yes, the papers reported the story," she said coolly.

"The lady is my wife. I'm sorry I didn't tell you before the rumor mill started. It's been a...hectic few days and I felt I needed to see you in person."

"I see." She paused with a delicacy so finely tuned, Cam heard a clear ping in the air. "My congratulations, Your Grace. I hope you and the duchess will be very happy."

She was a stylish creature, he thought with sudden admiration. And brave. She deserved better than a cold, decorous marriage with a man who didn't love her. He'd offered her a shabby bargain, however shabbily he now broke it. She was better off without him.

"Thank you. You have every right to be furious, and—"

She raised one hand to silence him. "I've enjoyed your company, but there were no expectations on either side."

A face-saving lie. Guilt and regret flooded him, but her

subtly brittle air hinted that his apology was the last thing she wanted. He'd come to know her better than he'd realized during their circumspect courtship.

He felt like the lowest worm in creation. Because now that he looked closely, a tightness at the corner of her lips and a wariness in her eyes revealed that she was no happier hearing that he'd married another woman than he was telling her. And the hellish reality was that her jilting was no secret. The gossips wouldn't be kind to the woman Camden Rothermere had passed over.

Her slender throat moved as she swallowed, but her voice emerged with commendable evenness. "There has been no mention of the lady's name. Is she perhaps Italian?"

"No."

"An English lady, then."

The habit of protecting Pen's identity was so ingrained, he had to remind himself that everything would become public in a few days. "My wife is Penelope Thorne, Lord Wilmott's sister."

Shock turned Lady Marianne's expression blank. "I only know Miss Thorne by reputation."

Cam could imagine. "We grew up together. I went to Italy to tell her about her brother's death."

Lady Marianne studied him before comprehension lit her features. Cam had a nasty suspicion that she put two and two together and got thirteen. "A long-standing attachment, then."

"Yes," he said, meaning friendship and knowing that Lady Marianne pictured childhood sweethearts renewing their passion.

Why in Hades was the world obsessed with love? Surely there were more important things to worry about.

"The lady has been away from England for many years. Perhaps she'll appreciate a friend to help her navigate

London society. I hope Her Grace will call when she's in Town."

Good God, Marianne Seaton was tip-top quality from her smooth mink-brown hair to the soles of her yellow satin slippers. Cam was seriously impressed. He wondered why he wasn't also eaten with regret that instead of claiming this magnificent creature, he married willful Penelope Thorne with her blemished reputation.

"You're very kind." He meant more than the social platitude. Again he tried to express how sorry he was. "You and I—"

Again she waved one graceful hand. "Nothing further need be said."

Lady Marianne's generosity left him very much on the wrong foot. He'd behaved badly toward this woman, but now he was committed to Pen. He'd been committed to Pen since he'd saved her from the bandits. He'd been a fool to imagine anything else.

He stood. Lady Marianne wouldn't wish to extend this meeting.

"Is your father in London?" Cam doubted that the old man would take the news as well as his daughter had.

"No, he's at the family seat. I came up to do some shopping and attend a former governess's wedding. I'll return to Dorset next week."

"I wish you a pleasant stay, then," he said calmly.

As he left the Seatons' tall white town house, he exhaled with unworthy relief. Today proved that Lady Marianne was too perfect for him. Pen was woefully far from perfect, but she made his blood sing. That recommended her as a wife, if not a duchess. The promise of finally possessing her set an unaccustomed spring to his step on his stroll back to Rothermere House.

Chapter Seventeen

Fentonwyck, Derbyshire, late March 1828

The baroque glories of the Rothermere family chapel overwhelmed the small wedding party. On this rainy morning, the gilt and marble interior was icy and full of eerie reverberation. The housekeeper had done her best, lighting candles and arranging what flowers she could find. But even the famous Fentonwyck greenhouses had only produced a few straggly dahlias and half a dozen pots of hyacinths.

Before the altar, Pen shivered in the most suitable dress she'd discovered among the late duchess's effects. The high-waisted style left her bosom looking as flat as Lincolnshire; the silk was too light for the nasty weather; the pink that had flattered the duchess's Nordic fairness made Pen look pasty. Although perhaps she should blame her poor complexion on a run of sleepless nights and the elephants waltzing in her belly. The only good thing Pen could say about her dress was that it covered the bruises from drifting around the seabed.

The sound of Cam's voice speaking a steady "I will" wrenched her back to the moment. She braced to make the vows that condemned her to a lifetime with a man who would never love her. Her gloved hand closed hard around the snowdrops she held, releasing a burst of sickly scent.

Her churning stomach revolted as the vicar addressed her. She swallowed, praying she wouldn't be sick. Vomiting over one's bridegroom wasn't done, especially if one wished to avoid gossip. Losing the cup of tea which was all she'd managed to choke down this morning would stir speculation that the bride increased disgracefully early.

A charged silence extended and the elderly vicar regarded her with concern. She swallowed again. She could do this. She'd made the decision three days ago. The decision that had been inevitable from the moment Cam found her in Italy. She was as trapped now as she'd have been if she'd married him nine years ago.

The vicar coughed. Bile jammed Pen's throat. She glanced wildly at Cam, who had barely looked her way since she'd walked up the aisle. Beside her, her brother Elias jabbed her with his elbow. With Peter so recently gone, it was difficult to think of him as Lord Wilmott.

"Pen," he prompted.

Behind her, the sparse congregation of a few senior household staff and county gentry shuffled in their seats. The wind rattled the stained glass windows, demanding her response.

She clenched her bouquet so hard that she broke the stems. Then Cam's hand bridged the small distance between them. His fingers curled around hers, grounding her.

She inhaled and realized that she hadn't taken a breath in far too long. Cam's grip firmed in silent encouragement.

As if fearing that the new duchess was slow of understanding, the vicar repeated his questions, his reedy tenor resounding around the stone chapel. "Wilt thou have this man to thy wedded husband, to live together after God's ordinance in the holy estate of matrimony? Wilt thou obey him and serve him, love, honor, and keep him, in sickness and in health? And forsaking all others, keep thee only to him, so long as you both shall live?"

At last she found her voice. She was grimly aware that what she promised would drain her soul before she was done.

"I will."

"Congratulations, sis." Harry hugged Pen hard. "Although you could have chosen a more flattering gown."

They were in the drawing room before sitting down for the wedding breakfast. After the meal, the staff would spend the rest of the day celebrating the duke's nuptials. Pen was sure that the servants' party would prove more festive than this subdued gathering.

"It's lovely to see you too," she said drily, hugging him back. "I wouldn't have recognized you."

Last time she'd seen Harry, he'd been a gangly adolescent inclined to communicate in grunts. He'd shown little sign of growing into this handsome giant. Of her three brothers, he was the one who looked most like her, with his black hair and eyes, and tall, lean build.

"Best wishes, Pen." Elias turned from his conversation with Cam. "May I kiss the bride?"

"Of course." She presented her cheek. Elias felt like a stranger. She'd always been closer to Peter and Harry.

Vulnerable and unhappy as she was, she welcomed her family's presence. But she wasn't a fool and she could count. For Elias to reach Derbyshire for the ceremony, Cam must have sent the invitation before she'd accepted his proposal. How galling that His Grace, the Duke of Sedgemoor, had been so remarkably sure of himself.

She pasted a smile onto her face for the sake of her brothers and the local landowners. Pen wished desperately that Cam's sister was here. A sympathetic woman would dilute this overbearing masculinity. But Lydia lived far south in Devon with her husband Simon. Not even Cam's powers could waft her to Fentonwyck in time for the service.

"This scapegrace showed up at Houghton Park the day before yesterday, claiming he tired of London," Elias said. "When he discovered I was bound for your wedding, he wouldn't stay behind."

"Wouldn't miss it for the world," Harry said with the wicked smile that she didn't remember in his younger self.

She'd heard that he cut a swathe through society's ladies. Right now she believed it. "I'll need time to get used to seeing my unpromising lout of a brother with so much town bronze. You're almost presentable these days, Harry."

"Too kind. If you ask nicely, I'll take you round the modistes and show you the latest rigs."

She cast him an annoyed glance. "I'm sure you heard about the shipwreck. I only reached Fentonwyck yesterday. There wasn't time to have a gown made."

"I'd take her in her petticoat." Cam's smile looked almost natural. She was impressed. Nobody seeing this superb man in his elegant clothing and with his easy manner would guess that this marriage wasn't his choice.

"You almost did," she said.

"It might be an improvement," Harry remarked.

She scowled at him. "Now I'm a duchess, I'll thank you to show some respect. There's a dungeon at Fentonwyck, young man."

Cam snagged two glasses of champagne from a footman and passed her one. As she accepted, she summoned another smile. Her brothers needed to believe that she was happy. She was bleakly aware that a lifetime of pretense awaited.

"The dungeons are now wine cellars, Pen. Tomorrow I'll take you on a tour of your new home."

"I'd readily commit the occasional *faux pas*, if it means you'll lock me away with your claret, Cam," Harry said.

Cam's arm slipped around her waist. Shock made her stiffen and withdraw before she recalled that they were in public. He caught her hand and gently rubbed his thumb over her wedding ring. The new ring felt alien, almost oppressive. She'd become accustomed to the weight of his signet, now on his hand where it belonged.

"Pen," he warned under his breath, releasing her.

She blushed at the reprimand, however deserved. And at the touch of his hand. She'd spent the last days bracing herself to share Cam's bed when he'd do much more than put his arm around her. How could she pretend that she didn't love him when he took her body? If he discovered she loved him, this current awkwardness would fade to nothing in comparison.

"Are you and Elias staying?" she asked Harry.

"No, we leave after the breakfast," Harry said.

"It's a long way to come just for the ceremony."

How cowardly she was, but her brothers offered refuge against Cam and what would happen in his bed tonight. Except that nothing would stop him possessing her. She'd spent her life trying to strangle her painful, unwelcome love. If he took her, that dependence would worsen. And now she couldn't run away to the Continent to avoid the constant reminder that he'd never love her.

She gulped a mouthful of champagne to dislodge the familiar lump in her throat.

"Steady on, old girl. You don't want to be tipsy on your wedding day. Cam doesn't need to know all the family foibles at once."

"Ha ha," she said sarcastically, although Harry's teasing stemmed rising panic. She'd hoped she'd accepted her lot. Apparently she hadn't.

"One of the nice things about marrying someone you met in their cradle is that there are few surprises," Cam said drily, sliding his hand around her waist once more. This time she made herself stand rigidly still.

"Elias doesn't wish to intrude on your honeymoon," Harry said.

They'd told her brothers the lie about the European ceremony. "We're an old married couple now."

Cam sent her a sardonic glance. "Hardly, my love."

The world stuttered to a stop. She only just saved herself from wrenching free. Those two words—"my love"—threatened to drag the whole façade around their ears. Those two words hurt. Dear God, they hurt. And she'd just signed up for fifty years or so of more hurt. Someone should shoot her now.

"Credit us with some tact, Pen," Elias said.

"I haven't seen you in so long," she said with a trace of desperation.

"Come and stay at Houghton Park once you've settled." Sadness shadowed Elias's expression. "It's shabbier than you remember. Old Peter wasn't much of a manager."

"He had a big heart and a generous spirit," Pen said quietly. "I'll miss him."

"I'll miss him too," Cam said softly, a reminder of the bonds linking her to this man. "There was nobody like Peter."

A somber silence extended as a benevolent ghost briefly hovered. A man who had been careless with money but never with people's feelings.

"He'd be happy today," Elias eventually said, smiling his approval at Pen and Cam. "He always considered you a brother, Cam."

"Thank you." When the butler appeared at the dining room door, Cam's grip on Pen firmed. "Breakfast is served."

With such a small and almost exclusively male gathering, social rules hardly counted. Still, Cam clearly meant to escort Pen. Through his glove and her dress, she felt the burning possession in his touch. The heat seared her, made her tremble with nerves. How on earth could she become his lover without revealing her feelings? The night loomed like a monster.

Harry touched her arm. "Pen, can I have a word?"

"Of course." She turned to Cam. "I won't be long."

She hung back while Cam ushered the guests away. Once they were alone, she faced Harry. However different he looked, something in her soul insisted that he was the same: impulsive, generous, sweet-tempered, surprisingly steady in his loyalties.

He fixed his black eyes upon her. "I need your help."

Oh, no. This didn't sound good. She could barely hold herself together, let alone take on Harry's problems. "Are you in trouble?"

"Not exactly." His tone didn't convince.

"Well, what, exactly?" She glanced behind to see if Cam returned for her.

"There's this girl—"

A grim premonition settled in Pen's stomach, souring the champagne. "You haven't done something dishonorable, have you?"

Harry drew himself to his full height and surveyed her down his straight Thorne nose. "Not yet."

Hardly reassuring. "Who is she?"

"Lady Sophie Fairbrother."

He paused as if Pen should immediately understand, but she'd been out of England too long. "I don't know her. Is she related to Lord Leath?"

"She's his sister," Harry said glumly.

"Harry, you can't make a marquess's sister your mistress."

Anger flashed in his face and she realized with a sinking heart that this situation was much more serious. If she recognized the signs—and how could she not?—Harry was in love.

"I don't want to make her my mistress. I want to make her my wife."

"That's aiming high for a third son with no prospects, Harry."

"I love her and she loves me."

Pen saw it was pointless saying that a young girl's fancy changed with the wind. There was even less point in saying that a young man's fancy was just as fickle. When Harry fell in love, he'd love forever. Just like she loved Cam. "If that's true, let's hope that Leath wants his sister's happiness. You'll have to offer for her."

Harry's mouth turned down. "I did. He showed me the door. Damned rudely."

"He must think you're a fortune hunter." A reasonable assumption. Leath's sister would be an heiress and Harry had little to recommend him, apart from his steadfast heart.

"He's picked a husband for her. A dry old stick with political connections called Lord Desborough."

"Do you want Cam to speak to Leath?"

Harry's laugh held no amusement. "No, that would completely scupper my hopes. You're out of touch with the tattle. Sedgemoor and Leath are at daggers drawn. Cam exposed Leath's uncle as an out and out villain. Leath's doing his best to stymie Cam's business ventures. Surprised nobody wrote and told you. The scandal has put paid to Leath's political ambitions. At least for the moment."

"Oh dear." She'd been right to worry. Harry was in a mess. "I do remember the news about Leath's uncle, now you mention it. In Italy, it hardly seemed important."

"Well, it's important now. At least to me."

"With your sister married to Cam, Leath will place you in the enemy camp."

Harry nodded gloomily. "And I was less welcome than a flea at a feast anyway."

"What can I do?" Today she'd signed up to a lifetime without love. How could she bear to condemn her brother to a similar fate? And perhaps her involvement might temper Harry's recklessness.

Harry smiled with a relief she couldn't feel she deserved. "You always were a great sport."

She had an ominous feeling that being a great sport in this instance was likely to incur her husband's wrath. "All I can advise is wait. It's not the Middle Ages. Leath can't haul his sister kicking and screaming to the altar. Once he understands that her feelings are real, he may relent."

"But he won't let me see her," Harry said on a despairing outburst. "He's sent her to Northumberland. Even when she comes back, he'll keep us apart."

"You want my help arranging a rendezvous?" Pen asked without enthusiasm.

Harry looked brighter. "Would you?"

She stared at him in frustration. "I'm in Derbyshire. What do you think?"

"I think you won't be in Derbyshire for long. Cam will go down for parliament and to introduce you to society."

She didn't hide her displeasure with her brother. "And you want me to act as your go-between?"

Harry displayed not one whit of compunction. "Yes."

"I... see."

Her reluctance surprised him. "Pen, you were always up for a lark."

"This is hardly a lark," she said sharply. She suddenly felt the gulf of five years in their ages. "Cam won't want a scandal."

Harry's black brows drew together. "Do you mean to dwindle into a mere wife after all your adventuring? I never thought to see it."

She glowered at her younger brother, wishing for the days when she could give him a good clip around the ear. "You know Cam's concerns for the Rothermere name. I don't want him to regret marrying me."

Harry regarded her strangely. "You speak as though he's taken you on approval."

Hell's bells. She needed to be careful, even with her family. Nobody could know about the cold center of her marriage. Nobody except the two parties most intimately involved.

"Don't be silly." She struggled to sound like the suggestion was absurd.

"Pen, don't let me down. You're my only hope." Harry's sulkiness reminded her poignantly of his younger self. "We'd be discreet."

"That's what people always say." This time when she checked behind her, Cam stood in the doorway. She couldn't blame him for his impatience.

"I must go, Harry." The affectionate irritation she felt was familiar from childhood. "It's the outside of enough to spring this on me today."

He had the grace to look abashed. "I know. But with Elias so determined to travel this afternoon, it was my only chance to ask."

"And you couldn't have waited?" She lowered her voice so the words wouldn't carry to Cam. An hour married and already she deceived her husband. What was to become of her? "How long is Lady Sophie in Northumberland?"

Woe descended upon Harry like a cloud upon a mountain. "At least a month."

For a young man of Harry's passionate temperament, a month must feel like eternity. "Let me think about it."

"Thank you, Pen." Harry beamed. "I knew you'd come up trumps."

She frowned. "I'm not promising anything. I can see this turning into a disaster for everyone involved, including Cam."

"Pen, our guests await," Cam said.

"I'm coming." She narrowed her eyes at Harry. "Don't do anything rash until I'm back in Town."

And not then either, she prayed. The last thing Cam needed was his ramshackle Thorne connections kicking up trouble.

She hadn't had long to come to terms with the truth that despite years of running like a scared rabbit, she was Cam's duchess. But one thing she swore was that she'd do her best to make him proud. Now before the ink on her marriage lines had dried, Harry's chaotic affairs threatened scandal. But if Harry genuinely loved Sophie and she genuinely loved him, could Pen deny them a happiness that she'd never find?

"Pen?" Cam's tone would have set the servants scurrying.

"I'll see, Harry. That's the best I can do," she whispered. Feeling beleaguered and inadequate, and not remotely bridal, she turned. With heavy steps, she walked in her unbecoming borrowed clothes toward her husband.

Chapter Eighteen

Carrying two brandies, Cam entered the duchess's apartments. Candlelight flickered over the birds and pagodas on the unfashionable silk wallpaper. The last woman to sleep in these luxurious rooms had been his tempestuous, troublesome mother, who had died when he was seventeen.

The cavernous space could house an army. A crackling fire in the hearth warmed the air. The four-poster bed on its platform looked as wide as a parade ground. By contrast, the woman propped against the piled pillows appeared small and fragile.

Warily Pen watched him cross the acres of floor between door and bed. Nor could he miss how her long, slender fingers curled like talons in the brocade counterpane covering her to the waist.

She'd been as brittle as a dry twig all day. He could kick himself for making his bride so nervous. His clumsiness on the *Windhover* had much to answer for. He wasn't unhappy about this marriage, but he was damned unhappy that Pen was. He prayed that he could awaken her passion and make her forget everything except the desire that had raged unsatisfied between them for weeks.

Her glorious night-dark hair cascaded over her slender shoulders. Her white batiste nightgown was sheer as mist. While it tied decorously where her pulse fluttered in her neck, that was the limit of its modesty. Her high, firm breasts pressed against the transparent material.

His hands twitched as if he already touched her luscious flesh. Beneath the crimson velvet robe embroidered with gold dragons, he was naked. And ready.

He felt more uncertain than usual with a paramour. But Pen wasn't just a paramour. She was his wife. His duchess.

Tonight he meant to convince her that she wanted no lover but him. Any niggle that he didn't bed a virgin faded as her black gaze burned a line down his body. Her lingering survey might convey caution rather than desire, but his body surged. If her eyes had such power, God help him when she laid those pale hands upon his skin.

"Is that brandy for me?" Nerves added seductive huskiness to her voice.

"Yes." With a pang, Cam noticed how unsteady her hand was as she accepted the glass. Another reminder to take this gradually. He mustered a reassuring smile and gestured to the edge of the bed. "May I?"

Her lips twisted, not in a smile. "It's your bed."

"*Our* bed. I endowed thee with all my worldly goods today." His gaze unwavering, he sat. He should have expected this ambivalence. She wanted him, but she was far from reconciled to a lifetime with him.

"Thank you," she said dully.

"You're welcome." Hell, he needed to lighten this oppressive atmosphere.

Her lush mouth glistened with brandy. He burned to lick

away the liquor, then drink the headier wine of her kiss. But instinct urged him to go carefully. "Pen, please smile. You're terrifying me."

To his relief, her lips curved with faint amusement. "The great Duke of Sedgemoor, afraid?"

"I want to do this right."

"You'll manage perfectly well. You always do."

He didn't understand the bitterness edging her response, although at least she looked less frozen. "I'll request a report."

Trying to read her mind, he stared into her eyes. He'd hoped to find desire. Instead he was shocked to see secrets.

What were they? Would she ever trust him enough to share them?

"Do that," she said faintly. She lifted her glass and drained her brandy.

"You're treating me like a dangerous stranger when you've known me all your life." It was the tone he'd use to soothe a half-broken horse.

Her expression didn't ease. "Somehow that makes it worse."

He'd expected Pen to take this wedding night in her stride, the way she'd taken bandits and arrogant dukes and hurricanes in her stride. Her fear was disconcerting, troubling. He'd hoped that mutual hunger would carry them through any initial awkwardness. "Pen, we needn't do this tonight."

Her skittishness didn't abate and her fingers tightened on her glass. "That's astonishingly generous."

She made it sound like generosity wasn't in character. His lips flattened with displeasure. "Not really. You look ready to shriek if I touch you."

She blushed. It always surprised him when this worldly woman went as pink as a peony. "You want an heir."

"Yes, I do." His laugh was sour. "But I can wait a day or two for that happy eventuality."

Her gaze dropped with a shyness that surprised him. "I have a horrible feeling that putting off the evil moment will make things worse."

For a blank moment, he stared at her, torn between unwilling amusement and outrage. Amusement won. He burst out laughing and reached for the glass twirling so furiously between her long fingers. "You're a tonic for my vanity."

She looked tense enough to snap. "I wasn't trying to be humorous."

He rose to carry the glasses to the dressing table in the alcove. "That's what makes it amusing."

His room was stocked with wine and brandy. Pen had a vase of stringy dahlias like the ones from the church and a brush set that had belonged to his mother. A reminder that his joke about marrying Pen in her petticoat wasn't that funny. She'd lost everything with the *Windhover*.

Behind his back, he heard her sigh. She sounded like she carried the weight of the world. Despite his efforts at patience, temper stirred. Blast her, she was a bride. She was supposed to be cheerful. He wasn't sure what Pen was feeling, but cheerful definitely didn't describe it.

With a sigh to equal hers, he acknowledged defeat. Tonight at least. He was unreasonable to expect eagerness. His wife had had mere days to recuperate from the wreck and accept a radically different future from the one she'd planned. He wasn't a barbarian, despite the throbbing weight in his loins. He could give her time to view that future with a tad more optimism.

"You're tired, Pen. No need to stir early tomorrow. When you're up, I'll show you around the house."

She regarded him with palpable disbelief. "That's it?"

He straightened his shoulders from their discouraged slump and struggled to smile. Frustration stung like acid in his veins. "I know you won't believe it, but I'm very happy that you married me."

To his surprise, the black eyes sparked for the first time today. He had a nasty feeling that this reprieve had lifted her spirits. Just as he had a nasty feeling that he'd spend his wedding night alone with an improving book and a bottle of brandy.

"You're right, I don't believe it, but I appreciate your gallantry." Her jaw no longer looked likely to shatter if she spoke one untoward word.

"In time, you will. It's been a devil of a ride since we met. We're both at sixes and sevens." He spoke what he prayed was the truth. "We'll get there. Goodwill and kindness will take us a long way."

Her expression changed, although he was too far away to read her fathomless eyes. Damn it, he didn't want to skulk back to the ducal chambers. He particularly didn't want to lie in the big, cold bed alone.

No, he wanted Pen in his arms. He wanted to scale the ladder to heaven that had beckoned since he'd found her again. He wanted to kiss her and touch her and ignite her passions. More than that, he wanted to slide inside her long, glorious body and forget everything except pleasure.

Tonight, want took him nowhere.

He turned toward the door.

"Cam?"

He didn't turn, partly because he didn't trust himself not to leap on her, whether she wanted him or not. "Sleep well, Pen."

"Cam," she said more urgently. "Wait."

He frowned at the polished mahogany door before him. Did she know how near he was to breaking point? She played a dangerous game.

He heard a rustle behind him. The thick carpet in a pattern matching the delicate chinoiserie wallpaper muffled the soft pad of her feet.

Every hair on his skin rose at her approach. He deliberately hadn't touched her since coming in, afraid that if he did, restraint would vanish. Also something about her watchfulness warned him that if he pushed too far too fast, he'd destroy all trust between them.

He'd cajoled her into marriage. For her sake. And for his. He couldn't claim unselfishness. Now Pen, or malign fate, or demons from hell paid him out for his self-interest.

He clenched his fists at his sides and faced her. She stood a foot away. Every sense was alert to her. Her violet scent drifted toward him. "Do you need anything?"

As she inhaled, her breasts shifted against her transparent nightdress. Dear God, she tortured him.

"I think…" Another excruciating pause before her words tumbled out in a heated rush. "I think I need to sleep with my husband."

Pen watched blazing excitement replace Cam's resigned grimness. Despite her invitation, she was still nervous, but her heart gave a great swoop of anticipation as he swept her up against him. He swung her high and strode toward the bed.

"Are you sure?" She'd never heard that raw tone before, even in those fraught, incandescent moments on the *Windhover*.

Before she could answer, he bent his glossy dark head and kissed her hard and hungry, as if he starved. She kissed him back with despairing abandon. The rich flavor of brandy mixed with the even richer flavor of his mouth.

Cam had wanted her as a mistress, not as a wife. Cam desired her. Cam would never love her.

With his lips plundering hers and his arms lashing her close, she hardly remembered why any of that mattered. What mattered was that he touched her with mad desperation and he held her as if she was the only woman in creation.

She was doomed. But this was a doom of heated caresses and fevered moans and kisses that made her head swim with pleasure.

He'd kissed her like this on the *Windhover* before he'd broken her heart—yet again—with his insulting proposition. After those heady moments, the wild rush should feel familiar. It didn't. She felt as if she'd never been kissed before.

The world dipped as he set her on the bed and lowered over her, shrugging off the crimson robe. She had a far too fleeting glimpse of his long, lean body before he caged her between his arms, his bare chest filling her view.

Dizzy with unprecedented, overwhelming excitement, she gasped as his weight descended. Automatically her legs parted to cradle his hips. She started up against him when she felt the insistent pressure against her belly. Huge. Demanding. Inescapable.

His mouth devoured hers, then nipped and licked her neck and shoulders. Roughly he shoved the frail batiste aside until he could kiss the ball of her shoulder and the line of her collarbone. He rushed her into a turbulent current of passion that permitted no pause. She flowed into his demands. She didn't want to think. She just wanted to feel.

Her heart thundered so loudly that she hardly heard the sharp rip as he tore the nightdress away.

"Cam!" With her last modesty, she tried to cover her sex

and her breasts. Everything happened so quickly. She hadn't come to terms with one sensation before another crowded to replace it.

"Let me see you," he groaned, staring down with glittering green eyes. "I've dreamed of seeing you."

She knew his dreams had involved passionate possession and nothing more. But she had no defenses against his pleading. Shaking with nerves, she lifted her hands away and buried them in the rumpled sheets.

"You're so beautiful," he said, bending his head to her breasts.

When he suckled, she cried out at the heat rocketing through her. Arousal tightened and coiled, making her writhe. With unsteady hands, she grabbed his forearms, fingers digging into the taut muscles. Once before, he'd pushed her to the edge, but this time, her responses were stronger, deeper. She could hardly think. This was like living inside a furnace. He'd burn her to ashes. All the time he muttered words that she'd heard so often in her fantasies.

You're so beautiful.

You're like fire in my arms.

I've wanted you so long.

I want you. I want you. I want you.

He rocked against her stomach, setting her blood shifting like the tides. She edged closer to an exquisite pinnacle. The musky smell of aroused male overwhelmed her. The torrid intimacy astonished her, even if in her imagination, her body had thrilled to his hands and lips and voice ten thousand times.

Oh, what wicked things he did to her. Arching, she bit him on the shoulder, wanting him to know a fraction of this painful joy. He jolted under the rough caress and bit her nipple hard enough to make her shake like the dice in a gambler's cup.

Like his kisses on the *Windhover*, this mating held little tenderness. She didn't want tenderness. Tenderness would cut too close to her lonely soul.

He raised his head and gazed at her blindly. His pupils were so enlarged, his eyes were as black as her own. The skin across his face looked too tight to contain the hard, exquisite bones: so male, so strong, so noble.

Fleetingly her aroused trance receded and she stared lost into his face, knowing she'd remember this moment as long as she lived. The burning gaze. The powerful arms straining beneath her clutching hands. The weight against her belly. The vulnerability betrayed in the line of his mouth. A vulnerability that she knew he'd deny.

She saw something else too. Something that pierced her like a sword. For all Cam's excitement, there was a distance behind those brilliant eyes. He might want her to yield unconditionally, but if he felt anything beyond physical urgency, it remained forever locked inside him.

As he tightened his hips and plunged into her, she released a broken sob of anguish.

Pen's harsh cry pierced the air, but it was too late. As he seated himself full length, Cam felt the delicate membrane tear.

Appalled realization crashed down and he went utterly still. Beneath him, Pen lay stiff as a board. All the lithe looseness had vanished the moment he took her.

Incredulity and shame battled inside him.

Incredulity. Shame. And unforgivable pleasure.

Because lying here, the strongest sensation was pleasure.

"Pen?" he asked shakily. He loathed that he loved being inside her. He loathed that his deepest physical nature wanted him to stay. With clumsy tenderness, he brushed back the hair clinging to her damp face.

"Pen, I'm sorry." His apology was thick with regret and raging arousal.

"Finish," she forced out in a guttural voice that he didn't recognize. "For God's sake, finish."

Every muscle in her body hardened against him as if her very skin rejected him. The hands that circled his arms were tight as manacles. She breathed in broken little gasps.

Damn, damn, damn.

"I'll hurt you," he said, frantic with remorse.

"You're hurting me now," she snarled, nails digging deep enough to draw blood. The sting was the least he deserved.

He'd been so tragically, fatally, criminally wrong. Why the devil had he listened to the vicious lies? Hell, if anyone knew not to credit spiteful tattle, he should.

Like a coward, he buried his head in the warm nook between her neck and shoulder. What he'd done was reprehensible. The result of arrogance, prejudice, stupidity, and selfish lust. Not to mention lacerating jealousy of her imaginary lovers.

But he'd wanted her so badly that he'd been blind to the signs of inexperience. Her skittishness on the journey. Her volatile reaction when he'd suggested an affair. Most of all, tonight's crippling nervousness.

All this knowledge came too late, too late.

He'd been so convinced about the string of lovers. Whereas everything he knew of Pen declared her fastidiousness. Sod it all, at nineteen, she'd been too fastidious to marry him.

The compulsion to finish beat in his blood. His heart crashed against his ribs. Every hot clench of her body awakened shudders of delight.

His mind insisted that her body tightened to expel the invader. His mind insisted that he must withdraw, beg forgiveness, leave her alone. His mind insisted that he'd never make recompense for his actions tonight.

Even so, he lingered. Drew the scent of hot, aroused Pen into his lungs like incense. She smelled like the woman he'd kissed, but different. As though lilies suddenly blossomed on a favorite rosebush. As though he'd worked some deep change in her, beyond the mere matter of two bodies colliding in pain and pleasure.

The crackle of the fire played soft counterpoint to her panting distress. Somewhere outside a night bird called, a high, melancholy sound that echoed her cry as he'd entered her.

Gradually she gave him what he waited for. Her shocked rigidity softened. So infinitesimally that unless he'd tuned his attention to her so closely, he'd miss it.

She was woefully removed from squirming urgency. But she was no longer so tense that she'd likely break if he made the slightest twitch.

Every muscle howling for release, he rose on his arms. He opened his eyes and saw her bite her lip to stifle a protest at his movement. Hell, he knew he hurt her. Guilt sliced at him like razors.

She stared up at the tester, embroidered with gilt Rothermere unicorns. Tears trickled from the corners of her eyes to soak the black hair spread around her like tangled silk. Compared to her ashen cheeks, her lips seemed startlingly red, bruised with his kisses.

"For pity's sake, end this." Her demand rasped across his nerves. "I want this over."

"My dear—"

He faltered into silence. After his ruthlessness, he had no right to speak endearments. His lips brushed hers in a kiss meant to comfort, but her nearness defeated him and he deepened the contact. He tasted tears.

Dear God, he was a swine. Self-disgust struggled to rise above his craving to complete the act.

Gingerly, he retreated. Her breathtaking tightness made every inch excruciating and rapturous. Then very carefully, he eased inside, hearing her muffled grunt of surprise at the unexpected smoothness. She didn't stiffen against his invasion, although he caught the flinch she tried to hide.

Brave Penelope.

He moved again, gently, although the need to lose himself shook good intentions. He hooked a hand beneath her knee, bending it to aid his entry.

Another withdrawal. Another careful thrust. Rewarded with a sigh, this time conveying something other than discomfort.

He shifted again and again, desperate to grant her some scrap of pleasure to make up for his sins. But with every moment, control frayed.

On a long groan, his hips surged forward and his seed flooded his wife's virgin womb.

Chapter Nineteen

Cam's body crushed Pen into the mattress. Shock receded, but every breath reminded her that he hadn't been gentle. She still couldn't believe that the wild crescendo ended in such awkward intimacy.

Astonishment kept all other emotions at bay. Although resentment, regret, frustration, wretchedness, confusion all hovered.

She tried to make sense of what had happened. She'd always imagined that Cam would please her as a lover. She'd feared that he'd please her too much. His hold over her was already terrifyingly powerful.

The overture to Cam's horrible invasion had been extraordinary. Better than being in his arms on the yacht. Better than anything in her life.

If the prelude was so breathtaking, surely the act itself must be even better. Then he'd thrust inside her. The union had given her no joy. Which seemed so unfair when she'd edged beyond discomfort and toward satisfaction before he brought everything to an abrupt end.

She made herself look at Cam, then wished to heaven that she hadn't. Now the worst ache resided in her soul. He looked completely devastated and self-loathing clouded his green eyes.

"Pen, I'm so sorry," he whispered brokenly, and kissed her forehead with a grieving tenderness that slashed her heart into tattered shreds. His tenderness was much more painful than his possession. She had no defenses against it.

He eased out, setting off twinges through her body. Stupidly she missed him the moment he withdrew to collapse beside her with an unhappy grunt.

"It was my duty," she said dully. Now that the pain faded, she was aware of a heavy restlessness, like Cam had held her high in the air and couldn't decide whether to drag her to safety or drop her to destruction.

"It should have been more." Regret deepened his voice. "I was a clumsy oaf."

"I'll live." With every minute, her aches subsided. The physical ones at least.

"Pen, don't be gallant. I can't bear it." Then in a shaking voice, he asked, "Why the hell didn't you tell me you were a virgin?"

She started. "Why would you think I wasn't?" Then shame filled her. "It's because I let you touch me on the yacht, isn't it?"

Shocked denial made him grimace. "No!"

She stared into Cam's face and wondered just what he'd imagined she'd been up to. The possibilities made her sick. She looked away and mumbled, "I don't want to talk about this now."

"We'll have to talk about it sometime," he said implacably.

"Just…not now." Through her misery and exhaustion, anger stirred as she recalled him asking her to be his mistress.

He'd obviously spent the last weeks convinced that he traveled with a woman who rivaled Jezebel for wickedness.

While nothing had matched the pleasure she'd found in his kisses and caresses, she hadn't absolutely hated the act. She wished desperately she knew more about what men and women did together. After all those racy conversations in Continental salons, she'd considered herself worldly. None of those sly, witty exchanges had hinted at the raw, earthy reality of a man's body pushing into a tight female passage.

She stared up at the tester. She'd never see the Rothermere unicorns without remembering how Cam had thundered into her. Given she'd just signed up to a lifetime as the Duchess of Sedgemoor, those unicorns would remind her over and over.

"You should go back to your room." She rose against the pillows and dragged the sheet up. Lying naked beside him, she felt too much like a ritual sacrifice. She winced. Changing her position launched a barrage of new twinges. Between her legs, she felt sore and sticky.

He'd flung one arm over his eyes, so she had no idea whether he'd drifted off or whether he merely avoided his dissatisfied bride. Except the dissatisfied bride couldn't help stealing this opportunity to study the superb masculine form beside her. Long, lean, powerful. Intriguingly hairy on his chest and . . . down there.

Surreptitious interest stirred in places that she thought could never react again. The heaviness between her legs turned hot and insistent, instead of purely uncomfortable.

One question beat at her over and over. *Was the act always like that?*

"Do you really want to be alone?" Cam sounded weary and reasonable, a different man from the passionate seducer. "I'll go if you like, but I need to make amends and I can't manage that from behind a closed door."

"As long as we don't have to do it again," she said stiffly, sidling toward the edge of the bed.

"You're safe," he said grimly. Without taking his arm from his eyes, he caught her wrist with his other hand.

She tensed, but as his hold was loose enough to break, she didn't shake him off. "I don't feel safe."

His expressive mouth, visible beneath his forearm, thinned. "You used to."

"That was . . . before."

Sighing, he lowered his arm and released her. She'd seen his expression after he'd taken her. He'd looked ready to slit his throat to save the world the trouble of shooting him. He still looked like he'd forsaken his last hope for happiness. Her heart twisted with a stupid female need to assuage his cares.

She battered down the impulse to take him in her arms. What comfort had he offered when he'd so ruthlessly used her? Then left her incomplete at the end.

"I can apologize again, Pen," he said bleakly.

She avoided his desolate jade gaze and stared down to where her fingers folded and unfolded the sheet with idiot compulsion. "Don't."

A silence fell, then she felt the mattress move as he rolled away. She should be glad he went, but something in her was disappointed that he didn't stay to persuade her. Not into doing . . . that. But she'd appreciate him making an effort.

Oh, devil take her, she was a complete mess. She wanted this. She wanted that. None of it made any sense. After what Cam had done, she shouldn't want to see him again. However impractical that might be, given today's marriage ceremony.

She was almost as annoyed with herself as she was with Cam.

Which didn't prevent her watching as he walked away. The back view was just as spectacular as the front. The proud set of the head, even now when his pride smarted because he'd failed to satisfy his bride. The wide powerful shoulders. The straight, well-muscled back. The firm globes of his buttocks.

Like her, he still bore the shipwreck's marks. Healing bruises and abrasions, including a slash of dark purple across his ribs. Anger ebbed out of reach, although disappointment remained. Whatever tonight's disaster, he'd nearly died saving her.

She waited for him to enter the duke's apartments, but instead he veered off into the luxurious bathing room. Disgruntled, Pen straightened against the pillows. If he wanted to wash, couldn't he do it in his own rooms?

He emerged carrying a bowl and towel, and with another towel slung low around his narrow hips. He set a small mahogany table beside the bed and placed the bowl upon it. He turned and with one hand, hooked up the heavy red robe, covering himself.

"Lie down," he said softly.

"Why?" she asked suspiciously.

"I'm going to make you feel better."

She bit back a sniping response that his absence would achieve that most effectively. Anyway, it wasn't true. As her discomfort faded, she felt lonely and teary and desperately in need of kindness. Even if the kindness came from the man who had hurt her.

Very gently he pried the covers from her clinging hands and drew them down, revealing her nakedness. Tonight she'd cursed her stupidity more than once. She cursed it again when she realized that she should have gone in search of a fresh nightdress while he was in the other room.

She acted a complete ninny. A brazen ninny at that.

"Leave me alone," she said, grabbing uselessly after the covers.

"Pen, a wash will help." He paused, and she knew he hated having to reiterate his good intentions. "I promise, only a wash."

The urge to curl into herself and hide from those probing eyes was strong, but something in his face told her that if she did, she'd hurt him, as she'd hurt him when she'd claimed that she no longer felt safe. Yet again she derided her soft heart.

"Very well," she said reluctantly, stretching out.

She watched him wring out the cloth and lift it over her stomach. Before he touched her, she grabbed his hand. "This doesn't mean I've forgiven you."

His gaze darted up to meet hers and she read his profound remorse. Unfortunately, remorse didn't strike her as a particularly strong foundation for marriage.

"Pen, let me do this." He made no attempt to break away. "Please."

Pen wasn't proof against Cam's uncharacteristic humility. Reluctantly she released him. He took the gesture as permission to continue. Very carefully, he began to wash her. Starting with what should have been unexceptional places like arms and neck. He winced every time he touched one of the yellowing bruises from her ordeal after the *Windhover* went down.

She should be immune to Cam's touch, but her skin tingled as the warm, damp flannel wiped away the night's sweat and, she had to confess, much of the bitterness.

When he trailed the cloth over her midriff, every muscle clenched. By the time he reached her breasts, she breathed unsteadily. He didn't linger, but the soft friction had her nipples hardening as if he kissed them. She mistrusted the wayward responses that left her lightheaded as though she'd had too much claret.

Methodically, he moved to her legs, washing thighs and knees and shins and feet. This felt like slow seduction, although she caught his flinch when he saw the blood on her thighs.

He dipped the cloth in the water and gently parted her legs. She made a soft sound of distress.

Slowly he raised his head as if emerging from a daze. He'd concentrated so hard on what he did, he'd barely looked beyond the area of skin he washed. His eyes were as lifeless as malachite in his dark, intense face. "Trust me, Pen."

She bit her lip. She'd trusted him earlier and had come to grief. But she couldn't deny a lifetime of love. She let her legs fall open, although no man had seen the private hollows of her body. He thoroughly washed each fold and valley, soothing every sting. His gentleness squeezed her heart into a tiny ball.

She bit back another whimper, not this time of discomfort. Although this intimacy made her more embarrassed than she'd ever been in her life. How could her body respond like this? After years of imagining a man in her bed, of imagining *this* man in her bed, she knew now what happened. Pain. Shame. Regret. Powerlessness.

Yet with every stroke, he smoothed the disagreeable memories and replaced "never again" with "perhaps."

With trepidation, she watched him wring the cloth. She'd been afraid that his passion might have left her a bloody mess. She was reassured to see only a trace of pink in the water.

Finally the torture that had transformed into dangerous allure ended. He dropped the cloth into the now cool water, dried her one last time, and lifted his hands away.

The silence preyed on her nerves, but she couldn't force words through a throat jammed with tears. Not from pain this time, but because whatever pain he caused her, she loved him. She'd always love him. His care only proved that never having him love her in return would eat at her until her dying day.

The slow washing, like a ritual, had calmed him. Just as it had calmed her. His jaw no longer looked chiseled from stone and the lines around his mouth and eyes had relaxed.

He bent toward her. She thought he bowed to say good night. The atmosphere between them had become strangely courtly.

But his head lowered and lowered.

Before she could think to move, he placed his lips on her pale stomach, just above the navel. She felt the warm, damp brush of his kiss. Her skin tightened, although the kiss felt more an act of homage than a sensual invitation.

Questions flooded to her lips but died unspoken when he lifted the bowl and turned toward the door. Pride and confusion kept her from asking him to stay. She felt piercingly alone watching Cam walk away. But not so alone that she was ready to endure his use of her body.

Cam went through the door, leaving it ajar. A gesture of reassurance, the way one left a candle burning for a child in the dark. He must guess that she found this cathedral of a bedroom intimidating.

Awkwardly, still sore despite Cam's ministrations, she struggled to stand. She needed a nightdress.

When she emerged from the dressing room wearing another of the late duchess's seductive peignoirs, Cam leaned against one of the carved oak posts at the base of the bed. He still wore his robe and his expression was calm.

Perhaps he came to say good night. Then she noticed the

decanter of red wine on the dressing table near the empty glasses. Given how he'd arrived with brandy, the wine struck an ominous note.

She stopped so abruptly that the blue silk nightdress slipped from one shoulder. "What do you want, Cam?"

He prowled across to pour the wine. He passed her a glass. "I think we've done things completely the wrong way around."

She frowned in confusion. "You mean you should have got me intoxicated before you joined me in that bed rather than after?"

Despite the tense atmosphere, his lips twitched. "No."

Warily she studied him. "Then what do you mean?"

He gestured toward two chairs beside the hearth. "I mean, my wife, that we need to talk."

Chapter Twenty

Cam watched Pen's wariness deepen, but at least she appeared willing to listen. As she sank into the chair, she looked fierce and sensual, like a ravished goddess. Her black hair flowed around her. The blue nightdress was cut like a Greek tunic and emphasized the otherworldly quality of his wife's beauty.

In the firelight, he noticed a red mark on her collarbone, just below where her pulse pounded like a trip-hammer. He'd branded her as his. Desire rippled through him, but he stifled any impulse to push his luck. He'd done that earlier and catastrophe had resulted. Guiltily he remembered the blood marking her thighs. Her cry as he'd pushed inside her still rang in his ears.

She watched him as if expecting him to pounce. "I told you I don't want to talk about your...assumptions." She gave the last word a bite that made him flinch.

"I'm sorry, Pen. But we must."

She raised her chin and glared at him. "I suppose you mean to apologize again."

He slid a chair from the other side of the hearth closer, but not close enough to crowd her. After he sat, he tasted his wine. The claret filled his mouth, rich and heady and complex. Nothing to compare to Pen's kisses.

Beneath his composure swirled a turbulent stew of emotions. Anger at himself. Compunction at his clumsiness. Uncertainty that he could make up for what he'd done. Surprise—how had this sensual, beautiful woman remained untouched? "Would it do any good?"

"Probably not."

Inwardly he winced. "You've been away from England a long time."

"What's that got to do with it?" Her temper lifted his spirits. He never again wanted to see her hurt and crying. Especially over something he'd done to her.

"You must know there's been gossip."

She looked unconcerned. Dear God, he wished he could be as nonchalant about spiteful talk as the Thornes. "Occasionally someone would write and say that they'd heard about something I'd done. But why should the ton care about me? I never had a season."

"That's part of the appeal. You're a mystery. A well-bred girl who chooses to scandalize the Continent rather than make her debut and find a husband. Peter's profligacy and Harry's tomcatting kept the Thorne name on everyone's lips. Your antics added spice to the mixture."

She sipped her wine. "There were no antics."

His eyes sharpened on her. "What about the Grand Turk's harem?"

She looked startled. "What about it?"

For years, outlandish tales of Pen's adventures had piqued both his chagrin and curiosity. The rumors had become pure torture once he'd met her again. "Don't try to be funny."

Her lips firmed with impatience. "I'm not being funny. A woman is safer in a harem than she is in a nunnery. Apart from the eunuchs and the Sultan, the harem is a female preserve."

"What about your affair with Count Rosario?" An affair which had never taken place, Cam realized.

Hostility sparked her gaze. "The Count is seventy if he's a day."

"You and he traveled together for weeks."

"I joined a party of scholars to see the excavations on Rosario's estate outside Palermo. The weather was bad and the count was kind enough to take me into his carriage. His arthritis has stopped him riding."

How thoughts of the count had tormented Cam. Now Rosario loomed in his imagination as a geriatric bookworm. "What of the Prince of Castrodolfo? He's a young man. And you two spent a night alone in the Apennines."

Amusement lit Pen's annoyance. "At thirteen, the prince is certainly young. Most people consider him hopelessly bookish. His mother fears difficulties in securing an heir, unless she can awaken his interest in the fair sex."

"What about Goya? Word is that he painted you wearing what only the most intimate associate would wear." Which meant wearing nothing at all. The idea of another man feasting his eyes—and other things—on Pen's glorious nakedness made him livid. He knew he was a primitive, but despite everything, he looked at this woman and his heart beat *mine, mine, mine*.

Her cheeks went pink. "He's a great artist."

Cam started to feel like a schoolmaster quizzing a troublesome pupil. "So that rumor is true?"

"He swore that he'll never show the painting to another living soul. I believe him."

"And Sir Andrew Melton?"

Pen laughed dismissively. "Now there's a fellow whose mother has definitely given up hopes of awakening his interest in the fair sex." Umbrage sharpened her voice. "My refusal on the yacht must have stung, given you believed that every man in Europe has shared my bed. And a few in Asia too."

He struggled not to squirm under her taunts. "Not so many. Definitely one or two."

"You kept careful note of my supposed paramours."

Another jibe that hit home. "Our childhood connection spurred my interest."

He was mortified to admit how agonizingly jealous he'd been of Pen's lovers. Especially when she showed no interest in Camden Rothermere.

Her lips tightened. "If I'm so notorious, nobody would think you a cad if you didn't marry me. I only gave you what I'd given a hundred men."

"There have been plenty of wanton duchesses."

When she caught the bitterness in his voice, her expression softened. "Cam, not every woman is like your mother."

"You're not."

The thaw ended abruptly. "You thought I was."

"No, never," he said emphatically. "My mother's every act was a betrayal. Of her husband. Of her rank. Of her family."

"I had no idea that people thought me such a trollop. You sacrificed yourself to this marriage to save my good name. Now I discover that I have no good name to save."

As her indignation faded, Pen looked tired and wretched. He should let her go back to bed—without him—but he knew how quickly she'd rebuild her defenses. He needed to get to the truth now.

"Don't forget that I was preserving my good name too.

A man who seduces a girl he's known from childhood then abandons her to insult is beyond the pale."

Her smile held no amusement. "Even if the childhood friend goes to the dogs?"

"You're still a Thorne."

"And now I'm a Rothermere." Clearly a fact that gave her no pleasure.

Why should it? She'd exchanged independence for life with a man who had treated her like a doxy. Remorse twisted his guts anew. He sighed and ran his hand through his hair. "Hell, Pen, you're twenty-eight years old. For nine years, you've run wild with a louche crowd under your aunt's inadequate supervision. Not to mention that any man would want you. What in Hades was I meant to think?"

Bleak humor flickered in her black eyes. "Don't sound so peevish, Cam. Most men would be delighted to discover that their bride was a virgin."

Was he blushing? "Perhaps so, but not in the circumstances that I did."

"Poor boy," she said sarcastically.

"You have every right to anger. There's no excuse for my behavior. I should crawl on my knees to you and beg forgiveness." Cam gestured with his free hand. "But we're together for life and we need to reach some understanding."

Her expression was cynical. "So you can touch me again."

Devil take his blundering, she spoke of his possession like dire punishment. "Do you mean to bar me from your bed?"

"I made promises to you." She twirled the glass in her hand until the wine flared ruby.

It was the same dead tone she'd used when she said that she'd done her duty. Disappointment pierced him. But what could he expect after his rough wooing? "If duty alone compels you, our marriage bed will be a cold place. I think we can do better than that."

"You're an optimist." She sighed and the resistance seeped from her body. "Cam, can you give me some time? Surely we don't have to decide everything tonight. It's been a long and difficult day."

Guilt, his constant companion, stabbed deep. It had been a long and difficult few months. She'd lost both aunt and brother, and faced death several times. He'd risen to take her in his arms before he remembered that his embrace was the last thing she wanted. He subsided into his chair and surveyed her discontentedly.

A bride proved more bewildering than any mistress. His sympathy went out to the Grand Turk with his hundreds of wives. Then all impulse to amusement fled when he saw his wife's closed expression. "Pen—"

She raised her hand. "Not...yet."

With that he must be content. It had been a devil of a wedding night.

Chapter Twenty-One

After dinner, Cam accompanied his wife upstairs. For a day and a half, he'd been a married man. The experience bore no resemblance to his expectations. For a start, he'd kept his hands to himself. Being with Pen without touching her—when he had every legal and moral right to roger her from here to China—was a torture he wouldn't inflict on his worst enemy.

He'd woken with the dawn in his own bed, rigid with longing, miserable, lonely, feeling like a dog someone had kicked into the gutter. And sick with guilt over hurting Pen. At breakfast, to his bewilderment he'd encountered a stranger. This tranquil, restrained woman wasn't Pen. Pen was impulsive and opinionated and ready to shoot a man if he wronged her. Yet this morning she'd played the perfect duchess. It could have been Lady Marianne facing him over the marmalade.

And Cam had loathed it.

He'd burned to wrench his wife from her chair and muss her neat perfection. Then fling her across the polished table and do things likely to make the butler resign.

But he'd behaved himself, although just being in the same room was torment.

The only logical choice, given his bride's reluctance for his company, was to devote the day to business that had accumulated during his absence. So why then had he found himself showing Pen every nook and cranny of the vast house? And in return, all she'd expressed was polite interest. Not once had she called him a blockhead or objected to an arrogant remark. He worried if perhaps last night he'd done her brain some injury.

Now, confused, unhappy, and shamingly randy, he trailed after her into the duchess's cave of a bedroom.

Pen turned with an expression of well-bred surprise that he'd never seen before. "Your Grace, what are you doing?"

Cam glared at her. "Why the hell are you 'your grace'-ing me? You've called me Cam since you were toddling."

She flushed. "As you wish. But I'd still like to know what you're doing."

He shut the door with a sharp click. "I'm coming to bed with my wife."

Her eyes widened with alarm. "Now?"

He stalked toward her, tugging off his neckcloth and tossing it to the ground. "Now."

"You said you'd let me think about it."

Clearly a welcome was too much to expect. He shrugged off his coat and flung it across the room. "Have you?"

She retreated again. "Have I what?"

Impatiently he flicked open the silver buttons on his silk waistcoat. "Have you thought about it?"

She frowned as if questioning his sanity. "Of course I have."

He let the waistcoat fall where he stood. "Good. No need to call your maid. I'll undress you."

At last Pen stood her ground. "Why are you doing this?"

His smile was mocking. "My dear, you might be innocent, but you're not *that* innocent."

She raised her chin and regarded him like he'd crawled out from under a rock. In a sewer. "I'm not ready."

"It's like falling off a horse. You need to get straight back on." He was deliberately crass to provoke a reaction. She'd been a blank slate all day.

"I'm not your horse," she said cuttingly.

Briefly she disappeared from view as he tugged his shirt over his head and tossed it near the crumpled blue waistcoat. "If we wait too long, you'll convince yourself that the experience was so awful that you never want to repeat it."

She arched an eyebrow, although he didn't miss how her eyes focused on his bare chest. Last night he'd found grounds for hope in the way she'd looked at him. His nakedness had intrigued rather than disgusted her.

"Too long is more than a day?"

"Yes."

She backed until she bumped into the high bed. "I don't think so."

Briefly he considered undoing his trousers, but a glance at her outraged expression told him that might be a step too far. "I do."

"Hurrah for you," she said sourly, clasping her hands before her. She breathed unevenly.

Cam suspected that despite her nervousness, she was interested, however reluctantly. But he'd learned to be careful with assumptions about Penelope. "Yesterday you promised to obey me."

Rebellion darkened her eyes. "Yesterday you said you wanted more than mere duty."

He was grateful to see a spark of spirit. "I've changed my mind. If mere duty is all you're offering, I'll take it."

"You'll regret this." She sidled along the bed.

He stepped closer, deliberately crowding her without touching her. "I doubt it."

If Lady Marianne had given him mere duty, he'd have accepted it. From Pen? Never. Before he'd blasted everything to hell, he'd tasted her passion. He meant to do more than taste her tonight.

"Cam, I don't want to do this," she said shakily, still twisting her hands together.

He cupped her jaw. Self-disgust flooded him when she jumped. She'd enjoyed his touch on the yacht. Until he'd been an idiot. She'd enjoyed his touch last night. Until he'd been an idiot.

The lesson for tonight was not to be an idiot.

Cam sucked in a breath, striving to calm his racing heart. He had time. He had patience. He had the skills. And tonight she wouldn't take him by surprise. The new Duchess of Sedgemoor didn't know it, but her world was about to change. Forever.

In a subtle caress, he moved his hand against her face. "Courage, Pen."

She broke the contact. "I'm not feeling brave."

He reminded himself that coaxing his wife to pleasure wouldn't be quick or easy. But the reward was worth it. He didn't do this only for himself. He did it for Pen. Such a sensual woman shouldn't fear a man's touch. She should revel in it. He'd make her forget that he'd ever hurt her. "Tonight I'm going to show you paradise."

That remark elicited a derisive snort, but at least she stopped edging away. He was close enough to see her trembling. "I wasn't anywhere near paradise last time."

He raised his eyebrows. "Really? Even before I spoiled everything?"

He was gratified to see her color rise. She avoided his searching regard. Damn it, why hadn't he had the brains to understand that her shyness signified more than coyness?

"Pen?"

With a flash of temper that pleased him even more than her blush, she jerked her head up. "I've forgotten."

He laughed appreciatively. "Little liar."

"Stop trying to inveigle your way into my bed."

"Everyone deserves a second chance."

She folded her arms and surveyed him without favor. A night of self-castigation and a day of struggling to keep his distance lent him the wisdom to remain silent.

"If I say no?"

He sighed, defeat beating around him like a hundred angry ravens. "I'll leave you alone."

"How reassuring," she said sarcastically. Her arms fell in surrender to her sides. "I'm at your service, Your Grace."

If anyone but Pen's husband had asked her to revisit yesterday's disaster, she'd threaten him with the nearest fire iron.

But she owed Cam more than she'd ever realized. She'd always known that for her sake, he'd relinquished the perfect bride, a big society wedding, a connection with an influential family. She'd had no idea that he had wed a woman whose name was synonymous with sin, however ill-deserved her reputation. This marriage had done Cam a greater wrong than she'd imagined.

She swallowed to moisten a mouth dry with nerves, and told herself she could endure his possession. But dread hollowed her stomach. Along with a roiling soup of other emotions that included unwilling attraction, contrition, resentment—and ineradicable love. When during her sleepless night, she'd resolved to become a proper duchess even if it killed her, she'd known that her proud spirit wouldn't bow easily. But imagining oneself a conformable wife and playing the part proved very different.

His green eyes were grave. "Trust me."

"I'll have to, won't I?" she said grumpily, before recalling that a conformable wife wouldn't snipe.

He caught one of her clenched fists. "We'll go slowly."

She shivered. Not entirely with fear. "I'd rather get it over with."

He kissed her knuckles until her fingers relaxed. "You'll change your mind."

She didn't believe him. Her belly lurched as she recalled the dizzying drop from the heights of excitement to the act itself.

He released her. "Turn around."

"Why?"

His lips twitched. "I'll help you undress."

"Is it necessary?" All the same, she turned. It was a relief to escape his glittering gaze. He looked smug, like he knew a great secret. He also looked like he wanted to make a meal of her. Neither quieted her jangling agitation.

He untied the wide olive satin ribbon that cinched the gown so unnaturally high. "Absolutely."

She caught the gown as it sagged over her bosom. "We need to do something about my clothes."

Skillfully he unlaced the back. "I am doing something about your clothes."

She felt no desire to laugh. Her knees trembled as she stepped from the crumpled gown. "You know what I mean."

"Yes, I do." Deft fingers released her corset. "And, yes, I will. But not tonight."

Her stomach quaked as his hands brushed her bare shoulders. Then quaked again at the salute of his lips on one shoulder blade, then the other.

"No, not tonight." Her voice was thready. "Shall I . . . shall I take off my shift?"

"Not yet."

She couldn't help noticing how his voice deepened on "yet."

His fingers slowly sketched a cobweb of heat over her skin. She'd never counted her back or shoulders as erotic zones, but he set her tingling. Under her upswept hair, he massaged her nape. Warmth flooded her right to her toes. Goose bumps broke out and her nipples tightened into aching points.

Surprise held her motionless under his touch. After last night, she'd thought arousal impossible.

Tonight he treated her like the virgin she was no longer. As he stroked her body, pleasure flowed through her like warm honey. She knew this tremulous anticipation led to humiliation, but something stupid and stubborn inside her refused to believe that.

At her sides, her hands closed and released. Her toes curled in his mother's satin slippers. Her breasts swelled. She'd been jumpy when he'd followed her upstairs, but as he touched her softly and asked no more, she drifted into a glorious dream. On a sigh, she shut her eyes and leaned back against him.

"Ouch!"

Cam's bite on her shoulder zapped through her like lightning across a summer sky. She stumbled upright.

"Don't go to sleep." He nipped at her earlobe. This time when she swayed, he pressed against her back. She stiffened and a whimper escaped. His insistent weight reminded her where this delight headed.

"Shh, Pen," he whispered.

He treated her like a restive horse. But rebellion sank

under a wave of response as he caressed her breasts. His hands abraded her nipples through her shift until she squirmed.

"I love your breasts," he murmured, rolling the peaks between his fingers. "I love how your nipples harden with desire. I love their taste. I love how you shake when I touch them."

"Cam—" she choked, not sure whether it was a plea or a protest.

A whisper of fabric as he slipped her shift off. His exhalation expressed delighted surprise. "You're not wearing drawers."

Standing half-naked in a man's arms and squeezing one's buttocks against his rod should extinguish blushes, but still her face went bright red. "Your mother didn't own any."

His laugh cracked, proof of burgeoning hunger. "I wish I'd known at dinner."

"I'm not trying to titillate you," she choked out.

"Nevertheless, I'm titillated." His hips bumped her.

She gasped. She should run shrieking, but pleasure had vanquished fear. His hands traced her sinfully bare stomach and thighs. Her fingers dug into his thighs, crushing his trousers. She thought she'd understood the imperatives of attraction. Tonight's siege demonstrated that she was a mere novice.

"I won't stop you now," she confessed huskily. She waited in suspense for him to push her down onto the bed and thrust inside her.

"There's no hurry." He scraped his teeth across a nerve on her neck until she saw stars instead of the duchess's old-fashioned apartments.

"What do you want?" she asked, bewildered. Holding a conversation while he set fire to her senses tested her.

"You have to desire me."

"I desire you." After last night, she'd never thought she'd say that.

"Not enough."

"Any more and I'll explode."

"If you explode, I'll put you together and begin again."

"You make me suffer."

"I'm not taking chances," he said with a hint of grimness.

With sudden ruthlessness, he cupped her mound. He made a deep sound of masculine gratification and lashed an arm across her middle, holding her hard. His fingers slid between her legs and he brushed a sensitive spot. She shuddered under a flood of reaction.

For what felt like hours, arousal had tangled inside her. Now her response focused. Moaning, she quivered, wanting more delicious pressure.

To her frustration, he withdrew. Behind her, his chest heaved.

"Cam!" she protested. She was slick and ready.

For a breathless moment, he pressed her to him. His breath gusted harsh against her ear.

Then roughly he whirled her around and slammed his mouth into hers.

Chapter Twenty-Two

As Pen's mouth opened beneath Cam's, he tasted blind hunger. She was like living flame, clinging so close it was as though she tried to join her body to his where they stood. Her generous response made his heart leap. A powerful wave of thankfulness swept him.

He nudged her until she toppled onto the mattress. He longed to feast his senses, etch her into his memory. But instinct insisted that if he hesitated, she might recall the last time they'd shared this bed.

Pen stared at him, eyes languorous. Her full lips parted, awaiting more kisses. Her arms spread across the sheets. Her shining hair fanned around her.

Whatever the risks, Cam paused to capture this moment for when he was old. She was beautiful. More beautiful, even, than he'd thought. Perhaps the most beautiful woman he'd ever seen.

"Move over, Pen," he said softly, lifting one foot to tug off his shoe. She obeyed instantly, with a wriggle of long, elegant legs and pale skin.

He removed his second shoe and kicked it away. His hands hovered over the buttons fastening his trousers before he decided that for now, he was better keeping them on. Reining himself in nearly killed him. Lying beside her naked would push him over the edge.

He slid onto the bed. When he'd kissed her, his blood had thundered with urgency. Somewhere since, he found that, however he burned, he wanted to cherish her. Sweetness flooded him as he lay on his side, head supported on one bent arm. He stroked tendrils of hair back from her brow.

Avidly she examined his features. He didn't know what she sought. He hoped whatever it was, she found it. Standing by the bed, he'd read her desire. Now only inches away, he read vulnerability. His kiss conveyed admiration and gratitude and a silent promise to make her happy. "Pen—"

"Don't talk."

Once before he'd ignored that command and he'd paid for it ever since.

She took her time exploring his mouth. And he, transfixed, let her. He collapsed onto the pillows and she rolled over him, kissing him with leisurely enjoyment. He buried his hand in the tumble of black hair. Without breaking the kiss, he turned to lean above her. She gasped as he voluptuously rubbed his hips across hers.

Fear or pleasure?

Last night he'd mistaken enthusiasm for readiness. He'd rather smash onto Goodwin Sands again than repeat that mistake.

Carefully he parted her thighs and stroked her. Dear Lord, she was wet. When he found the center of her pleasure, she jerked against his hand.

Again he touched her and her eyes opened wide with surprise. "That's ... wicked."

He smiled, deepening the pressure until she squirmed. "It is indeed."

Gently, fighting his blood's pounding command to take her, take her, take her, he slid his middle finger inside her. As carefully as a jeweler setting a diamond, he inched forward. He studied her face, alert for discomfort.

She looked strained and intense. When she tightened against his incursion, he struggled to contain the urge to push her further, faster. He curled his finger, rubbing the sleek passage with his knuckle. On a choked sound, she lifted her hips. When he kissed her, her ardent response demanded more.

With a slow, suggestive slide, he withdrew. This time, he tested her with two fingers, subtly stretching her. She bit her lip, eyes flaring at his intimate caresses. The craving to taste her sex made his mouth water, but he restrained himself. He bore down with the heel of his hand, making her buck against the mattress. She grabbed his arms with frantic hands. When he pulled free, she released a disappointed whimper.

Her hands fluttered across his chest, setting off blasts of heat wherever they landed. He kissed her again, plunging his tongue into her mouth. As she yielded, the seemingly random brush of her hands became more purposeful. When she flattened her palms against his nipples, he started.

"Do you like that?" She trailed her lips up his cheekbone.

"Yes," he said, not sure if he did. Her slightest caress threatened incineration.

He gritted his teeth as she circled her palms. Those fiendish hands drifted lower. One curved over his right buttock. The other covered his cock. He groaned with a painful mix of elation and frustration.

Her fingers tightened until he saw stars. "Take off your trousers."

He reared up on one arm. "You need to be ready."

To his surprise, she laughed. "Any more ready and I'll be flying."

When she pressed the underside, white heat blinded him. "Pen—"

"Do you need help undressing?"

Before Cam could respond to her impudence, she tugged at his trousers. In her haste and inexperience, she was breathtakingly clumsy. Finally his throbbing cock bobbed free.

"Good heavens..." Pen breathed, looking down.

"You saw me last night."

"You look bigger." She licked her lips, ratcheting up his arousal. "I think I'm nervous."

He wrenched her up and kissed her, holding her with one arm while his other hand shucked his trousers. Her mouth was hot and wet and desperate. As he followed her down onto the bed, he slid between her legs and nudged her humid heat. She sighed against his lips and shifted on him. A tilt of his hips and he edged inside.

She caught her breath and stiffened.

In an agony of need, he stopped. He couldn't bear to hurt her again.

She lay unmoving beneath him.

No, he wouldn't accept this. Penelope was created for pleasure. And he intended her to achieve it. Or die trying.

With a shaking hand, he touched her sex. Every nerve close to snapping, he caressed her into trembling urgency. She arched and drew him into her. The sudden acceptance had him thrusting before he recalled the devastating price of impatience.

On a sigh like the sweetest music, she twined her arms around him. Her body flowered into glorious welcome.

* * *

Pen braced for pain, but between last night and now, her body had adjusted to Cam. This sensation was closer to completion than invasion. After all her running and dodging, she was in Cam's arms and she'd stay here.

His head dropped to the curve of her shoulder. His soft hair tickled her cheek. His skin was damp and hot.

The long muscles in his back tautened and released under her hands as he moved. To her surprise, the glide of his body set off a faint quake. A quake that intensified when he kissed her neck.

She inhaled sharply as he withdrew to plunge again. Immediately that sweet fullness returned. His spicy scent was the air that she breathed.

Another glorious stasis before he moved once more. This time, he changed the angle. A spiral of tension stirred inside her. Half pleasure, half torment.

He established a powerful rhythm. She clung as the spiral twisted tighter. Instinct made Pen raise her hips. This time, impossibly, he went so deep, he must touch her heart. He groaned encouragement into her shoulder.

Roughly, he raised her knees, changing the angle again. She was shaking and sweating and clawing at him. The tension in her belly coiled and uncoiled. She reached for something she'd never experienced before, some relief from this agonized striving.

Moving faster, Cam's thrusts became choppy, urgent. His body hardened. She tilted her hips, begging with incoherent sighs for him to fill her.

She was so close. So close.

He bit down hard on her shoulder and flung her over the shining horizon into the melting heat of the sun. Crying out, she shuddered under the onslaught of astonishing, overwhelming, inescapable pleasure.

Brilliant light blinded her and she closed her eyes to retain the rocketing colors. Fire ricocheted through her, searing every corner, making her anew. Through the wild clamor, she felt Cam jerk against her. His groan filled her ears.

She opened hazy eyes to see him rise on his arms. As he spent himself inside her, the strain leached from his face and his eyelids drooped with sensual satisfaction.

Briefly he looked happy, younger, less burdened. As if Camden Rothermere during these seconds became just a man, not the embodiment of centuries of duty and tradition.

Sensual reaction still pounded through Pen. If he'd done this to her on the yacht, she'd have drowned for sure. Right now she didn't have strength to roll over, let alone swim for her life.

I love you, Cam. I've always loved you.

The words welled up. She knew he didn't love her, but after the shattering honesty of what they'd just shared, she couldn't keep such a vital secret.

Cam's kiss was tender. She tasted satiation.

"Thank you," he said softly. "Thank you for trusting me."

She stroked the side of his face. "Of course I trusted you, Cam."

Tears loomed close, making her voice sound rusty. But she didn't feel like crying. She felt like wrapping this precious, magnificent man in her arms and holding him safe.

He shook his head to deny what she said and she watched his joy retreat. So quickly the familiar self-possession returned. Although physically they were as close as two people could be, she sensed that somewhere in his mind, he established a distance.

That breathtaking consummation had convinced her that they were bonded forever. For him, it threatened defenses that he'd spent a lifetime building.

Her impulsive declaration of love died unspoken and her happiness seeped away even as she still quivered with reaction.

Cam had sealed eternal dominion over her soul. In return, she'd fed his physical hunger.

Dear God, she needed to keep her wits about her. All her life, she'd known that confessing her love would at best create restraint, at worst send Cam fleeing what he viewed as impossible demands.

To be fair, he wouldn't want to hurt her. Although the sad truth was that because he didn't love her, he hurt her again and again.

The true hell of her marriage struck like a blow. Disgrace and scandal could never match the damage that awaited now that she'd irrevocably tied her life to Cam's.

She was a damned fool.

And the largest part of her damned foolishness was that despite all she knew, all she'd seen, in some corner of her mind she'd hoped that over time, he might find it in himself to love her.

She stared into his eyes and recognized that the barriers against her, against anyone threatening his self-containment, would always be there. Although she felt like crying, she summoned a smile. "Cam, I promise to be the wife you want. You'll never regret marrying me."

He grimaced as if her words held a sting. "I don't deserve you."

Even harder than that smile was dredging up the kind of remark he'd expect of sharp-tongued, independent Penelope Thorne. She'd enlisted for a lifetime of lying when she married Camden Rothermere. She refused to stumble at the first fence. "I intend to be the world's greatest duchess."

He regarded her searchingly. She saw the moment he

decided to accept her humor at face value. "High hopes indeed."

"Why aim for the ordinary?"

His soft laugh vibrated through her. Despairingly she wondered how he could lie inside her, yet feel a million miles away.

"My dear Penelope, you couldn't be ordinary if you tried."

The passion in his kiss made her blood pump. The world's greatest duchess would never deny the duke his pleasure, even if her heart cracked into a thousand pieces.

Chapter Twenty-Three

Whence Cam passed the blue salon on his way inside from checking his new colt, he heard gusts of feminine laughter. Since his sister's marriage two years ago, Fentonwyck had been a bachelor establishment, so the sound struck him as unexpected. Pen, to his bitter regret, hadn't laughed much lately.

Curiosity made him pause. Curiosity and a determination to rescue his wife. If county society descended, having decided that a week was sufficient privacy for the newlyweds, this would be Pen's first solo encounter with the English upper classes since her return. His wife would be a lamb in a den of wolves.

Cam had spent a lifetime countering spite, starting with savage bullying at Eton over his mother's adultery. He'd learned the hard way how to handle trouble. His gut knotting with worry, he stepped into the room's azure and gold splendor. And stopped dead.

The neighbors ranged around the tea table. The Countess of Marley. Lady Greene and her two daughters. The three

Misses Moulton-Brent. Lady Gregory Fulham and her spinster sister. All cats to their last breath. All hanging entranced on whatever Pen described in an uncharacteristically quiet voice.

She'd been uncharacteristically quiet all week. He almost wondered if he'd married two completely separate women. One by day was prudent and obliging and almost demure—a word he'd never thought to associate with Penelope Thorne. By night, the other Pen was endlessly responsive. It was like living with the perfect wife and the perfect mistress, all wrapped up in one spectacular package. Every man's dream.

And Cam could hardly endure it.

This new version of his wife confused him, sparked his impatience, obsessed him—which bolstered his impatience. Both with Pen and himself.

He'd attempted to break through to the vibrant woman he'd known in Italy. But she'd greeted his fumbling efforts to establish some ease between them with cool disinterest. Even when he was so far inside her he felt like their blood flowed through a single heart, Pen held herself tantalizingly separate.

The real Pen, the Pen who infuriated and fascinated and challenged him, remained hidden behind those brilliant black eyes. And every breathtaking climax seemed to edge her more out of reach. It was enough to drive a man to drink. Longingly Cam thought of the brandy in his library, even if it was only early afternoon.

While he'd never wanted an emotional connection in his marriage, he had imagined that sharing a home, however large, would result in friendly intimacy. But he felt further from Pen than he had when he'd saved her from the bandits.

Despite this polite estrangement, their sexual encounters transcended his experience. Every time he spilled into her body, he felt like he surrendered part of his soul. He hated to be in thrall to a woman determined to remain elusive. She turned his nights to flame, and his days to mere intervals of waiting before he joined her on that wide bed upstairs.

He felt like a satyr. He felt out of control. He felt like she hovered just beyond his grasp, even when she stirred to his most daring caresses. Nighttime Pen never denied him, physically at least. Daytime Pen seemed set on establishing a life completely apart from his.

Now daytime Pen coped perfectly well with the intrusive curiosity of Derbyshire's ladies. He prepared to retreat, but Lady Greene saw him. "Your Grace!"

So much silk fluttered as the ladies curtsied that a breeze ruffled Cam's hair. He greeted them, starting with the countess who considered herself local society's leader. The Duchess of Sedgemoor trumped the Countess of Marley. Lady Marley wouldn't like that.

"Her Grace was describing your heroic rescue in the Alps," Lady Marley said. "No wonder you two fell in love on the spot."

As usual when he heard the word "love" in relation to himself, Cam's stomach curdled. How ironic that he'd given his friends romantic advice. Camden Rothermere talking about love was like a blind man describing a rainbow.

"The tale seems to have roused your amusement, my lady."

With a neutral smile, Pen set down the teapot. She presided with a sureness of touch that even his mother would have envied. She wore one of the dresses she'd ordered from Sheffield to carry her through until they left for London next week. It was conservative in style and color. He'd never have imagined Pen could look dull, but in this drab gray gown, she looked...dull.

"How dashing," one of Moulton-Brent girls sighed.

"Just like a novel," Miss Greene added in an equally saccharine tone.

The swooning made Cam bilious, but as he glanced around the group, he commended Pen's cleverness. These ladies had arrived prepared to despise her, until the stories of his courtship presented this marriage not as a woeful mésalliance but a romantic triumph.

Damn it. He'd been a fool to fret over Pen. He forgot how she'd charmed her way through Europe. He forgot that she was a Thorne. While the Thornes might neglect life's prosaic elements, they could always woo an audience.

"I told the ladies how shocked I was when my childhood idol marched in at such an opportune moment, Your Grace."

Daytime Pen always addressed him formally. Each time she said "Your Grace" in that sweet, soft voice, he felt like she struck him with a hammer.

Cam shouldn't be piqued that she'd been perfectly all right without him. He shouldn't be piqued, but he was.

His wife smiled at him over the tea as if meeting a mere acquaintance. London's most perfect gentleman stifled the impulse to fling the priceless china into the fireplace and tell the duchess's new acolytes to sod off.

He'd known Pen all his life, yet every day, she felt more a stranger.

Merrick House, Mayfair, early April 1828

Cam descended from the luxurious Sedgemoor town coach painted with the Rothermere unicorns. He extended his gloved hand to escort Pen up the short flight of marble steps.

"Thank you," she murmured in a very un-Penelope voice to the footman who held the carriage door open.

As she surveyed the magnificent home of Jonas Merrick, Viscount Hillbrook, and his beautiful wife, Sidonie, Pen's grip on Cam's hand tightened. He glimpsed something in her face that looked like genuine emotion. It said something for his state that her trepidation made him feel better. She'd become such a cipher that he frequently wanted to pinch himself to make sure he wasn't dreaming. Or perhaps pinch Pen to check whether she was alive and not just a lovely automaton.

Because she was still officially in mourning, Cam wasn't giving a ball to launch her into society. Instead, the new Duchess of Sedgemoor made a low-key arrival. Tonight, Lord and Lady Hillbrook hosted a dinner before the party attended a musicale at Oldhaven House.

"They'll like you," he murmured, leading her toward the door, which opened at their approach. "Don't worry."

Without hope, he waited for some humorous response. Pen didn't speak. How lowering to remember that he'd wanted a quiet, perfect wife. Now that he had one, he itched to throw tantrums and shake her until she shouted back.

The odious truth was that Pen was everything that Cam had wished in a duchess. Tranquil. Undemanding. Well behaved. Polite. Cooperative. Who knew unusual, dashing Penelope Thorne would prove such a conformable spouse? Damn it, she'd even been a virgin when he'd married her.

If he told anyone about his increasing dissatisfaction, they'd call him a lunatic.

As Cam handed her into the black and white tiled hall, she stepped ahead wrapped in her new velvet cloak. They'd been in London since Easter and rapidly established the kind of marriage that proliferated in society. Cam saw his wife at breakfast and dinner where they swapped inconsequential information. With every hour, she retreated further.

But what could he say to her? *You're too good, You're too obedient. You're like a textbook description of the perfect lady and I loathe it. Do something shocking. At the very least, tell me off when I'm my asinine self.*

This husband business was a conundrum. One that deepened every day.

And not one he'd solve in Jonas's impressive front hall while Pen watched with the faint curiosity that counted as interest these days. The old Pen would have told him in no uncertain terms to hurry up. The new Pen waited patiently.

"Your pardon, my dear." He stepped forward to lift her cape from her shoulders. Briefly he fantasized about Pen in ruby red or deep sapphire. Something to complement the ardent soul that he still, despite all evidence, believed she possessed.

But the dress was gray with long sleeves and a bodice that covered her to the collarbones. Logic insisted that not every gown she'd ordered from the ruinously expensive modiste was gray. It merely felt like it.

He was sure he'd seen some beige.

Pen was still technically in mourning for Peter, although she could wear colors after three months, and her marriage meant that only sticklers would count the days since her brother's death. But damn it, Cam had married a beautiful, sensual woman, and she dressed like a blasted nun.

The irony struck him that he'd asked fate for a wife who was the opposite of his mother. Fate had very generously granted his wish.

He wanted to plant fate a facer, then kick it in the ribs for good measure.

"Your Grace?" Pen asked softly.

He realized he stared blankly at her. "You look lovely," he said with the deathly politeness that had infected his behavior too.

Regally she inclined her head. "Thank you."

Again, Cam questioned his discontent. No woman had ever appeared more the duchess. Yet he wanted to wrench the diamond combs from Pen's black hair and rend the French silk dress and kiss her until her lips were red and swollen and she never called him "Your Grace" again.

He offered his arm. In bed, her exquisite body was his to do with as he willed. During waking hours, she kept physical contact to a minimum. Her hand lay so lightly on his arm that he hardly felt her through his black superfine sleeve.

As if on a royal progress, they ascended the staircase. Cam had no idea what lurked in Pen's mind. Once he thought he knew her as well as he knew the men awaiting them. Now, thanks to the wedding ring on her slender finger, she'd become an enigma.

The butler flung open the drawing room door. "The Duke and Duchess of Sedgemoor."

Cam mustered a smile appropriate to a newly married man, even if it threatened to crack his jaw, and ushered his bride forward to meet his dearest friends.

Chapter Twenty-Four

Every person in that drawing room cared for Cam, more than he deserved.

Jonas, Lord Hillbrook, turned from his dark-haired wife Sidonie and strode forward, hand outstretched. A smile lightened his scarred, saturnine features. "Cam! About time you introduced us to your duchess. Sidonie and I were about to set up camp at the gates of Fentonwyck."

"I suspect your definition of camping would differ from most people's." Cam clasped his friend's hand with a warmth that contained a shaming measure of relief. The last time he and Jonas had met, the encounter had ended in a bitter quarrel over his plans to marry Lady Marianne. "Silk tents, servants, and champagne at the least."

"I was afraid you didn't invite us to your wedding because you thought I'd scare your wife." The humor sparking in his dark eyes softened the remark, although Jonas's face aroused unease, even now.

"I wanted to keep my bride to myself." Cam released Jonas's hand. "Penelope, this is our host, Jonas Merrick, Viscount Hillbrook."

"My lord." Pen dipped into a curtsy so graceful that Cam's heart stopped. The coolness between them didn't lessen her power over him.

Jonas bent over Pen's hand with an aplomb remarkable in such a big, heavily muscled man. "Your Grace, welcome to my home." He straightened and gestured to Sidonie who slid her hand around his waist with a natural affection that pierced Cam's barricaded heart with envy.

When he'd married Pen, he'd hoped that they'd establish such physical closeness. Whereas for all that they stood together, an invisible chasm a hundred yards wide separated them.

"Your Grace, I've been in a fever of curiosity since Cam wrote to tell us of his wedding," Sidonie said. "And in such haste that we couldn't attend the ceremony."

Cam caught Pen's hunted look, although the meaningless smile remained. It was a smile Cam had never seen until Pen became his duchess. Once, she would have responded with a witty remark. The expression in her eyes now hinted that she considered heading for the hills.

Cam saved her from replying. "Our marriage isn't as sudden as it appears. Pen and I have known each other since childhood."

Sir Richard Harmsworth stepped forward to take Pen's hand. "Pen, dashed good to see you. I thought you were lost to us forever. You'll adorn London as you've adorned Paris and Rome."

"Richard." There was no mistaking Pen's pleasure. An unforced pleasure that Cam couldn't remember her targeting toward him since her adolescence. "I doubted you'd remember me."

"Remember you? Why, when you sailed for Calais, you broke my heart." With his famous urbanity, Richard pressed his lips to Pen's cheek, the privilege of long-standing friendship.

For one fraught moment, Cam glared at the golden-haired fellow kissing his wife, and he wanted to thump the man who had been his best friend since their miserable days at Eton. With a shock he recognized two unwelcome facts. The first was that despite his plans for a sensible, calm marriage, his wife aroused a jealousy that wouldn't discredit his father. The second was that the roots of this estrangement with Pen extended to long before his wedding.

"I see you still talk a lot of nonsense." For the first time that night, Pen's smile looked real. Cam's jealousy stirred anew, even though he knew their flirting meant nothing and Richard was devoted to his wife.

"He does indeed," Genevieve Harmsworth said drily. "Welcome to London, Your Grace."

Richard kept Pen's hand, curse him, while he turned to the lovely blond woman he'd married six months ago. "Pen, allow me to introduce my clever wife, Genevieve. The only silly thing she ever did was to marry a dunderhead."

"Good evening, Lady Harmsworth," Pen said.

"Your false modesty convinces nobody, darling," Genevieve told her husband.

"I'm trying to be charming," he retorted. Luckily for his continuing health, he released Pen's hand.

"And succeeding," Pen said quickly. "Lady Harmsworth, I'm a great admirer of your work."

Genevieve smiled. "You know just the right thing to say. I'm still feeling my way in London. Fortunately everybody is so enamored of my husband that my odd ways go unnoticed."

Cam glanced across to Jonas and Sidonie. To his dismay, both looked troubled. Did they disapprove of his wife? He had an unwelcome inkling that they didn't find Pen unsatisfactory, but their old friend Camden Rothermere.

Cam broadened his smile until he grinned like a damn effigy at a fair. Still he knew that his show wouldn't convince Jonas and Sidonie. They knew how to glean emotion from mere pretense.

Richard and Genevieve still glowed with wedded bliss. It must be perfectly obvious that Cam and Pen...didn't. Bugger it, he should have avoided introducing Pen in such intimate surroundings. In a public setting, the cracks in their union might be less apparent.

Thank God for Genevieve, who turned out to be familiar with Pen's writing. She drew his wife toward a chaise longue, asking about some excavations outside Rome.

Cam sucked in his first full breath since arriving. At least Pen wouldn't feel a complete outsider. Genevieve's welcome made Pen less the pallid Duchess of Sedgemoor and more like the vivid woman he'd known in Italy.

"Cam?"

Cam started from studying his wife to see Jonas extending a glass of champagne. He hoped that his expression didn't betray his thoughts, but he had a nasty feeling that it did. He accepted the wine. "Thank you."

Richard and Sidonie chatted beside the fireplace. Jonas showed no concern. But then, Jonas knew that Sidonie adored the ground he walked upon. Sourly Cam wondered what that felt like, before he reminded himself that the absence of love in his marriage was a blessing, not a curse. A wife who adored a man who couldn't love her back would make a damned uncomfortable companion.

After ensuring that his guests had wine, Jonas returned to Cam. Cam braced for an inquisition. Jonas could be ruthless. Otherwise he'd never have survived the horrors of his childhood. But Jonas sipped his wine, then said in a neutral tone, "It's a pity Lydia and Simon couldn't join us."

To save himself from having to discuss his wife, Cam leaped on the subject of his sister and her husband. "Lydia's doctor has advised her to avoid travel until after her confinement in June. I doubt they'll be in London for the season." Not that his sister and Simon gave a fig for society. They were perfectly happy to rusticate on Simon's estate in Devon.

"Do you plan to visit? I assume the duchess knows them both."

"Probably in the summer. As girls, Pen and Lydia were as thick as thieves, although usually Pen was behind any trouble."

Jonas quickly masked his surprise. Tonight's decorous version of Pen seemed an unlikely hellion. "You'll wait so long?"

Cam's lips tightened. "I've got business in Town."

"You're worried about Leath?"

"Shouldn't I be?" Cam sipped his wine and cursed the interfering marquess. "He's working to oppose my canal bill. I can weather the loss, but Elias Thorne has invested in the hope of restoring the family fortunes."

"You made a bad enemy in Leath."

"*We* made a bad enemy." Cam scowled into his champagne. "He's always had a reputation for upholding the law. One would assume he'd want to end his uncle's criminal rampage."

Jonas's expression remained brooding. "I doubt it's sympathy for his uncle that ranges him against you. Neville Fairbrother was a blackguard of the first water."

"Leath should thank us for lancing the infection at the heart of his house."

Jonas's laugh was grim. His humor tended toward the black. "You know as well as I do that Leath wants to rip out your liver because you made everything public. Gentlemen handle scandal between themselves."

"Fairbrother's evil extended beyond the scope of a quiet handshake."

"We didn't give Leath the option. I suspect he particularly resents our failure to contact him before involving the authorities."

"Are you saying his campaign is justified?"

Jonas shrugged. "I'm saying that a scandal of this magnitude so close to a man who's spent his life angling for political influence has done damage that the powerful marquess won't forgive in a hurry. Or allow to go unrequited."

"Let Leath maneuver. Nobody crosses me lightly."

The arrogant declaration, as Cam should have expected, won no points. "You might find Leath's enmity cuts closer to home than a few business schemes going astray."

Even knowing him as he did, Cam still sometimes found Jonas difficult to read. "What do you mean?"

"The word around Town is that Harry Thorne pursues Leath's sister."

"I didn't know Leath had a sister."

Another flash of sardonic humor. "She's new this season. Pretty blond chit who's got the fortune hunters in a lather."

Cam didn't smile. "I can't see Harry Thorne playing fortune hunter."

"The tattle is that he fancies himself in love. He's chased her all over London making sheep's eyes."

Cam was relieved. For a moment there, he thought Jonas might have some genuinely bad news. "He's a pup. He'll get over it."

"I hope you're right," Jonas said without great conviction. "The girl's making sheep's eyes back, although Leath's earmarked her for Desborough."

"Desborough must be forty if he's a day," Cam said in surprise. "Leath never struck me as a domestic tyrant."

"This scandal has shaken him."

Cam frowned. "It's unjust to blame Leath for an uncle who should have been hanged years ago."

Jonas's lips twisted with old bitterness that not even his current happiness had quite extinguished. "I hardly need to point out that when it comes to sin at the highest levels, people are too eager digging up dirt to worry about fairness."

Of course Cam knew that. So did Jonas and Richard. All had been branded bastards. All had countered the shame as best they could. Jonas was probably the luckiest of them all. The world now acknowledged his legitimacy.

Cam had given up hope of unraveling the tangled threads surrounding his parentage. All three players in the drama were long dead. Even if they weren't, hard facts were impossible to establish. When Cam had finally summoned courage to ask his mother who had fathered him, she'd claimed ignorance. His mother was a practiced liar, but on the subject of which Rothermere had planted the future duke in her womb, Cam had believed her.

Jonas went on. "If Leath wants to lead the country, he needs to keep his nose clean—even at a remove. Neville Fairbrother's crimes cast doubt on the entire line."

Grimly Cam remembered Harry's insistence on speaking to Pen at the wedding. Had that been about the Fairbrother chit? This unpleasantness with Leath was complicated enough. The last thing Cam needed was his wife encouraging two young fools to play Romeo and Juliet.

Chapter Twenty-Five

Harry slouched against the back wall of Oldhaven House's ballroom and moodily surveyed the crowd. Returning to the place where he'd met Sophie, memories inevitably assailed him. Since leaving for Northumberland, she'd managed three letters, each promising eternal love. All three rested in the pocket nearest his heart.

The concert was packed to the gunwales. Although the famous Dutch soprano and the Italian tenor had sung their lungs out, tonight's principal entertainment was always going to be the new Duchess of Sedgemoor.

His sister, Penelope, who sat in the front row displaying less animation than the average statue.

Harry had caught a few comments before the speakers noticed the duchess's brother within earshot. Surprisingly, most people had expressed grudging approval. Along with the inevitable dollop of spite. His sister's elevation to the highest levels wouldn't pass without a serving of jealousy.

When Harry was sixteen, he and Peter had met Pen in Rome. He recalled an independent woman widely admired for her sparkle. Even as a self-centered adolescent, Harry had recognized that all the men were mad for her. Penelope had remained strangely unaware of her effect.

Like everyone else, he'd heard rumors of love affairs. A few liaisons with glamorous Continental gentlemen would hardly blot the cloudy Thorne escutcheon. But occasionally he'd wondered about that curiously innocent girl in Italy. She'd always struck him as a one-man woman. Was she in love with her husband? At her wedding, she hadn't been a glowing bride. But she'd just survived a shipwreck and worn a dress twenty years out of date.

The marriage had surprised Harry. However hard Lady Wilmott pushed Pen at the Sedgemoor heir, Cam was always going to choose a wife who catered to his arrogance. Someone like Lady Marianne Seaton, who sat a few rows back from the Sedgemoors.

Tonight people had prepared not only to scorn Cam's unconventional duchess, but to gloat over Lady Marianne's disappointment at losing such a prize. But to the chagrin of the old tabbies, both ladies had behaved perfectly. In his sister's case, too perfectly. Seeing Pen like a doused candle, for all her diamonds and finery, deepened Harry's suspicion that the Rothermere marriage wasn't all rainbows.

Damn it, Pen deserved rainbows. If Cam hurt Pen, Harry would kill the bastard.

The Hillbrooks sat beside Pen. On Cam's other side ranged arbiter of elegance Sir Richard Harmsworth and his lovely new wife. If nastiness became overt, Pen had powerful defenders. Harry almost found himself in charity with his brother-in-law. Until he glanced again at Pen's set features.

Right now, she looked...

He struggled for some description that wasn't inexpressibly sad. But the only word that came to mind was "cowed."

He glowered at Cam, lounging beside her with his usual insufferable pride. Harry had a fancy that if he took a razor to the duke's aristocratic hide, iced water would flow.

"What the devil's biting you, Harry?" Elias asked from beside him. "You look ready to shoot someone. Or yourself."

Harry forced a smile to his lips. "I'd rather shoot the damned soprano."

Elias, the most musical of the Thorne siblings, regarded Harry with disdain. "You've always had a lead ear. Waste of time explaining why that was a transcendent experience."

"Transcendent?" Harry said snidely. "Good Gad, you'll be writing poetry next. Does Byron know he's got competition?"

Harry didn't know why he jabbed at his brother. Elias hadn't done anything wrong, apart from the inarguable fact that he wasn't Peter. If Harry was angry with anyone, he should be angry with Peter for being so bloody careless with his life.

Not that Harry's needling cast Elias down. "You're an ignorant puppy. Byron died four years ago, as you'd know if you expressed a shred of interest in anything beyond playing the dashed fool."

Elias was out of touch. Since Sophie's departure, Harry had only shown his face at the most respectable gatherings. He knew his reformation wouldn't change Leath's mind. Leath had undoubtedly dismissed Harry Thorne from his thoughts even more quickly than he'd dismissed Harry Thorne from his luxurious house. But behaving himself was all Harry could do at present to forward his courtship.

"Boys!" Pen said, coming up to them. Lost in his brooding, Harry had missed the end of the concert and the room clearing. "Stop it."

"Now you're a duchess, you imagine you can order us around," Elias said drily.

Harry bristled before he caught the amusement in Elias's face. Pen was smiling, although without the brilliance that Harry recalled from Rome.

"Only when you're likely to compromise my duchessly reputation," she said lightly as Cam joined her. "I hear you're making your maiden speech in the House this week."

Elias nodded. "Will you be in the gallery to support me?"

Because Harry watched so closely, he caught the quick glance she shot Cam, as if unsure whether to request his permission. Harry's displeasure with his brother-in-law deepened. Devil take Cam for bullying her.

"I hope she'll come to see us both in action." Cam slipped his hand around Pen's arm. Pen started as though her husband's touch was unfamiliar. Unwelcome?

Oh, Pen, what the deuce have you got yourself into?

Cam squeezed Pen's arm and released her, asking Elias about his parliamentary debut. The two wandered toward the door. It was the opportunity Harry sought.

Before he could speak, Pen leveled a glare upon him. "What on earth are you doing?"

"Doing?" A guilty flush rose in his cheeks. "I don't know what you mean."

"Yes, you do." She folded her arms and regarded him with a stern expression that made him feel about six. "You looked at Cam like you wanted to poison him."

"Poison's a woman's weapon," Harry responded with unconvincing humor.

"You always liked him."

"So did you," Harry retorted.

"I still do." She looked surprised and if he wasn't mistaken, uncomfortable. "He's a good man."

Harry grunted. Five minutes ago, he'd burned to punch the duke's nose. Now, he wasn't so sure.

"He's a good man, Harry," she repeated adamantly. "And I won't have family discord. Nor will I become a martyr to gossip. There's been enough talk about both the Thornes and the Rothermeres. You'll have to put on a better face than you've managed tonight. And quickly. People notice."

"Pen!" He tugged her into a tight embrace. Briefly he'd glimpsed the forthright woman he remembered. "I'm so glad you're back."

She struggled free and patted her hair. "You're quite mad."

She could call him a lunatic a hundred times as long as she lost that gray aura. "It runs in the family."

"Ha ha," she said. The mocking sound pleased his ears the way a harmonious chord pleased Elias. "Now if you can bring yourself to act like a gentleman and not a grumpy bear, let's find my husband and make our farewells."

He had more on his mind tonight than the state of his sister's marriage. "Wait."

Impatiently she paused. "What is it?"

"Have you thought about what we talked about?"

"No."

It was Harry's turn to be annoyed. "It's important."

"Harry, you're so young—"

"I won't change," he said steadily.

He saw the moment she realized that this wasn't a passing attraction. She sighed. "Leath won't let you near his sister. You're asking for an ocean of heartbreak."

"I don't care. I love her," he said stubbornly. "I want you to help me to see Sophie. Leath won't watch you. You can carry messages."

"Like a sneak."

"Like a loving sister."

Pen looked hunted. "Is Sophie back?"

"She returns next week. The aunt is in Edinburgh for some lecture series so Leath wants Sophie under his eye."

"I thought communication between you two was cut."

He shrugged. "Where there's a will, there's a way."

"You're reckless."

"Faint heart never won fair lady."

"If you're not careful, your rashness will bring a scandal down around our ears. Cam doesn't deserve it. And if you think Leath won't resent me for promoting this illicit flirtation, you're a blockhead."

Harry's jaw firmed. "I've considered the arguments. I can even bring myself to agree with a few of them. Sometimes."

She looked relieved. "Then stop this before someone gets hurt."

"Never," Harry said adamantly. "Nothing will convince me that Sophie's better off married to a man who doesn't love her. A man she doesn't love."

"I suppose she fancies herself in love with you." Pen considered him. "I'll concede that you're serious. But she's young too."

"She knows her heart. With all the trouble involved, it would be easier to give me up."

"Perhaps she's swept up in the excitement. Secret meetings and the drama of family opposition can turn a chit's head."

"It's not like that," Harry said obstinately. "Sophie loves me. We're going to get married."

Pen sighed again. "Over Leath's dead body. I don't know the man, but everything I've heard says that he won't yield. If he's decided you're not the right husband for his sister, you'll never get his approval."

"Then we'll act without his approval," Harry said sharply, causing a footman stacking chairs at the other side of the empty room to glance up.

Pen looked shocked. "Harry, you'll ruin us all."

He sucked in a breath and lowered his voice. "Right now, all I want is a chance to see Sophie." He read his sister's reaction. "You have my word that my intentions are honorable. You won't be assisting a rake's stratagems."

Pen's expression was pensive and something went on behind her eyes that he didn't understand. Then to his relief, after a long delay that had him nervous as a cat on a stove, she nodded. "Very well. For the moment, you have my cooperation. God help us if this comes undone."

"What did Harry want?" Cam demanded, once they were in their carriage away from listening ears.

Nervously Pen glanced across at him. Of course that perfect gentleman Camden Rothermere sat with his back to the horses. God forbid he should ignore etiquette and sit beside her.

"Well?"

Pen was grateful that the lamps inside the carriage remained unlit for the short journey to Rothermere House. Cam always knew when she lied.

"You're sounding very lordly," she responded, bristling at his tone. And eager to evade the question.

Her eyes had adjusted enough to see him fold his arms across his powerful chest. She didn't need to see his expression. It would inevitably be implacable. "Humor me."

"Why should he want anything? After all, we've been separated for the best part of ten years."

"If he didn't want anything, you'd tell me."

Devil take him, he had a point. Pen reminded herself that she'd promised obedience. Still, she couldn't betray her brother. "What do you think he said, Cam?"

Cam stretched his long legs across the well between

the seats. He'd looked magnificent tonight. Tall and distinguished, a striking man even in the company of spectacular Richard Harmsworth. Pen had fought desperately hard to hide her bedazzlement. Unfortunately, she had a feeling she'd overcompensated and convinced Cam's friends that she didn't care a fig for him.

Genevieve had been friendly and Richard had always been a darling. Sidonie and Jonas Merrick clearly thought that Cam's marriage was a mistake.

She reminded herself that anything, even a cold reception from Cam's friends, was better than the exposure of her secret. How the world would laugh at the awkward duchess unable to hide her adoration for her indifferent husband. Worse, Cam would feel sorry for her.

"Tonight I heard a disturbing rumor that Harry sets his sights on Leath's sister," Cam said.

"I don't know Leath or his sister," Pen responded with perfect honesty. To hide how her hands trembled, she slid them under her velvet cloak.

"Leath's ranged himself against me."

"Surely he can't do much harm," she said.

"Surely he can. Support has dwindled to nothing on a number of my projects, not least that canal scheme that Elias has invested in. I have wool and coal in Derbyshire and a mill in Manchester that I'd dearly like to link, not just for my own prosperity but for the people of Fentonwyck."

"But you're Sedgemoor."

"And Leath's spent his life building political influence, whereas I've been out of the country for the last few months."

She hid a pang of guilt. Cam had neglected his interests because he'd been haring after her. "You're back now. You'll sort it out."

"Sorting it out means smoothing his resentment," Cam

said austerely. "Your brother's plans to seduce the man's sister won't help."

"I imagine not." She kept her voice calm. "I have no control over Harry."

"Just don't encourage any delusions about his courtship."

"I'm hardly likely to promote the joys of matrimony to someone I care about," she said bitterly.

A blistering silence crashed down.

Shock at her unguarded response had her stiffening against the carriage's sway and peering through the darkness at Cam. Her voice quivered with remorse. "Cam, I'm sorry."

A passing street lamp revealed his devastated expression. At that moment, she loathed herself.

She loathed herself more when he caught her hand and stared at her with piercing concern. "Pen, I'm so sorry that you're unhappy." His regret made her poor, aching heart cramp. "Tell me what I can do."

Love me.

She bit back the inevitable answer and forced an unconvincing laugh. Surely they must be nearly at Rothermere House. She could retire to her room for a serious conversation with herself about making one's bed and lying in it.

"I'm so sorry, Your Grace." She pulled free. "I'm a fishwife. I hope you'll pardon me. The evening's been difficult."

His sweeping gesture conveyed impatience. This situation bore down on him too, even if he didn't live with the object of an impossible passion. "Hell's bells, stop it, Pen."

"I don't understand," she said in a leaden tone, retreating against the seat and huddling into her cape.

"For God's sake—"

To Pen's craven relief, the carriage turned into Grosvenor Square. "We're here."

"We're *home*," he snapped. "Don't imagine this discussion is over."

Most men wouldn't notice that she was yet to call any of the Rothermere properties home. She cursed his perception. But none of his houses felt like home. Amidst all the oppressive splendor, she felt like an interloper.

She fell back on the standard excuse. "I'm tired—"

"I'm sure you are," he flashed back. "And I'm tired of being called 'Your Grace' and treated like a pariah. I'm tired of seeing you shy away from me as if you expect a kick for the slightest show of spirit."

"I hardly think—" she began heatedly, before she reminded herself that an argument would shatter their fragile truce.

The door opened. She hurriedly gathered her reticule and stepped out of the carriage, leaving Cam fuming behind her. In his usual dignified style.

Cam watched sourly as his beautiful wife sailed into his imposing London house. He felt like a toad for haranguing Penelope. None of this was easy for her.

It wasn't easy for him either. Ever since he'd discovered her in the Alps, Penelope Thorne had demonstrated an unprecedented and decidedly disagreeable ability to stir his emotions.

He'd spent weeks burning up with lust. Foolishly he'd imagined that appeasing his hunger would end it. Yet he wanted her more now than before. Somehow the simple fact that he wanted his bride—surely a good thing—became just another tangle in the knots she tied him in outside the bedroom.

It was a damnable situation.

He stared like a moonling after his wife. Even worse, he

did it in view of the servants. He caught Thomas, the footman's eye, as he descended from the carriage. The man's neutral expression must hide a wealth of speculation.

Disheartened, Cam trudged inside. Although the night had been a success. Society seemed willing to wait and see if Pen was ready to put her wild ways behind her. Even the sticklers had admired her poise. His friends had rallied around her. There was some sign that the scandalous Thornes mightn't be quite so scandalous from now on. Elias had always been the steadiest of the family and his behavior tonight had been commendably restrained. Harry remained unpredictable, but even so, the evening could have gone worse.

So why did Cam feel like his dog had died?

He paused in the hallway under the cold stare of the marble Roman worthies. His habit since his marriage was to have a quiet brandy in his library, then undress before seeking Pen.

Thomas opened the library door. Cam stared into the starkly masculine room as his mind sifted the quarrel—or what they'd managed of a quarrel before reaching home. It was clear that Pen regretted her frankness. Which cut at his heart. Once he'd thought they could share anything. But that was long ago.

She was upstairs preparing for bed, even though within the hour, if every other night was any indication, her nightdress would be a tangled heap on the floor. Right now her maid was brushing out Pen's shining hair and turning back the covers. There Pen would lie waiting for him. After they'd got past their disastrous wedding night, he'd assumed she enjoyed their encounters, but tonight's acerbic comment made him wonder.

Damn it, did she welcome him to her bed only to make the best of a bad job?

Sick anger flooded him. Not with Pen. With himself. He couldn't bear to be a bad job.

He shook his head at Thomas and climbed the stairs two at a time toward his wife's ornate bedroom. Fleetingly in the carriage, the possibility of genuine honesty had hovered. Then Pen had backed away. Cam couldn't accept that.

Tonight he wouldn't give her a chance to prepare for him the way a city prepared for siege. Tonight, he'd mount a surprise attack and see what lay hidden behind the city walls.

Chapter Twenty-Six

Pen sat at her dressing table as her maid brushed her hair. The activity didn't soothe as it usually did. Instead a headache beat at her temples and the gaze she met in the mirror was defeated. Three weeks married and she felt like she'd aged twenty years. Heaven help her if she lasted to Christmas.

Troubling memories from the night circled like growling dogs. Harry's palpable desperation. The Hillbrooks' politely concealed wariness. The avid curiosity in every face at the musicale. Her noxious argument with Cam. The familiar emptiness in her soul.

The door opened and hit the wall with a very un-Cam-like bang. Pen started, wrenching against Jane's downward stroke. "Ouch!"

"Your pardon, Your Grace," Jane stammered to Pen. She curtsied to Cam. "Your Grace."

In the mirror, Cam's expression wasn't reassuring. Still Pen's voice emerged with commendable steadiness. "You may go, Jane. I'll finish here."

"Very well, Your Grace."

Cam hardly glanced in the girl's direction as she slipped past. Instead his attention fixed on Pen.

Sick of confused emotions, she set the heavy brush down with an audible click. "There's no need to terrify the staff, Your Grace."

With his jaw set in adamantine lines, he shut the door. He was careful closing it, which struck her as more alarming than another show of temper. She recalled the days when she'd believed that Cam had no temper to lose.

"If you ever call me 'Your Grace' again, I'll have the press-gangs kidnap Harry and send him to a mosquito-ridden swamp in Panama."

That didn't sound like a joke. "I'm trying to be a proper duchess."

To fit in with his image of the ideal wife, tonight she'd minded her manners, she'd smiled like a fool, and she'd kept any controversial opinions to herself. Even worse, she'd worn a dress for her London debut that she wouldn't put on a scarecrow.

Everyone had seemed to approve. Everyone except Cam. Clearly he had impossibly high standards.

"A proper duchess pleases her duke."

Once she'd have treated that arrogant statement with the contempt it deserved. But that was before she'd saddled Cam with her wanton reputation. "I'm sorry I'm not ready," she said dully, standing. "Would you like help undressing?"

He scowled as he leaned against the door frame and folded his arms. "I'd like you to talk to me," he said in a tone that brooked no argument.

Her jaw dropped in astonishment. "Talk?"

For three weeks, he'd come to her room in a lather of passion. His unsteady breathing and the color lining his slashing cheekbones betrayed that he wanted her now. Yet he wanted to talk?

"Yes."

She backed against the dressing table, hooking her hands over the polished mahogany edge. "What on earth can we talk about?"

His eyebrow rose in that superior expression that always made her itch to clout him. Or at least it had before she'd sworn to become a conformable spouse. "I don't know," he said sarcastically. "What could two people linked together for life and with no idea of what the other one is thinking say? Perhaps we could discuss the weather."

"There's no need to be rude."

"I think there is." He sauntered in her direction.

To her relief, he stopped a few feet away, although his searching regard stirred terrified flurries in her belly. She'd learned to hide her emotions in bed, and she stayed out of his way during the day. His actions tonight set a precedent, one that troubled her.

"You're never rude," she said despairingly. "You're a model of behavior."

He frowned. "I never thought you were."

"I'll do better." She bowed her head and studied the pink embroidered slippers peeping from under her voluminous white nightdress.

He didn't immediately respond. He advanced until she saw the toes of his black shoes at the edge of her vision. "Pen, you don't have to turn yourself inside out," he said softly.

The patch of floor became watery at the edges. She blinked to clear her sight and mumbled, "I don't want to talk about this."

"I do." He spoke almost musingly. "Not long ago, you'd

have sent me to the devil if I'd said that mutton-headed thing about pleasing me."

"We weren't married then," she said sadly.

The regret in his sigh crushed her soul. "Pen, look at me."

"I'd rather not."

"Do you know what I've always admired about you?" The sudden change to tenderness slid over her, softer than her lovely velvet cloak.

She tensed. How she wished he'd go away. Or throw her on the bed and thrust into her. Or yell. "I can't imagine."

He laughed, still with that affectionate note that reminded her that he was the only man she'd ever held in her heart. Now that he was there, he was like a worm in an apple, gradually destroying her from within. "Well, there's your complete lack of vanity."

Eventually curiosity forced her to speak. "Is that what you admire?"

"I admire that. But it's not what I admire most."

She sucked in a breath. He was so close that she smelled his sandalwood soap. "Won't you say?"

"Not unless you look at me."

Her throat was so tight that it hurt to swallow. "I can't bear the disappointment I see in your face," she said on a mere thread of sound.

"Oh, Pen..."

She jumped when one hand caught her chin. "I'm making a mess of this marriage thing."

"No, I am. We rushed into this."

She tried to retreat, but the dressing table trapped her. "We didn't have any choice." She paused. "*You* didn't have any choice."

This time his sigh held a hint of frustration. "God give

me strength, woman. Don't tell me you're eating yourself up with guilt."

Now that he didn't sound so likely to fold her in his arms, she let him tilt her face up. Then wished to God she hadn't, that she'd taken to her heels the minute he'd stormed in.

Cam stared at her as if she was his single concern in the world, as though her happiness mattered more than his next breath.

It was a lie, she staunchly insisted. But how could she heed common sense when the man she adored regarded her with such care? She licked her lips again and noticed with sparking heat how his eyes focused on the betraying movement.

"I didn't realize how much it cost you to save me from ruin until you told me about the gossip. By then it was too late. We were married."

A flash of bitterness lit his green eyes. "All your escapades were innocent. Nobody knows that better than I."

She leveled her shoulders and confronted him with the truth. "After a life devoted to restoring the family name, you've attached yourself to a woman with a questionable past and rebellious habits."

Comprehension lit his expression. "So you're trying to become the ideal duchess." She flinched at the sarcastic edge he placed on "ideal duchess." "By calling me 'Your Grace' and trying to fade into the wallpaper."

"I don't want to do any more damage." She swallowed. "I can't do anything about being a Thorne or about the stories or about not being the woman you wanted to marry, but I can try to be a credit to you."

His lips flattened in vexation. "You are a credit to me."

Her glance was disbelieving. "Obviously."

He caught her shoulders. "Pen, you are the woman I wanted to marry."

This was too much for even her besotted mind to accept. A hollow laugh escaped. "Cam, you're such a gentleman, but there's no point lying."

"You're the only woman I've proposed to. And I did it twice. What further commitment can a man demonstrate?" His grip tightened and she wondered if he meant to shake her. He looked like he wanted to. "How can such a clever woman be so stupid?"

She glared at him. "How can such a clever man expect a woman of the slightest intelligence to accept this flannel? We both know that your heart was set on Marianne Seaton."

His jaw squared in rejection of her accusation. "Hardly my heart."

He warned Pen to tread carefully and not bring messy emotions into their dealings. But he'd forced her into this awkward, revealing conversation. He could damn well take the consequences. "She was your choice."

He shrugged as if it hardly mattered. "She was a suitable bride."

"And I'm not."

"Actually I find myself surpassingly grateful that you married me."

"I can't imagine why."

Impatiently he ran his hand through his hair. "A gentleman shouldn't say this, but much as I admire Lady Marianne, life with her might have lacked...excitement."

Gloomily Pen surveyed him. "Excitement can be uncomfortable."

"And it can make a man glad to be alive. It can make him look forward to waking up every morning. And going to bed every night."

She flushed. "Sexual attraction will fade."

He frowned. "I want you more every day."

Be careful, Pen. If you pay too much heed, he'll break your heart again. "It's early days yet," she said sourly. "You'll become jaded with my charms."

"You're looking at me."

She frowned, not understanding the change of subject. "So?"

"I promised that when you did, I'd tell you what I admired most."

"So I assume that's what you like most, your desire for me." She tried to sound displeased. Whereas the pathetic truth was that she basked in his attentions like a cat in a patch of sunlight on a cold day.

"Well, it's no drawback. You seem compelled to concentrate on the disadvantages of our union. After three weeks, I'd say the benefits far outweigh the inconveniences. Even with you moping like a schoolboy stuck inside on a wet holiday."

"I haven't been that bad," she said, stung.

"Yes, you have. But I'll set you right tonight."

How could she love him and want to punch him at the same time? "I await your wisdom."

He brushed his lips across hers. It was an affectionate kiss, different from the deep, passionate, hungry kisses he gave her in bed. She was on the verge of sinking against him when he raised his head.

"What I admire about you, dear Penelope, what I've always admired, ever since you rode that half-broken pony at the age of three, is your courage."

Her heart dipped like a swallow in flight, leaving her dizzy. Oh, dear, she was in so much trouble. When he said things like this, when he made her feel that he and only he peered into her soul, she wanted to melt. Worse, she wanted to confess how desperately she loved him.

"It was a courageous act to marry you," she said with that same edge, hoping he wouldn't hear how she struggled to sound unaffected.

Her response didn't stir his temper. She wondered where his anger in the coach had gone. "It was indeed."

His intense stare made her shift uncomfortably. It was all very well for him to peer into her soul, but she had secrets. Old ones like her love, and more recent ones like her promise to Harry.

"Now I want you to find the courage to be yourself. I want you to find the courage to build something from this marriage, something strong and safe."

"London won't approve of me," she snapped back. She didn't trust this turnaround. All her life, she'd known Cam wanted a biddable duchess. He must know that if Pen was true to herself, biddable was the last description to apply.

"I will. Remember, a proper duchess pleases her duke."

"You won't say that when everybody's pitying you for marrying an outspoken hoyden."

One black eyebrow arched. "If you stop dressing like a damned grandmother, London will be so dazzled, nobody will care what you say."

She scowled, even as she wondered if perhaps he was right about her meekness being impossible to maintain. "Tonight's dress cost you a fortune."

He laughed softly. "A damned rich grandmother."

She drew herself up and spoke the unpalatable truth. "Cam, you don't want a scandalous Thorne as your duchess. You want Marianne Seaton."

Growling low in his throat, he sat on the bed and removed his shoes. A strange thrill shivered through her. This intimacy was new. He always undressed in his own rooms. "Pen, I'll say this once more, then the subject's forever closed."

"If I'm to be myself, you know that I'll object to orders."

"One last order."

Still wary but unable to resist, she drifted across to lean against one of the bedposts. "I'd be naïve to believe that."

He tugged his neckcloth loose. The gold signet ring glinted as if it was alive. He addressed the air above her head. "To think I asked this woman to speak her mind."

"To think," she retorted.

He stared directly at her and to her surprise, his eyes were serious. "Since you became my wife, I haven't regretted losing Lady Marianne once. You're the woman I want. I didn't travel to Italy intending to marry you." He raised a hand to forestall her protest. "But I'm not sorry that I did. I hope that you'll allow me to prove myself as a husband so that you're not sorry either."

"Cam—"

"At least you're not calling me 'Your Grace' anymore," he said wryly and went on before she could speak. "You keep talking about what I gave up to marry you. Yet you gave up as much or more. I know that you're unhappy. I'd do anything to change that. But first I want you to acknowledge that you're not some unsatisfactory substitute for the woman I should have married. If you imagine I come to your bed every night cursing the fact that it's you in my arms and not Marianne Seaton, you're completely unhinged. The demons plaguing you are chimeras. I hope that in time you'll trust me."

"I do trust you," she mumbled without meeting his eyes.

"Obviously. So much that you jump a mile when I touch you in public."

"I'm not used to—"

Compassion softened his eyes until they glowed soft emerald. "I know. This marriage business is new to us both, but with goodwill, we can create something glorious."

He said all the right things. She should be glad. But she couldn't help noticing the one glaring omission in all his talk about their bright future. She commended his honesty, but still her idiot, yearning heart craved to hear the word "love."

But "love" was a word that Cam would never use. He respected her too much. The irony of that statement left her wanting to break something.

Still, she recognized how he'd humbled himself. "I'll do my best."

His lips curved in the sweet smile that made her melt just the way his sweet kisses did. She was so susceptible. It was downright terrifying. "Your best will be magnificent."

"Thank you," she said with such uncertainty that he smiled.

"Pen, come here and make me happy. That's your only duty tonight."

She stared at him, dissent sparking. She wanted to make him happy. But more, she needed to seize some control. Starting tonight in the big, elegant bed where her big, elegant husband lounged, eyeing her like a sugared almond that he wanted to snap between his straight white teeth.

She'd been so eager to prove herself worthy that she'd abdicated all power. Including over what they did in bed.

He told her that he wanted her. That was a significant admission from someone as reluctant to surrender the advantage as Cam.

He'd never love her. She needed to accept that finally and forever. Once, she had. Nineteen-year-old Penelope had been wise beyond her years. Twenty-eight-year-old Penelope was a sentimental fool.

As she read Cam's stirring desire, she realized that in this if in nothing else, they were equals. He'd told her she was brave. She'd need to be brave to gain what she set out to achieve.

Their nights would become a kingdom where she reigned supreme.

Chapter Twenty-Seven

As Cam rose to shrug off his coat, he caught the excitement in Pen's face. And something else that he didn't understand.

These glimpses of a stranger in her eyes always disoriented him. It was like seeing a ghost standing behind an old friend. Slightly eerie. Fascinating. Irresistibly tempting.

But then, everything about Pen was irresistibly tempting.

This raging hunger was unsettling. He was grimly reminded of the straits his parents and uncle had found themselves in when private feelings overflowed into the public arena.

He tugged his shirt over his head and as he emerged from the folds of white linen, Pen leveled an assessing stare upon him. The way her gaze fed upon his body made his gut knot with anticipation. And more unease. She was definitely up to something.

One slender hand curled in a damned suggestive way around the carved bedpost. Blatantly her gaze dropped to the front of his trousers. This time when she licked her lips, it wasn't nervousness, but salacious appreciation. Arousal thundered through him, making him deaf to warnings.

"Take off your trousers, Cam." Her tone was sultry, setting his bones vibrating with desire.

Startled, he paused, shirt dangling from one hand. "What did you say?"

She shrugged, still staring at his crotch. "You told me to be myself."

"Yes," he said warily. "In society."

"Everywhere." She licked her lips again. Each time she did that, his blood heated another ten degrees.

"Come here and I'll help you with your nightdress."

She smiled as if recognizing his offer for the weak foray that it was. "First I want to see you naked."

She pointed one elegant finger at his stiff cock. Cam, as master of his household, didn't approve of Pen seizing control like this. His dick, however, thought it was a brilliant idea.

"I didn't mean that you can order me around," he protested, even as he unbuttoned the front fall.

That mysterious smile still curved her lips. Seducing Odysseus, Calypso must have worn such a smile. Then Cam realized that this was no sorceress. His bride was named for Odysseus's faithful and loving wife. If mythical Penelope bore any resemblance to this Penelope, no wonder the wanderer had been desperate to return.

"You complained that I was too amenable. It's too late to change your mind."

"Perhaps I miscalculated."

"Recalculate naked."

Surprised, excited, delighted, he released a huff of laughter. This was the woman he'd found so endlessly fascinating in Italy. Although in Italy, she'd never have told him to take his clothes off.

Perhaps his marriage progressed better than he'd thought. "Is there a penalty for noncompliance?"

She shrugged, although the glitter in her black eyes belied nonchalance. "If you don't play the game, you don't win the prize."

"You've convinced me." Hurriedly he tugged off his trousers.

Then because he knew that she tested his commitment to wanting her real self, he stood and let her stare at him. However much a numbskull he felt with his necessaries waving in the wind.

To his chagrin, his cheeks heated under her thorough inspection. "My manly magnificence can't strike you dumb. It's not as if you haven't seen everything before."

Her attention didn't waver. He shivered, although the night wasn't cold and a fire burned in the grate. "You usually don't give me time to look at you."

Guilt pinched him. So far in their married life, he'd swept Pen into bed. He'd aroused her, but he'd been ruthless about it.

"Lie down." At last she raised her eyes. Her eyelids were heavy and her cheeks were flushed. He felt less powerless now that he knew this seduction played on her control too.

He surged forward, taking her arm. As cool lawn bunched beneath his hand, he felt her lithe strength. He hadn't married a frail lily. He'd married a lioness. "Lie with me."

"Eventually." She stepped back, shaking him loose.

"Pen, don't tease."

"Teasing does you good. You've become odiously imperious in your old age." Her voice firmed. "Now on the bed, if you please, Your Grace."

"Don't call me that."

"Tonight I'll call you what I wish." She paused. "Your Grace."

He wasn't sure whether he wanted to kiss her insolence away or put her over his knees and spank her. Both. Still, she'd promised him a prize. He shot her a telling glance before stretching across the bed.

In the quiet room, he heard Pen exhale. With relief? With nerves? With anticipation?

He shifted on the sheets. They'd been packed in lavender and the sweet scent tickled his nose. "I feel absurd."

The silence extended, charged with suspense. Eventually he could bear it no longer. "Pen, for God's sake, touch me."

She continued to study him from the base of the bed. "Later."

"What the devil?" He started to lunge toward her, but she shook her head.

"Stay where you are."

For a long moment, he met the challenge in her eyes. She wanted him to prove that he couldn't handle this raw version of Penelope Thorne. Well, bugger that. If breaking through to something real between them required his abasement, he'd damn well accept abasement.

She crossed to the decanters waiting on a gilded table. Cam slumped back with a groan and stared at the intricate plasterwork on the ceiling. The clock downstairs chimed two. They'd been home little more than an hour. He felt like he'd been hard for days.

He heard the clink of glass. "Dutch courage?"

"Need some yourself?"

He was past politeness. His voice emerged rough and urgent. "The only thing I need is you. Wet. Ready. Under me. Moaning."

He turned his head quickly to catch what would surely be disgust on her lovely face. Instead, she looked intrigued. But not, blast it, intrigued enough to relent.

Pen wandered the room, sipping her claret. She paused in a shadowy corner. "I dislike this picture of Apollo and Daphne. We should replace it."

Little red hot ringing bells of hell. To think that he'd condemned her docility. She wasn't driving him insane. He'd been insane when he'd suggested changing the status quo. If she'd remained that compliant cipher, he'd already be plunging between her milky white thighs.

Still, two could play at this game.

He rolled onto his side to study her. In her long white nightdress, she looked like a gorgeous priestess of some exotic religion. "By all means, let's talk about art. We have until dawn."

Ha, that surprised her. He plastered an imperturbable expression on his face as she focused a startled gaze upon him. She'd ambushed him with this torture in the guise of seduction. See how the lovely witch liked a dose of her own medicine.

Her eyes narrowed as if she guessed his tactic. "There's a nice landscape downstairs that would suit."

"The Turner?" He began to sit up and was pleased to see Pen move to forestall him. "Let's try it in place."

She stopped a few feet from the bed. "You can't run around the house naked."

He subsided upon the pillows. "It's my house."

"The servants won't like it."

"They're asleep. And we must resolve this question of the painting in that corner immediately."

"I can wait until morning."

She might be able to. He wasn't sure he could.

Maintaining his casual manner required a mortifying effort. "Perhaps we should bring some pictures from Fentonwyck. My grandfather's best acquisitions are in the long gallery there."

She regarded him suspiciously. "I know. You showed me. Remember?"

"I remember." After he'd botched his wedding night. She'd jumped every time he'd touched her. Just as she'd jumped tonight when he'd taken her arm at the musicale.

The thought reminded him that he was at least half responsible for their difficulties. Pen had every right to prod and snipe. If it meant an end to the constraint between them, she could take an ax to him. He made himself smile. "I wonder if perhaps the Titian in the library might be better. Do you want to go and look at it?"

She sipped her wine as if considering his question. He had her measure now. Despite desire gnawing like a hungry tiger, he began to enjoy himself.

"Perhaps not immediately," she said neutrally.

"Then how else shall we pass the time? Do you still play chess?"

A quirk of her lips. She definitely guessed his scheme. "Not recently."

He nearly laughed. His amiability irked her. Although surely a moment's glance at his body must reveal that neither art nor chess was uppermost in his priorities. "There's a board in my room. Shall I fetch it?"

"You *want* to play chess?"

"You *want* to discuss art?"

To his relief, she burst out laughing, the sound sweet and silvery. He loved the wholehearted way she surrendered to amusement. If he could only gain her wholehearted participation in the conjugal act, he'd be a happy man.

With a click, she placed the half-full glass on the table and advanced toward the bed, every line of her slender body conveying purpose.

Cam kept his expression quizzical and his posture relaxed

while his heart thundered so fast, surely she must hear it. One hint of triumph and she'd retreat.

"You want to play?" She stopped beside the bed and swiftly tugged her nightdress over her head. Before he could mask his shock, she kneeled on the mattress and with a determined gesture, pushed him back. "Let's play."

Chapter Twenty-Eight

Butterflies the size of ponies cavorted in Pen's stomach. She wasn't nearly as confident as she pretended. Even worse, she suspected Cam recognized her uncertainty.

But beneath the playfulness, what happened tonight was important. To her. And to her future with her husband.

She'd been a fool to think that she could sustain her submissive spouse act. How unexpected that Cam asked her to be herself. Somewhere he'd developed an appreciation for unconventional females.

"Come here, my wife." His voice was hoarse with need. The desire in his gaze could set London alight.

He caught her in his arms, but she slid out of reach. "No."

She'd held the upper hand until now. She had no intention of surrendering it until she achieved her aim. Tonight she'd made Camden Rothermere strip naked physically. Little did he know she launched a campaign to strip him naked emotionally.

Dark brows lowered over his deep-set eyes, shadowing them into mystery. "What's this?"

Her laugh was mocking as she lolled shamelessly against the pillows. "Cam, haven't you understood yet?"

"I've done what you wanted."

"Nowhere near," she said lightly, and wondered if he heard the implicit threat. She hoped not. If he guessed her plans to pierce his armor, he'd be out the door before she could blink.

His hands opened and closed at his sides. The air sizzled with frustration. And arousal. He stared at her like he was starving. She flicked her hair behind her shoulders. Cam's attention immediately leveled on her breasts.

Only a brazen hussy would respond to that rapacious stare by arching her back. But then, only a brazen hussy would succeed on tonight's reckless quest.

Suspicion darkened his expression. "Pen, what are you up to?"

"I promise to be gentle." Actually she didn't promise that at all.

He looked so magnificent spread naked across the bed that Pen's courage faltered. Then she reminded herself to stop thinking like a starry-eyed virgin. She recalled discussions in France and Italy, late at night, when the wine flowed, when the gentlemen weren't present.

Squaring her shoulders, she kneeled above Cam. This time he didn't make the mistake of reaching for her. He'd always been a quick learner.

Assessingly, she stared at her husband. She knew from many a scandalous *duchessa* or wanton *comtesse* that men requested services from a mistress that they'd never impose upon a wife. She even, thanks to those frank ladies, had an idea of what some of those services entailed.

The question wasn't whether she could imagine those acts. The question was whether she could bring herself to initiate them.

Then she recalled the way Cam closed her out, even at the height of passion. Her heart slamming against her chest, she started with what lay within reach.

"Pen, what are you doing?" he asked sharply, tugging at the foot she held.

"I'm tasting you." She carefully avoided looking at his erection as she pressed her lips to his ankle.

"Then kiss me."

She stroked his foot. She'd never before taken time to consider what a marvelous piece of natural engineering he was. "I am kissing you."

"On the lips."

"Soon." His body was fascinating, so different from hers. A scattering of black hair covered his skin. She tested the difference between bone and muscle, feeling him flex under her touch.

"We'll be here all night if you examine me like a damned quack," he said despairingly.

She slid her fingers between his toes. "Do you have another appointment?"

"You'll kill me, you know," he said almost conversationally.

A smile tugged at her lips. "All in a good cause."

"And what's that?"

"My education, for one thing." She straddled his legs and kissed up past his knees to his thighs.

His muscles went as hard as rock, and heat sizzled off his skin. She cursed herself for not exerting her power earlier in their marriage. Turning him helpless with need was mightily enjoyable.

Cam's scent had been her definition of heaven since she'd been a little girl and he'd carried her to safety from one mishap or another. Now that she lingered over him, she discovered subtle undertones. As she slowly wended her way across him, closer and closer to the part that rose hard and demanding, male musk intensified with every inch.

His animal arousal stirred her. She shifted to relieve the slick ache between her legs.

"Holy God in heaven," he groaned, quaking under her lips.

Stroking his hips, she kissed random trails across his torso, feeling as much as hearing his breath catch when she played a sudden variation, like a bite where she'd licked or a scratch where she'd stroked. His hands tangled tighter and tighter in the sheets beneath him as he struggled not to grab her.

Of course he wanted to grab her. What she did offended all his notions of command.

"You push me too far."

She laughed against his sternum. "If you can still talk, you've still got a way to go."

He tugged at her hair, hard enough to compel attention. She stared up past his sharply cut jaw to eyes as black as her own with excitement. He must be gritting his teeth. His cheeks looked tighter than the skin on a drum.

"What are you doing, Pen?"

"Seducing you."

"Into complete subjection?"

She shrugged, her breasts tingling as they brushed his ribs. "This is war."

Cam was a man gifted with almost unnatural perception. Even teetering on the edge of control, he recognized that she was serious. "I don't want a winner and a loser."

"Unless you're the winner." Despite anticipation turning the air to invisible flame, she couldn't altogether contain her bitterness.

He stared at her. "I want to make you happy. That means we both win."

How she wished she believed him. With all the longing in her heart, she kissed him. She'd expected rapacious passion, but his lips were tender.

The frantic crescendo of desire fleetingly paused and something else hovered near. Something sweeter, more enduring, more powerful.

Then the moment dissolved as she broke away and slid down his body.

She took him in her hand, feeling the vital leap of his flesh. The man capable of speech only moments ago responded with a guttural groan.

Listening to her friends describe this act, Pen had been completely revolted. But a quick glance at Cam's face told her that right now he was in her thrall.

Curiosity gripped her. Curiosity and daring. And a profound wish to give him pleasure.

This was a gift of love. Cam would never know that. But Pen would. That must be enough.

She bent and took him into her mouth.

Cam watched Pen's silky dark head move down his chest, his abdomen, then lower. All night, she'd stretched him on a rack. Now she tightened the ropes until she threatened to rip him apart.

The nearer she edged to his aching cock, the more frantically his blood pounded. Wanton images tumbled through his mind. Even as he watched her position herself, he knew that a not-much-past-virginal lady wouldn't use her mouth on a man.

She wouldn't do it...

His world exploded into a million blazing stars. "Hell's bells, Pen," he grated out in shock.

His belly hollowed in despair as with a hot wet glide that nearly blew his head off, she lifted her mouth away from him. "Don't you like it?"

He focused on her lips. Pink. Plump. Glistening. His brain struggled to comprehend what she did. Or almost did.

"Cam?" Those witch's lips curved into a smile. He searched her face in vain for shyness or disgust. He saw neither, just a sensual eagerness that made his heart crash against his ribs.

"How—" Dear Lord, why was he wasting time talking? "Pen, you were—"

She laughed low in her throat and he realized that his wife's days of succumbing in wide-eyed wonder to his worldly experience drew to a close. "You don't usually have trouble finishing your sentences."

Damn it, she was right. He wasn't a schoolboy with his first sweetheart. He swallowed. He still didn't trust his voice. He swallowed again and grabbed a breath. Only then did he dare speak, hoping against hope that he didn't sound as bedazzled as he felt. "How does an innocent girl know to do this?"

That smile still flirted with her lips. "I'm not exactly an innocent girl."

"Not far off."

Her eyelashes fluttered down. "The gossips were right about one thing. Conversations in Rome's salons were more risqué than at Almack's."

Still straddling him, she slid upward until her sex brushed his aching cock. He bit back an agonized groan. Heat seared every thought from his brain but one. He must have her. He must have her now.

Through the ferment in his head, he heard her speak. He was in such a state, it took a few seconds to translate the sounds.

"I thought you'd like it."

He dragged his mind back from his need to plunge inside her. "I did." He paused in case she misunderstood. "I do."

"I'm working purely on hearsay."

She looked so serious that even half-demented with desire, Cam couldn't contain a laugh. "My sweet wife, whatever you do will please me."

Triumph lit her face. "I'm glad to hear it, Your Grace."

Tonight sarcasm had edged her use of the formal address. Each time, the bite in her mellow contralto set his desire spiking.

"I'm so mad for you, this house could burn down around my ears and I'd still choose to stay in this bed."

When she kissed him, she tasted of woman and desire and everything he wanted. He devoured her mouth, plunging his tongue deep. "Let me have you," he whispered against her lips.

"Not yet."

In an excess of frustration, he dug his hand into her mane of hair and held her still. "You really do want to kill me."

Her eyes glittered with excitement. "Perhaps."

With a blatant eroticism that set his heart galloping, she pressed down. She was so close. He tilted his hips, but before he could slide inside her, she retreated.

"I should finish what I started."

He couldn't trust himself not to spill into her mouth. "Have mercy. You test my control."

Her eyes flared with unholy interest. "I don't mind."

Pen shifted to take him inside her luscious mouth. His vision dissolved into a long dark tunnel. Her name emerged as an incoherent protest.

She licked the sensitive head and any impulse to stop her went south, along with every drop of blood in his body. Then—dear God—subtle suction.

She increased the pressure, squeezing her fingers around the base. Despite her clumsiness, this level of pleasure ranged beyond his experience.

The act blazed through him like fire through dry tinder. She moaned with enjoyment. Another jolt of excitement. Another thread ripped from his frayed control. He strained against losing himself.

"Pen, stop." His voice emerged as a raw husk. "Enough."

Tauntingly slowly, she rose, lingering at the tip. His neck muscles were so tight, he feared his head must break off. He closed his eyes. Speaking was painful. "Let me take over. You've made your point."

Whatever that point had been. He'd forgotten it the minute she'd used her mouth. Her hand still curled around him, warm and firm. She needed to let go or she'd get a nasty surprise.

Warm silk tumbled over his belly and she took him again.

Heat. Pressure. Pleasure.

Demand. Resistance.

The throbbing necessity of need.

Release…

Every cell in his body screamed for surrender. On a choked curse, he gave up the struggle, bowed toward the ceiling, and spurted his hot seed into her mouth.

Chapter Twenty-Nine

H er actions the previous night still occupied Pen's
thoughts the next evening when she accompanied
Cam to the Duchess of Matlock's ball.

Despite the power that had surged through her when
Cam had lost control, her victory had been hollow. Yes, he'd
acceded to her wishes. Yes, he'd relished what she'd done.
But when he'd taken her afterward with unashamed command, she'd recognized her failure. Cam had surrendered
physically, but behind his green eyes the barriers still rose.
She'd conquered his body, not his soul.

She had to be stalwart. One night, no matter how passionate, couldn't shatter defenses laid in earliest childhood and
shored up ever since. Cam wouldn't yield without a fight.

She sprang from a long line of warriors. Thornes never
lacked for nerve, whatever other qualities were wanting.
This quest to bind her husband to her would prove as hazard-
ous as any of the battles littering her family history.

Since they'd entered the ballroom, Pen had felt the reassuring warmth of Cam's hand at her back. It reminded her

that while she hadn't won the war, Cam had been unusually affectionate today. He'd kissed her at breakfast and he'd spent the day showing her around London. Odd that she knew cities like Paris and Rome like a native, yet the capital of her own country was fresh territory.

The Matlock ball was a highlight of the social calendar, making it the sort of crush that counted as a success. Guests included the Marquess of Leath and his newly returned sister, Lady Sophie Fairbrother.

Pen was surprised at her first sight of James Fairbrother, the man Harry painted as such a villain. Leath was handsome in the saturnine style. He was more heavily muscled than her husband, a prizefighter rather than a swordsman. She didn't miss how Leath's eyes narrowed on Harry, who ostentatiously kept his distance. Nor how he watched the golden-haired girl who was in such demand as a dance partner.

Pen hadn't been sure what to expect of Sophie either. The girl was lovely and clearly the toast of the ball. She paid no regard to Harry. Had she decided that a penniless younger son, however devoted, was beneath her touch? Or was she playing it safe in public?

According to Harry, Leath wanted Sophie to marry Lord Desborough. Pen knew hardly anyone in this glittering world. Several older men danced with Sophie. Perhaps one was Desborough.

Pen couldn't help feeling that tying such vibrant youth to a man approaching middle age verged on cruelty. Which didn't mean she disapproved of Leath's plans for a good match for his sister. Apart from his loyal and loving heart, Harry wasn't a good match.

But his loyal and loving heart should count. If Sophie loved him, Pen decided, she'd do her utmost to help. Cam had told her not to interfere, but how could she abandon Harry and Sophie if they were genuinely in love?

In this sea of unfamiliar faces, it was almost a relief to see Lord Hillbrook and his wife approaching through the crowd. Neither Jonas nor Sidonie Merrick had been particularly welcoming last night, but they were unfailingly loyal to Cam. And at least they weren't complete strangers.

"My lord. My lady." She forced a smile to her face.

"Good evening, Sidonie, Jonas." Cam sounded pleased. "I thought we might miss you in this brouhaha."

"Richard and Genevieve are here too. We met them as we arrived, but haven't seen hide nor hair since." Lady Hillbrook lazily waved her fan before her face. She turned to Pen. "The Matlock ball is always nearer a riot than a party."

"You're probably used to wilder evenings than we are in staid old London," Jonas said. "I remember public balls in Venice where they brought the army in to restore calm."

Pen wasn't sure if this was a dig at her itinerant past, but as Cam's friend, she gave him the benefit of the doubt. "I attended a masquerade during last year's *Carnevale* where I was lucky to escape with my life."

"I like your dress." Tonight Lady Hillbrook's reserve was less overt.

"Thank you." After Cam's unflattering description of her clothing, Pen wore her favorite gown from her new wardrobe. Cam's eyes had lit with approval when she'd come downstairs before the ball. The Nile-green silk was demure in style, but the color suited her and it complimented the Rothermere emeralds.

Cam extended his hand. "Sidonie, may I have this dance?"

Pen stifled an instinctive protest at remaining behind with the terrifying Lord Hillbrook. She desperately tried to catch the eye of Harry or Elias. But Elias danced with, of all people, Lady Marianne Seaton, and Harry was nowhere to be seen. He was probably on the terrace, sulking because his sweetheart was dancing with another man.

None of which helped Pen. This was her second society event. At the musicale, new acquaintances had clamored for an introduction. Tonight her novelty value had faded. Or perhaps Jonas Merrick's presence at her side discouraged interruptions.

"Perhaps you'd do me a similar honor, Your Grace," Lord Hillbrook said with a sardonic smile, as if he guessed Pen's apprehension.

"Please, call me Penelope." It seemed ridiculous to stand on ceremony with Cam's long-standing connections.

"With pleasure. I hope you'll call me Jonas."

He led her onto the floor where a quadrille started. At least it wasn't a waltz. Apart from the fact that her foolish heart wanted to share the waltzes with Cam, she flinched from an intimate *tête-à-tête* with the formidable viscount.

Cam and Lady Hillbrook joined another square. There was an ease between them that spoke of old affection. Pen couldn't summon a shred of jealousy. It was clear that Sidonie Merrick was profoundly in love with her intimidating husband. Which meant either the beautiful brunette was recklessly daring or Lord Hillbrook—Jonas—wasn't quite the beast he appeared.

"You've known Cam all your life, I believe," Jonas said as they waited for the lead couple to perform their pattern.

Pen hadn't been mistaken. He meant to quiz her. She answered as harmlessly as she could. "Our mothers were friends."

"But you've been away from England for many years."

Pen cast him a wary look. Even in Europe, she'd heard

about Jonas Merrick. She'd wager he already knew all about her. Had he discovered that the Continental marriage was a complete fantasy? Still, she kept her voice neutral. "I traveled with an aunt."

"Lady Bradford," he said, proving that he'd checked her background. "I met her in Greece twelve years ago. A redoubtable lady."

"I miss her," Pen said with perfect sincerity, relieved for a reprieve as she and Jonas took their part in the dance.

"I was sorry to hear she'd passed away," he said when they returned to their place. "I assume you stayed in contact with Cam."

"I kept up a large correspondence," she responded coolly.

This inquisition wasn't as off-putting as she'd feared. Continental courts were hotbeds of intrigue. Agents both for and against the authorities had sounded her out. Jonas Merrick was without doubt cleverer than those petty informers, but the pattern was familiar enough for Pen to cope.

"You'll pardon me asking. I claim the privilege of old friendship. While we're obviously delighted with Cam's choice, everything happened very suddenly. He disappeared for a couple of months, then returned with a bride. Via a shipwreck. It's the story of the year."

"My brother Peter brought us together," she said with complete honesty before the dance claimed them again.

When they reunited, Pen slightly breathless after keeping up with a young man who mistook the quadrille for a race, Jonas continued as if there had been no interruption. "I hope you and Sidonie will become close."

"So do I." Pen meant it. "I'll welcome a friendly face. London differs from free and easy Continental circles."

To her surprise, humor warmed his craggy features to attractiveness. "Sidonie wasn't used to society when we married either, as I'm sure she'll tell you. And you have the unutterable advantage of being a duchess."

"And Camden Rothermere's wife," Pen said with a touch of pride. Even after two outings, she'd realized that the ton held Cam in high regard, despite his scandalous parentage and the irregular circumstances behind his marriage.

"Yes, being Cam's choice will smooth most paths."

The square broke into movement and she and Jonas didn't meet until the end of the dance. "You can count on our support."

Although it sounded like an endorsement, Pen wasn't silly enough to take his words at face value. What she heard was "You can count on our support—as long as you do nothing to shame or discomfit our dear friend."

She could have told him that hurting Cam was the last thing she wanted. In fact, if she felt confiding, which she didn't, she could have told Jonas that marrying Cam was the worst injury she could do him.

Except she had an unwelcome perception that during the short conversation, the viscount had winkled out secrets she'd kept for a lifetime. Including the biggest secret of all: that she'd lay down her life for her husband.

Chapter Thirty

I n the Duke of Matlock's luxurious library, the ball's music and chatter formed a distant buzz. At a mahogany sideboard, Jonas poured brandies for Richard and Cam, as well as himself. Cam leaned his elbow on the alabaster mantel. Richard lounged with his usual louche grace upon a leather sofa.

There was no trace of the acrimony that had marked his interactions with Jonas and Richard before Christmas. Cam had been so busy since, he'd had little chance to lament the break. Now that they were reunited, he realized how much he'd missed his friends.

He'd only reluctantly abandoned Pen in the ballroom. In fact, they nearly hadn't made tonight's party. Seeing her in that devilish becoming dress, he'd wanted to drag her upstairs, rip away the green silk and pound into her until she screamed his name.

But he was Camden Rothermere, Duke of Sedgemoor, model of behavior, arbiter of manners, and his recent actions had prompted enough talk. The last thing he wanted was the world saying that he was so besotted with his bride that he couldn't last five minutes at a public event before rushing her home.

Even if it was perilously close to the truth.

After a nervous beginning tonight, she seemed more at ease. Perhaps because Jonas and Sidonie had smoothed her way. Cam appreciated their efforts. Jonas could be a managing bugger, but once he'd pledged loyalty, he didn't waver.

Cam had restricted himself to one waltz with his wife and the promise of the supper dance. He'd even maintained an expression of polite interest while a line of scoundrels claimed her as a dance partner.

Eventually, because they were overdue for a conversation he didn't want overheard, he and his closest friends had retreated to this quiet room. Pen was safe with Genevieve and Sidonie and her brothers.

"I vow these melees get worse," Richard drawled. "I don't know why we came. Genevieve took one look at the crowd and nearly turned tail."

"It takes a lot for your wife to show scared," Jonas said with a wry twist of his lips. He passed the glasses across. A fire and a couple of lamps illuminated the elegant room. The flickering light softened his scars. These days, Cam hardly noticed them.

"Speaking of wives," Richard said, "Cam, we must raise a glass and wish you happy."

"You did that last night," he said.

Richard shrugged with characteristic nonchalance, although since his marriage, there was a substance to his presence that was new. He no longer tried to conceal his sharp brain, or the kind heart beneath his superlative tailoring. "When he forsakes bachelorhood, a man can't have too many good wishes."

Cam mustn't have hidden his wince fast enough, because Jonas sent him a sharp look. "All not bliss in Eden, my friend?"

"Jonas, leave the poor devil alone," Richard said. "A man's comrades shouldn't poke their noses in."

"They should if they can help," Jonas responded softly, watching Cam like a cat watched a mouse hole.

Cam shrugged and lied. Although after last night, it wasn't quite as much a lie as it had been. "Everything is fine."

"Didn't look fine yesterday." Jonas ignored Richard's glare. "The duchess was afraid to say a word and you acted like you'd made an appointment with the hangman."

"He's exaggerating," Richard said. "Don't listen to the officious blockhead."

"Officious?" Jonas raised his glass in Richard's direction. "Convey my compliments to Genevieve. She's doing wonders for your vocabulary."

Richard didn't smile. "If only Sidonie did wonders for your manners."

Cam sighed. "Pen doesn't deserve your criticism."

Jonas's gaze was unimpressed. "I'm sure she doesn't."

"You think I do," Cam said grimly, wondering why the devil he'd missed his friends. Although he gave Richard credit for trying to divert Jonas's awkward questions.

"You're the only other candidate." Jonas stood at the mantel's opposite end.

Cam frowned. "I'm not here for an inquisition."

"Yes, you are," Jonas said shortly.

"To be fair, Cam, given you flounced off in a huff because we weren't keen on Lady Marianne, then the next time we see you, it's with a different bride in tow, you must expect a few questions." Richard sipped his drink.

"Whose side are you on?" Cam snapped.

Richard took his time swallowing his brandy, then smiled. "Yours, although you probably don't believe me."

"I don't."

"Do you want some advice from an old married man?"

"No."

"All right." Richard drank some more brandy. "Damn fine drop, this. Must find out where Matlock buys it."

A prickly silence extended, until Cam could bear it no longer. Jonas had the patience of Job, but Richard's forbearance surprised and annoyed him.

Cam sighed and spoke less belligerently. "What's your advice?"

"I'm rather astonished to be counseling the font of all wisdom." Richard's mouth stretched in a reminiscent smile. "I remember Pen as a girl. She was plucky and impulsive and full of life."

"Yes, she was." Cam too found himself smiling.

Richard's smile faded. "That wasn't the woman I met last night."

"You knew her many years ago."

"You need to convince her that you won't come down in a hail of reproach if she steps out of line. She's clever; she'll soon work out what she can and can't do without upsetting the old biddies."

"You make me sound like a despot," Cam protested.

Richard shrugged. "You chose a woman of spirit. Or at least she will be, once she stops fretting about any whisper of disapproval that might inconvenience you. She's a Thorne. I can't imagine she's terrified on her own account. The Thornes drink recklessness with their mother's milk."

"Her reputation precedes her," Jonas said quietly.

Cam set down his glass with a click. "Shall I knock your teeth down your throat, chum?"

"Threaten all you like—not that there's much of my hide left to mark. I'm just speaking the truth we all know, Cam," Jonas responded calmly. "You always said you'd marry a woman of unsullied reputation. In fact, that was why you chose Lady Marianne, if I recall our discussion."

"Not entirely why," Cam said uncomfortably. Despite his apology, despite fate selecting another bride, he felt guilty about Marianne Seaton. He'd seen the sideways glances directed at her. Society interpreted Cam's marriage to Pen as a rejection of his first choice.

"She met your standards of beauty and intelligence. But if she'd had the slightest brush with scandal, you'd never have gone within ten miles of her."

"Then you arrive home with Penelope Thorne, who's kicked up her heels from Cairo to Stockholm," Richard said. "You can't blame us for being curious."

Cam sucked in a breath and realized that he had to tell his friends the truth. They knew him too well to believe the tale of falling madly in love. He straightened his shoulders. "Pen is the only woman I've proposed to."

Jonas looked unimpressed. "Obviously. You married her."

Richard already knew the sorry facts, or most of them. Cam had never confessed his unwelcome yen for nineteen-year-old Pen. "Well, yes, I proposed before the wedding. But nine years ago, I asked her to marry me."

"You've been engaged all this time?" Jonas looked astonished, either at Cam's delay in claiming his bride or, more likely, at discovering something he didn't already know. Jonas Merrick prided himself on his omniscience.

"Of course not." Cam disclosed one of his few failures. "She turned me down."

"Good for her," Richard interjected, toasting the absent Penelope. "Didn't I say she had backbone?"

"Penelope Thorne wouldn't marry you?" Jonas asked. "The family must have already been in financial straits. There's always been a whiff of notoriety about the Thornes. Superb soldiers in times of crisis. Nothing but trouble in peace."

Cam's lips tightened, although it was an opinion he'd grown up hearing. "Peter was my friend."

"I know the fellow was charming. Too charming for his own good. And they're a handsome family. You've caught yourself a beauty, Cam."

"Lady Marianne isn't exactly a pill," Richard protested.

"Not at all," Jonas said. "But even an old married man like me can tell that the new Duchess of Sedgemoor will turn heads. Once she gets some confidence and—forgive me saying so—buys some decent clothes, she'll be so spectacular you won't get near her for admiring swains, Cam."

Hell, that was the last thing Cam wanted. He'd decided young that he didn't want a duchess whom other men panted after. Yet here he was under the sway of a woman who set masculine hearts racing. His lifelong ambitions for a quiet domestic life were doomed.

He bit back a surge of jealousy to think of anyone else touching Pen, of her doing to another man what she'd so breathtakingly done to him last night. His stomach clenched tighter than a fist. Anyone trying to poach Pen away would face annihilation.

He paused in lifting his glass, wondering when he'd turned so primitive. Passions were dangerous, unless leashed. Yet he'd kill any bastard who came sniffing around his wife.

"Are you all right, Cam?" Richard asked.

Cam must be staring at his friends in a complete daze. He felt out of kilter, as if someone had chopped a couple of inches off one leg.

"Of course." They'd recognize the lie, but surely they'd never guess the reason behind it.

"You looked like you wanted to rip Jonas's guts out through his waistcoat."

Cam struggled to smile. "Pen is my wife. She merits my loyalty—and your respect."

Jonas frowned as that devilish mind whirred. "Of course she does."

Cam hadn't expected such ready agreement. "You'll like her when you know her."

"I'm sure I will."

This level of amiability verged on the fantastical. Cam scowled down his long nose at his friend. Unfortunately, Jonas was at least as tall so the withering stare didn't have its usual effect. "Are you being sarcastic?"

Jonas looked genuinely surprised. "Not at all. I'm delighted that you didn't marry Lady Marianne. I was against the match from the start. I hated to see you enter such a coldhearted arrangement."

Cam started to say that his match with Pen was just as coldhearted until something stopped him. Perhaps an inkling that Jonas waited for an open declaration of his feelings. Or lack of them.

"Pen will make a splendid duchess," Richard said peaceably from the sofa. "It's still a puzzle that she didn't marry you in the first place if the Thornes were in a mess."

"Are you both suggesting that she'd only marry me for worldly advantage?" Cam's tone bristled.

Richard regarded him disapprovingly. "You're deuced touchy, Cam. That's not what we mean. Anyway, you know that even if you were off your head with opium or inclined to slobber into your dinner, chits would still line up for the duchess's coronet."

"Thank you," Cam said grimly.

"You're welcome."

Jonas remained keen to explain himself, which didn't happen every day. Cam controlled his temper enough to listen. "All those years ago, her family must have pressured her to accept you. Was she in love with someone else?"

"Not that I know." Cam found the idea distasteful, although he couldn't say why. If Pen had been in love at nineteen, the affair hadn't had a happy outcome. "There was never any talk."

"There was talk on the Continent," Richard said soberly.

"It was purely talk," Cam said. He only realized after he spoke how his confidence hinted that he had reason to know. Heat tinged his cheeks and he sipped his brandy to hide his embarrassment. Pen's innocence was nobody else's business. He quickly changed the subject. Unfortunately the topic was almost as discomfiting. "Her mother nagged her to the point where Pen canceled her season and scarpered for Italy."

Jonas burst out laughing in one of those quicksilver changes of mood so characteristic of him. "Oh, Cam. You have my commiserations. But damn it, that's priceless."

Cam glowered at his friend. "I fail to see the funny side."

Jonas took an infuriatingly long time to stop laughing. "You would if you'd been subject to your perfection all these years. I'm liking your bride more and more."

"Cam, don't go all haughty on us." Richard rose and lifted the decanter. "Even I find it a tad amusing that the woman who met your criteria was so horrified at the prospect of marrying you that she fled the country."

"She escaped her mother," Cam said stiffly.

"I'm sure." Richard refilled Jonas's glass and turned to Cam. "None of this explains how you tied yourself to her after so long and after she'd led a fascinating life, never sparing you a thought."

Whereas Cam had devoted too much energy to a setback that shouldn't have mattered. He hid a sigh as he extended his empty glass toward Richard. He should be grateful to have friends brave enough to prick his arrogance. If only they knew that they were nowhere near as skilled at skewering him as his lovely bride.

"Peter asked me on his deathbed to escort Pen to England." He waited for some response, but he'd captured his friends' attention so completely that they remained silent. "I found her in the Alps and brought her back."

"Alone?" Richard replaced the decanter on the table.

"Yes." Cam paused. "Don't look like that. I kept my hands to myself."

"That must have been bloody difficult," Jonas said.

Cam bared his teeth at Jonas, who seemed remarkably taken with another man's wife. "She's my friend's sister. I'd grown up with her." He paused. "She didn't offer much encouragement."

As he returned to the sofa, Richard studied Cam. "That must have rankled."

Cam nodded before he thought better of it. He rushed into the rest of his story. "We pretended we were married and avoided places where anyone might recognize us."

"Until?" Jonas asked.

"Until the ship went down, I imagine," Richard said. "Good God, Cam, talk about destiny taking a hand."

"Pen wore the Rothermere signet. The people who fished us out assumed we were married. There was no way to keep the story quiet."

"So no passion-fueled wedding in an Italian chapel?" Jonas asked.

"No." Cam resented Jonas's amused superiority.

"No wonder you didn't wait to invite us to the wedding. I must admit to being rather...piqued." He paused. "I worried you'd taken our last discussion to heart."

Cam's laugh held no humor. "I was ready to shove your ill-considered opinions down your gullet. But not enough that in normal circumstances, I'd neglect to ask you to my wedding."

"That's good to know," Jonas said without a trace of irony. "I'm not so flush with people I trust that I can afford to lose one."

Cam's resentment faded. And his jealousy. Jonas had eyes for only one woman, and it wasn't Penelope Rothermere. "You spoke with good intentions—and your usual need to run the show."

"That's the pot calling the kettle black." Richard laughed and drained his glass. "Life has been adventurous lately, my friend."

"Indeed." Cam finished his own brandy.

Richard was his friend. So was Jonas. After the recent hiccups, he was relieved that the bonds they'd formed at Eton hadn't weakened.

It was time to return to Pen. Especially if Jonas was right about her becoming a focus for male attention.

Chapter Thirty-One

After the Matlock ball, Pen waited in Rothermere House's hall while the footman took her cloak. Cam glanced back at her from the doorway to his library.

She was always aware of his arresting male beauty, but something about the way the chandelier cast a sheen across his black hair and set his green eyes gleaming made her heart swoop. She became briefly the innocent girl who had pined after him, instead of the woman of twenty-eight who knew his body better than her own.

Especially after last night.

Anticipation sparked at the prospect of testing his resolve again. All day, their battle had been in abeyance, but his intent expression now hinted that he too contemplated pleasure.

Her eyelashes flickered down, not altogether with shyness. Guilt itched like ants crawling over her skin. In the ball's retiring room, she'd passed Sophie a message from Harry. A message whose contents marked Pen a conspirator against her husband's wishes.

The marble statues lining the hall stared down in disapproval. She hated those cold, white Romans with their supercilious expressions to rival Cam at his most ducal.

"Will that be all, Your Grace?" the footman asked.

"Thank you, Thomas," Cam answered. "Her Grace and I will have a brandy in the library before we go upstairs. You may finish for the night."

"Good night, Your Grace." The young man bowed and left.

Surprised, Pen turned to Cam. "Ladies don't drink brandy."

"You do." He paused. "Or at least you did."

"I wasn't a duchess then."

Weariness bracketed his mouth. Weariness or irritation. "Pen, if you want a brandy, bloody well have a brandy."

On the way home, she'd wondered whether she'd displeased him. He'd been quiet and he hadn't touched her. His bristling tension had convinced her to keep her distance. "I don't understand you, Cam."

He leaned one arm high on the door, making her overwhelmingly conscious of his lean, strong body. "Unfortunately I suspect that's true."

She made a frustrated gesture. "You've spent your life repairing the damage your parents left behind. Yet you encourage me to kick over the traces."

"My parents acted without honor." A smile lengthened his lips. "You're the most honorable person I know."

She was too astonished at the compliment to be pleased. She stared at him, mouth open, until she realized she must look half-witted. She snapped her jaw shut. "Thank you."

He stepped aside to let her pass. She paused in the center of the room. This was very much his territory, furnished in leather and gleaming dark wood. Pen took in the rows of leather-bound books, the shining scientific instruments, and the paintings on the walls. Her eyes focused on the magnificent Titian above the fireplace, the painting Cam had mentioned last night. Venus and Mars. Mars was clearly completely besotted. Lucky Venus, Pen thought sourly.

"You know, I might have been teasing last night, but that painting would look good in my apartments."

Behind her, the door closed with a finality that made her wonder whether Cam meant to chastise her for breaking some arcane social rule. Life in Italy had been much simpler.

"Bugger the Titian," he muttered.

She had a chance to turn with a gasp, then Cam grabbed her arms and his mouth crashed into hers.

Shock held her unmoving. When he raised his head, desperation glittered in his eyes. Heat all but steamed off him.

Oh, she was such a fool. His behavior in the carriage suddenly made sense. Relief flooded her. Relief and excitement.

He wasn't angry. He wanted her.

Beyond reason, by the look of him. The skin of his face stretched taut and his eyes shimmered with sensual purpose.

"Cam, what—" she managed to say before he swung her around and backed her against a bookcase.

"Don't stop me, Pen. For pity's sake, don't stop me." The hands on her arms clenched and unclenched in an involuntary caress and he breathed gustily as if he'd climbed a mountain instead of walked through his front door.

"I wasn't—"

"I've burned all night." His voice was raw and low. "You're lucky I didn't haul you into the Matlocks' garden and ravish you under the laburnum."

She choked on appalled laughter. "You'd have caused a sensation."

Cam was beyond amusement. "All day I've struggled to

keep my hands to myself. Then seeing you tonight, glittering like a queen, and knowing that you're mine; it's too much for mortal man to resist."

His desire thrilled her. She'd never seen him like this. He'd wanted her before. Of course he had. Even before church and state had blessed their couplings.

But this was a man losing control.

Hope sparked that at last she pierced his defenses, then crumbled to dust just as quickly. Staring into his feverish green eyes, she recognized that despite his agitation, she encroached no further into his soul than she ever had.

Roughly he twined one arm around her waist and jerked her against his hips. Through her skirts, she felt his hard power. This wasn't seduction. This was conquest.

Swift arousal weighted her belly, made her hot and needy. Her wriggling incited a guttural groan.

"You're audacious," he grated out, kissing a searing path up her neck, nipping at the places that he knew drove her to madness.

"I am," she admitted breathlessly, hooking her hands over his shoulders and feeling the friction of fine wool under her palms. "Shall we go upstairs?"

"No," he muttered, his breath in her ear stirring a liquid response. Clumsily he hitched up her skirts.

"Cam, we can't."

"Pen, we must," he groaned, and this time when he kissed her she responded, sucking his tongue deep into her mouth.

Demurs vanished under molten pleasure. Vaguely through her thundering heartbeat, she heard material ripping. She hoped it wasn't the only London dress that she almost liked.

Cam thrust his hand between her legs. When he found her core through the slit in her drawers, she decided that she'd happily sacrifice an entire wardrobe for this bliss.

"This is…revenge for last night, isn't it?" she choked against his lips.

"Precisely." His voice was even huskier than hers.

Before she worked out if he was joking, his tongue invaded her mouth and he penetrated her with one long finger. She jolted, bumping the bookcase.

He stroked hard and her muscles contracted. He swore softly, angled her up, and tore her drawers until they sagged in tatters around her ankles. With urgent purpose, he returned to her sleek passage. He found a place that set sensation clanging with the pure note of a hammer on gold.

She cried out in wonder. He kissed her again. Wet, succulent kisses that promised a mating without civilization or restraint.

When he finally lifted his mouth, she struggled to focus. Cam looked ferocious and determined, his jaw as hard as rock. As hard as the part of him pressing into her belly.

His musky scent was so powerful she felt drugged, lost in a narcotic haze of Cam. She sagged against the bookcase, grateful for its support. Her legs threatened to collapse.

"You want me," he growled.

She didn't know whether it was question or statement, although he had no reason to question her readiness. The glide of his fingers confirmed that she was primed.

"Yes, I want you," she forced through a throat that tightened along with the rest of her.

Her breath emerged in rhythmic sighs matching his incursions. Before long she was shaking and whimpering. She was almost there when abruptly he stopped.

"Cam?" she asked uncertainly.

"Hold my shoulders," he grunted, pinning her to the bookcase. His hands slid between them, releasing his trousers.

Stomach churning with longing, she firmed her grip.

With both hands, he grabbed her hips and lifted. To prevent a fall, her legs circled his thighs.

She released a soft cry of surprise at how defenseless she felt in this position. Then another cry when he shifted until she impaled herself upon him.

He buried his face in her shoulder. Her hands clutched his back, feeling his uneven breathing. His heat surrounded her, filled her. From this angle, she had no control over the depth or speed of his entry. The sensation verged on uncomfortable, however greedily her body clung to his. Another whimper escaped and she jiggled to adjust to the thickness inside her.

He nudged his hips up and the dizzying climb that had started when he'd used his hand flared into blinding light. She convulsed in his arms, digging her fingers into his coat as she sought some anchor in this reeling, brilliant world.

It cost him not to move. Through her peak, she felt his quivering rigidity. His back felt like a steel column, his shoulders like planks of oak.

Drifting down from that astounding climax, she opened her eyes to see deep lines bracketing his lips. He looked furious.

She smiled her satisfaction. She'd learned that look could denote something other than anger.

She let herself dangle in his arms. If he released her, she'd melt into a puddle on the extravagant carpet. She rested her cheek on his coat, hearing the fierce heartbeat under her ear. There was something breathtakingly decadent about the fact that they were both dressed—mostly.

"You're still fighting me," he said unsteadily.

She started, trying to force her sluggish brain to make sense of what she heard. Her head was too heavy to lift. Honestly, at this rate, he'd have to carry her upstairs. Or call Thomas to help. Which could be interesting. "What?"

"You're holding back." His voice was a bass rumble, vibrating against her cheek. His hands gripped her hips, holding her in place.

She muffled a weary laugh. "Don't be an idiot, Cam. You just sent me to the stars."

"It's not enough." She felt him inhale. What sweet intimacy to be close enough to count his every breath.

"I don't understand."

Except she did. Didn't she feel exactly the same when she stared into his eyes at the peak of intimacy and knew that he held himself separate?

How odd that he too felt the faint distance, minute but unmistakable. The fear of revealing her love always hovered, even when she was lost to pleasure.

"I'm deep inside you, deep enough to touch your heart, and I feel—" He broke off. She could imagine why. He didn't deal in emotions, especially his own. "I feel like you elude me."

"I'm right here." Except they both knew she wasn't.

"In body."

"That's enough." She shifted to ease the fullness. Her shoulder dislodged a book and sent it tumbling to the carpet with a dull thud.

"It's not." He sounded confused. And frustrated.

"Cam, you have me."

"Not completely," he said stubbornly and jerked his hips to confirm his claim.

Another cracked laugh. "Cam, you've got me against the blasted wall, for heaven's sake. Anyone who heard you would think you mad."

Except, most tragically, Penelope Rothermere.

It suddenly struck her that they both wanted the same thing. Access to the other's soul. Without risking their own vulnerabilities.

"I know what I mean," he persisted, shifting. Almost unwillingly, her exhausted body adjusted.

She crushed her face into his shirtfront, breathing his rich scent. His lips brushed the crown of her head. After such passion, the unexpected tenderness stabbed like a knife. Before she reminded herself that longing mustn't infect this moment, she released a soft, unhappy sigh.

The hands under her bottom hardened to bruising. She tightened her legs around his hips, feeling the slide of his trousers against her bare skin. The sensation was wildly erotic. Everything about this encounter was wildly erotic.

"Hold on, Penelope," he whispered.

He slid from her body, then slammed back. The thrust crashed her into the wall. Three more books toppled. That stretching sensation returned. And to her astonishment, a flicker of arousal.

Cam's slow withdrawal fired every nerve. He took her again. And again. One final rise and he went taut and still. With a rough groan, he pumped into her.

It turned out that she had more than a flicker left. Caught in the conflagration, all Pen could do was hold him and pray that she'd survive the ride. She felt pummeled by pleasure, stripped to essentials, re-created as Cam's creature.

She'd had no idea that the physical world encompassed such wonders. Or that the physical body could endure such extremes of delight. If she thought she'd yielded before, this sizzling connection proved that Cam could draw more from her. More reaction. More pleasure. More wildness.

More love.

He staggered and lost hold of her hips. Her feet slipped down and their bodies separated. She grabbed his shoulders. She had no hope of standing on her own.

"I hope Thomas went to bed," she said shakily, staring

at Cam and seeing what she expected. A man flushed with satisfaction, his gaze lazy, his clothing in disarray.

A man who still concealed his true self behind his eyes.

She still hardly believed what he'd said. They fought the same battle. After tonight, she recognized how cruel that struggle would become. Why was he so set on gaining her surrender? Was it about power? Pride?

Cam laughed softly. "I love to hear you cry out."

"I love to hear you grunt," she retorted.

"Come upstairs and I'll grunt some more."

As she straightened, her skirts slithered to her ankles. "I don't think I can walk."

Cam held her loosely by the waist. "Catch your breath."

Despite the declaration of war—for what else had that been?—they stood leaning into one another for a sweet interval. Gradually Pen's breathing settled, her awareness of something other than physical sensation returned.

"I'll get you that brandy." He kissed her briefly on the lips.

To save herself sinking into his arms and revealing exactly how besotted she was, she drew away and bent to collect the books that had cascaded around them at the heights of their passion.

"Cam?" she said in shock.

He turned from the side table where he poured their drinks. "Yes?"

Her voice shook as she extended a book toward him. "I wrote this."

"You did indeed," he said as if his ownership of one of her travel memoirs meant nothing. "And very good it was too. If you check the shelves, you'll see your other books as well."

Still holding the book, she slumped onto a chair. "I'm... surprised."

Damn him. What hope did she have of resisting? There was a poignant pleasure in knowing that he'd read and enjoyed words she'd written.

He brought her the brandy. "Let's drink to your talent."

He spoke so casually when she felt completely over-turned. And not just because of that headlong seduction. It was an effort to keep her voice light. "Which talent in particular?"

His brows arched. "Let's just say that the last half hour has given me a new appreciation for my library."

She met eyes alight with humor and found herself laugh-ing with an unfettered amusement that she hadn't felt since her aunt's death. Careless of the brandy, Cam drew her up into his arms as he laughed with her.

Briefly, despite this being the depths of night, sunlight warmed her world.

Chapter Thirty-Two

When Harry heard the carriage stop outside Aunt Isabel's house in a narrow street off Russell Square, his heart threatened to explode with excitement. He drew a deep breath of the dust-laden air and strained to hear Sophie's steps approaching the door.

Bang. Bang. Bang.

The triple knock signaled her arrival. She sounded impatient. Almost as impatient as he.

He flung open the door to see the dark, unmarked carriage and Pen's anxious face peering out the window. He waved to reassure her, before his attention focused on the veiled woman on the step.

Without speaking, he caught Sophie's wrist just above her short glove and dragged her into the hall. Under his fingers, her pulse pounded madly.

The slam of the door echoed through the unoccupied house like a gunshot. He tipped back her bonnet and flung away the veils concealing her beautiful face. Then he was kissing her and she was kissing him. The long, lonely weeks suddenly didn't matter.

His darling was here. He was alive again.

Three afternoons he'd waited since Pen had delivered his note. Three afternoons alone in this neglected house left empty for years while Aunt Isabel toured the Continent. In this middle-class neighborhood, nobody was likely to discover him with Sophie.

He kissed Sophie's lips, chin, cheeks, nose, brow. Hundreds of words tumbled out, boiling down to three essentials.

I love you.

I missed you.

Don't leave me.

He took far too long to realize that Sophie was crying. He caught her face between his hands. "Sweetheart, what is it?"

She sniffed and regarded him with swimming blue eyes. "I'm just so happy to see you. I thought James might leave me in that frozen wilderness until he drove up with Desborough and forced me into the chapel for the wedding."

"You said your brother wouldn't bully you."

"He's so set on this match. Desborough is coming to propose tomorrow."

Dread oozed down Harry's spine. "Hell."

She nodded. "If I say no, I'm afraid that James will send me away again."

"But your aunt has left Northumberland."

"There's always Alloway Chase."

He strove to lighten the atmosphere. "At least it's not in Northumberland."

Sophie didn't smile. "It may as well be. It's in the middle of the Yorkshire moors and my mother will watch me like a hawk." She stared at Harry as if he had every answer. If only he did.

"Can you put Desborough off?"

She shrugged unhappily. "Given that his suit is an open secret, any delay will make James suspicious."

Harry hated to see Sophie so defeated. He kissed her until she clung. By the time he'd returned to earth, she looked less distraught.

"Play for time." He seized her hand and stripped off the glove. He pressed a fervent kiss to her palm before leading her into the heavily curtained drawing room.

Sophie's spurt of hope faded. "It's only delaying the inevitable."

"Say you're considering the proposal favorably. It might make Leath less vigilant."

"If I marry Desborough, all is lost."

On a stage, the statement might sound melodramatic, but she spoke nothing less than the truth. His Sophie wasn't made to be his mistress. She deserved better than to become an adulterous wife.

"We've only got an hour," she said bleakly, slumping onto the chaise longue.

"I'd hoped for longer." Harry catalogued each fair feature. An hour? It seemed too cruel. Although only a lifetime would suffice. Even then, he'd feel cheated.

"It was difficult enough getting away from Lady Frencham's tea party. The duchess said she wanted to take me to her modiste." Sophie removed her second glove. "Although anyone with half a brain must realize that Her Grace hasn't been in London long enough to recommend a dressmaker."

From what he'd seen of Pen's drab ensembles, no girl of style would take up her offer. That gray monstrosity she'd worn at the Oldhavens' would frighten the horses.

The mention of clothing focused his attention on Sophie's costume. "Good God, is that a tent?"

Despite her turmoil, a broken giggle escaped. She untied

the toggles fastening the cloak. "Your sister lent it to me, as well as the bonnet and veil. But she's so much taller than I am."

"You look like you're drowning." If they only had an hour, he didn't want to spend it stewing over their tribulations. "I doubt your own mother would recognize you under all that material."

Gracefully Sophie slipped the cloak from her slender shoulders. In this cheerless room, her pink muslin gown was as fresh as cherry blossom. Harry could no longer bear to keep his distance. In two paces, he was on his knees beside the chaise, her hands in his. "Now you look like my girl."

"Your sister is wonderful." Her sweet, brief kiss made his heart caper. "She looks like you."

"Poor thing."

Sophie giggled again. He was pleased to see the back of her tragic air.

"Stop fishing for compliments." The amusement drained from her expression. "She's very good to help us. I can't imagine her husband approves. Last night at the opera, James and Sedgemoor glared at each other like a pair of snarling lions."

Harry sighed. "My sister couldn't have married anyone less likely to raise me in your brother's favor."

Sophie's hands tightened. "It's so unfair that Uncle Neville's wickedness has blackened anyone called Fairbrother. Especially as I never liked him and James positively despised him."

"You know how society works, Sophie. People still talk about Sedgemoor's parents, and he's always been a model of propriety."

"Harry?" Sophie asked uncertainly. "What are we going to do?"

He suspected she wanted him to come up with a long-term solution. Unfortunately, he hadn't found one yet. "Pen's given me a key for this house. Night or day, I can meet you here."

Sophie looked no happier. "James watches me."

"He'll grant you more freedom if you agree to marry Desborough."

Sophie wrenched her hands from his and lurched to her feet. "I can't marry Desborough. Not when I love you. How can you ask it?"

Harry stood and swept her into his arms, feeling how she trembled. "I'm not asking it."

"Then you want me to lie?"

He growled low in his throat. "Once we're married, there will be no more hiding, no more secrets."

"I hate it too," she whispered, nestling into him in a way that made his heart expand with pride. How had this glorious creature come to love him? He wasn't worthy, although nothing in heaven or hell could stop him loving her.

"We can't go on like this. It's tearing us both to pieces."

Tears filled her eyes. "And our hour must be nearly over. I'm so lonely without you."

"Me too," he said glumly, tightening his embrace and kissing her.

Sophie's lips were so soft and her sighs so sweet that minutes went by before Harry recalled that he had something important to say. And not much time to say it. He smiled into her flushed face. She looked like she floated in a blissful dream.

He heard a church clock in the distance strike the hour. "Sophie, we must make plans. If Desborough proposes, say you don't want to rush things with him."

She gripped his waist as if resisting their parting. He

prayed this separation would be brief. "I *don't* want to rush things with him."

"Well, that's good," Harry said with a short laugh. He kissed her quickly, but withdrew before heat engulfed him.

She looked displeased. "Kiss me again."

"I dare not. This is an empty house and that chaise longue fills my head with naughty thoughts."

"I don't mind." Her voice wobbled. "Harry, I don't want to go."

"I don't want you to go. But you must." Very gently, he wrapped her in the voluminous cloak and replaced her bonnet, arranging the veils. "Pen's outside." He'd heard the rattle of the carriage a few minutes ago.

"I know," Sophie said miserably.

"Be brave, my love." He kissed her hands tenderly then passed her the gloves. "I swear we'll find a solution."

"I hope so." He couldn't see her expression, but he heard how emotion thickened her voice. "Because, Harry Thorne, you've been reckless with my heart."

"Never," he said in shock.

Her tone hinted that she smiled through tears. "You've made me fall so deeply in love that I can't live without you."

"Oh, Sophie…" His voice wasn't much steadier than hers.

She whirled away and rushed down the hall. He didn't follow. Instead he stood in the empty room and listened to the door click shut.

Chapter Thirty-Three

B ad blood will always out, you know."

The low, insinuating female voice reached Pen on her return to the crowded ballroom from the ladies' retiring room. Shock more than curiosity made her pause. The tone was repellently malevolent. Just hearing it made her want a thorough wash.

What on earth could engender such spite?

A palm tree concealed the speaker—Lady Frencham's soiree had a tropical theme—so Pen had no idea who she was. Even after a fortnight in London society, she had difficulty identifying people. Although if she'd heard that nasty voice before, surely she'd remember it.

A second woman replied before Pen could do the decent thing and move out of earshot. "He's done a grand job of convincing the world to forget his slut of a mother. I'd mention his father, but nobody knows who that is. There are two likely candidates. But given the late duchess's depravity, hundreds more could have sired him."

The late duchess? Although no names had been mentioned, a sick foreboding coiled in Pen's belly.

"He gives himself such airs that one might almost believe him the gentleman he apes. Almost."

"Until he turned up with that Thorne strumpet."

Dear Lord, they *were* talking about Cam. And her.

Horror kept Pen trapped beside the palm tree. Was this what everyone thought?

She flattened a trembling hand against the wall and told herself to leave. The proverb about eavesdroppers hearing no good of themselves came to mind. That clearly counted double for hearing no good of those one loved.

"A marriage in Italy? I for one don't believe a word of it. Don't tell me she wasn't sharing his bed. After the ship-wreck, the game was up, so they married in haste. I see trouble already. They act more like strangers than newlyweds. There's more Rothermere scandal ahead, my dear. That hussy Penelope Thorne won't limit herself to one man. And Sedgemoor will tire of her soon enough and seek entertainment elsewhere. It's in the family line, isn't it?"

Humiliated color seared Pen's cheeks. The witch's remarks contained enough truth to cut. She and Cam had struggled so hard to contain any gossip about their wedding. She supposed it was inevitable that they'd failed. But this squalid meanness nauseated her.

"I heard they were at it like rabbits even before she went abroad." Pen wouldn't have believed that the first speaker's voice could become more waspish, but it did. "Everyone knows why she left England before her debut. You mark my words. There's a Thorne bastard with Rothermere eyes somewhere in France or Italy. I wouldn't be surprised if there's talk in a few years of them adopting some obscure cousin's child that nobody's heard of. A bastard spawning another bastard. It would be amusing if it wasn't such a blow to society's standards. Heaven knows, one pays respect to the title when one meets the villain face to face, but it becomes tiresome pretending to honor a mongrel, whatever his noble pretensions."

Pen could take it no longer. She forgot every promise she'd made never to shame Cam. She didn't care that the ballroom was packed with observers. Such lies couldn't go unchallenged. Drawing herself up to her full height, she sailed around the palm tree to accost the women.

"Just as it becomes tiresome to follow the dictates of good manners," she snapped, unfolding her fan in a single movement and waving it as though the air reeked in the vicinity of these two old cats.

To her surprise, she recognized both of them. They'd fawned over her, angling without subtlety for invitations to Fentonwyck.

"Your Grace..." Mrs. Combe-Browne rose and started a curtsy before recalling that if Pen had overheard them, the gesture was misplaced. Instead she staggered like she'd had too much to drink before landing so awkwardly on her spindly chair that she nearly tumbled to the floor. Pen felt no urge to smile.

"Ladies." Pen focused a hostile eye on the first speaker, Lady Phillips, a woman notorious as the late Duke of Kent's mistress. "Although I use the term advisedly."

"Your Grace!" the woman protested. "I have no idea what prompts such discourtesy."

Pen glared. "Don't you?"

Lady Phillips was less easily rattled than her companion. Her eyes narrowed as she stood. "Were you eavesdropping on a private conversation?"

"No conversation audible from the other side of the room counts as private." Pen matched tone to actions by closing her fan with a contempt that the old bat couldn't miss. "How ironic that a woman of your blemished reputation sees fit to malign the finest man in England."

Lady Phillips didn't retreat, although Mrs. Combe-Browne whimpered like a sick piglet and huddled into her chair as if trying to melt into the wall. "A noble title does not of itself denote honor. Nor in this case breeding."

Pen stepped forward. Unfortunately Lady Phillips was almost as tall and twice her weight. This might be like confronting a bad-tempered rhino, but nothing could calm Pen's outrage. How dare this raddled hag insult Cam?

"Perhaps a noble title doesn't. But character and honesty and heart do. And my husband has those in abundance. If courage and intelligence and generosity form no part of a gentleman's character, he's no gentleman, whatever his parents got up to. And that counts for ladies too."

"Well, I never!" Mrs. Combe-Browne bleated behind her friend.

"You never should have, either of you," Pen snapped. "My husband is a man of influence."

Lady Phillips sneered. "You dare to threaten me, you trumped-up whore? Don't imagine your brazen antics across the Channel are any secret."

Pen squared her shoulders, ready to do battle, but before she could engage, Cam spoke behind her. Usually she was preternaturally aware of his presence. It was one of the burdens of loving him. But she'd been so furious, nothing else had registered.

"That's quite enough, Lady Phillips," Cam said in an icy voice.

Pen shivered. She hated that tone. The few times Cam had used it on her, it had scraped the flesh off her bones. She could see that he was seething. Perhaps, she thought with a weight settling in her belly, he was angrier with Pen than with Lady Phillips and her friend. They only repeated rumors that the gossips had spread before and would embroider in the future. Whereas Pen was obliged to uphold the Rothermere name.

She knew that she'd made a horrible *faux pas*. In society, one rose above insults. Hadn't Cam and Richard tried all their lives to prove that the sad old stories had no power? Not that anyone believed that, including Cam and Richard.

At Cam's reprimand, the woman paled. "Your Grace, I'm sure you misunderstand."

Pen should have realized that while the Duchess of Sedgemoor wouldn't foil this tough old vulture, the duke would put her in her place.

"I'm sure I don't, Lady Phillips, Mrs. Combe-Browne," Cam responded in a clipped voice.

"I didn't—" Mrs. Combe-Browne said shakily.

Whatever defense she'd meant to mount evaporated under Cam's frigid stare. She shrank into herself and looked likely to burst into tears.

Pen was dismayed to notice that this fraught encounter stirred general interest. She cursed her impulsive Thorne blood. She wasn't born to be a duchess, cool and composed under social fire. And she had a horrid suspicion that Cam reached the same conclusion, despite her efforts to make him proud.

"Your Grace, you've fallen in with bad company." Lady Hillbrook approached to take her arm. "Come, my husband is eager to discuss your brilliant article in last month's *Blackwood's Magazine*. He wants your advice on acquiring artifacts from that excavation in Messina that you describe in such fascinating detail."

Although she couldn't imagine that a reminder of her unfeminine interest in scholarship would mollify Lady

Phillips, Pen turned to Lady Hillbrook. "I'd be delighted." The huskiness in her voice betrayed her gratitude.

Cam stared at her, green eyes opaque. Of course, he'd delay a lecture until they were alone. They'd caused enough talk. His anger would likely take the path of coldness rather than a blistering tirade. He couldn't be nearly as disappointed in her as she was in herself. Harpies like Lady Phillips and Mrs. Combe-Browne weren't worth fighting. Their poison was so deeply rooted that nothing would excise it.

"Sidonie, my wife and I are leaving. Jonas can talk antiquities some other time." Like his voice, Cam's expression was neutral. He was a master at hiding his feelings. From earliest boyhood, he'd had to be.

He extended his hand. Pen swallowed what felt like a boulder stuck in her throat and told herself she could survive this. She'd survived refusing the proposal she'd dreamed of all her life. She'd survived nine years without him. She'd survived his company in the Alps and the travesty of their marriage. She'd even survived pretending that she felt nothing but physical pleasure when he'd shared her bed.

Compared to what she'd been through, tonight was a minor bump in a union that would prove rockier yet.

She lifted her chin, determined to conceal every scrap of vulnerability from the hungry predators otherwise called polite society. She accepted Cam's hand. The heat of his skin radiated through their gloves.

"Your Grace—" Lady Phillips started in a peremptory tone.

Cam's glance would wither apples on the branch. His bow was a masterpiece of disdain. "Good evening, my lady."

"Thank you, Lady Hillbrook," Pen murmured.

Sidonie smiled without reserve. "I'll call tomorrow."

"Please do."

To her amazement, Sidonie kissed her cheek. The gesture of support bolstered Pen's failing courage.

Under ranks of avid eyes, Cam tucked Pen's hand into the crook of his elbow and at a stately pace that was a mark of defiance, he led her toward the doors. The musicians scratched away at an ecossaise, but hardly anyone danced. Instead the guests craned their necks to observe the Duke and Duchess of Sedgemoor.

Cam's muscles were rigid. The man whose arm she held burned with deep emotion. Pen didn't need to be especially perceptive to recognize anger.

Inside their carriage, Pen battled to suck air into starved lungs, but every second's delay only tightened her nerves. "I'm sorry—"

He raised his hand. His other hand, much to her surprise, still curled around hers. "Wait until we're home, Pen."

Apprehension clawed at her, but she supposed that if he intended a full-scale row, he'd want time and privacy. His silence alarmed her more than censure would.

Pen slumped beside her husband and wished she'd had the sense to keep her mouth shut. But it was too late for regrets. She'd said what she'd said. Cam had heard. Sidonie had heard. She had a sneaking suspicion that everyone in that packed ballroom adorned with bedraggled palm trees had heard. Those who hadn't heard would soon receive an accounting of the duchess bearding the ton's most vicious gossips.

An accounting only likely to grow more flamboyant in the telling.

Her sigh escaped before she remembered to muffle it. To her surprise, Cam's grip firmed.

Far too quickly, Pen faced Cam in the library where a few nights ago, they'd shared such blazing passion. She tried not to remember how he'd pounded into her. But it was impossible. The experience had marked her soul. She'd treasure it until the day she died.

"Cam, I can't tell you how sorry I am," she began, still clinging to his hand. Silly to find that innocent contact so affecting after the wanton things they'd done to each other.

He stood close, blocking her view of everything but him. What was new? Since she was a little girl, she'd only ever seen him.

"You're sorry?" His voice sounded choked.

Oh, no, he really was livid. She braced for temper and closed her eyes.

"Are you afraid?" he asked, still in that raw voice.

She swallowed to moisten a mouth dry with terror. And lied. "Of course not."

"You looked like you weren't afraid of anything when you told that cow Lady Phillips to shut her mouth."

"She made me so angry." Pen spoke quickly before her courage evaporated. "I know I said I'd behave. I know I said I'd do my best to be a proper duchess. But she was so mean."

"And you couldn't bear to hear her deriding me."

"No." She opened her eyes, dreading what she'd find.

There was a light in Cam's eyes that she'd never seen before. He raised his hand to cup her face. "Nobody's ever defended me like that. You were magnificent."

Chapter Thirty-Four

"My darling, you took such a risk coming here." In the drawing room of the Russell Square house, Harry flung his arms around Sophie. Outside, everything was quiet. This wasn't an area that bustled after dark.

"I know." Trembling with innocent fervor, she pressed against him. "If my brother finds out where I am, he won't send me to Northumberland, he'll send me to the moon."

"When I got your message, I couldn't believe it." Harry kissed her softly, then returned to taste her more thoroughly. Her sweet, floral scent made him feel like he'd overindulged in champagne.

"I couldn't stay away." Sophie was supposedly at a lecture at the British Museum with a party of friends. At least so she'd told her brother. She'd cried off at the last minute and made her way to this house.

He stared into her face. Guilt darkened her lovely eyes.

"The lies make you feel bad."

Her jaw firmed. "I'd feel worse if I didn't see you. Since I promised to consider Desborough's proposal with a view to acceptance, James hasn't been nearly so watchful."

"Which makes you feel worse."

A hint of her delightful smile curved her pink lips. Pink lips he wanted to spend an eternity kissing. These stolen meetings wore on him too. "I'm hopeless, aren't I? I pursue a romantic intrigue, but I can't bear secrets. Yet secrets are at the core of an intrigue."

Harry laughed, although only the lowest worm in creation would tarnish this girl's honesty. Then he asked the question that always made him want to smash his fist into the wall. "How long do we have?"

She stroked his face. "A couple of hours."

"I've got things to tell you." He caught her hand and brought it to his lips. If she kept touching him, any hope of sensible discussion would vanish like dew in sunlight. Or perhaps, given his heated reaction, like paper in fire.

"Talk later. I want to kiss you."

He smiled at her, dazzled by her beauty and ardor. "Sweetheart, if I kiss you, I'll forget I'm a gentleman."

"I'll remind you."

He regarded her with a cynical eye. "I don't trust you."

"Of course you do." She pouted theatrically.

The sight of those rosebud lips pursing heightened his arousal. He stifled a groan. He must return Sophie to her brother's house a virgin or know himself a blackguard.

Love could be hell.

He gave in, as he was always going to, and kissed her. Her mouth opened immediately. Because she'd teased, he'd expected her kisses to tease too. But she responded with wild abandon.

He had enough trouble controlling himself when she was playful. When she acted like the uninhibited woman who haunted his dreams and left him waking ashamed and needy, his principles collapsed.

He tore his lips from hers. "Sophie—" he protested, hands clenching in her blue silk dress.

"Don't stop," she begged, ripping clumsily at his neck-cloth.

He went rigid. All over. And told himself to stop before he did something irrevocable.

Since those torrid moments in that woodland glade, he'd struggled to keep their physical interactions light. That day, the dangers of unrestrained desire had been agonizingly apparent. The problem was that he didn't feel light with her. He felt like significance weighted every moment.

But Sophie Fairbrother was pure and good. No man had the right to sully her outside the bonds of marriage. Harry must hold back even if he disintegrated into a million smoking embers.

He grabbed her hands. "Sophie, no."

Her expression was urgent. "I think about you all the time. I think about the things you've done to me. I think..." She licked her lips and he closed his eyes and prayed for strength. "I think about the things I'd like you to do."

"Darling—"

"You want to do more. I know you do."

"We can't," he said in despair, stroking her wrists until she pulled free.

"We can." She tugged his neckcloth off and tossed it over a chair.

God give him strength. She intended seduction. Then where would they be? Leath would want his guts for garters. And rightly so. "Sophie, you'll be ruined."

Damn it, he should pack her into a hackney right now and send her back to Leath House where she was safe from over-excitable young men. But still he stood, breathing her scent as though it kept him alive.

"I don't care," she said stubbornly, tearing at his waist-coat buttons. Whatever happened tonight, he'd emerge looking like he'd fought a bear single-handed. "Tonight we have time."

"How do you know?" He tried to resurrect the teasing, but the question emerged as a strangled yelp.

"I don't," she snapped, sounding frustrated and so desperate, his bones dissolved with longing. At this rate, he didn't have a hope in Hades of resisting.

"Sophie, I can't deflower the Marquess of Leath's sister."

To his surprise, a knowing smile curved her lips. Blazing sensation incinerated scruples when she placed her hand on the front of his trousers. "If you mean you're incapable of deflowering Leath's sister, I doubt that's true."

He choked and despite every dictate of the code he followed, tilted his hips to increase the glorious pressure. "What the devil is a man to do with you, Sophie? I thought you'd be nervous."

Lashes flickering, she glanced down to where she touched him. She didn't look frightened. She looked like she anticipated a wonderful treat. Harry's blood pounded hard and heavy as though he'd swallowed a big, noisy drum. Whatever his head commanded, his body prepared for pleasure.

She curled her hand around him. "You'll think me a wanton."

"I think you're beautiful. You know that." His voice lowered to a growl. "And if you don't stop touching me, you'll find you've taken on more than you can handle, my girl."

He grabbed her hand and, ignoring the howling protest of the devil who conspired against every ounce of goodness, he pulled her away. Then he released her. Even holding her hand threatened his resolve.

When he caught the purposeful glint in her blue eyes,

he was smart enough to be nervous. In fact, he was bloody terrified.

Because of course, Sophie had an ally. The devil inside Harry that had slavered after her from the first.

She seized the lapels of his coat and pulled him closer. "Let me do what I want, Harry."

The innocence in her eyes made her brazen statement more provocative. He tried to fight, but they both knew that his honor hung by the slimmest thread. "I'm trying to protect you," he grated.

"I know you are." She stared at him like he was Sir Galahad complete with Holy Grail. An impression that sat oddly with the inferno of desire blinding him to everything but Sophie.

"Then let me keep you safe," he said on a frantic plea.

"I'm safe with you." She placed her hand on his shirt, where his heart thundered with love for her.

He shook his head. "No. You're not."

She didn't seem to hear. Instead her hand crushed the fine material as she brought him closer. He kissed her, not holding back for the first time since that close call in Wiltshire. He caught her sweet face between his palms and plundered her mouth, sliding his tongue between her lips in imitation of the act he burned to complete. He finally gave himself permission to touch her the way he'd imagined. He shook with the bliss of it.

Even now, he held back from undressing her. Until she stole the initiative. Unsteadily she shoved her bodice down. He caught her breasts as they tumbled forward. He pressed and stroked and kissed the impudent tips. She tasted like flowery honey and her perfume filled the air like a musky garden.

He was past denying her. This moment had been ordained

from the instant he'd caught her crying in the moonlight. He couldn't fight his desire. Not when her desire was just as ravenous.

The tension leached from him. Frantic nips and licks and kisses steadied to leisurely exploration. He even found the control to unlace her gown without tearing the delicate material.

He wasn't ashamed of what he did. With love this powerful, there was no sin, however the world viewed what happened.

"Let me undress you, darling," he whispered between kisses on her satiny neck.

She raised her arms like a small girl. Tenderness flooded his heart. Tenderness that made his hands shake as he pulled her gown over her head and laid it carefully on the chair.

She took less trouble with his coat. It crumpled onto the floor. She was impatient. But like him, her wildness gradually faded and in its place, a glowing calm lit her eyes to sapphire.

Carefully he unfastened her corset. After he'd slipped it off, he pulled her shift over her head.

She stood naked, every inch of pale, perfect skin flushed with gold from the fire he'd lit before her arrival. Her breasts were round and firm, crowned with rose-pink nipples. The firelight created mysterious shadows around her nest of dark blond curls.

He stepped back and drank in the sight. The emotions flooding him were complex, difficult to define. Joy. Desire. Those went without saying. But there was also the heady realization that he claimed this girl. After tonight, they were forever linked.

From the first, he'd pledged himself to her. But tonight when he introduced her to sensual pleasure—dear God, let him be adequate to the task—the promise went deeper than the ocean.

She was his and he was hers.

Somewhere in all the solemn eternities filling his heart lurked gratified satisfaction. That Harry Thorne stood with Sophie Fairbrother. That Harry Thorne had the privilege of touching her.

Her brilliant eyes met his and he knew that she made the same vows. When she slid the pins from her hair, her grace made his heart falter to a besotted stop. The shining mane cascaded around her bare shoulders, playing hide and seek with her breasts.

Harry swallowed to shift the emotion jamming his throat. "You're so beautiful."

Her self-confident smile set his soul singing. He caught a glimpse of the striking woman she'd become. "You're wearing too many clothes."

With a carelessness in marked contrast to his fussing over Sophie, he kicked off his shoes and ripped away shirt and trousers, casting them wherever they fell.

Slowly he moved forward. Outside, London continued on its busy, ruthless, crowded way. Inside this room, a golden bubble of love enclosed him with Sophie.

He buried his hands in her hair and tipped her face up. Her lips parted and her eyes sparked with excitement.

In a daze, Pen let Cam lead her up the elaborate marble staircase. None of this made sense. She'd been so convinced he was furious. Yet he'd just called her magnificent. Not only that, he'd kissed her so sweetly, if she wasn't careful, she'd persuade herself that he loved her.

When of course he didn't.

She needed to remember that. Something almost impossible when he stared at her as if she'd brought him the sun for his lantern.

He swung her bedroom door open and drew her inside, pausing on the threshold for another heart-stopping kiss. She responded helplessly. How could she do otherwise? She loved him and somewhere during this topsy-turvy night, he'd lowered his barriers against her. She didn't dare put a name to his feelings, but this untrammeled passion felt different. Less calculated. Less a triumph of skill over emotion.

Glittering green eyes transfixed her. His voice emerged as a hungry growl. "No games tonight, Pen."

"I don't—" she began, although she knew exactly what he meant.

He kissed her again, sucking her lower lip into his mouth and flicking it with his tongue. Arousal spiked. The blatantly earthy kiss set her aflame.

"Let's start again, as two people who desire each other." His smile conveyed a warmth that she hadn't realized until now had been absent. "Hell, as two people who like each other."

"I've always liked you, Cam." What a coward she was. She used his lukewarm word when lukewarm was as far from her feelings as London was from Tahiti.

"I wanted to cheer tonight when you told that old cat to go to blazes."

"I thought you'd hate me for making a scene."

"I've never felt so proud. If you could have seen yourself, fire all but shot from your eyes. If you weren't on my side, I'd have been quaking in my boots."

She smiled. "Nothing frightens you."

An unreadable expression crossed his face as he drew her toward the center of the room. "You do."

She touched his face. Usually, fearing she'd betray

herself, she curtailed affectionate gestures. "Yet you say you like me."

"I'm damned glad you married me."

He didn't love her. But tonight he committed to her in a way that he never had. She should be satisfied.

"So am I." She was astonished to realize that she meant it.

He was surprised too. "Are you?"

She felt like she stood naked in sunlight. The radiating heat reached to her bones, thawing the chill in her heart. "I meant what I said. You're an exceptional man and I'm proud to be your wife."

"Darling—" He sounded like her declaration touched him beyond words.

She decided to rescue him. He wasn't accustomed to expressing emotion, but it was clear that he pledged his loyalty and affection. It wasn't enough, but it was a lot. "Now take me to bed."

He looked happier. She'd long ago realized that sensuality offered him an escape from self-containment. On a physical level, he held nothing back. His soul had always been the closed kingdom.

But staring into his eyes, she was astonished to see that was no longer true. Tonight the gates to his deepest heart lay open. He trusted her. For Camden Rothermere, that was as close as he'd ever venture to love.

Chapter Thirty-Five

S upporting Sophie's back with spread hands, Harry gently lowered her onto the chaise longue. His conscience gave one last squeak at the idea of debauching the Marquess of Leath's sister in his aunt's house and with his sister's unknowing connivance. But the warm, lithe reality of Sophie beggared caution.

Sophie's arms twined around his neck and she covered his face and neck and shoulders with enthusiastic kisses. Harry followed her down, sliding between her legs. She wriggled, brushing him with her mound. The feathery touch threatened to undo him. He gritted his teeth and prayed for control. This was her first time and he wanted her to enjoy it.

"Sophie, easy now," he gasped as she tilted her hips in invitation. "This can be uncomfortable if you've never done it before."

"It doesn't feel uncomfortable," she said and, God help him, curled her bare legs around him until her feet caressed the backs of his thighs.

Seeing her—flushed, aroused, excited—sent good intentions flying. "Do you know what's going to happen?"

"Yes. My governess was a widow who thought girls shouldn't be kept ignorant." Her soft laugh set off vibrations that added another layer to Harry's torment. "She made me promise never to tell my brother."

"I can imagine. What did she say?"

He waited for Sophie to repeat the accepted advice to blue-blooded young women approaching marriage. About obedience and pain and procreation.

"She said that if I loved the man and he loved me and we were kind and patient with each other, nature would work its magic."

Shock made Harry rear up. He stared at the gorgeous creature beneath him. "Your brother should have paid her double."

Their mouths molded together. When he raised his head, he heard her unsteady breathing. "Now touch me," she whispered.

He didn't succumb, whatever frantic approval his cock sent to his blood-starved brain. "Are you sure?"

Laughter lit her face, but profound emotion underlay the humor. "Harry, I'm naked in your arms. That means I've surrendered."

The gleam in her eyes was irresistible. "All hail the victor."

When she stretched up to kiss him, he couldn't hold back. He'd wanted her so long.

He stroked her. Now she was naked, it felt like exploring a new country of gentle hills and valleys and plains. He concentrated on sensitive regions. Behind her knees. Her sweet, beaded nipples. Her nape. Deliberately he didn't touch her sex, although her female scent made him shake with need.

He kissed the tip of her breast, then drew it between his lips, hearing her sigh of pleasure. He rolled the other nipple between his fingers.

She shifted restlessly. "Oh, Harry..."

His tongue teased her nipple as his hands drifted down her flanks to her waist and the alluring flare of her hips. Finally, unable to wait, he slipped his hand between her legs. He stroked the satiny folds, finding the place that made her gasp and tremble. Taking encouragement, he touched her over and over until she cried out and gushed over his fingers. When he raised his head, her eyes were dark and her face was flushed. Her parted lips were full and red.

"Sophie?"

She blinked as if returning from far away. "I liked that." Her slender throat worked as she swallowed. "Can you do it again?"

Triumph surged. "Shall I try?"

Her flush became more hectic. "Harry, I feel...empty without you."

Immediately he understood. Hunger vied with his over-whelming need to cherish her. For all her vitality and eager-ness, she seemed fragile. "I don't want to hurt you."

She pressed so close to where he wanted her. Every time she moved, he struggled not to penetrate her. "I want you."

Rapidly he reached a point where he needed to take the final step in this dance or leave the house. Given his state of undress, that would give the good residents of Russell Square something to talk about.

Very gently, he slid one finger into her. His belly con-tracted at how tight she was. He stroked her deep, feeling her clench. He used two fingers, making her pant for air. She was sleek and wet and her scent sharpened with need.

He stroked her until she quaked under the intimate caress,

then he withdrew and propped himself above her. She raised her knees and tilted her chin with a defiant gesture that was so familiar, so beloved, that his pounding heart skipped a beat. Still, careful of her innocence, he eased forward. He inched inside until she'd accepted the head completely. She quivered and dug her fingers into his arms.

He kissed her until she relaxed. He pushed further. She breathed in gusts. A line appeared between her fine blond eyebrows.

"Should I stop?" he grated.

She shook her head and he felt her brace. Her tightening body blasted him with pleasure. "You'll split in two if you stay this rigid."

"This isn't very...nice." She closed her eyes on a wince.

"Sophie, I can stop." He wasn't sure he could. But he'd try. Dear heaven, he'd try. His carnal nature yelped denial at the prospect of chaste adoration. Having touched her body and witnessed her pleasure, it seemed the direst punishment.

"Don't...stop." To back up that choked command, she angled her hips, drawing him deeper.

"I must." Sweat covered his skin and his muscles ached. His teeth must be ground to powder.

"No." She clasped his buttocks. Her touch made him shake.

"Sophie, I'm sorry," he muttered in a mixture of despair and unworthy pleasure. "I'm so sorry."

On a deep groan, he thrust forward. She jolted at the invasion and released a soft cry. He closed his eyes and basked in heavenly completion. He felt part of her. They were united in a way that extended beyond words. No man could sunder them now.

He lowered, supporting his weight on his hands. Nuzzling her cheek, he pressed his chest into her breasts. She remained still and silent. He told himself to retreat. But he'd exhausted control. Instead, he stretched above Sophie in delight and self-hatred, and wondered despairingly whether she'd ever forgive him.

She moved. She probably wanted to shove him away and order him never to touch her again. He couldn't blame her. The fact that it was good—beyond good—for Harry was irrelevant. Or at least so he told himself.

Then unbelievably, she slid her arms around his back. And Harry, who thought he couldn't love this girl more, broke into a whole new universe of love. "My darling—" he sighed against the curve of her neck.

Not satisfied with that one astoundingly generous act, she shifted, settling him deeper. Heat speared him. He stared down at her. "I love you, Sophie."

She was pale and still didn't look like she enjoyed herself, but she summoned a smile. Not her most convincing effort, but he appreciated her trying. "I love you, Harry."

He pulled away then pushed in. She hid a wince.

"I'm hurting you."

"A little, but it's better than it was." She tightened her grip on his back as though afraid he meant to leave.

As if he could. He kept up the gentle undulation. It gave him blazing pleasure. Surely it must work on her. But still she lay like a frozen doll.

He was about to give up and spill himself on her belly when she released a sob that sounded more like delight than pain. He kissed her and this time she responded with a hint of enthusiasm. When he moved, she clenched in welcome.

With the next thrust, she rose to meet him and joy exploded behind his eyes like victory fireworks. She released a long moan that was a plea for more.

At last.

He couldn't hold on much longer. Her eyes closed. Her features were strained. She started to shudder. Her nails scraped his back. The sting seared like flame.

On a massive groan, he pumped hard and furious, sealing their union.

Chapter Thirty-Six

Cam stepped closer to Pen and cradled her marvelous face between his hands. There was such character there. Beauty of course, but much more. Intelligence. Generosity. Strength. She'd been an exceptional child and she'd grown into an exceptional woman. The right woman for him. Too good for him, by God, but he wouldn't complain to destiny about that.

Nine years ago, he'd known himself better than he'd realized. Proposing to Penelope Thorne was the smartest thing he'd ever done.

His earliest memories were of lies and conflict and his parents' selfishness. In the perpetual war between the late duke and duchess, their child's welfare hadn't counted for a farthing. Cam had learned young that people deceived and betrayed and destroyed. As he'd grown up, a few outstanding men like Richard and Simon, and later Jonas, had earned his friendship and trust—up to a point. But the deepest core of him always remained closed to intimacy.

Until tonight. Until Penelope had described a man he

didn't recognize as himself and with a ringing sincerity that had melted the ice in his soul. She'd been chipping away at that ice since they'd met in Italy, but now he could no longer keep her out of that bastion of isolation deep inside him.

He trusted his wife. Completely. Unconditionally. Unquestioningly.

His heart expanded as he remembered her standing up to those shrews. "You made me feel like a hero tonight, Penelope," he whispered, kissing her between her dark eyebrows. "Thank you."

She shook her head. "Cam, you've always been my hero. You must know that. When I was a little girl, I followed you around like a duckling follows its mother."

"That was many years ago."

Characteristic humor lit her seriousness. "Not that many!"

"I rather like hearing that I'm still your hero."

"You saved me from the bandits." She sent him a glance beneath her lashes.

"I did indeed."

"And from the waves."

"That too," he said, although he couldn't laugh about nearly losing her to the sea. He still had nightmares about catching uselessly at her hair before the current ripped her away. He'd wake sweating and terrified.

"And I'm hoping you'll now save me from a dull evening."

He smiled at her, enchanted anew. "Let me remedy your boredom, Your Grace."

He kissed her with openmouthed enthusiasm. She kissed him back with unfettered eagerness. She gave a soft squeak of surprise as he lifted her and carried her to the huge bed where they'd already rattled the gates of heaven.

"You look so smug," she said with a delicious gurgle of

laughter. She linked her hands around his neck and tugged at the hair brushing his collar.

"I'm a hero. My wife told me so." Gently he laid her across the bed, her legs dangling over the edge. She rose on her elbows and slid back until he caught one slender ankle. "Don't move."

"Cam?" she asked uncertainly.

"I want to give you pleasure."

"You have."

"There's more."

"I doubt I'll survive more."

He smiled as he untied the ribbons around her ankle and slid one green silk slipper off. "Be strong."

She lay back in silent acquiescence. He released her garter and slid her stocking down, then lifted her foot to kiss her instep. The fragrance of her skin filled his senses, a tantalizing hint of what was to come. He hid a sly smile and gave the other foot the same attention. He flicked his tongue across her toes until she shivered.

The glassy look in her eyes betrayed her enjoyment. Anticipation surged like a cavalry charge. He tossed her skirts up, revealing her drawers. With one rip, they were in shreds.

"Cam!" she gasped in shock, jerking up on her elbows.

"I'll buy you more." He drew her forward until her hips balanced on the edge of the mattress. Her dark curls glistened and the scent of her arousal rose to tease his nostrils.

"Good thing I married a rich man." She lay back, tangling her hands in the sheets.

"Very wise, my dear."

He wasn't entirely joking. This week, he'd torn three pairs of drawers, ruined two gowns, and left a nightdress in tatters. Their battle for supremacy had been tough on her wardrobe.

Yet tonight he discovered that he'd always sought an equal, not a subordinate.

"What are you doing?" she asked nervously.

He kneeled on the floor between her legs. Her scent was earthy, luscious, familiar. Like her daytime self, but richer, more evocative. "Admiring the duchess."

He lifted his head from contemplating her secret places. She really was lovely. She was particularly lovely sleek with desire.

"The duchess is blushing." She reached to shield herself.

He caught her hand and placed a kiss on each fingertip, then set her hand beside her hip. Before she could protest, he bent his head and licked her cleft.

Her flavor flooded his mouth. Salty and female and succulent. Like a delicious exotic fruit.

She shuddered and her thighs spread wider. He loved that she didn't hide her reaction. He licked her again, lingering at the sensitive flesh above her sex.

She whimpered and wriggled. "That's indecent."

He smiled into this hidden place and began to nip and suck and kiss her, taking her so far but stopping short of release. She dug her fingers into his hair, pulling hard.

"You leave me no inch of privacy," she protested.

He smiled into the soft skin of her thigh. "I'm a very thorough man, darling."

Her choked laugh ended on a gasp as he nipped her and returned to his exploration.

"Please, please," she moaned, rippling toward him.

He fluttered his tongue and felt her clench. The sounds of her pleasure filled his ears. Despite his fantasies, he'd never imagined how powerful this act would prove. Holding her thighs, he plunged his tongue into her. He increased the pressure, biting gently at the sleek, swollen flesh until she moaned. Then he drew her into his mouth and she convulsed on a choked cry of completion.

Eventually he raised his head. With one shaking hand, he wiped his mouth. Pen sprawled sideways across the bed, looking completely debauched and more beautiful than he'd ever seen her. Her face was rosy. Her extravagant blue gown was rumpled. Her ebony hair tumbled about her shoulders. Her long white legs spread in ungainly abandon.

Surely a woman who gave herself so wholeheartedly to physical satisfaction could hold nothing back. He placed a kiss on one smooth white thigh and rose above her, his hands flat against the mattress.

Her black eyes found his immediately and he read warmth and trust and affection. And pleasure.

And far away in the starry darkness, a closed door.

Harry stirred from his doze. At his side, Sophie curled, warm, soft, and boneless. His hand idly traced patterns over her bare shoulder.

For two, the chaise was delightfully cramped. In the grate, the fire burned down. He should tend to it. The idea drifted into his mind and drifted out again. His contentment left no room for anything but the beautiful girl who had just shown him the shining path to ecstasy.

A carriage rattled past on the quiet street and like that, the imperatives of real life jabbed him to alertness. He had no idea what time it was and his pocket watch was in his coat across the room. But he knew that the hour approached when Sophie must return to Leath House if she meant to continue the pretense that she'd been at the British Museum.

"Why are you laughing?" she asked drowsily, snuggling closer and setting her slender hand over his heart in a possessive gesture. Why shouldn't she touch him like she owned him? She did.

"You missed Lady Harmsworth's lecture about Cistercian Abbeys."

"What a pity." She laughed too.

He buried his face in her tangled hair. Her scent made him drunk. Love surged up, choked him, made it impossible to speak. She was a total joy. He couldn't live without her.

When he caught his breath, he loosened his hold, although she hadn't complained. "Sophie, you distract me."

She sent him a look that jolted heat through him. "Shall I distract you again?"

For a moment, he stared at her, lost in the glorious thought of making love to her once more. Then the clock outside struck ten, reminding him how soon she must leave. He sat up and drew her beside him.

"Sophie, we need to talk. I didn't bring you here to ruin you." He waited for a twinge of guilt, but he was only happy and grateful.

She sobered and stared at him. "Are you sorry?"

He shook his head. "I should be, but I'm not."

She smiled at him. "I'm not either. I must be wicked."

"No, you're wonderful." He couldn't resist kissing her, but he stopped before they *distracted* one another again. "Perhaps you'd better get dressed."

To his relief, she rose and collected her scattered undergarments. Manfully he strove to ignore the sight of her moving naked around the room with an ease that made his heart somersault.

In between helping her back to respectability and dressing himself, he calmed down enough to think beyond the unforgettable moments they'd just shared. He joined her on the chaise, gazing into eyes still hazy with pleasure. He hoped like hell that she didn't run into Leath tonight. One glimpse at her radiant face and her brother would know she'd been up to no good.

"Sophie, we can't go on like this."

"Don't approach James again. Since your sister married Sedgemoor, he's more set against you than ever."

"I learned my lesson last time." He tightened his grip on her slender fingers. "We have to get married."

"Harry, I've just given myself to you." She stared uncompromisingly at him. "You'd better marry me."

She didn't say what they both knew, that if he'd placed a baby in her womb, the issue of their marriage became more urgent than ever. His heart gave a thud of excitement at the thought of her bearing his child. "I want us to run away together."

Shocked she tugged her hands free. "To Scotland?"

He inhaled and spoke the words that had increasingly seemed the solution to everything working against them. "To America."

"Harry—"

He rushed on before she could object. "We can start afresh. In New York, we'll be beyond your brother's reach."

"America," she said as if he'd suggested flying to the moon. "I don't know anyone in America."

"I don't either." He caught her hands, needing the physical contact. "That's the glory of it, my darling. We'll be free, free to become the people we're meant to be."

"I'm not sure." Her fingers twined around his as though he offered protection against her fear, when he was the one who had frightened her.

"Sophie, I know it's not what you dreamed. I know you wanted a wedding at St. George's, and James walking you down the aisle, and a place in society."

"Those things don't matter. But leaving my family and my country does. Can't we stay in England?"

He tried not to be disappointed at her lack of enthusiasm. "Your brother will hound us. I wouldn't put kidnapping past him. The gossip about our elopement will dog us for the rest of our lives. If we stay here, we'll never outrun the scandal."

"You ask so much."

"I know." He paused. "The decision is yours. You've got more to lose than I have."

She looked troubled. "We've become lovers. I have no choice."

He sighed and spoke the grim truth. "Sophie, I hate to say it, but you're a great heiress from an influential family, whatever your uncle did. Many men will overlook your lack of virginity in exchange for your fortune and your brother's favor."

Her lips turned down with disgust. "That's not how I want to live."

He raised her hands and kissed them, feeling like a blackguard. He really should have talked to her before he took the irrevocable action of sleeping with her. "You can't have the life you were born to lead and marry me, my love."

She regarded him somberly. In that moment, something changed within her. The girl who spoke had grown up in some subtle way. "You're forcing me to choose?"

He released her and stood. The urge to sweep her into his arms and kiss her into compliance was too powerful when he sat only inches away. "I must."

She scrambled to her feet, delicate jaw setting with determination. "Can you walk away from me?"

"If it's for your good, I can." The thought of never seeing her, never kissing her, hell, after tonight, never making love to her, cut like a blade. "I tried to do the decent thing. I asked your brother for your hand. But he'll never countenance me as a brother-in-law."

"We can wait."

"No, we can't." He sighed and ran his hand through his hair. "Sophie, we'll get caught. And when we do, the world will sneer at you and call you vile names. You deserve better than that."

He waited for her to disagree with what they both knew to be true. Instead she wrapped her arms around her chest and stared blindly into space. "But America?"

He fought the impulse to draw her close and say that none of this mattered. They'd found paradise in this house. They could find it again. If they ignored the outside world, the outside world would ignore them.

Sadly neither he nor Sophie was fool enough to believe that nonsense. "We could go to France or Italy. Pen has friends on the Continent."

"Friends who write letters to England."

He flinched at Sophie's stark assessment. She'd reached the same conclusion that he had. The Continent was both too far away and too close for them to establish themselves free of scandal.

"At least in America, they speak English," she said in a small voice.

"So they claim," he said drily.

Sophie studied him with an agonized yearning that made his belly cramp with denial. He saw her regret. He saw her count everything on his side and everything on her brother's side. He already knew which balance carried the most weight.

She meant to say no. After all they'd been through, all they'd been to each other, all that had happened tonight, she'd leave him and retreat to the safety of her brother's care.

She'd marry bloody Desborough and grace high society for the rest of her life. And in a few years wonder just what madness had possessed her that she'd almost discarded a secure future for the sake of Harry Thorne's bright black eyes.

Bloody, bloody, bloody hell.

But what did he have to offer? Love. Nothing else. Right now, he couldn't see why she'd make any other choice but to stay with Leath.

"When do we go?"

He was so sure she'd refuse that it took a few seconds to understand what her question meant. "What did you say?"

The shadows left her eyes and she gazed at him with a trust that made his heart swell. "I'm happy to go to America with you."

"Really?" he asked in a daze.

As if the impetus shifted from him to her, she placed her arms around him. She stared at him with that unconditional love that he knew he didn't deserve, but which he'd do his damnedest to perpetuate. "I threw my lot in with you months ago. Let's take the next step in our adventure."

He was too shocked to respond to her embrace. "What about your brother?"

Sadness dulled her gaze for the first time since she'd agreed to this impetuous scheme. "I hope he'll forgive me. I hope he'll come to see you for the wonderful man you are. But I love you. I can't lose you. I won't tamely give in to James's demands and marry a man I don't love."

The reality of Sophie's concession gradually washed over him, sweeping his doubts away on a tide of purpose. His arms lashed around her. "We'll go tomorrow night. I'll wait outside the mews at Leath House. If you can't get away, I'll try again the next night."

She laughed and if there was an edge of hysteria, he

couldn't blame her. He'd miss Pen and Elias. And some of his friends. But America brimmed with exciting possibilities. And he'd have Sophie. That above all made the future beckon bright and hopeful. She on the other hand gave up so much, including a beloved family and her reputation. He couldn't believe that she loved him enough to do this. The fact that she did made him love her even more.

She regarded him with a slight wobble in her smile, but a jaunty tilt to her chin. "Our new life starts today."

Harry spoke gravely, wanting her to know that he'd never take her sacrifice lightly. "I swear I'll make you happy, Sophie. You won't regret for one moment that you decided to come with me."

Chapter Thirty-Seven

The soft murmur of voices disturbed Pen's troubled dreams of pursuing Cam through rooms flooded with seawater.

Her body was heavy with pleasure. And exhaustion. They'd been to the opera, then a private supper party with the Harmsworths and the Hillbrooks. She hadn't stumbled home until two. She stirred and reached out for Cam, but his side of the bed was empty. Only recently. The sheets still held traces of warmth. She blinked dazed eyes. The door to the corridor outside was ajar and she saw the flicker of a candle.

"What the devil does he want in the middle of the night?" Cam muttered in a low voice just outside the bedroom.

"He was most adamant, Your Grace," their butler Dixon whispered back.

"At—" Cam broke off. "What time is it?"

"Just gone half past four, Your Grace."

Half past four? She'd been asleep an hour. No wonder she felt so groggy. Who on earth had called in the middle of the night? Curiosity struggled up through the thick-headedness of interrupted sleep.

"Tell him to come back at a civilized time."

"I suggested that his lordship wait until morning. He responded... discourteously."

Cam sighed with irritation. "I'll be down directly. Please show Lord Leath into the library."

Leath? Sick terror lurched through her belly and banished the last of her drowsiness. Pen was wide awake now and wished to heaven she wasn't.

Leath wasn't waiting in the library. Instead, dark eyes sparking with fury, he stood in the hall, glaring up to where Cam descended the stairs in his red dressing gown. The marquess tapped his riding crop against one palm. Cam stiffened as he recognized the action's controlled violence.

This visit would clearly be short—Leath hadn't even removed his topcoat. Why the hell was he here? The Neville Fairbrother scandal must have turned his mind.

"Where is she?" Leath barked as if addressing a slovenly groom in an inn yard.

"Good evening, my lord." Cam spoke calmly, despite his urge to toss the bumptious rogue out on his ear. "Or perhaps I should say good morning."

Leath's heavy brows lowered and he took a menacing pace forward. "Don't play with me, you condescending bastard. Where's my sister?"

"How the devil should I know?" His sister? What in Hades was this? Impatience roughened Cam's question. "If you can't keep track of your dashed relatives, why on earth should I?"

Leath's voice vibrated with rage. "According to her maid, she left the house after dinner and hasn't been seen since."

"I still don't understand what I can do about it." Cam walked down the last steps to face down the fuming marquis. Few men matched Cam's height, but Leath was well over six feet. "If she's missing, I'm sure there's an innocent explanation."

Leath's snort conveyed no amusement. "Innocent explanation, my arse. She's with that blackguard Harry Thorne."

Ah, at last he knew why Leath had singled him out for this visit. Cam's voice dripped hauteur. "The duchess isn't her brother's keeper."

Leath's attention skimmed past Cam. His glittering eyes narrowed. "No, she's his accomplice."

Pen spoke before Cam could dismiss the mad accusation. "I don't know where Sophie is."

Cam whirled around in surprise. Pen poised in frozen immobility a few steps above, one hand resting on the gilt banister. In her rich gold brocade dressing gown, with her shining black hair flowing around her, she stood like a queen.

He expected her to look appalled and shocked.

She looked appalled and shocked. And unmistakably guilty.

His heart slammed to a disbelieving standstill. "Pen?" he asked uncertainly, fleetingly forgetting their audience. He stepped back so he could see both Leath and his wife.

Pen didn't glance his way. Instead she regarded Leath with a horrified comprehension that spoke volumes about her deceit. Her grip on the banister tightened until her knuckles shone white.

"Pen, go back to bed," Cam snapped, feeling as though the ground crumbled beneath his feet.

"No, she needs to stay and tell me what she knows," Leath demanded. "Sophie's not at the Russell Square house. That's the first place I went."

"Cam, I'd like to help," she said shakily.

"Haven't you *helped* enough?" he muttered furiously for Pen's ears only. When she flinched, he hardened himself against any guilt. She'd brought this on herself.

Cam saw a crack in Leath's rage as he stared at Pen. He might be angry, but beneath his anger he was worried sick. "For God's sake, if she's here, tell me. I won't punish her. I just want to know she's safe."

"Pen, just what have you done?" Cam growled.

She cast him a desperate glance, then focused on Leath. "Sophie's not here. On my honor, I'd tell you if she was."

"Madam, I wouldn't trust your honor if my life depended upon it."

Blind rage bubbled up and Cam lurched forward to land a solid punch to the marquess's jaw. Whatever his wife had done, Cam wouldn't stand for anyone insulting her.

Leath must be built like an ox. The bugger staggered but didn't fall.

"Cam—" Pen gasped in horror, rushing down to hover behind him. Thank God, she didn't touch him. Right now he was so enraged, he didn't trust himself not to lash out at her too.

"You will apologize to my wife," Cam said in a voice that shook with outrage. He curled his stinging hand at his side. Leath had a jaw like rock.

Rubbing his chin, Leath glared back with unconcealed hatred. "Like hell I will."

"Please, I can explain," Pen said desperately.

"Don't bother," Cam said coldly. He was so livid that he couldn't look at her. Sick anger twisted in his belly like hissing cobras.

He clung to his rage. Beneath anger heaved an ocean of anguish. He'd believed Penelope Thorne was true gold. He'd trusted her in ways he'd never trusted anyone, not even his closest friends. And she'd betrayed him.

If those young idiots had eloped with Pen's connivance— and every sign indicated that they had—there would be an almighty scandal. The kind of scandal that would dog their families for years. Pen's interference had in the space of weeks undone Cam's years of work to restore honor to the Rothermere name.

Once, that might have counted as her greatest sin.

Once, before she'd weaseled her way past his defenses and made him believe that she was the one person who would never break faith with him.

Now while he cared about the scandal, he cared more that he'd trusted her and she'd proven unworthy. He'd ignored the lessons of a lifetime to believe that Pen was the exception to the rule that everybody lied.

Then she'd shown herself a liar.

She'd been underhanded and deceitful. She'd known the damage scandal could do, yet she'd gone ahead against Cam's express wishes and promoted her brother's seduction of an innocent girl. When her loyalty had been tested, Harry won out over her husband. Cam would never forgive her for that.

The marquess bared his teeth at Pen. "Where is my sister?"

Pen stepped down beside Cam. He resisted the need to move away. He was so incandescently angry, her merest presence made him shake.

"You have no reason to believe me, my lord—"

"How true."

"Watch what you say." One punch hadn't satisfied Cam's need to smash something.

Pen's hand curled around his arm to stop him hitting

Leath again. "His lordship is right to be upset." Her voice thickened with tears. "You are too. But we need to find Harry and Sophie."

Her touch inevitably reminded him of how minutes ago, he'd rested in her arms, congratulating himself on being the luckiest fellow in England. With lacerating bitterness, he wondered if his father had felt the same before learning that his duchess had tupped his brother. His wife hadn't turned to another man, but she'd betrayed him unpardonably all the same.

"A nice show of concern. I'd almost believe you if you and that whelp hadn't cooked this up to get his hands on Sophie's fortune." Leath's voice cut like a whip. "You know where they've gone, all right."

Pen's hold on Cam's arm tightened. Her touch felt like acid. "I'm as surprised as you are."

Cam still couldn't bring himself to look at Pen. She'd see his rage, but he'd rather be shot at dawn than reveal how she'd wounded him. He ignored her soft gasp of hurt when he shook her off and stepped clear.

"Even after you arranged the ruin of my sister?" Leath asked harshly.

"He loves her," Pen said stalwartly. "I believe she loves him."

"Sentimental rot," Leath snarled. "This was a cold-hearted plot to set your brother up for life."

"Harry's not a liar," Pen said.

Cam already suffered such a nauseating mixture of emotions. Anger. Grief. Regret. Surprise. Now he had to add piercing jealousy. She was so endlessly loyal to her brother. If only she'd been half as loyal to her husband.

"Of course he's a liar." Leath glared at Cam. "Is this part of your vendetta against my family?"

Cam's weary "I don't have a vendetta against your family" clashed with Pen's shocked "You can't blame Sedgemoor. He warned me against meddling in Harry's courtship."

"Courtship!" The word exploded from Leath's lips like a curse. "His cynical pursuit of a naïve girl, more like." He glowered at Cam. "You need to control your wife, sir."

Cam heartily agreed. If he only knew how. If he'd only stuck to his plans to marry a chaste cipher. Biddable. Trustworthy. A woman who would never engage his emotions and leave him wanting to die when she played him false.

"Recriminations won't find Harry and Sophie." Pen's dignity impressed, even now when Cam wanted to consign her to the lowest realms of Hades. "Did Sophie leave a note?"

Leath gave a contemptuous grunt. "Yes."

"Well, what did it say, man?" Cam asked roughly.

Leath's voice was flat. "That she was sorry to disappoint me and she hoped one day I'd forgive her. She didn't mention that cur Thorne, although he's behind this mess."

"Did she say where she was going?" Cam asked.

"If she did, would I be here?"

"Scotland is the usual destination," Cam said. Blast Harry for a rash fool. And a cad to play with a young girl's reputation. "Madam?"

"I don't know," Pen said miserably.

"I've got men on the north road looking for them." Leath suddenly looked deathly tired. "Sophie was meant to attend the theatre with Lady Gresham. I wouldn't have discovered her absence until breakfast, except Lady Gresham sent a note after the play asking after Sophie's headache."

"So they've got a good start," Cam said grimly.

"If they've left London."

Dixon cleared his throat to gain his employer's attention.

Cam realized that his butler waited near the library door, struggling to hide his fascination.

"What is it, Dixon?" Cam said, cursing himself for not taking Leath somewhere private whether the bugger wanted to go or not. The staff would know every detail of this brawl before the morning was out.

Dixon approached and extended a salver upon which rested a letter. "Your pardon, Your Grace. A note was delivered this evening for Her Grace and Thomas placed it with the other mail. When I heard the disturbance, I took the liberty of checking to see if Mr. Thorne had sent a message."

Cam reached out, but Pen was there first. "The letter is meant for me," she said with a touch of spirit, ripping it open with shaking hands.

"Give it to me." Leath snatched the paper. He quickly scanned the contents, then crumpled the page with a savagery that Cam knew he'd rather expend on Harry Thorne. Tossing the letter to the floor, Leath headed for the door without a farewell.

"Wait." Pen bent to retrieve the page and smooth it. "Before you go—"

"Time is of the essence." He didn't pause.

"Please," Pen called after him. "Surely, my lord, you can spare one moment."

"Thank you, Dixon." Cam said firmly. Reluctantly Dixon turned to go.

Leath faced Pen, his features a mask of disdain. "I owe you nothing. If you were my wife, I'd horsewhip you."

"Look to your own household and your hoyden of a sister," Cam bit out. "My wife isn't your concern."

"Thank God," Leath said fervently.

At last Cam glanced at Pen. She was paler than the paper she held and her black eyes were lifeless.

"I have no excuse," she said dully. Cam had never heard her sound like this. "But before you go, please, tell me how you know I was involved and how you know about Russell Square."

Leath's laugh was so cutting that Pen jerked back as if he'd hit her. "I'm surprised you haven't heard. Word is everywhere about the duchess playing pimp for her brother."

"But how—" Pen looked utterly horrified. "We were so careful."

"Not careful enough." He sighed and spoke less aggressively. "Just as I wasn't careful enough with Sophie. Believe me, I make no excuses for my own faults in this matter."

"I'm sorry." Piercing regret weighted Pen's voice.

"Too little too late." Leath inhaled, fighting to control his temper. When he spoke, he sounded more like the man Cam had faced in so many parliamentary debates. "A hackney driver recognized Sophie. The gossip rags pay for items of interest. A journalist dug up the rest of the sorry facts, including your ownership of the house where Thorne lured my sister. That journalist has trailed them all week. The story hit this evening's papers. I'm guessing the elopement will make a fine follow-up piece tomorrow."

"Couldn't you ask the damned scribbler about their destination instead of barging in here?" Cam asked sharply, even as visions of cataclysmic scandal battered him. While his deepest fury centered on Pen's breach of trust, he didn't discount what hell life would become for Fairbrothers, Thornes, and Rothermeres in the wake of this rash imbecility.

"I tried. For a few shillings, the man proved disgustingly voluble. Such is the worth of my sister's honor."

Cam had seen immediately that Leath's anger, while powerful, couldn't compare with his profound hurt. How odd that he and Leath were in exactly the same boat. A sinking one.

"He saw Thorne collect my sister in a closed carriage from the back gate of Leath House, but lost them in traffic."

"So publicity is unavoidable," Pen said bleakly.

Leath cast her a look of loathing. The mark on his chin looked red and sore and promised to become an impressive bruise. "My sister will be branded a harlot. Your brother's name will become a byword for dishonor. You will be derided as a bawd who promoted a young girl's destruction. The world will sneer at your husband as a fool in the hands of a brazen woman. A fine result for your interference, madam."

Pen looked brittle enough to shatter. Furious as he was with her, Cam couldn't bear it. He grabbed Leath's arm. "Get out before I throw you out."

Leath snatched free. "With pleasure."

His boot heels clicked across the marble tiles, and then he was gone, leaving the ruins of Cam's marriage behind him.

Pen watched Cam with a devastated expression. "I'm so sorry—"

He held up an astonishingly steady hand. In the last few seconds, he'd battened his raging, ferocious anguish into the dark depths of his soul. The same dark depths where his pathetic longing for parents who loved him still lurked. Even his voice was calm. Although flat and dead like a desert. "Just tell me where they've gone."

"Cam—"

He sighed and grabbed Harry's note from her shaking grasp. After reading the short message, he stared at Pen in shock. "The fool is taking Sophie Fairbrother to America?"

"He's not—"

"I told you not to bother excusing his behavior—or yours."

Her eyes flashed. "Cam, don't go all ducal on me. We need to fix this."

Her teasing about his ducal ways had—mostly—amused him. Now the reference grated. "As his lordship pointed out, you've done enough. Go to your room."

Her mouth flattened with defiance. "I'm not a naughty child, Cam. I'm your wife."

"More's the pity."

She whitened and staggered back, fumbling for the banister. Her eyes were like dull black coals in her strained face.

He sucked in a breath and struggled to rein in his anger. "That was unworthy. My apologies." His jaw was so tight that every word felt carved from stone. He bowed stiffly. "We'll discuss our future when I return."

"You're going after them?" she asked unsteadily.

"Of course I'm bloody going after them." His attempt at control frayed almost before he'd told himself to settle down, for the sake of his pride if nothing else. "I need to stop Leath from killing Harry, much as the sod deserves it."

He was Camden Rothermere, famous for his self-possession. How he longed to be that man again. Not this agonized, confused, enraged creature who wanted to march away from his wife and never see her again. And who wanted to seize her in his arms and kiss her and make her swear that everything he'd learned tonight was spiteful lies.

"I didn't think you cared what happens to Harry," she said heavily.

"I care that this scandal gets no worse than it bloody is already."

Unfortunately that wasn't nearly the whole truth. He cared about much more than that. He cared about Pen, although he intended to eradicate that affliction before the night was done. He cared for reckless, thoughtless Harry Thorne. He cared for silly, headstrong Sophie Fairbrother, who right now imagined the world well lost for love. She'd face a bitter awakening once she'd abandoned the privilege and protection of life as the Marquess of Leath's sister.

Love! The world would be a better place if there was no such thing.

"This is my fault," Pen said in a leaden voice.

He didn't answer. He didn't have to. When the silence extended, she turned away with a despairing gesture.

He needed to leave if he meant to overtake Leath. But still he lingered to watch Pen climb the stairs. Her head was up, her shoulders were straight and her spine could double as a ship's mast. But he didn't misunderstand that if she'd dealt him a killing blow, he hadn't been much kinder. If he had a heart, he'd feel sorry for her.

But he had no heart. She'd crushed it when she proved herself untrue.

Chapter Thirty-Eight

Cam ran down the front steps. His phaeton waited, his two fastest horses restless after being roused from a warm stable before sunrise.

He wanted to concentrate on his immediate need to find that blockhead Harry Thorne and his brainless inamorata. Not to mention prevent Leath from committing murder and making this elopement a matter for the authorities. But he couldn't help dwelling on the failure of his lifelong efforts to bury the old scandals. Scandal fattened on scandal, so all the stories about his mother and her taste for Rothermere brothers would do the rounds again.

Still, he'd rather think about scandal than about his duplicitous wife.

He'd already calculated the quickest route to Liverpool, where Harry had chosen to embark on this ill-considered adventure. There were closer ports offering passage across the Atlantic, but God forbid that his brother-in-law should make things easier. Perhaps the long journey was a blessing. It would give Cam a chance to cool down. At this juncture, if Leath didn't shoot Harry, Cam would.

Jenkins, who had served the Dukes of Sedgemoor all his life, held the restive chestnuts. "Are you sure I shouldn't come, Your Grace?"

"I appreciate the offer, but I'm going alone." He grabbed the side of the carriage and vaulted into the seat, seizing the reins. "Stand aside."

"Wait!"

With a sense of inevitability, Cam watched Pen rush from the house. She was dressed for travel and she carried a small bag. "Go back to bed."

"I'm coming," she said breathlessly, reaching for his hand to help her into the phaeton.

Cam didn't release his grip on the reins. "No, you're not." He nodded to Jenkins. "Release the horses."

"No!" Pen darted forward to block the carriage. "Not without me."

Jenkins looked at Cam, then at Pen, then at Cam. He didn't release the horses.

"Jenkins, you heard me," Cam said through lips made of ice. If only his heart was.

"You won't run me down," Pen said with a confidence he resented.

"You're making an exhibition of yourself," he bit out.

"I don't care."

His eyes narrowed. "You'll move if I drive the horses at you."

"Try me."

Cam raised his whip above the chestnuts' glossy rumps. "Jenkins."

"Your Grace," he protested.

"Now."

With obvious reluctance, Jenkins stepped away.

"Are you that angry with me?" Pen didn't shift as Cam urged the horses forward. Her face revealed no trace of fear.

Instead of setting off smoothly, the horses moved choppily in the shafts. One neighed its confusion, the other tossed its head.

Across the distance, Pen's eyes burned into his. At the last minute, as she knew he would, curse her, Cam turned the horses to avoid her.

She stepped into his way again.

"Stand aside."

"No."

"Damn it, woman," he muttered.

"Harry will listen to me. And you'll need a woman's help with Sophie."

It wasn't the best moment to remember Pen's stubbornness. If you gained her cooperation she'd go to the ends of the earth for you. If you didn't, bullying only made her dig her heels in.

"Cam, you need me."

No, he bloody well didn't.

He glowered at Pen while his horses stamped on the cobblestones and tugged at the reins to evade this madwoman. Would she budge if he tried again? She was so blasted mulish, he suspected that she wouldn't. He might want to strangle her, but he drew the line at cold-blooded murder.

Not that there was anything cold-blooded about his reactions. He wished to Hades there was.

"Come on, then," he said grimly, firming his hold on the reins.

He waited for some evidence of relief or gratitude, but Pen calmly stepped around his horses, patting them on the way. "Thank you, Jenkins."

His coachman bowed to her. "Your Grace."

She stood beside the carriage and passed Cam the bag. "Help me up?"

"Don't push it," he growled, but he reached for her. Once she was settled, he dug around under the seat and found a travel rug which he shoved ungraciously in her direction. It was a deuced cold night for early May.

"Thank you," she said quietly.

"Don't expect any more concessions to female weakness. This isn't a pleasure jaunt."

He glanced at her, but she stared straight ahead as if she didn't hear him. Although she did. She might suffer a poor grasp of ethics, but her hearing had always been excellent. Feeling he'd bartered his dignity enough, he clicked his tongue to the horses.

They were well out of London before he spoke. "You took a damned risk back there."

He still felt sick to think that he might have lost control of his highly strung horses. Sick, and furious with Pen for placing herself in such danger out of sheer obstinacy.

"Not really," she said steadily, staring at the road ahead.

"The horses could have charged you."

"You had them in hand."

Perversely her trust made him angrier. He'd trusted her and she'd let him down. "Running you down held a certain appeal," he admitted, even as he reminded himself that silence was safer.

"I know," she said in a subdued voice.

A quick glance revealed her desolate expression. He closed his heart against her. She was a deceitful snake. A man didn't hug a deceitful snake unless he wanted to be bitten. And Cam had had quite enough of Pen's poison.

After hours of traveling, Pen was stiff and frozen and queasy with regret and guilt. Cam hadn't spoken to her since their exchange about that fraught scene outside Rothermere House.

He did a wonderful impression of a man impervious to feeling, but she'd seen his eyes when he'd learned that she'd helped Harry. She'd only realized how much he'd opened up to her when he'd stared at her like a stranger. The uncompromising line of his jaw told her that he'd cut off his arm before he'd trust her again.

As they stopped at yet another inn and the ostlers rushed to change the horses, Cam jumped to the ground with an energy that made Pen cringe. They'd left the chestnuts behind two inns ago, not that she'd noticed much difference. At this speed, nothing countered the rough roads. At least it wasn't raining, but the wind was icy and belonged more to winter than nascent spring.

"Would you like something to eat?" Cam asked in a stern voice.

She sought some sign of relenting. But his eyes were colder than the wind and the smile lines that she loved so much were absent. Still, at previous stops he'd made no concessions to her comfort, so perhaps things weren't as bad as they had been.

"I don't want to hold you up." After the long silence, her voice sounded rusty.

"Half an hour won't make much difference."

"Very well," she said. "Thank you."

To save him from touching her disgusting self—he'd ostentatiously avoided contact, despite the phaeton's restricted space—she moved, wincing at her numb backside. But she'd misjudged the effects of sitting still so long. The moment her feet hit the cobbles, her legs folded.

She released a soft cry and grabbed for the carriage. Then strong arms caught her and lifted her high. It was like the time she'd collapsed after the shipwreck. Cam hadn't liked her much then either. But that had been because he wanted her and couldn't have her. This time, he didn't like her because she'd betrayed him. Despair clenched her empty belly.

"I can walk," she said, just as she had then.

"Shut up," he said frostily and carried her into the inn's blessed warmth. The innkeeper directed them to a private parlor. Over her head, Pen heard Cam questioning him about whether Leath had stopped here. Apparently he had about an hour ago. They still had hopes of catching the marquess.

"We can't wait," she said dully. The thought of facing the weather again so soon made her want to cry.

Cam set her on a stool near the hearth. His touch was efficient but without tenderness. She tried not to remember how last night in bed he'd lashed her to his body as if he couldn't bear to be more than a breath away from her. Knowing that he'd never hold her like that again made her want to curl up and sob.

"I'll order some food," he said, still in that emotionless voice.

By the time he returned, she felt more human. Ten minutes near the fire restored her blood to something like its usual temperature.

"I've arranged a room where you can wash."

Surprised, she turned. "That's very obliging."

He frowned as if suspecting sarcasm, but she was sincere. She knew he was livid. She was still amazed that she'd won that public battle of wills in London. Although if he hadn't taken her, she'd have followed on her own.

A maid arrived to escort her upstairs. Aching muscles protested at each step. They weren't even halfway to Liverpool. Heaven knew what state she'd be in when they arrived.

Although one thing she did know—Cam wouldn't have come any closer to forgiving her.

Chapter Thirty-Nine

Pen stirred. Although the bed shifted in a most bizarre fashion, Cam's familiar warmth surrounded her. She drew in a lungful of his delicious scent. Leather. Soap. Horses. Perhaps a little heavier on the horses than usual.

Then she recalled that she traveled to Liverpool to save Harry's hide and that Cam hated her.

Which made no sense when his arm held her safe as they galloped through the night. He'd wrapped his greatcoat around them against the biting wind.

Despite her best efforts, she must have shifted. Cam's arm stiffened, then in a gesture that cracked a rift across her heart, he disentangled himself and slid away.

"I'm sorry." She struggled to sit up against the rocking of the carriage. After hours in the phaeton, her muscles ached with weariness, despite her nap.

He didn't respond. He'd been a remarkably quiet companion. Pen felt so heartsick that at first his silence had been welcome. Now it became oppressive. Some hint that he was capable of speech would be welcome. "Where are we?"

Beyond the frail glow of the carriage lamps, everything was dark. There should have been a moon, but lowering clouds turned the sky black.

"We've just left Wolverhampton." He didn't sound angry. He sounded tired and fed up and disinclined to conversation.

Too bad. "How far to Liverpool?"

"Miles."

Well, that was informative. She sighed and huddled into the rug. When Cam withdrew, he'd taken his coat and his heat.

They covered several miles and she fell into a waking doze where the world melted into a dark blur and the only other person alive was the fuming, powerful man relentlessly driving the horses.

He was still angry. Waking in his arms, she hadn't felt it. But she felt it now. A blast of fury like heat from an open flame.

Eventually she could bear it no more. "Cam, at least let me explain."

Although he'd never understand why she'd helped Harry. To understand, Cam would need to realize what love was. And for him, that word had no meaning.

She didn't see him recoil, but the horses' gait broke. The betraying moment was over in a second, but it confirmed Pen's impression that his silence was like a volcano waiting to erupt.

"Cam?"

The horses resumed their gallop. Cam stared ahead as if the road provided the world's most fascinating view. "I don't want to hear, madam."

Madam again. The cold address stung. She had an inkling of how he'd felt when she'd Your Grace'd him to death. When she'd tried to play the proper duchess.

He'd told her to be true to herself. As a result, they faced disaster.

"You can't condemn me unheard," she said on a surge of desperation.

After a long pause, he said, "Yes, I can."

They reached Liverpool's best inn midmorning. Leath was still ahead of them. In fact, he'd made up time. At the last stop, they'd learned that he was at least four hours in advance.

Pen felt sick with guilt. If Cam had traveled alone, he wouldn't have stopped so often. Not that he'd precisely made the trip comfortable, but he'd pulled back from the punishing pace he'd established leaving London.

Their carriage bowled into the Bear and Swan's bustling yard. After the lonely road, the noise and crush were dizzying.

"Shouldn't we go to the docks?" It was the first time she'd spoken in hours. Cam's discouraging response to her ill-timed attempts to explain had daunted her.

"No."

She bit back a sigh. The silent treatment had lost its meager charm about twelve hours ago.

Then to her surprise, he went on. "I'll reserve our rooms and arrange more discreet transport."

It made sense. She ventured another question. "What about Leath?"

To her astonishment, Cam's lips lengthened in a smile. A grim smile, but his first sign of amusement since leaving Rothermere House. She wasn't fool enough to think he was thawing, but nonetheless, she was heartened.

"We have the advantage."

She was even more astounded to hear him say "we." But

when he looked at her, the real Cam had retreated far, far behind his eyes. So far that she knew she'd never reach him.

A wave of misery overwhelmed her. She'd made so many mistakes. Now she paid the price.

Any further chance for conversation disappeared in the business of arriving. Only when they were inside a closed carriage did Pen pursue the subject of Leath. "Why do we have the advantage?"

From the seat opposite, Cam regarded her with the shuttered gaze that she began to loathe.

Wait until you've lived with it for fifty years.

She ignored the bleak little voice and waited, without hope, for Cam's reply.

"I have shipping interests here. I know the city well. Leath's business is in mines and property. He'll need time to get his bearings."

"And you know where to go?"

He shrugged. "I've got a good idea."

"What if Harry and Sophie have already sailed?"

"Then the New World is welcome to that pair of nitwits."

Even as she spoke, she knew she wasted her time. "Harry loves Sophie."

His stare was frigid. "Don't."

She bit her lip. She hated Cam's contempt for love. All her life she'd cursed his self-centered parents for warping Cam's attitudes. Never so bitterly as at this moment.

He continued. "I doubt they'll get straight onto a ship. They're likely holed up in a boarding house." Another hint of grim humor, but this time she knew better than to take encouragement. "I wonder how Sophie likes life away from the luxury of her brother's home."

"Sophie's stronger than you think," Pen said, although she too had worried about the girl coping with hardship. The grand romance of running away with her lover might fade in squalid surroundings.

"We'll see."

Pen hoped for Harry's sake that Sophie proved steadfast. She also hoped for both their sakes that they hadn't left for America. Surely there was a way of unraveling this tangle without crossing the Atlantic.

As he and Pen approached the boarding house where a couple fitting Harry and Sophie's description rented a room, Cam wasn't surprised to glimpse a tall man striding ahead. Seeing the marquess, his anger welled anew. He blamed Leath for this farrago, almost as much as he blamed Pen. If Leath hadn't forbidden Sophie from seeing Harry and in the process, turned them into Romeo and sodding Juliet, the love affair would have petered out. Nothing like opposition to make young hearts beat faster.

Leath glanced back when he reached the door. In his elegant clothing, he looked incongruous against the peeling paint and cracked windows. The bruise on his chin had darkened to angry purple.

His eyes narrowed on Cam and Pen. "They're booked on the *Mary Kate*, sailing for Boston tomorrow," he said as though there had been no break in conversation.

"We're in time, then," Pen said.

Cam heard her relief. She'd already lost one brother. The prospect of losing another, even if to distance rather than death, must be agonizing.

Together they climbed the rickety staircase to the top of the tall house. The air outside reeked of rotten fish. The air inside reeked of mold, dirt, misery, and human ordure.

Cam's conviction firmed that Sophie would object to this foretaste of her new life. Leath should have no trouble persuading her home, after which she became his problem. The runaways couldn't have married already. Sophie was under twenty-one, and they hadn't had time to stop and talk a friendly vicar into performing a ceremony of doubtful legality.

"Let's take them by surprise," Leath whispered as they stood on the landing below the attic.

Cam was about to agree when Pen spoke. "No, let me talk to them."

"I'd rather kick the door in," Cam murmured.

Pen's quelling glance expressed disdain for dramatics. The exchange was a bitter reminder of their previous wordless communication. Regret pierced him as he counted what he'd lost. He'd been so intent on decrying her betrayal. He'd forgotten that without Pen, he was fated to arctic desolation.

The idea revived his impulse to smash something. Unfortunately, while the Marquess of Leath offered the perfect target, punching his lordship wouldn't help Sophie and Harry.

Pen pushed past Cam and Leath to ascend the last flight. She knocked on the door. "Harry? Harry, are you there? It's Pen."

The flimsy door squeaked open. "Pen, what on earth—"

Leath mounted the stairs two at a time, flattening his hands against the door and slamming it open. Cam pursued close enough to see the door crash against the faded wallpaper and a hunk of plaster fall from the ceiling. Sophie Fairbrother curled up on a narrow bed and watched with wide eyes as the tiny room filled.

"I'll kill you, you bloody worm," Leath gritted, grabbing Harry's coat and aiming a blow at his jaw. "How dare you come within an inch of my sister?"

Harry staggered. Sophie screamed and flung herself

between her brother and her lover. "James, no! Please, don't hurt Harry."

"Hurt Harry? I'll sodding murder him," the marquess hissed, flinging her out of the way and advancing on a reeling Harry. "Stand up and act the man. Nobody ruins my sister and lives to tell the tale."

Fleetingly forgetting his anger, Cam glanced at Pen. He'd been right to fear bloodshed. "Stop it, Leath," he said sharply.

"You can't kill Harry," Sophie protested. "I won't let you."

"I'll deal with you when we get home," Leath bit out, seizing Harry again.

"Stop it, I say." Cam tore Leath away before he inflicted more damage. "This serves no purpose."

"It makes me feel better; that's enough," Leath growled. He was stronger than Cam expected and keeping him from Harry, who still looked dazed, took a good deal of effort.

Sophie regained her balance and threw herself on her brother. "James, please, listen to me."

"Hiding behind my sister, are you, Thorne?" Leath snarled.

Harry shook his head, Cam thought more to order his addled senses than to contradict Leath's taunt. "What are you doing here?" he asked shakily, touching his jaw and wincing. "How the devil did you find us?"

"We're here to stop the two of you making the biggest mistake of your young lives, you fool," Cam said roughly. "Given the mistakes you've both made, that's saying something."

With a shocked expression, Harry looked past Cam to Pen. "Did you give us away?"

Pen took Harry's arm. "Harry, this isn't the way to win Sophie."

"He has won me," Sophie insisted.

Leath interpreted that in the worst possible sense. A sense that Cam, unfortunately, suspected was true. "You bastard."

Leath lurched free of Cam and raised a fist to slam Harry to the ground. The concentrated power in the gesture promised murder. Pen must have seen it too. With the reckless courage Cam knew so well, she darted between the two men.

"James, watch out!" Sophie screamed, but it was too late.

Fist thudded on flesh and Pen stumbled.

"Pen!" Cam pitched forward to catch her.

He went down on his knees, hitting the uncarpeted floor with a painful bang. He hardly cared. Pen looked as pale as she had when he'd accused her of betrayal. He cradled her against his chest and bent his ear to her lips. Was she breathing? Over the thunder of his heart, he couldn't be sure.

Panting, he glared at Leath. "You are a dead man."

Leath regarded Pen in horror, hands held stiffly open at his sides as if he couldn't bear the thought of them wreaking further harm. "My God, man, why did she do that?"

Harry hovered at Cam's shoulder. "Cam, for pity's sake, tell me she's all right."'

Cam clutched Pen more tightly. "Pen, darling, say something."

Dear heaven, don't let her be seriously hurt. With shaking desperation, he pressed her to his chest. She couldn't die. He wouldn't let her.

But as he stared into his wife's waxen features, his show of arrogance disintegrated. Instead, all he had was a wounded heart. And blind terror that she left him forever just as he discovered that he couldn't live without her.

Chapter Forty

This was like that delicious moment of forgetfulness when she'd awakened in the phaeton. Pen didn't want to move in case it was a dream. Or in case Cam pushed her away again.

Then red-hot pain sliced through her head and she groaned. Recollection crashed back. Leath had hit her. If Cam held her, it was *noblesse oblige*. She began to detest that phrase.

"Pen, Pen, say something." Cam's voice, yet not Cam's voice. Or at least not how she'd last heard him. Then he'd spoken like he hated her. Now he sounded like he cared. Perhaps she should ask Leath to hit her again.

"Pen, I'm so sorry," Harry fretted somewhere behind Cam. "This is all my bloody fault."

"Yes it is, you damned idiot." Even that lacked the bite of Cam's earlier remarks. "Pen, please..."

"I'm...I'm fine." It wasn't true, but pride was a powerful motivation. She opened dazed eyes. Cam, Leath, and Harry crowded her, sucking up all the air. She tried to move, although the slightest twitch made her head feel likely to fall off.

"I'd give the world to relive the last minute." Leath kneeled beside her. "Your Grace, how can I beg your forgiveness?"

"Get away from her," Cam snarled, his grip making her wince. "Name your seconds."

"Haven't we had enough violence?" Pen asked shakily, struggling to sit straighter in her husband's arms. Fighting the pounding in her head, she forced out a plea for good sense in a choked voice. "It seems we're all family or destined to become so. Can't we discuss what's happened calmly and kindly?"

Cam's arms tightened protectively. "Pen, don't try to talk."

"No, I must say this." She looked at Leath. "Do you really want to shoot Harry?"

Leath scowled at Harry. "Yes, I do."

Sophie spoke and to Pen's surprise, she didn't sound young or silly. "That's too bad, James. Because I'm marrying Harry Thorne, whether here or in America. In Outer Mongolia for all I care. I love him."

"You're not old enough to know what love is." Leath turned from Pen to Sophie almost with relief. She didn't mistake how appalled he'd been at hitting her.

"Yes, I am. You think I'm not because you've always looked after me." Sophie smiled at Harry, who still stared at Pen as though expecting her to expire any moment. "Now Harry and I will look after each other."

"In America?" Leath asked sarcastically.

"If necessary." Harry ran his hand through his black Thorne hair and met Leath's eyes with commendable steadiness. "You have every right to want to kill me. I acted badly.

Your sister's honor is as precious to me as it is to you, my lord. I'm unworthy of her. We both know that. But I love her more than my life and I'll do my best to make her happy."

"That means nothing." Leath rose, formidable in the cramped room.

Harry didn't back down. "It means the world."

Pen, who despite her fondness had always thought Harry a bit shallow, was impressed. She suspected that Sophie and Harry together were more than a match for the marquess.

Sophie took Harry's hand. "James, I don't want to marry Lord Desborough."

Pen's pain receded by inches. She realized that she clung weakly to Cam when he didn't want a bar of her. She straightened away from him, anguished at how easily he let her go. She struggled to steady her voice. "My lord, surely if you love your sister, you won't force her into an uncongenial marriage."

Leath frowned more in puzzlement than anger. "Sophie, of course I want you to be happy. But you never said you disliked Desborough."

"I don't dislike Desborough." Sophie's jaw firmed with stubbornness. "But I told you I *loved* Harry."

"I thought it was only a passing fancy for a handsome fribble. I was trying to save you from hurt." Leath looked devastated. After Harry's tales of star-crossed love, Leath's unselfish devotion to his sister still surprised Pen. "I wanted you to marry a man who could give you everything you deserve, who would love you faithfully, and protect you, and treat you like a queen."

"I'm that man, my lord," Harry said staunchly.

"Leath," Cam said quietly before the other man could deliver a blistering setdown about Harry's ham-fisted attempts to "protect" Sophie.

Leath faced Cam and for the first time, his eyes didn't flare with hatred. "This is a blasted mess."

"I agree." Cam's voice remained calm. Thank goodness, his temper had subsided. Pen couldn't bear to think of him risking his life in a duel. Especially over something that was the result of her impetuosity. "And don't forget that the whole world knows our business."

Guilt made Pen cringe. In Ramsgate, she'd foretold that if she married Cam, the result would be scandal and disgrace. There was no satisfaction in being proven right.

Sophie gasped softly. "How—"

Leath shot her a stern look. "You've been publicly ruined, my girl." Dislike stirred as he focused on Harry. "Thanks to this oaf."

Before the argument resumed, Cam spoke. "We need to scotch the scandal as best we can."

"Go on," Leath said warily.

Cam rose and very gently helped Pen up. "Can you stand?"

The pathetic creature who would sell her soul to stay in Cam's arms begged her to say no. The realist, her guide since she'd recognized that she'd yearn in vain after Camden Rothermere, told her to grow up. "Yes."

"How are you feeling?"

Like someone hit me with a rock. But her heart hurt worse than her head. "I'm fine."

Cam's expression was skeptical. Gratefully, she felt his hand curl around her waist, keeping her upright. With more of that heartbreaking gentleness, he led her across to sit on the bed. He released her and she assumed he meant to leave her alone. But his hand settled on her shoulder in silent support as he stood by her side.

Leath's expression was stark with remorse as he looked at

her. "Your Grace, an apology doesn't come near to making up for what I did."

Pen mustered a shaky smile. "Then help Harry and Sophie."

Cam turned to Leath. "Arrange a quick, quiet wedding. Make a show of accepting Harry. Get your cronies to rally around the newlyweds. Given my part in this, I'm willing to offer the match what countenance I can. I'm sure the Harmsworths and the Hillbrooks will help."

"But the scandal—"

A flash of Cam's wry smile. "I've lived with scandal all my life. You, my lord, are a mere amateur. It's too late to silence gossip, but a good face on proceedings will help."

"So best behavior all round. That includes not shooting each other." Pen glanced toward Harry and Sophie. "Or sailing to America."

Harry still looked wretched. His chin bore a bruise to rival Leath's. At this rate, they'd all return to London looking very sorry. "Pen, I never should have embroiled you in this."

Reluctantly she left Cam to offer Harry a gingerly hug. Every movement made her head throb. If Leath ever decided against becoming prime minister, she could recommend him as a boxer. "Be happy, brother."

Carefully she hugged Sophie. "Welcome to the family."

Sophie returned her embrace, then approached her brother. "James, I'm sorry I've caused all this trouble." Her voice wobbled. "But I love you and I hope you can forgive me one day."

Pen was sure that Leath would hate the way his expression betrayed every emotion. Anger. Frustration. Abiding affection. Guilt. Then reluctant acceptance. Up until now, Pen hadn't been sure that she liked the marquess. She didn't blame him for hitting her, but she couldn't excuse his arrogance.

Now when he beheld his sister as though he'd sacrifice anything for her, Pen's heart melted.

It was the old magic again. Love. Once more she faced the harsh truth that the magic would forever remain a mystery to her husband.

"I'll think about forgiving you." Leath's tone said that he already had. He kissed Sophie on the forehead, then faced her toward Harry. "Look after her."

Pen had never seen Harry so grave. "I will, sir. And thank you."

Incredibly, they might yet emerge without bloodshed. When Leath left Rothermere House, she'd been sure that he'd kill Harry.

Pen sagged with exhaustion. Now that the tension ebbed, she felt like Leath had punched her over and over, instead of landing one glancing blow to the side of her head.

"I'll take Sophie and Thorne to Alloway Chase," Leath said. "They'll be safe from curiosity there while we plan the wedding."

Sophie and Harry collected their few possessions—they'd traveled very light—and left with Leath. Pen and Cam remained behind in the dingy room, his arm around her waist.

She felt giddy and sick and sore and woefully unprepared for this reckoning. But she couldn't bear to wait any longer to decide her future. She'd reached a point where a short sharp cut seemed preferable to slow strangulation.

Cam's touch reminded her too painfully of all she'd lost. She broke away, fighting to keep her voice steady. "What happens now, Cam?"

He frowned. "I take you back to the Bear and Swan and summon a doctor."

"I'm perfectly all right."

He raised his eyebrows in disbelief. "Leath landed a hell of a blow."

"It was an accident."

To her surprise, a faint smile curved Cam's lips. "It wasn't an accident. It was your damned recklessness. You haven't changed since you were six years old and jumping into the river to save a drowning puppy."

Cam had rescued her that day. Cam always rescued her. What a crushing realization that he'd never rescue her again. This was like having a limb amputated. Slowly.

"He was going to kill Harry," she mumbled.

"Undoubtedly."

"I couldn't let that happen."

"So you put yourself in danger."

She sighed. "I wasn't hurt."

A flash in his green eyes reminded her of his incandescent anger when Leath clipped her. "Yes, you were."

"Not seriously."

"Good luck only."

"You can't still mean to shoot Leath. You two sounded almost friendly before he left."

Cam's mouth thinned and he sent her a direct stare that she couldn't interpret. "I won't shoot Leath. I may want to shoot you."

That was hardly news. Despairingly she realized that while Sophie and Harry might get their happy ending once they'd weathered the scandal, no such happy ending awaited her with Cam.

"Don't say that."

He frowned. "That was a joke."

"Not a very funny one."

He looked shocked. "I really don't want to shoot you."

No, he just wanted to freeze her out of his life. Shooting seemed kinder. She raised her chin. "You did earlier."

He shrugged. "I've had time to calm down."

But not to forgive her. She knew that. "Cam, I feel like I'm teetering on a tightrope. Tell me what we do now."

That oddly direct stare persisted. "We go on, of course."

She sighed. "I can't live with you if it means walking on eggshells forever."

He sighed impatiently. "Then don't."

She stiffened as a blade of ice pierced her heart. His rejection was clear. As clear as the shine on a headman's ax. She drew a breath and squared her shoulders.

"How do you see this proceeding?" She set out the options, every word slicing like a razor. "I can live at Fentonwyck or on another of your estates. Or I can return to the Continent. There will be talk if we separate, but let's face it, our marriage was always fated to fail."

Chapter Forty-One

Pen wanted to leave him?

Appalled, Cam stared at her. "What's this bloody nonsense?"

"Cam, I should never have married you." She stood like she faced a firing squad, pale as milk in her black traveling dress. He should find consolation in her lack of enthusiasm for deserting him. "The events of the last day and a half must convince you if nothing else does."

He sighed and reached for her. She edged away. "Damn it, Pen. There's no need for this."

"Yes, there is." She inhaled deeply. "I've tried. I've tried until I'm blue in the face. I've tried to be a proper duchess and proved a woeful failure. I've tried to be true to myself and in the process I've embroiled you in a frightful scandal. I'll never be the wife you want. I've known that since you proposed to me at Houghton Park all those years ago."

He regarded her steadily. "Just how hard did Leath hit you?"

She didn't smile. Instead her fists closed at her sides as if she resisted clouting him. He almost wished she would. At least that would make a scrap of sense. "Don't treat me like a fool."

"Can we leave decisions until after a meal and a few hours' sleep? Preferably in a place that doesn't stink like something died in the corner."

She still looked like a medieval martyr going to the stake. Self-disgust welled up. He'd done a brilliant job of convincing his wife that he despised her. How he regretted his temper. But then, he regretted so much. The question was whether he could heal the breach between them, wide as the Atlantic. Something profound and unhappy, a remnant of his horrid childhood, insisted that he couldn't.

He wanted to shout his denial to the sky.

"This won't take long," she said in a hard voice.

They were both exhausted. She was hurt—her head must pound like an anvil under a hammer. He couldn't bear to see his wife in such poor surroundings. But his arrogance had done enough harm. If she wanted to talk now, he'd talk, even if it felt like she scraped out his guts with a scalpel.

With a sigh, he slumped onto the unmade bed. "Say what you need to."

"Don't sound so long-suffering," she snapped.

Compared to stoic misery, her temper was welcome. He spoke the truth he'd discovered during those nightmare moments in the English Channel. And again when Leath had struck her. Still, he was a proud man. His voice emerged flat and hard. "I don't want to lose you."

She didn't seem to hear. "It's time to stop playing my knight, Cam. I'm no longer your responsibility."

"You damn well are," he said in a dangerous tone, lurching to his feet.

"By helping Harry, I deceived you. I knew how you

abhorred scandal and I went ahead anyway." She looked more a duchess than ever before, standing boldly in a run-down room in this shabby quarter of Liverpool. "And I'd do it again. So while I'm sorry you're angry and I'm definitely sorry the story hit the papers, I don't regret my actions."

"I forgive you."

A poignant smile touched her lips. "No, you don't. And neither you should. I'm doing what's best for you."

"Which entails falling on your sword, I gather," he said acidly. "Pen, I want you to stay."

"Very kind."

"I'm not bloody kind."

She cast him a pitying glance. "Of course you are. But I'm no longer taking advantage of your good nature. I set you free."

"I don't damn well want to be free." He fought the urge to snatch her into his arms and kiss her until she shut up. Instinct warned that he needed to win this battle with words alone.

Words weren't his *métier*. At least words about emotions.

"Perhaps I already carry your heir." With an expression he couldn't read, she placed one hand over her belly. "I know it's my duty to give you a child."

He stared at her aghast, even as the glorious idea of his child inside her shuddered through him. "Would it only be duty, Pen?"

She didn't answer. Instead she wrapped her arms around herself. The room was chilly, but he knew that more than the temperature made her shiver. "I'm sorry I've ruined your life, Cam."

"What rot."

Her face was wan. "And I'm sorry I betrayed you. At least let me tell you why I did it."

His slashing gesture dismissed explanations. "I know

exactly why." His voice deepened with the certainty that had struck him, vilely late, when she'd flung herself between Harry and Leath. "You did it out of love. You've done everything out of love."

Shock jolted Pen from self-flagellation. "But you don't believe in love."

"I believe in you," he said quietly.

"I don't understand." His avowal didn't soften her attitude. "Not long ago, you hated me."

He sighed and moved across to lean against the wall, hoping it held his weight. The whole building looked likely to collapse. A bit the way his pride was about to collapse around his ears. "I was angry."

"That's an understatement."

"And I was hurt," he said with more difficulty.

They were both aware what that confession cost him. From earliest boyhood, he'd done his best to deny his emotions. He had much to blame his parents for, not least the painful gossip about his bastardy. But only in the last hour had he realized that their worst crime against him was the way they'd made him mistrust his deepest feelings.

Pen didn't speak and Cam realized that to win what he wanted, he had to lay his soul out before her. "All my life I've kept people at a distance."

"I know."

"I can't keep you at a distance."

"That's desire," she said flatly. "Once you stop wanting me, you'll put me back into my place."

Her voice betrayed how he'd hurt her. Good God, what a selfish swine he was. "Your place is at my side."

She drifted toward the filthy window, staring outside, although the glass was so dirty he couldn't imagine she saw much. "You didn't think that last night."

He ran his hand through his hair. "Stop using my temper as an excuse to run away." He was unaccustomed to apologizing. The words emerged awkwardly. "I'm sorry for my tantrum. You're the only woman in creation who turns me into a lunatic."

She didn't turn. "Surely that's reason to separate."

He stepped forward. His voice resonated with urgency. "Damn it, Pen, surely that's reason for you to stay and finish the job of making me human."

She bent her head, staring down at where her hands flattened on the grubby windowsill. Her upswept black hair seemed too heavy for her fragile neck.

He wanted to bundle her into his arms and promise to be her knight, the man who would keep the monsters away. But again, that niggle of instinct insisted that if he pushed her, she'd walk out. So far, at least she listened. He was an expert on the impermeable doors against emotion. He didn't want to give Pen a chance to shut hers.

"You're human," she whispered.

"Only with you."

When she faced him, she looked angry. "Why are you saying these things? You don't mean them." Her voice lashed like a whip. "Lying won't change anything."

"I'm not lying," he said helplessly. "I've never lied to you."

"What do you want, Cam?" She folded her arms and her tone was uncompromising. The frailty had vanished. She looked like the fierce goddess who had defied the world on his behalf at Lady Frencham's.

He hadn't deserved her praise then, but he'd been damned glad to hear it. The memory fortified his resolve. She'd taken risks for him. He'd take risks for her. She was worth it. She was worth it even if he failed ignominiously.

He rubbed his jaw. "Once I thought I knew."

"Don't toy with me."

She'd dragged him into this, kicking and screaming. If he wanted to dawdle over the last few yards before tumbling over the cliff, he would. "I wanted a wife who acted with dignity and decorum, a wife who couldn't even spell 'scandal.'"

"You wanted a pretty little doll to decorate your playpen," she said sourly.

"An exaggeration, but only a slight one." He linked his hands behind his back to hide their trembling. That cliff edge loomed closer and closer. "Instead I got a difficult, pigheaded termagant."

"Then you should be glad that she's leaving."

He smiled. He liked this tougher version of Pen. "Oh, no."

"No?" she asked on a rising note. At last she stepped forward.

The instincts that guided him through this impossible maze insisted that if she bridged the distance, he'd win. If he pursued, she'd run.

He was a man who seized what he wanted. Playing the cool game nearly killed him. "Because while she's undoubtedly endless trouble, not to mention inclined to rebel against her lord and master—"

As he'd expected, that prompted a withering glance. To his relief, she was no longer the distraught, lost creature desperate to escape at all costs.

His tone wouldn't disgrace one of Genevieve's scholarly lectures. "—she also turns my nights to fire and makes me feel alive every minute of every day."

Something happened behind her obsidian eyes. He just wished to God he knew what it was. Her lips firmed. Those soft, pink lips he'd kissed until he was drunk with the taste of her. "So you want me in your bed. That means nothing. You've wanted me in your bed since we met in Italy."

He smiled. "I think it means a great deal. So do you. And if we're being accurate, I've wanted you since my first proposal."

Shock chased away what little color she'd regained. "I don't believe you."

He shrugged. "It's true. Hell, it scared the living daylights out of me. I proposed because we were friends and you understood my horror of messy emotions, not because you drove me mad with desire." She still struggled to respond. "As you did. As you do."

"Desire isn't enough." Beneath the chilly tone, he caught piercing regret.

"No, it's not. It matters. But it's not everything."

"Because it's not everything, I can never be what you want."

"How easily you give up, Your Grace."

"Don't call me that."

"What else should I call you? You're my duchess and my wife."

"Much as you wish otherwise."

By all that was holy, she was a tough opponent. While he'd learned to respect her strength, he'd never before realized how adamant she could be.

He poised on the cliff edge and stared at the sharp rocks below. Vertigo sent his belly on a sickening dip. If he jumped, odds were he wouldn't survive.

"You asked me what I want," he said slowly.

She stiffened as though bracing for a challenge. She wasn't nearly as composed as she struggled to appear. Her voice trembled. "Why don't you tell me?"

He resisted the need to touch her. "The strange thing is that I've known for years, even if I only just acknowledged it."

She sighed. "You speak in riddles."

"Cowards often do. And I am a coward. I've recognized that too."

Inevitably the time had arrived when he must jump. He prayed that he'd live to tell the tale. He expected his voice to shake, but his words rang with conviction.

He launched himself into space. "I know what I want, Pen. I want you to love me."

Since she was eight years old, Pen had imagined Cam asking for her love.

Except this scene wasn't quite right. In her fantasy, the words were different. *I love you, Pen. I will always love you.*

Although she saw what it had cost Cam to speak, his demand didn't inspire her to declare eternal devotion. Instead, it made her feel tired, as though a great weight pressed down on her.

In the last six months, she'd lost a brother and a beloved aunt. Once or twice, she'd nearly died herself. She'd shouldered Harry's troubles. She'd struggled to cope with becoming a duchess when she'd never aspired to the title. She'd always wanted Cam. She'd never wanted to be the Duchess of Sedgemoor.

Most crushing of all, she'd denied everything she knew to be true and married Cam.

Whatever physical pleasure she'd enjoyed, her soul had starved since their marriage. She had a grim feeling that her soul would continue to starve, even if she confessed her love, even if he trusted her again, even if he forgave her for this latest scandal.

"Did you hear me?" His expression was wary, almost like he expected her to throw herself out the window.

Pen realized that she must stare at him as if he spoke a

foreign language. She supposed that when Cam spoke of love, that was true. "I did."

He stepped toward her. When she backed away, his face contracted with anguish. "You've got nothing to say?"

She bit her lip. He was so handsome, especially now when his self-sufficient air crumbled to nothing. She couldn't doubt that he'd changed in the last weeks. The problem was that he hadn't changed enough. She came to realize that he never would.

"You can't make someone love you," she said dully. If she'd learned one truth, it was that.

His jaw firmed. "I can try."

"There's no point. Just let me go."

The slashing black brows lowered. "Do you want to leave me?"

She'd fled to Europe to escape Camden Rothermere. Right now, she wished she'd stayed there. "Yes."

He slumped back onto the flimsy bed and stared blindly ahead. "Have I done so much damage?"

Her stupid, stubborn heart wanted to reassure him. But hard experience had taught her that every step in his direction meant another step deeper into pain. "No, I have."

He didn't look at her. "I know I acted the complete ass about Harry, but, hell, Pen, I've acted the complete ass before and you've forgiven me."

She reminded herself that she did the right thing. "Don't you see, Cam? While we're together, there will be another scandal and another. Every time, you'll lash out."

He turned to her, stricken. "I promise I won't."

"That's not a promise you can keep," she said sadly, twining her hands together.

He straightened. "I won't give up."

She sighed, wishing this was over and she could go

somewhere dark and silent to grieve. "The whole world knows that we're an unsuitable match. London's perfect gentleman and harum-scarum Penelope Thorne."

He stumbled upright and this time when he advanced, he didn't stop. "I don't give a rat's arse what the world says."

Shock paralyzed her. "Of course you do."

"No, my sweet, misguided wife, I don't." He placed his hands on either side of her head, caging her against the wall.

Her voice shook. "You've devoted your life to proving that a Rothermere can be a man of principle."

"Rather I've wasted my life," he said bitterly.

Bewildered, she stared at him. "You'll rise above this scandal. Especially if I'm in Italy and you go back to being society's ideal."

"If you run away to Italy, I'll follow."

"Why would you do that?" She'd been afraid that if she touched him, her resolve might weaken. Now she pushed at his chest. Even a blow to her head couldn't addle her like Cam's nearness. "For heaven's sake, stop looming."

Desperation tightened his features. "Will you listen to me?"

She almost wished he'd retained his imperturbability. She still had no idea why her decision to leave touched not just his pride, but some deeper level. "Cam, if I stay with you, it will only sully the family reputation."

To her relief, he lowered his arms. He remained too close for comfort, but she didn't feel quite so surrounded. "Pen, I've come to realize that no man of character lives by someone else's leave. I'm not responsible for my parents' behavior. It's time to say I'm Camden Rothermere, take me or leave me."

Now that she observed him more closely, he did look different, as though he'd sloughed off a demon or two. Despite everything, she smiled. If he broke free of the old scandals, she could only rejoice. "Cam, if that's true, I'm happy for you."

"A man of character also stands up and says this is the woman I've chosen."

Regret bit deep. "You didn't choose me."

To her surprise, he smiled. "Now who's a fool? Of course I chose you. I think we were meant to end up together from the day we were born."

"You only married me to prevent scandal," she said miserably.

"I don't care about scandal." His voice lowered to a deep rumble that vibrated in her bones. "I care about you."

She stiffened. "It's not enough, Cam."

"I'll convince you that it is."

"I'll be in Italy."

His gaze was unwavering. "If I have to go to the ends of the earth, I'll court you as no woman has ever been courted. I'm going to win your love."

"But why?" she asked frantically. "This can't just be vanity."

The frown returned. "Pen, don't you understand what I'm saying?"

Vehemently she shook her head. "You've always treated love as the enemy."

His laugh was harsh. "Love was terrifying."

Confusion still fogged her mind. "Of course love is terrifying. If it's not terrifying, it's not love."

Another harsh laugh. "So terrifying that I still run like a coward."

"You're not a coward, Cam," she said woodenly, tiring of this bewildering conversation. Lack of sleep must make her stupid. Or Leath's blow.

"Mere words frighten me."

When he grabbed her shoulders, she started. "Let me go."

"Not yet. Not until you hear me out." He was ashen and the hands on her shoulders trembled. A muscle twitched in his cheek, always a sign of deep emotion.

"Cam—"

He spoke over her in a hard voice. "I love you, Pen. I love you more than I ever thought I'd love anyone in my misbegotten life. I love you so much that you make me shake. I love you so much that you have the power to consign me to eternal darkness if you leave me."

Amazed, speechless, devastated, disbelieving, Pen stared at him. Her heart stopped beating. Even in dreams, she'd never imagined that he'd say anything like this.

"You've brought me to this pass. It started years ago. Before I proposed. Before the world's longest wild goose chase to find another woman I wanted to marry. My affliction has only worsened since I found you again." His voice cracked as the words tumbled out. "I know your gift for love. I've seen it over and over again. I covet that love for myself. I humbly ask for the chance to become the man you want."

Cam was made to command. She couldn't believe that he loved her enough to beg.

"Please, say something. Even if it's to send me to the devil." His hands clenched on her shoulders before, with an apologetic gesture, he released her.

"Do—" She swallowed to release the scratchy words. "Do you mean it?"

"Damn it, of course I mean it," he said roughly. He reached for her, then reconsidered. That truncated, defeated gesture sliced at her heart.

"If you don't mean it, I'll never forgive you," she said in a rush.

"You have no reason to give me another chance, but if you do, I promise to make you happy." His eyes burned into hers. "Put me out of my misery. Tell me there's hope."

She blinked away tears. Despite the anguish and violence and drama, today turned into the best day of her life. She caught one of the hands he bunched at his sides. "I don't understand how this happened."

That muscle still flickered in his cheek. "I've loved you for weeks. But I'm such a novice to love, it was only when you leaped between Harry and Leath that I could admit to myself what you really mean to me." His Adam's apple bobbed as if he relived the horror. "You'd die for the people you love. I realized that I'd die for you. It's as simple as that. Once I accepted that, everything else made sense. Please, Pen, all I ask is one word to say that it's not too late."

She felt buffeted by his astounding confession. Not yet happy. Not yet secure. But as she met his gaze, she believed him. Tears won the battle and started to fall.

"Don't cry, Pen. Please don't cry." Shaking, he cupped her cheek.

"Cam—" Too choked to speak, she raised his hand and kissed his knuckles. A kiss of homage. A kiss of gratitude. A kiss, above all, of love returned. "You're wrong. You are the man that I want."

The confession was so low and so weighted with tears, she didn't expect him to hear. But he went instantly still. "What did you say?"

Dazzled, she gazed at him. "I said I love you." She sucked in a shuddering breath and finally confessed her oldest secret. "I've always loved you. You. Only you."

She saw hope leap, then subside under confusion. "But when I asked you to marry me—"

She twined her arms around him and kissed him with all

the love in her heart. His lips answered with an unspoken question. He wanted to believe her, but he didn't. She'd felt the same when he'd said he loved her.

Reluctantly she broke the kiss. "Of course I said no. How could I bear to live with you every day and know that you'd never return my love?"

The green eyes flared and his lips curved in an exultant smile. "You have such pride."

"So do you."

"I should have damn well realized that I loved you when the thought of you drowning made me want to die too." His eyes darkened. "Pen, I've hurt you for so long. I had no idea. How can you forgive me?"

She returned his smile with a joy that washed away regret and bitterness. "Say you love me again."

"I love you." He still pronounced the words as if they scalded. Staring at her like the most precious jewel in the world, he cradled her face between his palms.

"You don't sound very certain," she said shakily, at last sure enough to tease.

His smile widened until his face blazed with brilliance. "I love you, Penelope Rothermere."

"That's better."

It was. The declaration resounded like a fanfare.

"You love me." He sounded like that was a miracle. "You love me. And I love you."

Pen was so happy, she felt like she'd swallowed the sun. She was so happy that she couldn't stop crying. They'd come so near to losing one another.

With a wordless groan, he dragged her into his arms. She felt more a part of him at that moment than in all their nights of unfettered passion.

"So we get a happy ending after all," she whispered just

above where his heart thundered. The heart that he'd finally unlocked and presented to her. She'd never take that for granted. Never.

His embrace tightened almost to pain. "I'll always love you, my darling."

Curse these tears. She couldn't stop weeping all over him. "You've got some catching up to do."

"Give me the next fifty years to adore you and we'll be equal. You know how I hate to lose a contest."

"I look forward to that."

"So do I," he said fervently. "Now let me take you back to the Bear and Swan where I'll prove my devotion."

"That will make an excellent start," she said huskily.

They'd journeyed their whole lives to reach this point. They'd been through the storm. Now they found safe harbor.

After the years of wandering, Penelope finally came home.

Epilogue

Fentonwyck, Derbyshire, December 1828

Pen stirred from a doze to find Cam sitting on her bed in the shadowy room. He gently stroked the hair back from her face and smiled when she opened her eyes. A smile so full of love that she curled her toes under the blanket. Even now, months after the revelations in that squalid Liverpool attic, she marveled that her dreams had come true.

"Good afternoon," she said drowsily, smiling back.

"Good afternoon to you." He kissed her with a sweet thoroughness that set her toes curling again. "How are you feeling?"

"Like a grumpy elephant." She let him help her up against the pillows. "Your son stays awake all night and he expects me to keep him company."

Cam laughed softly. "My daughter is troublesome just like her mother."

The friendly argument over whether their baby was a boy or girl had continued for months. In Liverpool when Pen had said that she might carry his child, she'd spoken true. Soon after they'd returned to London, morning sickness had set in. Then for a few blissful months, she'd felt marvelous. But in the last weeks, she'd just been uncomfortable and exhausted.

"Boy or girl, this baby kicks like a mule." She caught Cam's hand and placed it where the next Rothermere emphatically made its presence known.

"Another powerful personality." He tried to sound ironic, but Pen heard his pleasure.

"What time is it?" she asked on a yawn.

"Nearly four." He kissed her belly and rose. He crossed to the windows and drew the curtains with a rattle. A snowy afternoon filled the ornate room with soft light. "Why are you smiling?"

He stared at her as if he beheld the most glorious creature on earth. Pen thought she looked like a hippopotamus, but she'd come to realize that her husband observed her with the eyes of love. The eyes of love found even the advanced stages of pregnancy beguiling. "The snow reminds me of our journey through the Alps. You have no idea how close I came to shoving you into a glacier."

He laughed again. "I deserved it."

"You did." She extended a hand. "But I'm glad that I didn't."

"Because you love me?"

"No, because you come in very handy when I need to stand up."

"Ah, the painful truth at last." He drew her from the bed.

She braced her hands against the persistent ache in her lower back. As she stretched, her attention focused on an oblong rectangle wrapped in black velvet and set against the wall. "What's that?"

"Your Christmas present."

"It's not Christmas yet."

"Should I take it away?" He wasn't smiling, but the deepening lines around his eyes alerted her to his game.

"No." She stepped forward. "It looks like a painting."

"Well, I know that you take art very seriously."

Even as her lips twitched, she cast him an unimpressed glance. "The Titian looks much better in the duchess's London apartments."

"I bow as always to your decision."

Another unimpressed glance. Their relationship retained a delicious push and pull, resulting in the occasional clash. It was inevitable when two such opinionated people lived together. But the reconciliations were wonderful, and no disagreement assailed the deep-rooted strength of their union. Cam was her lover and her friend and the finest man she knew. Not a day passed when she didn't whisper a prayer of thanks for his love. "Can I look?"

"Yes." He regarded the painting. "I want you to see it before our guests arrive tomorrow."

For their first Christmas as a couple, they played host to their favorite people. The Harmsworths. The Hillbrooks. Lydia and Simon and their baby girl Rose. Sophie and Harry who were so rapturously happy that they barely noticed society's disapproval. Elias. Marianne Seaton who had proven a good friend to Pen through the repercussions from Harry and Sophie's elopement.

Lord Leath even planned to stay a day or two. He and Cam weren't the best of friends, but there were signs of rapprochement. Cam's canal scheme had proceeded, to the benefit of the Thorne coffers. Leath's grudging acceptance of Harry gradually changed to genuine respect. Especially since Harry had taken over one of Cam's estates and showed every sign of making a success of it.

The beau monde might frown at Her Grace, the Duchess of Sedgemoor entertaining so close to her confinement, but these days the Rothermeres paid little attention to gossip.

Which was a good thing. The scandal after Harry and Sophie's elopement had been appalling. Insults, innuendos, and ribald lies had proliferated. The young couple still faced a degree of ostracism.

Pen knew better than to stew over the world's spite. To her satisfaction, Cam showed every sign of agreeing. The Camden Rothermere who teased her this afternoon was his own man. If the world didn't approve, that was the world's loss.

With a theatrical gesture, Cam lifted the velvet to reveal the painting.

The bristling silence extended until Cam's delight faded to concern. "Pen, are you all right? I thought you'd be pleased."

"I am," she said in a suffocated voice.

She couldn't tear her attention from the painting. She'd only seen it once before, after the artist completed it. On that single viewing, it had brought tears to her eyes. Now, six years later, she still wanted to cry. Because it was so beautiful. Because it was so true. So heartbreakingly true.

"How did you get it? He swore never to let it out of the studio."

"I set out to buy it after we got married. It seemed a suitable gift for a new duchess. But he passed away last April and I had to negotiate with his heirs."

"But why did he change his mind? He said it was his most precious possession."

"He always intended it to be yours, apparently. There's a note down in the library that came with the painting. He calls it a gift of love."

"He didn't love me."

"I think in his way, he did." Cam stared at the picture, reverently tracing its lines. All hint of teasing had vanished. He looked like the man who had begged her to stay, vulnerable and passionate and so dear. "You can see it."

"I can see love, but it's my love for you," she whispered, touching the graceful curve of the girl's naked shoulder. "What do you see?"

For a long time, Cam studied the beautiful woman in the Goya portrait and then the beautiful woman who, praise all the angels, was his wife. As she'd said with her usual perception, the love was clear to see. In both versions of Penelope Rothermere.

Cam hadn't realized until the painting arrived today that he'd proffered mere gold for something beyond price. A late masterpiece from a transcendent artist. A glimpse at Penelope in those years when she'd been lost to Cam.

He still shuddered to think that if chance had played differently, she might never have worked her way back to him.

"I see a lovely girl," he said slowly.

She glanced at him. "You're not shocked? After all, I'm one fur stole away from naked."

He shrugged. "Only a prurient mind would see sin here."

In the days when Pen's escapades had tormented him with jealousy, he'd devoted too much time to imagining the wanton images on this canvas. But despite the amount of perfect white skin displayed against the shadowy background, the woman radiated an innocence that vanquished criticism. If Cam had seen this portrait before he'd married Pen, her virginity wouldn't have been a surprise.

Pen kept her back to the viewer. Sable draped diagonally from one upper arm to her hips, baring her to the small of her back. She'd drawn her black hair in a rope across her shoulder to reveal the tender nape of her neck.

She turned to stare out of the frame, eyes huge and glowing, lips parted on a breath. The old painter had caught so much of Penelope. Her defiance. Her intelligence. Her sweetness.

And something else.

"Look at the painting."

With a puzzled frown, she obeyed. "What is it?"

Cam stared unwaveringly at the real Pen, curling his arm around her shoulders. "What do you see?"

Pen took a long time to answer. "I see a woman in love. Isn't that what you see?"

"Yes."

"I wasn't in love with Goya."

"No, you were in love with me." He said it without gloating, although her love always made him feel like the luckiest devil alive. "What else?"

He felt her start as she saw it. "The girl in the painting is in love, but she has no hope of happiness."

"That's it," he said on a long hiss of satisfaction that she understood.

The shining eyes of the girl in the portrait were sad. How had Goya captured the truth hidden from Cam until it was almost too late? A mystery of genius, he supposed. But the great Spanish painter had known that Penelope Thorne was young and beautiful and brimming with spirit. And desperately in love with someone who didn't care.

Cam crossed to the dressing table to retrieve the heavy silver mirror from his mother's brush set. He returned to Pen's side. "Look in the mirror."

For a long time, Pen stared at her reflection. Then she turned unsmiling to Cam. "Now I know what it is to love and be loved."

"You do." He paused. "I'll love you forever."

Her eyes glistened with tears. "And I have loved you forever."

He stepped behind her and laced his arms around her thickened waist. He adored this fecund, round version of Penelope. There was something so earthy and sensuous about her. "I'm so happy that you married me."

The wry smile contrasted with the moisture brightening her eyes. "I'm happy that I married a man who can give me a Goya painting with a mere flick of his fingers."

He laughed. "I'll need to come up with something even more spectacular next Christmas."

"You will at that." She placed her hands over his where they linked across her belly. "If you hang the portrait, you'll shock the neighbors."

"This painting belongs here." He smiled. "Your bedroom will soon rival the Royal Academy, my love."

She choked back a laugh. "So we'll only shock the servants."

"I suspect by now the servants are past shocking." While yet to catch their employers *in flagrante delicto*, the Rothermere staff must be perfectly aware of the duke and duchess's insatiable passions.

Pen turned to face Cam, twining her arms around his neck. She rose on her toes and kissed him tenderly. "Thank you, my darling. I love my Christmas present." The emotion that hovered just behind the teasing thickened her voice. "I love the woman I've become since you made me your wife. That girl was sad and lonely and unfulfilled, and you've given me so much joy."

"Oh, my darling," he whispered, too moved to say more. But when he kissed her this time, hunger mixed with tenderness.

Pen pressed against him with another broken laugh. "Oh, dear, Your Grace, we may be due to shock the servants all over again."